Daisy's Vintage Cornish Camper Van

Ali McNamara

sphere

SPHERE

First published in Great Britain in 2018 by Sphere

5 7 9 10 8 6 4

A CIP catalogue record for this book
is available from the British Library.

ISBN 978-0-7515-6623-9

Typeset in Caslon by M Rules

Printed and bound in Great Britain by Clays Ltd, Elcograf S.p.A.

Papers used by Sphere are from well-managed forests
and other responsible sources.

MIX
Paper from
responsible sources
FSC® C104740

Sphere
An imprint of
Little, Brown Book Group
Carmelite House
50 Victoria Embankment
London EC4Y 0DZ

An Hachette UK Company
www.hachette.co.uk

www.littlebrown.co.uk

For those who believe in the unbelievable ...

Prologue

September 2001

'What ya listening to?' the new girl asks, sitting down next to me on one of the benches that surround the schoolyard.

I look at her suspiciously, wondering if I should say. I usually got teased mercilessly when I admitted what was playing in my earphones, but something in the expression on this girl's face tells me she might understand.

'Wham!' I say hesitantly, still not trusting her or my judgement completely. 'Actually it's a compilation of eighties music.'

'Ooh, I love eighties music!' she exclaims happily. 'No one at my old school got it. They were all into the Backstreet Boys, NSYNC, and' – she pulls a face – 'Westlife.'

I feel her pain.

'I'm Daisy,' she says, introducing herself. 'I'm new here.'

'I know,' I tell her. 'I'm Ana.' I shyly offer her one of the earphones. Daisy takes it and in that moment we begin a friendship that will last for the next seventeen years.

Until the day it ended.

One

'And that concludes the will reading for the Estate of Rosalind Mary Williams.' The elderly, sombre man we'd been listening to for the past fifteen minutes shuffles the papers in front of him on the desk like a newsreader at the end of a bulletin and looks up at us.

There's silence in the small office we're all crowded into, not because there had been anything particularly shocking about Daisy's will, but what other way are we supposed to react? Our loved one has still been cruelly taken from us, and no words read by a solicitor with white hair and a questionable taste in ties were going to make us feel any better.

I turn to Peter, Daisy's grieving husband. He gives me a half smile which, just as quickly as it has appeared, disappears immediately from his face. I glance around the room at the other few people who have joined us today: Daisy's parents, Katherine and Tim, and her brother Elliot, all looking equally as upset and distraught as Peter and I felt.

'Thank you, Jonathan,' I hear Peter telling the solicitor. 'We appreciate everything you've done.'

Jonathan gives a dismissive shake of his head as he takes Peter's outstretched hand. 'Not at all,' he says, placing his other hand over the top of Peter's. 'Daisy was a fine young woman who sadly left us far too soon.'

Peter simply nods, and his head drops.

I stand up and go over to him. 'Pete,' I say, placing my hand on his shoulder. Peter turns to face me, allowing the solicitor to release his hand and move discreetly away to Daisy's mother, who is dabbing at her eyes with a tissue.

'Ana,' Peter says, and he kisses my cheek. 'That was fun, eh?' He pulls a wretched face, and the lines under his eyes that I swear have increased threefold since Daisy's death are pulled taut for a second.

I nod. 'She certainly knew what she wanted.'

'Daisy always knew just what she wanted from the first moment I met her.'

I smile in agreement. 'I know exactly what you mean. For someone who was so free-spirited, a rod of iron definitely ran right through her.'

'To my detriment a lot of the time,' Peter says wryly, and he smiles now too as we remember her.

'Try being her friend – Daisy was always the one who made the decisions on what we should do and where we should go on nights out. I never got a look-in!'

'*Best* friend,' Peter corrects me.

I shake my head. 'Only until you came along, Pete.'

'Will you do what she asks?' Peter enquires eagerly. 'She was adamant she wanted you to have it.'

'I— I don't know,' I say, looking away. 'I'm not sure it's really my thing, and the will said it's currently down in *Cornwall*.' I say the word 'Cornwall' like it was Mars.

'I know, in St Felix. Daisy loved it down there. She was never happier than when we took a holiday there with the boys. She called it her magical place.' Pete's eyes get a little misty as he talks, and I regret coming over to chat to him. Seeing Pete getting emotional only made things worse. 'This meant a lot to Daisy – you know it did. It was the only thing she talked about towards the end . . . the one thing that kept her going . . . gave her hope.'

I reach for his hand.

'Please, Ana,' he asks imploringly, looking into my eyes. 'Please do this one thing for Daisy, and do it for me too. It would mean so much . . . to both of us.'

I should have driven, I think for about the hundredth time since I left London this morning. What possessed me to take the train, *all* these trains down to Cornwall? It was taking for ever to get there.

But when you live in London, or on the outskirts like I do, public transport becomes your norm and I'd thought this would be the easiest option. I'd use the travelling time productively to get on with some work – it would be ideal. But as so often happens in life, what I'd planned and what actually transpired were two very different journeys.

It had started like most of my days did, with a train into Liverpool Street Station. I'd then hopped (well, I say hopped, I'd actually been dragging a small suitcase and carrying a rucksack) on to a Circle Line tube across to Paddington Station. This would have been fine – I'd allowed plenty of time to make my changes – until I discovered there had been a security alert and Paddington Station had been evacuated.

Again, this wasn't anything new as it happened a lot

5

these days. The security breach could be anything from a hoax phone call to a stray bag left on the platform, and even overcrowding was reason to evacuate a station nowadays. I roll my eyes – another delay – but I try to keep myself calm. Better to be safe than sorry. Anyway, at least by travelling later in the day than I usually did, I'd saved myself money on my ticket – something I always liked to do. Daisy, rather than being impressed, would have laughed at my thriftiness; she always found my penny-pinching hilarious. I just called it good sense.

I drag my case across the road to a nearby coffee shop. As I wait in line with some of my fellow delayed passengers, I think about Daisy. She was the reason I was here today about to embark on this journey down to Cornwall. I shouldn't complain – Daisy had been such a good friend to me over the years that this was the least I could do for her in return.

Travelling later in the day had not only saved me money but it had allowed me to avoid too many commuters as well. An excuse not to have to push on to a busy tube platform followed by standing in an even more crowded train was always welcome. Daisy had always been so good about my 'little problem' as we often called my anxiety. There had been many a time when we hadn't been able to go somewhere because of it: school discos in our teens, busy nightclubs in our twenties, mosh-pit-style pop concerts when we were just about old enough to know better. Only a few years ago, I'd had a bit of a wobbly when in a mad moment we'd decided to hit our local shopping centre on one of the first Black Friday sale days in the UK and it had been absolutely rammed.

But every time my little problem had occurred, Daisy had

understood and never complained. She'd simply found another way for us to deal with the situation, and it had always worked out fine, if not better, as a result.

God, I missed her so much.

Eventually the station is opened again without a reason being given for its closure, and by the skin of my teeth I just manage to board my train before it leaves for Exeter.

I find my seat, grateful I'd booked one in advance, and flop down into it with my untouched coffee, drinking it fast before it gets cold.

But just as I've emptied my cup and I'm thinking about getting my laptop out of my bag, we stop at a station and a grandmother and her two grandchildren board and sit in the three reserved seats opposite and next to me.

I smile politely at them and hurriedly retrieve my laptop from my bag before they cover the table between us in their comics, crisps and electrical gadgets. This was the longest stage of my journey – I would be on this train for over two hours and I'd planned on doing a fair amount of work in that time so I didn't waste it.

'What's that?' one of the kids asks, as I arrange my equipment on the table.

'It's a drawing tablet,' I reply, quickly plugging it into my computer.

'Cool, can I see?'

I look at the grandmother in the hope that she might intervene, but she's already absorbed in the pages of her *Woman & Home* magazine.

So the rest of my train journey is spent fending off questions from the children about what I'm doing. They take a bit of a break when they're allowed their crisps, but once the munching has stopped they then turn their attention immediately back to me again.

I could ask them to leave me alone or even ignore them in the hope they'll go back to their own gadgets, but I haven't the heart to do that because they remind me so much of Daisy's two children. They were always inquisitive too and fascinated by my life, so different to their mother's, and they would never seem to tire of asking me questions about it.

I'm relieved when we reach Exeter, but also a little sad to say goodbye.

'Thank you,' the grandmother says, as we all get up to leave the train. 'You've been very good with them. I do hope they haven't bothered you too much?'

'Oh no, don't worry,' I lie. 'They've been fine. Are you stopping in Exeter?' I ask, desperately hoping they aren't going to be on my next train.

The woman nods. 'Yes, I'm returning them to my daughter. They've been on holiday with me for a week.'

I smile, relieved to hear I won't have to answer any more questions on the next part of my journey. Perhaps I'd get some peace at last? I wave goodbye to the family then attempt to find the platform my next train is leaving from.

My change this time is smoother, and as I board my fourth train of the day for St Erth, I'm glad to see my seat is one of two and not four. There is no one in the seat next to me so I settle down again and get out my laptop, but I barely get my latest project open on the screen when I feel my eyelids begin to droop. I reach for the can of Red Bull I'd bought at the station and sip it, but even that fails to give me the energy or the inclination to stay awake.

I sigh. I'll have to close my eyes for a few minutes. I won't fall

8

asleep, I'm sure of it. I barely slept at night these days, let alone nodded off in a public place, but just the simple act of calming my mind for a few minutes was usually enough to freshen me up.

It was a technique Daisy had taught me. She, unlike me, was completely into alternative healing. Usually I'd listened politely to her ideas then immediately dismissed them, but she had persuaded me to try this particular technique and I had to admit this one actually did work. However, whereas usually I would simply close my eyes, do some deep breathing and then open them again a few minutes later feeling revived, today I actually fall asleep and I don't awaken again until I feel someone tapping me on the shoulder.

'Wake up, dear. The train has stopped – you need to get off,' an elderly lady says in a strong Cornish accent. 'This is the end of the line.'

I glance bleary-eyed through the window and to my surprise see a small station with a few people making their way from the train to the exit, where a guard is checking their tickets.

'Tha— thank you,' I tell her, looking from the window up into a pair of cornflower blue eyes.

'Are you changing for Plymouth or St Felix?' she asks, as I stumble to my feet and gather my things.

'St Felix.'

'Ah, lovely, that's a wonderful part of the line. It runs right along the coast. You'll have some gorgeous views along the way, especially on a beautiful day like this.'

'Great, thank you,' I mumble, as I make my way along the carriage behind her and lift my case – the last one – down from the luggage rack.

'Holiday is it, dear?' the lady asks, carefully climbing down from the train in front of me.

'Er, no, not really – it's a bit complicated.'

'Matters of the heart, eh?' she continues, as I follow her across the platform.

'No, definitely not. Well ...' I think about Daisy. 'Not in the way you mean anyway.'

'Ah, matters of the heart come in many guises,' she says knowingly, as we reach the guard.

I'm not sure what to say so I just smile.

'Well, have a lovely time, dear, *whatever* you're going there for. St Felix is enchanting at any time of year.' She walks straight past the guard, who doesn't seem to notice her, and then as she enters the small ticket office she turns back. 'Some might even say magical,' she adds, before giving me the briefest of waves and disappearing around the corner.

The guard reaches for my ticket. 'St Felix, is it?' he asks, looking at my case.

I nod.

'That's Platform Three, just over there.' He points to show me. 'You the last?'

'Yes, the lady and I were.'

The guard looks at me strangely. 'Okay, then ... the next train will be along in four minutes. You've just time.'

My fifth and final train journey is the easiest and by far the prettiest. I'm grateful the Cornish weather has been kind to me so I can appreciate the spectacular sea views as we travel the short distance down to St Felix, which looks picture postcard perfect as I get my first views of the little harbour town from the train window.

Right, I think, as we arrive and I drag my case along the platform behind a few others doing the same. *Now I'm actually here at last, I just need to find where I'm staying for the next few nights, then hopefully I can get this over with as quickly as possible and head home again.*

I glance up into one of the bluest skies I've ever seen.

The things you make me do, Daisy. You're not even here any more and I'm still following your orders!

But I find I'm smiling as I leave the station and head down into the little town still dragging my case behind me. From what I'd seen so far, St Felix certainly wasn't the worst place in the world I could have had to visit to collect this thing. In fact, from what I'd seen so far, it was exactly the opposite.

Two

I check into my room at one of the local pubs on the harbour front – The Merry Mermaid. A jolly woman with a beehive of red hair and vintage fifties clothing introduces herself as Rita and shows me up to my room – a light, bright double with a great view of the harbour from a comfy-looking window seat.

'It's a lovely room,' I tell her, placing my suitcase and rucksack down on the floor in front of the bed.

'One of our best,' Rita says proudly. 'You're lucky we had a late cancellation or I'm afraid you might have been in one of our rooms without a sea view. Still beautiful, of course,' she adds. 'But this room is always booked up a *long* time in advance. We're very busy.'

'I'm sure.'

'Last minute break, is it?' she asks, looking at my case.

'No … not really.' I hesitate. 'I wonder actually if you might be able to help me? I'm looking for a garage, er … ' I scrabble about in my rucksack for a piece of paper. 'Bob's Bangers?'

'Yes, my love, I know it. It's on your way out of town. Just off the main road up on Duke Street.' She looks puzzled. 'But if you're after one of Bob's cars, you're out of luck, I'm afraid. I happen to know he's away at the moment.'

'What?' I exclaim a little too loudly. 'But I rang a few days ago to check someone would be there. I've come such a long way for this.'

Rita waits expectantly for me to continue, but when I don't she offers, 'Bob often gets someone in to cover if he's away. Maybe that's who you spoke to on the phone?'

'Oh.' I breathe a sigh of relief. 'That must be it. He was quite insistent I come down to collect. I thought there might be some way to have it delivered, but he said no.'

Again, Rita waits hopefully.

'I'm here to collect a vehicle,' I tell her.

'Ah.' Rita sounds almost disappointed, as though something else much more exciting was taking place. I get the feeling Rita knows a lot about what goes on in St Felix. 'Well, I'm sure you'll find it okay. Like I said, just off the main road.' She looks around the room. 'So I'll leave you to it then if you're happy. Let me know if there's anything you want, my lovely, won't you? My husband Richie and I are always on hand to help.'

'I will do, and thank you, Rita, you've been very helpful.'

After I've unpacked and settled in to my room it's already getting late – too late to walk to a garage that would more than likely be shut for the day now – so I decide to take a stroll and discover more about this little seaside town that I'm staying in and that Daisy was so keen for me to visit.

I walk back down through the pub, which is already busy serving early dinners to families with small children, and I head through the front door straight out on to the harbour.

It's early July so the light is still good as I walk along the harbour front, stopping to look occasionally in the many shop windows I pass. I'm pleased to see most of them aren't selling the usual seaside fare of plastic windmills, rock and silly hats, but instead paintings, ceramics, and artistic bits and pieces.

You snob, I hear in my head, as I imagine Daisy's reaction to my thoughts. *What's wrong with a bit of seaside rock and a Kiss Me Quick hat?*

I shake my head and smile as I continue walking past the shops all the way to the end of the harbour wall, right out to a little lighthouse that stands at the far end. I pause for a bit, leaning on some iron railings to watch the waves crashing against the wall below me as they roll in towards the harbour. *The tide must be on its way in*, I think absent-mindedly, as I gaze down into the blue-grey water.

After I've stood and allowed my thoughts to race for a few minutes – something that was never a good idea these days – I turn and retrace my steps, weaving my way back through the holiday-makers still out enjoying the evening sunshine. A waft of fish and chips laced with salt and vinegar pleases my senses, and I realise as I pass a third family eating them with wooden forks from white polystyrene cartons that I haven't eaten for quite some time. In fact, I haven't eaten much at all today. Walking on, I spy that it's Mickey's Fish Bar from which so many are enjoying food and I head over to join the queue winding out of its door.

When I've paid for and received my delicious-smelling parcel, I look around for a bench on which to sit and enjoy my meal, but the lovely evening weather seems to have brought everyone out tonight and every single seat seems to be taken. So I wander a little further away from the crowds, and to my joy a seat suddenly becomes available as a family vacates a bench that looks directly out to sea. I rush over and sit down, delighting in the gorgeous view I'll now be able to enjoy with my dinner. I'm surprised in the few minutes I've taken my eyes away from the sea how far it has progressed into the harbour, so that nearly all the boats that I saw earlier moored with huge chains are now bobbing about happily in water instead of looking like they've been abandoned on the sand.

'Watch out for the seagulls!' a young man walking a small dog warns, as he passes by behind my bench. I turn around to see him better, and as I do I hear fluttering by my ear. I turn swiftly to see a huge seagull hovering next to me, about to pounce on my newly opened meal.

'*Shoo!*' I call, swiping at it with my hand to see it off, but the seagull is undeterred.

The man claps his hands, and his little dog barks. The seagull, realising his mission is impossible now I've re-covered my food, takes the hint and soars off into the evening sky again.

'Thank you,' I say gratefully to the man. 'I should have known better.'

'No worries at all. They're devils for it around here. They've snatched many an unsuspecting holiday-maker's treat away from them. Not just fish and chips – pasties, ice creams – they're not picky. That's partly why they're so big. Keep your food covered and your wits about you, and you'll be fine.'

I smile at him.

'Enjoy your chips,' he says as a parting gesture, but his little dog has other ideas. She decides at that very moment to do her business right by my bench. 'Oh lord, Clarice,' he says, groping for a plastic bag in the pocket of his cord trousers. 'Did you have to do it right here when this lady is having her dinner.'

'It's fine, don't worry about it,' I tell him, as I watch him expertly scoop the little mess up. 'My friend had a Burmese Mountain dog. Now, when he goes *that* is trouble!'

The young man knots the bag, then he pushes his glasses back up his nose where they've slid down while he bent over. 'I can imagine. What on earth made your friend get a dog that big? Clarice is enough trouble and she's only a small breed!'

'Company,' I say without thinking. 'She was ill. I mean she didn't get a dog that big because she was ill. She'd just always wanted one and we tried to do everything she wanted before . . .' my voice trails off, 'before . . .'

The man nods hurriedly. 'I completely understand. I'm sorry about your friend. Was she young?'

'Yes, well, my age.'

'Too young then,' he says knowingly. 'Makes you wonder sometimes, doesn't it, what it's all about?' He looks out into the distance as though he's searching for the elusive answer.

'Yes, it does.'

'Anyway, we should be on our way,' he says suddenly, looking back at me again. 'Enjoy your dinner. I'm sorry if we've disturbed you.'

'No, not at all. Thank you for saving me from the mutant seagulls.'

The man smiles. 'It was my pleasure.'

I can't help but watch him as he continues on his way with his little dog trotting along happily beside him. How nice everyone seemed here. It made a change from London, where if you tried starting a conversation with a stranger they thought you were mad, sad or about to mug them.

I try to eat some of my dinner, keeping an eye out for any errant gulls, but after my encounter I find I'm not that hungry after all and my mind is racing again.

Why have I spoken about Daisy to a perfect stranger? I never usually spoke about her to anyone – I found it far too upsetting. I might not have said much, but what I had sur-prised me.

I toss the remains of my dinner into a nearby bin, which annoys me – I don't like waste – but thoughts of Daisy often put me off my food these days and I'd lost a fair bit of weight as a result, not that that was an issue for me. I'd been trying, usually unsuccessfully, to lose weight for years. Daisy and I were always trying the latest diet craze in an effort to become what we thought would be the perfect version of ourselves. Sadly, in the end, we both got our wish and lost far too much weight – Daisy due to her illness, and I due to worry and now grief.

They say be careful what you wish for . . . It was not a weight-loss plan I'd recommend to anyone.

Before heading back to the hotel for an early night, I decide to explore a little more of the town. No doubt a strange bed in a strange room tonight wouldn't do anything for my insomnia so some fresh air first might be a good idea.

St Felix, although busy, is quite a small town so it doesn't take me long to look around. Other than the harbour, there are several beaches, which are still being frequented by holiday-makers even though it's now getting late in the evening. The beaches are linked by narrow, winding, usually cobbled streets, and it's one of those streets I now find myself on as I try to find my way back to the hotel.

The aptly named Harbour Street leads down from the more modern part of town, which among other things has a small supermarket and a bank. Like so many of St Felix's streets it is cobbled, but this one, instead of being full of holiday cottages and flats, is filled with shops – old shops – many of which I can imagine have sold the same types of goods for decades.

In addition to more galleries and gift shops, Harbour Street boasts a post office, a beach shop and a rather cute-looking florist called The Daisy Chain. *Nice*, I think, pausing for a moment to look up at the sign. A bit further along is a bakery intriguingly called The Blue Canary, its window now empty of all the delicious cakes and bread I imagine it's usually filled with in the daytime. Unlike the shops directly on the harbour, which have stayed open to make full use of the holiday-makers still wandering around the town, these shops are now closed for the day, but I decide I'll definitely pop back tomorrow, especially to the bakery ...

I feel myself yawn. It's been a long day and I'm now quite tired. For me, this doesn't necessarily equate to the need for sleep, but I head back to The Merry Mermaid and up to my room in the hope that I might nod off early. I get into my pyjamas and decide to sit in the window seat for a bit, sipping the water I'd picked up from the supermarket earlier and gazing out at a spectacular blood-red sunset.

'Daisy,' I say out loud. 'I'm still not sure about the reason you made me come all the way here. But I definitely see now why you loved this place so much.'

I feel myself yawn for about the seventh time in the last five minutes so I close up the curtains, and ignoring the constant cry of the seagulls and the faint drone of a singer down in the bar of the pub, I climb into bed, assuming like always I'll simply lie awake in the darkness trying to calm my overwrought mind.

But the speed at which I fell asleep is not the only thing that surprises me when I awake the next morning – it's the fact that I slept right through the night too.

It's the first time this has happened since Daisy left us.

18

Three

The next morning I'm up early, feeling surprisingly refreshed after my night's sleep.

I eat a hearty breakfast down in the bar of The Merry Mermaid with some of the other residents, and then I decide to head straight up to the garage; much as I was enjoying being in St Felix, the sooner I got this part over with the better.

Like Rita had said I might, I find Bob's Bangers easily, situated up a hill on the outskirts of the town. The large iron gates are, to my relief, unlocked and open to receive customers. So I wander through to find a neat, tidy yard with vintage vehicles for sale lined up all along one side of the fence that surrounds the garage.

As I walk over to take a closer look at them, I realise what fantastic condition all the cars and vans are in. They've all been beautifully restored, and their shiny bonnets and chrome bumpers gleam in the morning sunshine.

'That's a real beauty, that one,' I hear a voice behind me say, making me jump.

I turn around and see a tall but youngish man in navy blue

mechanic's overalls wiping his hands on an oily rag. He's looking not at me but at the car I'm standing in front of.

'1964 MGB Roadster,' he continues. 'She's in great condition. If you're interested, we can take it out for a test drive?'

'Oh no, I'm not here to buy a car. I'm here to collect one.
Well, it's a camper van actually.'

The mechanic looks at me curiously for a moment, his green
eyes scanning me up and down.

'I did phone ... ' I say, feeling most uncomfortable under
his intense scrutiny.

'Ah,' he says, still looking at me peculiarly. There's a distinct
Celtic lilt to his voice when he speaks, the lightness of which
is at complete odds with the look he's giving me. 'That would
be you now, would it?'

I nod.

'*Hmm* ... ' he says, looking at me again, this time with his
head tilted slightly to one side.

'Is there a problem?' I ask, feeling myself starting to bristle.
'Only I've come ever such a long way for this. All the way from
London.'

'*London*, really?' he says, not sounding all that impressed.
'Now that *is* a long way.'

I narrow my eyes at him.

'Australia, now, that would be a long way to come,' he says,
thinking about this. 'Or America maybe? But *London*, nah, not
so much.'

Is he deliberately being rude? Or is he just a bit simple? I
couldn't decide.

The mechanic grins at me. 'Ah, don't mind me, I'm just
havin' a laugh. No, there's not a problem, you just don't look
the type, that's all.'

20

What is he going on about now? What type?

'I'm not sure I follow ... The type?'

'Ignore me!' he almost sings. 'Me mam said me sense of humour would get me into trouble, and it does that – a lot.'

'Look,' I ask rapidly, beginning to tire of all his nonsense. 'Is the van here or not?'

'Oh, it's here all right. But it's round the back.'

'So ...' I add deliberately, hoping to prompt him into action. 'Can I see it?'

'Of course you can, follow me!' He sets off across the yard, so I do as he asks, trailing along after his skippy step. 'Me name's Malachi, by the way,' he says, as I follow him around the back of the garage building into another yard. 'I'd shake your hand, but as you can see' – he waves his grubby hands at me – 'I'm sure you don't want engine oil all over yours.'

The yard at the back of Bob's Bangers is much messier than the one at the front. Whereas all the vehicles at the front of the building are in a pristine and perfect saleable condition, the ones at the back are very definitely in the process of being repaired and restored. Some of them are barely recognisable as any type of vehicle – let alone a vintage one.

'Parts,' Malachi explains, seeing my face. 'Sometimes Bob buys old vehicles and strips them down to use as parts for other cars.'

'Oh, I see.'

'So, here she is,' Malachi says, as we pass a large truck missing one of its front wheels. 'Your new best friend!'

I look at what he's gesturing to, but all I see is a rusty dirty old van. It too is missing tyres and several other parts of its 'anatomy', including a steering wheel, a windscreen, a door, one of its front lights and number plates. It's in such a bad state that I can barely make out its colour under the dirt. I think it's red, but it could just as easily be a murky brown or a dirty grey.

'*No* ... You— you must be mistaken,' I say, gazing with horror at the junk heap in front of me. 'I'm here to collect a vintage VW camper van and drive it home to London in a couple of days. This can't be the right one.' I look around. 'Do you have others?'

Malachi laughs, then immediately corrects himself and attempts to look professional. 'This is definitely your van, I can assure you. I checked Bob's records when you rang the other day. But I very much doubt you'll be driving it anywhere in a few days. Maybe a few months ...'

I stare at the old camper van, and as I do its one remaining door swings open and then promptly half falls off as one of its rusty hinges fails to support it.

'Ah, don't you be doing that,' Malachi says, rushing to support the door. He gently swings the door back to its shut position. 'The lady won't be taking you if you start those shenanigans.'

'This *can't* be the one,' I say half to myself, half to Malachi. 'Daisy wouldn't have left me this old thing.'

'Daisy?' Malachi enquires. 'Yes, that's the name on the docket – Daisy Williams. I remember it now.'

'But why would she have bought *this*?' I ask, as Malachi hurriedly covers the vehicle's wing mirror like he's covering its ears. 'It's a heap of junk.'

'Shush, or you'll offend her,' Malachi says, looking worried. 'These old vehicles are very sensitive – especially camper vans. They're the worst, very temperamental they can be.'

I look at him to gauge whether he's joking with me again, but his expression suggests he's being serious.

'Sure ...' I agree, deciding the best way to deal with Malachi is to humour him.

'The look on your face suggests to me you were expecting to drive this little beauty away with you today, is that right, Ana?' Malachi asks.

'How do you know my name?' I stare at him in surprise.

'You told me on the phone?' Malachi replies in a *Well, duh* voice.

'Oh yes, of course. Er, maybe not today. I'd arranged to have a little break down here for a few days and then I'd planned on driving it back home.'

'I see ...' Malachi says thoughtfully. 'But you weren't expecting to find this poor soul.' He pats the van as if he's comforting it.

It's me that needs comforting, I think, *not a scrapyarder of a van*. What was Daisy doing buying something that was clearly going to need as much work as this vehicle was?

'Do you know when Bob is back?' I ask, wondering if I can negotiate some sort of refund on this. Daisy clearly hadn't known what she was buying, so perhaps I can get another van somewhere? One that's actually roadworthy to begin with.

Malachi shakes his head. 'He's away indefinitely. He's gone up north to look after his mam who's not too well – it sounds pretty bad if you ask me. I'm covering for him.'

'Ah, I see. That's a shame.'

Malachi nods. 'Isn't it? So, do you still want the van? It's obviously not what you were expecting?'

I look at the old camper van in front of me, and I'm about to say no, can I possibly get a refund, when I spot something in the window of the door Malachi had saved from falling a few minutes ago.

I walk over to it and take a closer look. It's a small, but brightly coloured sticker that says *I ♥ the 80s*.

'Is everything all right?' Malachi asks, watching me with interest.

I nod. 'Yes, everything is fine.' I think for a moment and then turn to him. 'I'm assuming that since you're working here while Bob is away you know how to do up old vehicles?'

'I do indeed.'

'Would you be able to do up this one?'

Malachi studies the camper van again. 'That depends.'

'On?'

'On what exactly you want doing to it, *and* how much you want to spend.'

I look at the van again. This *was* what Daisy had wanted . . . though heaven knows why?

If something is worth doing, Ana – I hear one of her favourite sayings echo in my ears – *it's worth doing well.*

'I want everything doing,' I suddenly announce. 'When this van leaves St Felix, I want it to look and run like a brand new vehicle.'

Malachi looks impressed. 'Nice one.'

'And, I'd like it doing as soon as you possibly can.'

Malachi nods. 'Not a problem at all. I can do it up all right. As it happens I'm a bit of an expert on VW camper vans – they're a specialist subject of mine. But it will cost you.'

'That's not a problem,' I say, swallowing hard. Spending the sort of money I expected this renovation would cost wasn't going to be easy, but Daisy had left me quite a large sum to cover the van's restoration. At the time I'd thought it far too much, but now, seeing this – I had to stop calling it a 'heap of junk' – this *project*, I wondered if it was going to be enough?

'Are you absolutely sure about this?' Malachi asks, as if he's reading my mind. 'It's quite an undertaking?'

I wince at his choice of words. Then I glance at the sticker again.

Daisy was always right, and if this was her final wish for me then I had no choice but to go through with it.

'Yes,' I say with more confidence than I actually feel. 'I'm one hundred per cent sure.'

Four

To my best friend, Ana, I leave the VW camper van that sadly I will now never get the chance to drive and enjoy. Ana, you know how much I always wanted to own one of these wonderful vehicles and what plans I had to enjoy spending time in it, and now I would like you to have those special times for me. Make sure you enjoy the camper van, enjoy the town of St Felix and everything I know you will find there, and above all, enjoy life!

As I walk back down towards the town, I think about what's just happened. Even though I wasn't too keen on this project, I was lucky to have stumbled upon Malachi. He might be a bit odd but he certainly seemed to know what he was talking about when it came to restoring an old van. After I'd agreed to go through with the restoration, he'd immediately started spouting all sorts of terminology at me that I didn't understand – something about bay windows versus split screens, and T1s and T2s. I'd just been pleased he'd agreed to do it. Apparently Bob hadn't left him all that much work to do while he was away because he'd had to leave so suddenly, and Malachi seemed ecstatic to have a project such as this one to get his teeth into.

Annoyingly, though, he'd been unable to give me any immediate prices or a timescale for the restoration. He said he needed to work it all out, but we'd agreed to meet in the pub later tonight to discuss everything, when he said he hoped to be able to give me more of an idea what was needed.

The weather isn't quite as bright now as it had been when I'd left the pub this morning; there are grey clouds beginning to cover the blue sky and I can feel a cool wind starting to blow in off the sea. But I like it – it feels fresh and breezy – so I decide to take a walk along the coastal path. I had ages until I had to meet Malachi later, so why not spend it blowing away a few cobwebs.

I walk for about an hour, dividing my time between enjoying the spectacular views along St Felix's coastline and worrying again about my decision to spend a lot of money doing up an old camper van.

After a while I sense there might be rain in the now quite dark clouds that are fast approaching across the sea, so I head back into the town in case shelter is rapidly required.

I pause at one of the shops as I enter the top of Harbour Street and glance at the pretty postcards that are displayed in a rack outside, but it isn't the sunny photos of St Felix that catch my eye, just how many of the postcards contain artists' impressions of camper vans.

None of the jolly, colourful vehicles look much like the one I left back at the garage though. These vans shine and gleam as the sun beams down upon them – they look happy and jubilant to be at the seaside, not wretched and miserable like mine. Malachi really would need to be some sort of wizard to work enough magic on it to make it look anything like these glorious specimens.

I sigh, and wonder again if I've done the right thing.

It had been the sticker that had changed everything. One sticker – probably stuck in haste to the van window by the previous owner – had made me change my mind. I'd been on the verge of giving up on the whole idea before I saw it.

I didn't really believe in these things, but I had to admit it did seem like a sign.

After Daisy and I had bonded at the start of the millennium as two slightly unusual teenagers, we had continued to love everything eighties throughout our friendship. In recent years the eighties had come back into fashion again, and this had made it much easier for us to continue our passion. One of the best things had been the many bands that had re-formed for come-back tours, and one of the last outings we'd had together was going to see Spandau Ballet in concert at Wembley Arena. Daisy had loved every minute of that night even if it had exhausted her for days afterwards.

Leaving the postcards, I walk further down the street and pause again outside the window of the bakery that last night had been empty but now was filled, as I had rightly predicted, with delicious-looking cakes, breads and Cornish pasties. Like the fish and chip shop last night, there is a queue winding its way out of the door on to the cobbles outside.

I hesitate.

'It's worth the wait,' a friendly American voice says.

I turn to see a flamboyantly dressed young woman smiling at me. She's clutching a white paper bag in her hands.

'We try not to buy cake every day,' she explains. 'It's not good for the figure,' she pats her stomach. 'But my boss is heavily pregnant and she gets these weird cravings for Cornish pasties!'

I smile at her.

'The boys' baking is delicious – I thoroughly recommend it. Got to dash!' she says, waving her bag in the air. 'We're almost as busy as they are today. The town is jam-packed right now.'

I watch her as she walks a few doors down and heads into the florist, then without further hesitation I join the queue at The Blue Canary, which I'm pleased to see has lessened slightly.

'I'll have a wholemeal bap with tuna and cucumber please,' I tell the jolly-looking man behind the glass counter, when finally I reach the front of the queue. I'm secretly pleased with myself that I've been able to resist the scrumptious cakes and pastries that cover the shelves and display cabinets inside the shop.

Instead of agreeing with my request the man cocks his head to one side and looks at me suspiciously. 'Are you sure about that?' he asks.

'Yes . . .'

'Sure it's not a Belgian bun you're hankering after?'

It *was* actually, but I'd been trying to give up sugar lately. Well, at least cut down . . .

'How do you know that?' I admit.

'Call it an occupational hazard!' He chuckles at his joke. 'I can match the cake to the person ninety-nine per cent of the time.'

'What about the other one per cent?' I ask, playing along.

'They're good liars!' he winks.

'I guess I'd better order a Belgian bun then!'

'Good choice!' he grins. 'Declan will be bringing some fresh buns out at any minute – you can't get better than that, can you? Are you okay to wait for a second while I just serve this gentleman, who by the look of him' – he glances at the old man, who seems to be a holiday-maker judging by his shorts and sandals – 'wants a traditional Cornish pasty. Am I right, sir?'

The guess is obviously correct, because the man is as surprised as I had been.

I look around the shop while I wait for my bun, and I notice a sign behind the desk that reads: *Welcome to the Blue Canary Bakery where your hosts Ant and Dec will be pleased to serve you today.*

While I'm smiling at the sign, a smaller man wearing kitchen overalls appears from the back of the shop carrying a tray of freshly baked wares. 'Another tray of custard tarts on their way in a few minutes, Ant,' he announces, putting the tray down. 'Anything else we're running low on?'

'Chocolate tarts and mincemeat lattice, love,' Ant says, without having to look. 'We usually only have a run on mincemeat in December,' he tells me, expertly bagging up my Belgian bun, 'but people are buying everything at the moment! Dec can barely keep up.'

'Then I'll pay you for this and get out of your way,' I tell him. The shop was getting very full now, and I was keen to escape out of the door again. I hand him the right money.

'Make sure you come back!' Ant says, passing me the bag. 'You're here for a while, yes?'

'A few days,' I say non-committally.

Ant looks at me knowingly. '*Hmm* ... we'll see. Now enjoy your bun and we'll see you soon, my lovely!' He turns away to deal with his next customer.

I take my bun, buy a takeaway coffee from a stall by the harbour, then find a bench to sit down on and enjoy them.

Like yesterday the town is busy again today, and even though the sun has chosen to hide itself behind a bank of dark grey cloud, with its pretty bunting fluttering gaily in the breeze and the fishing boats bobbing about the rapidly filling harbour, St Felix still manages to remain bright and cheerful.

'*Clarice!*' I hear a voice call, when I've just finished my bun and am enjoying my coffee. '*Clarice, you come back here!*' The voice manages to penetrate through the cries of seagulls and holiday-makers' chatter.

I look around to see a small dog running along the harbour with its red lead trailing behind it along the ground. It races along in front of where I sit, so I quickly put my foot out and step on the lead, pulling the dog to an immediate halt.

Then I reach down and pick up the lead, and encourage the dog over to me. She comes willingly, allowing me to stroke her and acting as if there's nothing wrong with her behaviour at all.

'Thank you!' I hear the voice pant, as a pair of shiny red Doc Marten boots arrive next to me. 'Thank you so much. Noah would have killed me if I'd lost her.'

I look up past the boots to see a young woman. She's wearing black tights and black shorts with a white T-shirt that has *Choose Life* emblazoned upon it in black letters. Her dark hair is cropped short, and she has a nose piercing to match the several she has in each ear.

'We've actually met before,' I tell her, ruffling Clarice's head. 'Last night. Is Noah her owner? Youngish chap, glasses?'

'*Hmm.*' She screws up her face. 'I wouldn't call him young, but he does wear glasses. About your age, I guess.'

I smile at her unintended insult.

'Whoops! Sorry,' she says, realising, her pale face blushing as her hand clamps over her mouth. 'I didn't mean— I'm always being told I need to think before I speak!'

'It's fine. We both likely seem old to someone of your age.'

'Actually, you don't really,' she says, considering this. 'Not in the greater scheme of things . . . ' She appears to think about this for a few seconds, then she shakes her head hurriedly. 'Sorry, now where were we? Oh yes, you're right, Noah *is* Clarice's owner, but I'm walking her today because the shop is *really* busy.'

'Which shop do you work in?' I ask, amused by the girl's quirky nature.

'It's called Noah's Ark – it's just up off Harbour Street. We sell junk—' She slaps her hand over her mouth again. 'Noah says I'm to call them antiques or' – she smirks – '*vintage treasures.*'

'It does sound better than "junk".'

'But that's what it is,' she says matter-of-factly. 'Other people's old junk.'

'I'll have to come and have a browse sometime. Do you sell more modern stuff, like things from the eighties?'

'The eighties? That's hardly modern is it – it's like decades ago!'

She was right, of course. 'But your T-shirt is from the eighties,' I point out, 'and you're wearing it? Well, maybe not the actual shirt, but the slogan is. It's an iconic eighties design.'

The girl looks down at her top. 'Is it? Well, I never knew that. My mate Angie knocks them out and flogs them on the market. I wonder if she knows?'

She goes off into another dreamlike state and Clarice impatiently shakes herself next to me.

'Oh, I'd better be getting her back,' the girl says with a start.

'Thanks again for rescuing her.' She takes the lead from me. 'Pop in and see us in the shop sometime, won't you? I'm Jess by the way.'

'Thanks, Jess, I will. Goodbye, Clarice,' I say to the little dog. 'Be good now, won't you?'

I watch them walk back the way they came, and as I do I feel something cold and wet on my arm, and then on my face too as I turn to look at it – spots of rain.

Then I notice how dark it has suddenly become, and how few people there are about now. Mainly because the dark grey rain clouds that hovered ominously in the distance a short while ago have now come all the way in with the tide and are directly above St Felix.

Quickly I gather my things and hurry back to the pub, but I can't quite outrun the weather, and by the time I get there huge raindrops are pelting down from the sky, rebounding from the cobbles like little bouncing balls of water.

Taking shelter in the pub seems to have been the first thought of many, and the bar is crammed with people pulling off rain jackets and towelling down wet hair. To avoid them I head straight up to my room to get dried off. Sheltering in a pub in wet weather could be fun if you were with a group of people you knew, but I was on my own and didn't fancy trying to make small talk with strangers this afternoon, especially not in a bar as packed as the one downstairs. No way.

So I get changed, wrap myself in a warm sweater and settle down in the window seat with my book, intent on reading for the next half hour or so while I wait for the rain to stop. Then, if it was still raining, I would catch up on the work I hadn't done on the train journey yesterday.

Happy that I've planned my time accordingly, I open my

book, but the slow, steady, rhythmical sound of the rain on the window makes me feel quite drowsy and I find my head drooping forward several times before I give in and drift towards my comfy bed, where very quickly I doze off and find myself dreaming of arks, floods, camper vans and a dog called Noah.

Five

When I awake, I'm yet again surprised to find I've slept for some time. Reluctantly I roll out of my warm bed and wander over to the window, where I'm pleased to see the rain has now stopped and people are beginning to venture from their shelter.

To wake myself up I hop in the shower, then blow dry my hair and get myself ready to meet Malachi downstairs. We'd agreed to meet at just past six in the bar after he had closed up the garage.

A few minutes before six o'clock I wander down to a much quieter bar than the one I'd walked through earlier. Now the weather was better everyone had escaped back outside. Relieved I don't have to fight through a crowd, I order myself a Diet Coke, and then take a seat by the window to wait for Malachi.

At 6.15 he still hasn't arrived. I'm starting to feel a little awkward sitting here in the bar on my own, and I'm pleased I've chosen a window seat so at least I can amuse myself watching the comings and goings along the harbour while I wait.

If I'd known he was going to be this late I'd have brought my laptop down from the room and done that work while I'm waiting, I think, tapping a beer-mat on the table in annoyance. I prided myself on always being on time and I didn't like people who weren't.

I wasn't good at wasting time these days either. Some people could while away hours on end not really doing anything, but I liked to use my time constructively. Pleasant though it is watching the world of St Felix pass by, it's not, in my book, constructive.

'Sorry, I'm a wee bit late,' I hear above me. Immediately I turn away from the window to see Malachi standing casually at the table next to me.

'No problem,' I lie. 'Glad you could make it.'

'Can I get you a drink?' Malachi asks, looking down at my nearly empty glass.

'Oh, er ... yes. Another Diet Coke will be lovely, thanks.'

'A Diet Coke with ... ?'

'Just a Diet Coke, thanks. It's a bit early for anything else. Plus I haven't eaten yet.'

Malachi smiles. 'Of course. Right ya are. Back in a mo.'

I watch him walk up to the bar. Now he's not wearing his navy overalls he looks different than he had earlier. He obviously showered and changed before he got here because along with a clean white T-shirt with a sort of bird motif on the front and smart black jeans, his black wavy hair, combed back off his face, is still a little damp, and I couldn't help but notice how nice he smelt when he was standing by the table just now.

'One angelic Diet Coke,' Malachi says, putting my drink down on the table when he returns. 'And one not so virtuous pint of Guinness.'

He sits down in the seat opposite me, takes a sip from his

glass and pulls a face. 'Never tastes as good anywhere as it does in the homeland, and I've tried a few pints over the years.'

'Which part of Ireland are you from?'

'Ah, here and there. I've lived in many areas over time.'

'So what brings you all the way to Cornwall?'

Malachi studies me over the top of his glass with a pair of sharp green eyes.

'Let's say I got the call,' he replies ambiguously.

'The call?'

'From Bob!' He grins. 'Asking if I could look after his garage.'

'Oh, I see. So . . . ' I say, not impressed by his joke, 'did you manage to get some figures together for me today?'

'Straight to the point, I see.' Malachi puts down his pint glass. 'There are no flies on you, are there?'

'I like to get on with things, yes, if that's what you mean. I can't see any point in dilly-dallying around.'

Malachi smiles.

'What now?'

'Did you know the phrase "dilly-dally" is commonly attributed to the English music hall singer Marie Lloyd, but was actually in use much earlier than her 1918 song, as far back as the seventeenth century?'

I stare at him.

'Wonderful performer, Marie,' he continues. 'You should look her up sometime.'

'Sure . . . ' I say hesitantly, wondering what that was all about, 'I will, thanks for the info. Now about this camper van . . . '

I was beginning to wonder yet again if I'd done the right thing in agreeing to let Malachi help me, but now my concern wasn't to do with the money, it was more about him. Even though earlier he'd seemed a little … unconventional at the garage, with his overalls on he had at least seemed professional. Now with his relaxed demeanour, his casual clothes and the tattoos I can just about see poking from underneath his T-shirt sleeves, he seems anything but that.

'So,' he says, pulling a notebook from his back pocket and laying it on the table. 'Let's talk camper vans.'

'Let's.'

'First of all I need to know *exactly* what you require from the van.'

I look at the notebook Malachi has produced hoping to see pages of copious notes and complicated numeric equations, but the notebook remains unopened.

'How do you mean? I just want it roadworthy.'

Malachi shakes his head. 'No, you said, and I quote, "I want everything doing. When this van leaves St Felix, I want it to look and run like a brand new vehicle."'

I have to smile as Malachi is doing a very good impression of my voice.

'That's quite the talent for mimicry you have there.'

'And, if I may say, that's quite the smile you have there too, *when* you allow it to appear.'

I glance down at the table and hurriedly take a sip of my own drink.

'So, I'll ask again,' Malachi says, not appearing to sense my embarrassment. 'What *exactly* do you want doing?'

I'm relieved he's returned to talking business. 'Okay, so most importantly I want the van doing up so it runs reliably and doesn't break down.'

'Not a problem.'

'Then, I want it to look good too,' I improvise. 'I want it to look like those camper vans do on the postcards outside the shop up the road – all shiny, gleaming and happy.'

I glance at him after I've said *happy*. Had I gone a bit too far?

But Malachi doesn't look fazed. 'I can do all that, no worries at all. But what I think you've failed to grasp is just how many different specifications there are when it comes to vans.'

'Are there? Like what?'

'Like whether you want a pop-up top or a roof rack? The model you have would have had a roof rack originally, but I can add a pop-up if you want one?'

'Why would I want a pop-up roof?'

Malachi looks me up and down. 'How tall are you?'

'Five foot seven, but I don't—'

'Do you want to stand when you cook?'

'What?'

'If you have a pop-up you can stand to do things inside the van like cooking and washing up.'

'Oh, I see. I hadn't really thought about it.'

I won't tell him I've only thought as far as driving it home.

'But if you have a roof rack you have more room to carry things like surfboards and bikes.'

'Ah . . .'

'I have a pop-up so I carry my surfboard on the back. It just depends on how much equipment you have.'

'You have a camper van too?'

'Yeah, mine's just a T2 Bay. Much as I adore her, I'd love a classic Splitty like yours.'

'A what?'

'A Splitty. It's what we call a split screen camper van. All pre-1967 camper vans have a windscreen split in two. After that the new models all had the solid bay windows.'

'Right, there's quite a lot to it, isn't there?'

Malachi nods. 'And we haven't even started to talk about air-cooled engines, bullet indicators, or whether' – his eyes twinkle – 'you'll be needing a full-size rock 'n' roll bed ...'

Annoyingly I feel my cheeks flush. 'I won't be needing any sort of bed,' I hurriedly insist. 'I'm not going to be sleeping in it.'

'You're not? But how will you camp – will you need an awning or do you have your own tent?'

'No ... to both. I'm just going to be driving it home, that's all. I'm not sure what I'll do with it after that.'

There's a sort of stunned silence from across the table as Malachi sits back in his chair and stares at me.

'What now?' I ask huffily. 'What camper van law have I broken this time?'

Malachi shrugs. 'It's none of my business what you choose to do with her when I've finished my refurbishment.'

'I'm sensing a "but"?'

'*But* ... you'd be mad not to at least try camping in her. It's a wonderful experience. You can drive where you like, set up camp and cook your dinner in the open air, even bed down under the stars if you're lucky. The freedom is amazing.'

'I'm sure.'

'*It is*,' Malachi insists. 'You'll never have a night like it. You come from London, right?'

I nod. 'Not originally, but I live there now.'

'How much freedom do you have in London?'

'I'm hardly imprisoned when I'm there, if that's what you mean?'

'Oh, you are,' Malachi says softly. 'You just don't know it.' He pauses and then returns to his usual tone. 'What do you do for a living? Let me guess – you work in an office?'

'No, wrong!'

'What, never?'

'Well, sometimes, when I have to go in for meetings.'

Malachi looks triumphant.

'But I don't work in one. I work from home most of the time actually – I'm a graphic designer. *Free*lance,' I add for emphasis.

'That explains a lot.'

'What does it explain? You just berated me for not having enough freedom in my life, and yet I'm a freelance worker. I have all the freedom I need.'

'Not that, the graphic bit. All a bit tight and conformist, is it, your work?'

'No.'

'It's hardly avant-garde, though?'

'Look, I'm sure this is all relevant – to *you*. But to me this is getting us nowhere. You're supposed to be giving me estimates, not life advice.'

'Sorry, occupational hazard. Right,' Malachi says, opening the book on a blank page I'm disappointed to see is the first of many. 'Do you have a pen?'

I find one in my bag.

Malachi takes it from me then looks up at the pub ceiling for a few seconds as though he's working something out. Then he scribbles a number down in the book and shows it to me.

'How much?' I exclaim.

'Obviously we still need to discuss the finer points, and you have to bear in mind just what a state the van is in right now. It's a ballpark figure.'

I look at the figure again, and notice this time that it ends very specifically in two figures.

80.

Swallowing my desperate need to tell him to forget the whole thing, this was going to be far too expensive, I hold out my hand to Malachi to seal the deal.

Grinning, he takes it, and as we shake hands the strangest feeling runs right through me. It's not an unpleasant feeling at all, but it's definitely a feeling I've never ever felt before.

Six

'So now we've agreed everything,' Malachi says, after we've been discussing the renovations to the camper van for some time and seem to be pretty much in tune on what's to take place, 'let's talk about you.'

'Me? Why do you want to do that?' I can't help but feel a little flattered. Even though Malachi is somewhat eccentric, it's impossible not to notice how good-looking he is.

'Because these renovations aren't going to be over and done with in a few days, are they? I'm fast, and if I may say, *very* thorough.' He winks at me. 'But sadly I can't work miracles – yet. I was wondering where you were going to stay while I complete the work. You said you'd only booked in here for a few days.'

'Yes,' I reply feeling foolish, 'that's right, I have. I guess I'll have to go back to London and come back again when you've finished.'

'Why?'

'Because I have a life back in London – a job to do, things to take care of. I can't just abandon everything for weeks on end to watch you tinker about with engines and stuff.'

'I can assure you this renovation requires a lot more skill than simply *tinkering about*. If you think that,' Malachi says, sitting back in his chair with a hurt expression, 'perhaps you should find someone else to help you.'

'Okay, okay, take that look off your face. I'm sorry. Of course I don't want anyone else. You've been most helpful . . . so far.'

Malachi nods, and seems to readily accept my apology.

'But that doesn't change the fact I can't just chuck everything in and live here while the renovations are going on.'

'Why can't you? You just told me earlier how *free* your job allows you to be. Why can't you do it from here if you're so *free*lance?'

I think about this. I didn't actually have all that much on in the next few weeks – not that needed me to be in London anyway. I had a couple of big projects I needed to get finished but no meetings. I could work on my laptop and over the internet easily enough. Perhaps taking some time away might actually be helpful.

'And these things you need to *take care of*,' Malachi continues, 'what are they – pot plants?'

I look at him. Scarily he was spot on. I had no pets, children or boyfriend that needed tending to. I was actually a lot freer than I cared to admit.

'Perhaps I could stay for *a while*,' I reply, choosing to ignore his jibe.

'Great!' Malachi grins. 'We'd better find you somewhere to stay then.'

'Oh no, I'm sure I can do that. I'll ask Rita if she has any rooms free.'

'She won't have,' Malachi states without hesitation. 'They're fully booked.'

44

'And how could you possibly know that?'

Malachi shrugs. 'Why don't you ask her?'

'I will!' I stand up and go over to the bar. After a short conversation with Rita, I return to the table.

'Well?' Malachi asks, his eyes shining.

'She *is* booked up—'

'Told ya!'

'*If* you'd let me continue ... *but* she thinks she knows someone who might have a cottage for let.'

'There now! You're all sorted.'

'Possibly. I'll have to wait and see about the cottage first – that might be booked up too.'

'It'll be grand,' Malachi says confidently. 'You worry too much.'

'And *you* are very sure of yourself,' I tell him. 'How did you know the pub would be booked up?'

'Ah ...' Malachi says, draining the last of his pint. 'If I tell you that, you'd know all me secrets, wouldn't ye?'

'Hardly.'

''Tis easy.' He leans in conspiratorially towards me, and I get another whiff of his fabulous scent – it's like no aftershave I've ever smelt on a man, not that I get close enough to many to know these days.

Malachi looks either side of him. 'School holidays next week, isn't it?' he whispers. 'They were bound to be fully booked.' He grins. 'What were you thinking I am, some sort of soothsayer?'

I roll my eyes.

'Another drink?' Malachi asks, lifting his empty glass.

'Actually, I was thinking of getting some food.' My Belgian bun seems a long time ago now, and my stomach has started to complain. 'Would you care to join me?' I ask more from politeness than want. Malachi was fast becoming one of the most irritating people I'd ever met, even if he was quite fun too. However, I didn't want to sit here alone and have dinner, and he was the only person I knew in St Felix.

'I like your style.' Malachi gives a small bow and a flourish of his hand. 'I should be delighted, my lady!'

'*You* are such a loon!' I say standing up. 'My round,' I add, grabbing his glass before he can complain. 'I'll get us some menus while I'm there.'

I order us both a drink, and I ask Richie, Rita's husband, for two menus, one of which I peruse while I'm waiting for Malachi's Guinness to settle.

'Hello,' a voice next to me says.

I turn to see a tall man with glasses smiling nervously at me. 'I hear I have you to thank for saving my dog today?'

'Oh, *hello*!' I say, recognising Noah from last night. 'Well, I didn't save her exactly. Let's just say she'd got a bit overconfident off her lead!'

'Clarice is usually a little too overconfident in every situation! But thank you anyway, Jess said you were very helpful.'

'No worries. Really.'

'I didn't think I'd get to thank you properly. People tend to pass through St Felix pretty quickly. Then I saw you here at the bar and I thought I'd take my chance.'

I nod. This was beginning to feel a little awkward. I glance back at Malachi and I see he's grinning at me. He gives me a sly wink.

'Are you staying here long?' Noah asks. 'Or just passing through?'

'Longer than I first thought,' I reply, suddenly deciding to give Noah my full attention. 'I'm actually looking for somewhere to rent – like a holiday let?' I add, in case he thinks I'm moving here. 'I don't suppose you know of anywhere?'

I figure two possible leads are better than one, and Rita's might not come to anything.

'Funnily enough, I do. Poppy, who owns the flower shop on Harbour Street, has a cottage she rents out. I was in her shop this morning buying some flowers and I heard her say that the people who were due to rent next week have pulled out at the last minute in very odd circumstances. I'm sure she won't have been able to re-let it already. Perhaps you could pop along to see her?'

For reasons I don't understand I find myself wondering who Noah was buying flowers for, instead of jumping at the opportunity of a holiday cottage.

'Yes!' I suddenly reply, in the midst of my musings. 'I mean, yes, that sounds ideal. I'll do that first thing tomorrow, thank you.'

'No need to wait until then if you don't want to,' Noah says helpfully. 'Poppy's husband Jake is over there. We could ask him if you like? I know him quite well.'

'Oh, I wouldn't want to bother him when he's having a drink,' I say, looking over towards a tall sandy-haired man standing by the bar. 'I'm sure tomorrow will be fine.'

'Up to you, of course, but hotel rooms and self-catering properties don't tend to stay vacant for long here in St Felix.'

Richie places Malachi's Guinness down next to my Diet Coke and I pick up the two glasses. 'Thanks, Richie.'

'Oh, are you with someone?' Noah asks, looking at the two glasses. 'I'm so sorry, I didn't realise.'

'Only Malachi,' I say, nodding in his general direction. 'He's the mechanic looking after Bob's Bangers while Bob is away.'

'Ah . . .' Noah looks over towards where I'm gesturing, but

there are quite a few people filling the bar now and his view is blocked. 'I can't really see who you mean, but I don't think I've met him. The name doesn't ring a bell.'

'I think he's new to St Felix,' I explain. 'Look, shall I take these drinks over to our table, and then perhaps you'd be kind enough to introduce me to this Jake? I can introduce you to Malachi afterwards if you like?'

I push my way through the crowds to Malachi carrying the drinks and deposit them on the table.

'You don't waste any time, do you?' Malachi says, grinning at me again.

'How do you mean?' I ask, pulling the menus from under my arm.

'You and Noah over there – very cosy!'

'We are not *very cosy*. Noah might know someone who has a cottage, that's all – he's going to introduce me to the owner's husband.'

'Then it's him who's the fast mover!'

'*Stop!*' I tell him. 'It's not like that. I'll be back in a few minutes. Why don't you look at the menu while I'm gone?' I'm about to walk back towards Noah, but I pause and turn back. 'Noah said just now you two hadn't met before, so how did you know his name?'

'Been in his shop,' Malachi says, picking up a menu. 'I guessed.'

'Oh, oh, all right then. I'll just be a couple of minutes, okay?'

'Take all the time you need!' Malachi answers, waving his hand dismissively. 'I have all the time in the world.'

When I turn back towards the bar I find Noah isn't where I left him, but has made his way over towards Jake and is already in conversation with him.

I wander over feeling a bit awkward.

'This is the lady in question,' Noah says, welcoming me to the group.

'Hi, sorry to bother you,' I say apologetically. 'My name's Ana.'

'Jake,' he says, holding out his hand. 'And you're in luck, our cottage is still free. Well, it was when I left home – my wife was still fretting about letting it. She really shouldn't be in her condition,' he says to Noah. 'But what can you do? I try to keep her from stressing but she still wants to be in control of everything. She's pregnant,' he says, turning back to me. 'Due in two weeks.'

'Yes, I heard,' I tell him. 'I met her colleague outside the bakery. She'd been buying pasties.'

'That would be Amber. I think we spend all our time in that bakery. Poppy can't get enough of a Cornish pasty right now. She'll be beating old Stan's record soon if she's not careful, God rest his soul.'

I glance at Noah. He shrugs.

'Oh, sorry, is that before your time, Noah? I forget you haven't been here that long. Stan was an old chap who could eat a dozen giant Cornish pasties in one sitting – he held a record here in St Felix. Quite a character,' Jake says wistfully. 'I miss the old fella.'

'I do remember him actually,' Noah says. 'He came into my shop not long after I'd taken it on. He was full of what turned out to be very helpful advice about St Felix and its history.'

'He loved his stories, did Stan. Anyway,' Jake says, smiling at me, 'if you'd take the cottage on, you'd actually be doing me a huge favour. Hopefully Poppy will stop worrying about it if we have a tenant. How long did you want it for?'

'Oh, I— I'm not too sure. How long is it available?'

'Three weeks. The person who was due to take it is an artist – they were coming to St Felix, as so many do, to paint, but they had an unfortunate accident with a ladder and a cat apparently.' He shrugs. 'They fell and broke their wrist so, no painting!'

'Three weeks will be perfect,' I tell him, wondering if it will be. 'When can I see it?'

'The current tenants move out tomorrow, Saturday, so by all means pop along and take a look then. No pressure if you don't want to take it, but it's in pretty good nick. Poppy lists it on one of those boutique cottage websites and they have pretty high standards.'

'I'm sure it will be absolutely fine,' I say, wondering in my head how expensive this was going to be. 'Thank you so much for this – both of you.' I turn to Noah now. 'You've both been very kind.'

'Not a problem,' Noah says, 'I guess we're even now.' He holds out his hand. 'You saved my dog, and I saved—'

'—my bacon,' I finish, shaking his hand. 'Thanks!' I look back over towards Malachi. 'I guess I'd better be getting back to my . . . to Malachi. Do you want to come over?'

'No.' Noah glances quickly towards the table, then back at me. 'I wouldn't want to intrude.'

I nod, pleased I don't have to introduce them. I wasn't quite sure what Malachi might say. 'I'll be sure to pop into your shop if I'm passing.'

'I'll look forward to it,' Noah says, and suddenly we both realise he's still holding my hand.

Noah hastily releases my hand; we smile awkwardly at each other, then I hurry back over to Malachi, my face still flushed.

'Well,' Malachi says, as I sit down opposite him and hurriedly pick up a menu. 'Three handsome men in one night. Like I said, fast mover!'

I look over the top of my menu at him, and decide instead of arguing to play him at his own game for once.

'I assume the three men you're referring to are Noah, Jake and ...'

Malachi grins smugly as he waits for me to say his name.

'Richie behind the bar?' I offer triumphantly, and I grin into my menu at the part-amused, part-horrified expression that appears on Malachi's expectant face.

Seven

The next morning I awake in my room at The Merry Mermaid feeling quite positive about the day ahead.

Last night, Malachi and I had eaten together in the bar, and once I'd got used to his often erratic behaviour, I'd quite begun to warm to his company. Underneath the constant jibes and carefree ways was a very smart, perceptive individual, and I enjoyed listening to his amusing and spot-on observations about life.

Noah had stayed for a short while in the bar, just long enough for him to finish his pint with Jake, and then he'd left, waving casually to me on his way out. I had tried not to watch him too much while he'd been in the pub, but I'd often found my eyes wandering in his direction.

I'd told Malachi about Jake's offer of a cottage, and he thoroughly approved, saying he thought three weeks might just be enough time for his mission – as he'd curiously named the renovations to the van.

After breakfast, I set off in search of Jake and Poppy's holiday cottage. Before Jake had left the pub, he'd popped over to our table and told me exactly where to find the house so I could take a look before committing to anything.

I find the prettily named Snowdrop Cottage on a narrow cobbled street leading up from the harbour. The bright red geraniums cheerfully planted in azure blue window boxes, which match perfectly the bright blue of the front door, turn this terraced fisherman's cottage into a colourful and welcoming home. I take a quick peek through the front window and see a small but modern kitchen with all the latest appliances standing on granite worktops. A box of cleaning equipment rests in the centre of the wooden kitchen table, and there is an unused mop and bucket filled with soapy water standing in the middle of the floor.

I look at my watch – it's just gone 10.30 a.m. *The previous inhabitants must have left and the cleaners are getting ready for the next set of holiday-makers to arrive*, I think, as I stare through the window at the quaint little cottage.

A woman pushing an unplugged hoover suddenly appears in the kitchen. I swiftly try to move away from the window without her seeing me, but she spots me and waves. Then she beckons me over as she goes to the front door and opens it.

'Hello, dear,' she says, smiling. 'Are you Ana by any chance?'

'Yes, I am.'

'Ah, good. I'm Doris. Jake told me to expect you. Would you like to come in and look around?'

'Sure, yes, that would be great. Thank you.'

Doris leads me through the front door and gives me a very quick tour of the kitchen. Then we go through to a small twin-bedded room with wooden beds covered in pretty floral duvets. In the tiny hall there is a narrow staircase which leads up to a second bedroom – a king-size bed this time, with clean, crisp white bedding that Doris has obviously just changed. This room has modern Swedish-style furniture making it feel light and airy. Next to the bedroom Doris opens a door and leads me through into a light, bright living area.

'The living room is up here because of the view,' she says, walking over to a pair of French windows, which are already open, allowing a fresh breeze to pour into the room. 'Come and see.'

I follow her over to the window and out on to a tiny balcony which commands stunning sea views over one of the bays that I'd discovered on my walk yesterday.

'Wow!' I exclaim. 'I didn't expect this.'

'It's one of its selling points,' Doris says proudly, 'gets a lovely bit of sun most of the day. Poppy doesn't usually have much trouble renting this place out – you're lucky she's had a cancellation.'

Twice on one trip it seems. It makes a nice change to be on Lady Luck's good side.

'It's beautiful,' I say, gazing out at the sea. 'I'm surprised she doesn't want to live here herself. I'm sure I would if I owned a house like this.'

'It was Poppy's grandmother's originally,' Doris says. 'Poppy did live here for a while after her grandmother died, but when she moved in with Jake she went to live in his house – it's much bigger, see, what with him having kids already.'

Doris was obviously one of these people who liked to share all the information she had with you.

'She's pregnant now, isn't she?' I ask politely. Doris had been so nice in showing me around, I was sure she'd have something to say about it.

'Ooh, yes,' Doris coos, 'so she is. It was lovely news when I

54

heard. I can't wait to meet the little one. I've already knitted four pairs of bootees and two matinee jackets.'

I had no idea what a matinee jacket was, but Doris seemed pleased with them.

'So,' Doris asks, shaking herself from her baby thoughts. 'Do you think you'll take the cottage?'

'Oh yes, it's lovely. It will be perfect for me.' *I just hope it's not too expensive*, I think, as Doris gathers some of her cleaning equipment. I had some of Daisy's money to tide me over if I should need it, but I got the feeling most of that was going to be used up on the camper van the way Malachi was talking.

Doris nods approvingly. 'Good. I'll be in to clean for you weekly and change your sheets and towels. I'm almost done here, so if you pop over to the shop and speak to Poppy, you can move in later today if you like?'

'That sounds great. Thank you for showing me around, Doris. You've been very kind.'

'No trouble at all, my dear. Just let me know if you need anything, won't you, while you're here. My number's on the board down in the kitchen, but I only live up on Lobster Pot alley, a couple of streets away.'

'I will.'

We make our way back downstairs, and Doris sees me to the front door.

'I almost forgot to ask,' she says, as I'm just about to leave. 'Are you here to paint like the person who fell off the ladder? If so I can find you some old sheets and stuff to put on the floors upstairs?'

I shake my head. 'No, I'm not a painter. I'm a graphic designer. I'll be doing work while I'm here, but only on my laptop – so no mess!'

'Ah, good – that's what I like to hear!' Doris nods approvingly. 'I'll see you very soon then, lovey. Goodbye!'

'Bye and thanks!' I call, as I set off happily down the street.

This was all going very well. I almost felt pleased that the renovations on the van were going to take so long now. I hadn't planned on staying in St Felix this long, but now I was going to, Snowdrop Cottage would do very nicely indeed.

I walk straight to the flower shop and pull open the door of The Daisy Chain; as I do a small brass bell rings above my head.

'Won't be a minute!' a voice calls from the back of the shop.

I take a look around while I wait. Aside from the usual buckets of fresh flowers, this florist also sells some other interesting bits and pieces like pottery and colourful items of jewellery. They're displayed on whitewashed dressers and the whole effect is very shabby chic and eclectic.

'Hi!'

I recognise the young American woman from our encounter outside the bakery as she appears from a room at the back of the shop. 'We've met before, haven't we?' she asks, looking at me with recognition.

'Yes, outside the bakery,' I tell her. 'And you were right, it was worth the wait!'

She laughs. 'Indeed it is. It's much easier on us in the winter months when it's not so busy. We can go straight in then and get what we want in no time at all. In the summer we have to wait in line like everyone else! So what can I do for you?'

'It's actually Poppy I've come to see. It's about her cottage – I'm going to be renting it for a few weeks.'

'So you're Ana,' she says, nodding. 'I'm Amber. Poppy isn't here at the moment as she's had to pop out, but I've been left with instructions.' She rummages under the desk and produces several pieces of paper. 'Here,' she says, passing them to me. 'It's mainly just the terms and conditions of hire. If you could fill in the form, sign it and give it back to me, that would be wonderful.'

I take the paper from her and read. If I was lucky, what money was left from the renovations on the van might just cover the rent for the cottage, which was actually very reasonable for such a nice place. 'That all seems fine, thank you. Here's my credit card to pay for the rental.'

Amber takes my card and passes me a pen, which I duly use to fill in and sign the form while she swipes my card.

'There, all done,' she says, when we've completed all the necessary paperwork. 'Now, let me just find the keys for you.' She reaches under the counter again and passes me a small bundle of keys. 'There are instructions everywhere in the cottage so you shouldn't have any problems,' she adds. 'Poppy and Jake are very organised. I hardly recognise the place these days as it's changed a fair bit since I lived there with Poppy.'

'You've lived there too – it's a popular place, isn't it? Doris the cleaner was telling me a few things when I was there earlier.'

'Ah, good old Doris, I do love her. Yes, Poppy and I lived there when I first came to St Felix and we set up this shop together – it's quite a long story,' she explains. 'I live with Woody, my fiancé, now. He's the local policeman. You'll no doubt see him around while you're here.' She turns away for a moment to speak to a customer who's just come into the shop. 'Just let me know if you need anything in particular – the lilies are beautiful right now.' She turns her attention back to me. 'Three weeks is quite a long time for a holiday,' she says, without seeming nosy. 'Any particular reason you're staying that long?'

'Another very long story.' I grin. 'Let's just say I'm involved in renovating an old vehicle.'

'Really?' Amber sounds genuinely interested. 'Is Bob helping you with that?'

'Bob's away at the moment. He has someone in to help him out, though – Malachi? Do you know him?'

Amber shakes her head. 'No, I can't say I've seen him around. But it's good that Bob has got someone in – that place is always so busy.'

That's funny, Malachi had said he didn't have much to do right now. Maybe he'd meant he hadn't much to renovate and the sales side of things was still ticking over nicely.

'St Felix is such a great place for renovation,' Amber muses. 'Not just for physical things like vehicles, but for the soul too.' She looks meaningfully at me. 'That's an interesting name you have.'

'Ana?'

'No, your full name, I couldn't help but notice it on the form – Anastasia. It means "resurrection", doesn't it?'

'I believe so – yes.'

'Well, if you need resurrecting, or any sort of restoring, St Felix is the place to come. It's been helping people for years like that. Me included.'

'I'm glad to hear it,' I reply lightly. I used to get enough of this sort of mystical nonsense from Daisy, so I tried to avoid it now if I could, and Amber, lovely though she seemed, looked like just the sort of person that would be able to spout this particular type of nonsense for hours. 'Thank you for these,' I say swiftly, holding up the keys as another customer enters the shop. 'I won't keep you any longer – I can see you're getting busy. Thank Poppy and Jake for me, won't you. They've really helped me out.'

'As you have them, Anastasia,' Amber says, as I open the door of the shop to leave. 'As you have them.'

Eight

I wait a little while before moving my things out of The Merry Mermaid and into Snowdrop Cottage, just to make sure Doris has finished cleaning.

Rita is surprised to see me going so soon. 'I'm amazed you managed to get anything around here at such short notice,' she says, as I hand back her room key. 'My contact didn't have anything, that's for sure. Snowdrop Cottage *is* lovely, though – you've fallen on your feet there.'

'I know. I think someone must be looking down on me.' I smile, but Rita considers this.

'You're probably right. Finding accommodation at the last minute in peak season is surprising enough, but to do it twice! You must have the luck of the Irish on your side.'

'There's no Irish in me. Perhaps I'm just in the right place at the right time.'

'Perhaps. You'll pop in and see us again while you're here, won't you?' Rita asks. 'We're having an Indian night next week. Richie makes a mean masala.'

'Definitely. I'll look forward to it, and are you sure you

don't want me to pay for tonight? I did book three nights with you.'

Rita waves me away. 'No, it's fine. Any friend of Noah's is a friend of mine. Lovely boy, that one.'

'I thought I might pop up to his shop later and say thanks for helping me out.'

'You should. He has everything up there – a real Aladdin's cave, it is.'

'I thought it was Noah's Ark?' I wink at her.

'Ah, very good, very good. Now, be on your way. My Richie's jokes are bad enough, I don't need two of you in here!'

I wave to Rita as I leave the pub, pulling my suitcase behind me, but as I trundle my case along the cobbles, it suddenly dawns on me that I've only brought enough clothes for a few days, and I'm now committing to spending a few weeks here.

I spy a familiar face walking towards me along the street. 'Hello again,' I say to a deep-in-thought Jess just before she passes me.

'Wha— Oh, hey,' Jess says, jumping with surprise. 'Sorry, in a world of my own there. Whoa, not leaving us, are you?' she says, looking in horror at my suitcase. 'So soon? But I thought you were going to be staying now?'

I wonder for a moment how Jess knows this. Surely even Noah hadn't heard I'd taken the cottage yet? But word seemed to spread fast on the St Felix gossip network, so I don't dwell on it for long.

'I am. I'm just taking my stuff over to Snowdrop Cottage. I'm going to be renting it for a while.'

Jess looks relieved. '*Phew!* I mean, that's good. Good that you're staying here a while longer.' She grins a bit manically.

'Yeah ... Actually, you could be just the person I need.'

61

'Really?' Jess looks happy to hear this. 'What can I do for you? I'm here to help!'

'Yes ... Well, I was just thinking that I'd only packed for a few days and now I'm going to be here for a bit longer I'll need to buy some more clothes to tide me over. Any ideas of the best places to go locally?'

'Clothes ... right. Er, to be honest, unless you want to dress like a fisherman or striped tops are your thing, there's not too much around here.'

I'm quite partial to a striped Breton-style top, but I don't say anything.

'Oh, that's a shame. Where do you get your clothes then?' Jess seemed to have a wonderfully eclectic taste. Today she's wearing blue denim dungarees with pin badges attached haphazardly all over them, a silver lamé vest, silver DM boots to match and her short hair is tied up with a red polka dot scarf.

'Here and there. I pick up bits and pieces wherever I go really.' Jess looks me up and down. 'Perhaps you'd be better off trying the internet? Most of the more *traditional* stores deliver all the way down here.'

I grin at her. Jess had a wonderful way of putting her foot in it without actually realising what she was saying.

'Yeah, maybe I'll do that, thanks.'

'I mean obviously you're not traditional or anything like that,' Jess says hurriedly, suddenly realising she might have offended me. 'I didn't mean you were dull or anything.' She raises her eyes up to the sky as she feels herself digging even deeper. 'But there's just more choice – you know?'

'Of course.' I smile at her. 'Thanks for your help.'

'You'll still pop in and see us at the shop though?' Jess asks keenly. 'I'm sure Noah would like to see you again.' Her hand goes to her mouth and she stamps her boot on the ground. 'I mean we'd *both* like to see you.'

'Of course. Perhaps later today? Let me get my stuff moved in to the cottage first.'

'Later would be *great*! Right, bye for now then,' Jess sings happily as she heads off down the street. 'Happy moving!'

I grin as I set off in the opposite direction. Jess did make me smile, and that was a very good thing these days.

I reach Snowdrop Cottage, and I'm about to put the key in the blue front door when I suddenly realise how impulsive I've been in making this spur-of-the-moment decision to stay here in St Felix. It wasn't like me at all. Usually I liked to plan things, to turn over every eventuality before I made any decision, big or small.

'Are you proud of me, Daisy?' I ask, glancing up at the sky as I turn the key and open the door. 'It used to be you who was the spontaneous one!'

I pull my case into the kitchen and up the stairs, then I go about unpacking the few things I have with me.

'Right,' I say, when I'm finished. I look around the empty house. 'Now what?'

I think about heading to Noah's shop, but I decide I'll walk up to the garage first and see Malachi. I had a feeling I was going to have to keep a tight rein on him if the van renovations were going to be complete in the three weeks I had in St Felix. I'll pop over to see Jess and Noah later.

The garage is quiet as I walk through the gates. I'd assumed on a Saturday it might be busy with people wandering around browsing the old vehicles, but it appears I'm the only customer as I walk through the yard.

'Malachi!' I call, as I walk around the back. The camper van is still in the same place I saw it yesterday. It looks in slightly better condition than it had then, but that might just be the bright sun shining down on it today – everything always looks better in the sunshine. 'Malachi, are you here?'

But it's not Malachi who comes scurrying out of one of the sheds; instead I see a large golden Labrador.

'Hello!' I say, as it bounds over to me. 'Who are you?'

'*Woof!*' The dog licks my hand.

'I see you've met Raphael,' Malachi says, following the dog out of the shed. He's back wearing his navy overalls and wiping his hands on a rag again.

'Raphael? That's quite a name for a dog,' I say, ruffling his head.

'Yeah, I call him Ralph. It's easier.'

'And much better. Is he your dog?'

'We sort of got thrown together. But we've been with each other a fair while now, haven't we, boy?'

Ralph barks.

'So what can I do for you today?' Malachi asks. 'You don't expect me to have made much progress since I saw you last night?'

'No, of course not. I thought I'd just pop over and tell you I took the cottage, and I've already moved my things in. So you're stuck with me now for a few weeks.'

'Not at all, we'll enjoy showing you how we turn this lady into the beauty she deserves to be – won't we, Ralph?'

Ralph shows his support by cocking his leg against one of the van's tyres.

'Ralph! That's no way to treat a lady!' Malachi admonishes.

'How do you know the van is female?' I ask. 'Men always call vehicles "her" and "she" – what's that about?'

'She told me,' Malachi says seriously.

'She told you?'

64

Malachi nods.

'The van did?'

'Yep. Anyway, can't you tell just by looking at her?'

I look at the battered old camper van. I could barely tell what shade of red it was, let alone what gender it wanted to be.

'Her only problem is she doesn't have a name yet,' Malachi says, moving towards the vehicle.

'She can tell you she's female but not what her name is? Contrary, isn't she?'

'She is that,' Malachi says, rubbing his overall sleeve against the bonnet in an attempt to add a bit of shine, but all he does is make his sleeve even dirtier. 'It's camper van tradition that the new owner must name her.'

'Is it?' I ask, wondering if he's making this up. 'Do I have to?'

'Ana, Ana,' Malachi says, shaking his head sadly. 'Could you at least try to make out you're enjoying being the owner of a classic VW camper van? People pay a lot of money for these vehicles, and they're very sought after and much loved. I'm sure your friend must have wanted one dearly. To leave instructions in her will for you to have it in the event of her death – it must have meant a lot to her.'

I begin to nod in agreement. 'Wait, how did you know that?' I ask, looking at him accusingly. 'About Daisy's will?'

'You told me,' Malachi says, without hesitation.

'No, I didn't.'

'Yes, you did – yesterday.'

I think about this. 'No, I didn't, I'm sure of it.'

'All right, I guessed,' he admits. 'You mentioned something about wondering why someone had left you this when you came here the first time. Then last night you mentioned a friend and then you looked sad. I just put two and two together.'

I look at him suspiciously. 'That's very perceptive – even for you.'

Malachi shrugs. 'What can I say – luck of the Irish.'

'You're the second person today to say that to me. It must be catching.'

'So – have you decided yet?'

'Have I decided what?'

'What you want to call her, of course – it's very important and could set the tone for the whole project.'

I sigh and look at the rusty old vehicle in front of me. Malachi seems to have repaired the door that fell off yesterday, but because its paint has been rubbed against it's shinier and cleaner than the rest of the van, and I can see more clearly the shade of red that lies underneath. The sticker is still in the window, and it's as I stare at it that it hits me.

'Daisy,' I say, almost to myself.

'Did you say "Daisy"?' Malachi prompts.

I nod. 'I'm naming her after my best friend.' I gaze steadily at the vehicle in front of me. 'Yes, I think that name will suit a camper van, but more importantly I think my Daisy would have approved.'

'Daisy the Second it is then,' Malachi says, looking at the van. 'What do you think of your new name, Daisy?'

But Daisy II is silent in her reply. Just like my Daisy always is now when I speak to her.

After a bit I leave Malachi and Ralph with Daisy II, with Malachi promising to start work on her later this afternoon. Then I walk back into town and grab a sandwich, which I eat outside in the sunshine while thinking about everything that has happened since arriving in St Felix.

It was strange, I'd only been here a couple of days and I

already felt like I'd been here for ages. I'd made a few acquaintances – I could hardly call them friends – and I had somewhere more permanent to stay than a hotel room. All in all this trip was turning into something quite unexpected and something quite delightful at the same time.

When I finished my lunch, I set off in the direction of Noah's Ark. It's just where Jess had described – a little way up a street that extends off Harbour Street. From the outside the shop looks smart and well kept. The signage above the door is painted in a pretty Wedgwood blue with ornate white writing, and the two big bay windows either side of the entrance are spotlessly clean. Through them I can see carefully placed vintage items, antiques and objets d'art, all arranged into neat window displays.

I open the door, and just like the flower shop a tiny bell tries to ring above my head, but instead of making a clear chiming sound, it sort of purrs a little in its casing.

There are a few people already browsing the many items inside, so I close the door behind me and decide to take a look around. I hardly know where to start, there are so many things squeezed into the space, but even though there are items spilling from display cabinets and piled high on wooden tables, I get the feeling that everything is a lot more organised than it appears and no doubt perfectly catalogued too.

'*Hello!*' I hear a cheery voice call from behind a heavy-duty shop counter, the like of which you might have found seventy years ago in a pharmacy or a haberdashery store.

I turn to see Jess popping her head around an even older-looking ornate cash register. 'You made it!' she cries happily. 'What do you think?'

'Very interesting. You have a lot of stuff in here.'

'We certainly do, and Noah insists we catalogue every single thing!' She rolls her eyes. 'Takes flippin' ages.'

I smile – I thought as much. Noah seemed far too methodical and particular to run a chaotic, disorganised business.

'What are you whining about this time, Jess?' Noah asks good-naturedly, as he appears through an open door at the back of the shop. He's wearing cords again, a cream shirt with a fine check and the addition of a khaki green cardigan. 'Oh, hullo again,' he says, his pale blue eyes lighting up behind his glasses when he spots me. 'How nice to see you.'

'I thought I'd pop by and have a look around. Also, I came to say thanks. I moved into Snowdrop Cottage this morning. It's perfect.'

'Yes, Jess was telling me earlier. I'm pleased everything has worked out for you.' Noah takes off his glasses and gives them a polish on his cardigan. 'So is there anything we can help you with? Have you seen anything that takes your fancy?'

Jess giggles behind the till, and Noah blushes.

'Not yet, no,' I say, pretending I hear nothing amusing in his words. 'I'll take a look around, shall I, and let you know?'

'Yes, yes, you do that,' Noah says hurriedly. 'I'll just be over here if you need me.' He turns quickly and almost knocks over a large vase in his haste, but luckily he manages to catch it in time and steadies it from falling.

I see Jess grin.

I take a brief wander around the shop. I'm not really an antiques person – I prefer more modern up-to-date fixtures and fittings for my small flat, so I really didn't expect to find anything in Noah's shop that would interest me. Apart from the eighties, which Jess had so succinctly informed me yesterday were now definitely vintage, the past wasn't somewhere I was keen to hang out. Daisy had always been the antiques nut, and would often drag me around fairs and shops wherever we went. The trouble was she never really knew what she was looking for, but according to her that was half the fun.

As I suspect, I don't find anything that interests me, but I'm surprised at just how big Noah's place is. Aside from the main shop there are several smaller rooms that lead off it, all equally packed with vintage china, paintings, furniture and collectibles.

'Thanks for letting me look around,' I say politely to Noah before I leave. 'You have a very interesting shop.'

'Nothing you found interesting, though?' Noah says, sounding a little disappointed.

'Ana likes the eighties,' Jess pipes up from the other side of the shop, where she's hanging a cluster of small prints on the wall.

'The eighteen eighties?' Noah asks. 'I think we do have some Victoriana; it's in one of the back rooms. I can show you if—'

'No! The nineteen eighties, you 'nana.' Jess grins.

'Oh.' Noah blushes again. 'Of course. My apologies.'

'Don't be silly,' I say lightly. 'It's an easy mistake to make. I doubt you have much call for nineteen eighties things in here – probably a bit too modern for you.'

'On the contrary, if it's collectable, we sell it. I don't turn my nose up at any decade if it's an area of the past that people enjoy remembering.'

'That's good to hear,' I say, smiling at him. I pause for a moment. 'I like what you said just now, the way you described it.'

'About people remembering?'

I nod.

'That's how I see what we sell – a way of people remembering but also enjoying the past. There are a lot of memories in the things we sell here as they were all special to someone once.'

We look at each other for a few seconds, then Noah hastily looks down at the desk. He brushes some imaginary dust away with his fingers.

'Well, let me know if you come across anything in the next few weeks, won't you?' I say, sensing this is a good time to leave. 'From the eighties, I mean.'

'Of course,' Noah says, looking at me again. 'I certainly will.'

'Right. Goodbye, Jess!' I wave across the shop at her. 'Bye, Clarice,' I say to the little dog snoozing in her basket behind the desk. I look at Noah again.

'Call again, won't you?' he says in practised fashion.

'Yes.' I nod briefly, then I head quickly towards the door. The bell tries to ring above my head again and I look up at it.

'It's broken!' Noah calls from across the shop. 'Has been for some time. I need to get it fixed.'

I just smile and close the door behind me.

But as I'm about to walk away I can't help but hear Jess reprimanding Noah. '*Call again, won't you?*' she says, repeating what Noah has just said. 'What sort of a chat-up line is that? No wonder you don't have a girlfriend!'

As I hurry away down the street, I wonder why that piece of information should make me feel quite so happy?

Nine

I've only been here a few days, but already I'm getting used to the ever-changing weather conditions in St Felix.

The rest of the afternoon swings between showers and sunshine, and at one point there's a beautiful vibrant rainbow arcing over the sea.

I view this phenomenon from the balcony of Snowdrop Cottage when I'm taking a break from work. I'd finally got my laptop set up and my head down, and I'd found myself being quite productive throughout the afternoon and unusually creative as I worked on my latest assignment.

I take a picture of the rainbow on my phone, but find myself wishing that I had a decent camera with me with which to photograph the wonderful scene. Just as I'm gazing down at the photo I've taken, my phone rings in my hand making me jump.

Malachi's name flashes on the screen.

'Hi, Malachi,' I say, answering. 'How are you?'

'What are you up to at the moment?' he asks bluntly, dispensing with formalities.

'Not much, just taking a break from work. There's a

beautiful rainbow outside my window. Can you see it from where you are? It's just starting to fade a little here.'

'What do you want me to do, run out and hide me crock of gold at the end of it?' Malachi asks, and I know he's grinning when he says this.

'Ha, ha, very funny. I just thought it was pretty, that's all.'

'Ah, a rainbow is more than just pretty. It's full of meaning.'

'What sort of meaning?'

'That depends on where your belief lies. It means different things to different people. The Buddhists believe one thing, the Chinese another, and so on. But rainbows are always a sign of good things to come. Even Noah knew so.'

'Noah?'

'Yes, Noah,' Malachi says slowly as if he's addressing a child. 'You know Noah … The one with the ark? In the Bible … Book of Genesis? Saved-the-animals-from-the-flood Noah?'

'Yes, of course I know *that* Noah.' I berate myself. For a moment I'd thought he'd meant antique shop Noah.

'Ah, did you think I meant Noah from the pub? Knight-in-shining-armour Noah? Is *he* on your mind a lot recently?'

'No, of course I didn't,' I lie. 'And he's hardly a knight in shining armour. He wears a cardigan.'

'Nothing wrong with that,' Malachi says. 'Some of the greatest scholars and scientists the world has ever produced wore cardigans.'

'Did you want something, Malachi?' I sigh. 'You did ring me.'

'Ah, yes, I've found something – in Daisy the Second.'

'What sort of something?' I ask, thinking he's going to say rust or something even worse.

'Some postcards.'

'Postcards? Why are you telling me this? Just dump them.

72

I'm sure that's not the only rubbish you'll find in there while you're doing it up.'

'I think you might want to see these particular postcards.'

'Why?'

'They're not just any postcards. They're a bit old.'

'So?'

'At least come and look at them before I throw them out, will you?' he insists. 'Or shall I bring them down to you?'

'No, it's okay, I could do with a break. I need to pop out to get some food before the shops close tonight anyway. I'll call in on you on my way to the supermarket.'

'Grand, see you in a bit.' He hangs up.

I sigh. If Malachi needs me to come and look at every little thing before he discards it from that vehicle, I'll be spending more time up at the garage than here in Snowdrop Cottage.

But the evening air is pleasant as I make my way up the hill towards the garage. There's a burnt orange sky over the sea as the sun begins to think about going down, so again I take a photo with my phone, and again I wish I had a better camera.

The CLOSED sign is on the gates as I make my way up to the garage, but Malachi has left one of the gates unlatched so I can enter.

I head immediately around to the back where I find Malachi sitting on an upturned bucket with his face turned to the sun. Ralph lies happily next to him also basking in the evening's rays.

'I see you're busy!' I call. Ralph barks and comes bounding over, and Malachi opens his eyes slowly, blinking a couple of times to get his focus.

'Everyone needs to relax occasionally,' he says lazily. 'Even you, Ana.'

73

I choose to ignore his dig.

'So where are these postcards you want me to look at?'

'Calm down,' he says, standing up and stretching. 'They're in the office. Wait there and I'll get them.'

I sit down on the bucket and stroke Ralph while I wait for Malachi to return from the office. The side door of the camper van has been slid open and I can see where Malachi has already begun to clear and remove some of the worn interior.

The red leather seats that once would have carried the previous owners on their many journeys are now tattered and torn, and the brown Formica surfaces of the tiny kitchen units have definitely seen better days. There is a hole in the living area where a small refrigerator might once have stood, and the rings on the little gas cooker are dirty and covered in grease. An indiscriminate stain on the well-worn carpet could be from anything at all and the whole spectacle makes me feel quite sad as I gaze upon it.

'You are a sorry sight,' I murmur to the van as I stroke Ralph. 'I bet someone really loved and cared for you once. I wonder how you ended up in this state.'

'Here we are,' Malachi says, returning. 'What do you think to these?'

He passes me a few slightly tattered postcards.

'They're old postcards, so?'

'Why don't you read them before you pass judgement,' Malachi says, looking keenly at them. 'You might find something interesting.'

I look down at the three in my hand. They're all fairly typical seaside postcards: one shows a beach, the second a long white pier and the third some cliffs with seagulls soaring above them. I turn them over and read the first one aloud:

'My Darling Frankie,

I'm staying on the Norfolk coast for a few days with Rose.

The weather is simply gorgeous, and the sun has shone every day.

I saw a man riding a tricycle along the street yesterday, and it so reminded me of you, and the year you rode one around the town just to get everyone talking!

Oh, how we laughed that summer.

Forever yours,

Lou x'

I look at Malachi. He nods at the next postcard.

My Darling Frankie,

What do you know? Rose and I are down in Eastbourne, not that far from you.

I have an exhibition on here right now, so I'm hanging around trying to eavesdrop on what people are saying about me ... So far it has all been good!

As we passed the junction for Brighton I so wanted to turn Rose's steering wheel and come to visit you. But I don't know what you'd say if I turned up on your doorstep after all these years ... Maybe one day I'll be brave enough to.

Forever yours,

Lou x

'It's the same person!' I exclaim. 'What are the chances?'

'Read the next one,' Malachi encourages. 'It's the best of the three.'

> My Darling Frankie,
>
> I miss you so much since you went away. I knew I would be sad when you left, but I had no idea it would be this painful. Mother and Father have no idea of my feelings; I'm sure I have hidden them very well. In fact, I've hidden my sadness from everyone.
>
> I think it's only George who truly understands, but then animals always do, don't they? I'm sure he misses you terribly as well.
>
> I truly hope one day I will be able to share my feelings with you in person again.
>
> Until then, I'll be
>
> Forever yours,
>
> Lou x

'This is pretty amazing,' I say, looking in more depth at the cards. I hadn't really noticed before, but the seaside pictures vary more than I'd originally realised. They are not only from different seaside towns but different decades too. 'There's a postcard here that looks fairly modern,' I tell Malachi, holding up the card from Eastbourne, 'but this one must date from ... maybe the sixties or seventies?' I wave the one from Norfolk at him. 'And then this card from St Felix is much older, possibly the thirties or even the forties!'

'I know – I looked at the dates,' Malachi says practically.

'Oh yes,' I say, feeling a bit silly, 'there *are* dates. I see them now, just above the writing – 1976, 1988 and wow, 1945! That *is* an old one.' I look across at the other side of the cards where there would usually be an address, a stamp and a postmark, but they're all blank. 'That's odd – there are no stamps or addresses on any of these.'

'That's what I thought,' Malachi says, taking the cards from me again. 'Why would you write a card to someone and then not post it?'

'Not only that, but three times?'

'Perhaps Lou didn't want this Frankie to read them?'

'Why ever not?'

'Well, it's quite obvious she's in love with the guy. Perhaps she didn't want him to know.'

'But why write postcards to him then?'

Malachi shrugs. 'Humans are a strange species. They never stop amazing me.'

'Where did you find these?' I ask, looking inside the van.

'I was pulling one of the seats out so it can go to be re-upholstered. There's a huge rip in this particular one, and they were poking out of the back.'

'How strange. Do you think there might be more in there? These cards were written so far apart – there could be even more hidden away.'

'Why don't we take a look?' Malachi says. 'I've only pulled out one seat so far.'

'Where's that one?'

'It's just round the back of the van, propped up against it.'

'I'll check that one again, and you look inside the van.'

'Yes, sir!' Malachi salutes. 'Right away, sir!'

'Jump to it, then,' I instruct, playing along.

I head around to the other side of the van, and find a shabby red leather seat sitting forlornly on the ground. I turn it over and find the huge rip Malachi mentioned. I can't see anything so I gently slide my hand inside. All I can feel to begin with is coarse stuffing and metal springs, but then as I slide my hand a little further in between the springs I touch something that feels very much like card.

As gently as I can I pull it free from the seat. It's a little battered but I recognise immediately the florid black ink handwriting. I put my hand in again, a little further this time, and feel around a bit more. This time I retrieve two postcards at the same time – same handwriting, same sender.

'How are you getting on?' Malachi calls from the van.

I look up and see his face peering at me through the dirty window.

'I've found three more!' I tell him excitedly.

'Four here!'

'Really?'

'Yeah, and I've only opened up the back of one seat so far.'

Over the next hour we manage to retrieve an incredible ninety-two further postcards from the van. They are mostly stuffed into the back of the remaining seats, but we find a few tucked behind cupboards and in the lining of the ceiling.

'Wow!' I say, looking down at the pile we've amassed outside the van. 'These cards span more than fifty years. The earliest I've seen is dated 1945, and the latest 1999. It's madness.'

'Madness that we've found so many postcards or madness that they're all written *by* the same person *to* the same person?'

'Both!' I say breathlessly.

Malachi smiles at me.

'What?'

'I don't think I've seen you look so alive since you arrived here.'

'What do you mean?'

'You look flushed and excited by our little find, and if I may say, very attractive as a result.'

I feel my cheeks flush all the more. 'Stop it with all your blarney,' I tell him, looking away, pretending to examine the cards again. 'Full of it, you.'

I expect him to come back with a quip about me stereotyping the Irish, but Malachi is unusually silent.

'Cat got your tongue?' I ask, hoping he'll bite.

To my relief he does. He pokes his tongue out at me. 'Ah, you wish. Prefer the strong silent type, do you?'

'Er . . . no, I don't have a *type*.'

'Not even a rakishly handsome Irishman?' Malachi grins.

'Sadly, I don't know any of them.'

'Ah, the mortal wounds me.' Malachi pretends to retrieve a dagger from his heart.

I shake my head dismissively. 'All right, Romeo, let's get back to these postcards. Do you think the previous owner of the van was the same person who wrote these? What was her name again?' I look down at the cards at my feet. 'Lou.'

Malachi shrugs. 'It's possible.'

'She might like them back.'

'Would you stuff something you wanted to keep inside a seat or at the back of a cupboard?'

'I would if I wanted to hide it. If this camper van belonged to Lou, the postcards were likely precious to her but she didn't want anyone to see them.'

'So why leave them in a rusty old— Oops, my bad,' Malachi corrects himself, 'a *classic* VW camper van?'

I smile at his faux pas while I think.

'Perhaps the van was stolen from her and she didn't have

time to retrieve the cards? Or perhaps she was involved in an accident and the van was written off, only to be discovered years later hidden in a forest, covered in leaves.'

It's Malachi's turn to smile now.

'Hidden in a forest, covered in leaves?' he repeats. 'Wow, you actually do have an imagination, and a good one too.'

'Of course I have an imagination – I'm a designer, aren't I?'

Malachi pulls a sort of *meh* expression.

'What's that face for? I am.'

'Graphics are hardly art, are they?'

'Of course they are. I went to art college for three years to qualify.'

'I'm sure you did, but I bet everything you do now is computerised. When was the last time you picked up a paintbrush and let your imagination run free? At your college, I'd bet.'

He was right, but I wasn't going to give him the satisfaction of admitting it.

'I have a very creative mind,' I tell him instead. 'Otherwise I wouldn't be as good at my job as I am.'

'Ooh, get you.' Malachi puts his hands on his hips. 'That told me, didn't it?' He pretends to slap his hand.

'All right, clever, what do *you* think happened to the owner?' I ask, changing the subject back to what we were originally discussing, instead of allowing myself to be carried along on one of Malachi's tangents.

'I think the owner simply sold the van and forgot that the postcards were hidden in there.'

I shake my head. 'No, Lou wouldn't have forgotten. It's clear this Frankie meant a lot to her.'

'You're assuming that Lou *was* the owner of the camper van. She might not have been.'

'Do you have some sort of record here of who sold Daisy this van?'

'Do you mean the vehicle's log-book – that would have the original owner's name in it?'

'Yes, that would be perfect!' I say excitedly. 'Do you have that?'

'No, sorry, it didn't come with one. I think Bob must have just bought it from a junk-yard or found it derelict on someone's land before he sold it to your Daisy, as she has no paperwork whatsoever.'

'Oh.' My excitement diminishes somewhat.

'It's a shame she doesn't have a number plate either,' Malachi says, looking at the van, 'as we might have been able to trace her previous owner from that. You're a bit of an orphan, aren't you, girl,' he adds, patting her fondly. 'Let's think.' Malachi looks at me again. 'Perhaps someone else might have found those cards – a collector maybe – and simply transported them around.'

'So why hide them away?' I shake my head. 'No, I'm abso-lutely certain Lou was a previous owner of this van.'

'How in Lucifer's name can you know that?'

'Come with me,' I say, beckoning Malachi as I walk back around to the other side of Daisy II. 'Look at this …' I pull the leather seat away from where it rests against the dirty red paintwork.

Malachi leans down to peer at what I'm looking at, then he stands up again and smiles.

'You see?' I say with satisfaction.

'I see.' Malachi grins.

This side of the camper van is particularly grimy, even more so than the other. It's as if it has been left someplace where dirt could accumulate more easily on just one of its sides – like a road where it had been constantly splashed with dirty water from passing cars – but where Malachi had originally rested the seat when he'd pulled it out, some of the dirt has been worn away, and while I'd been looking for more postcards I'd noticed that painted in ornate white letters was the name *ROSE*.

Ten

As the late evening sun pours through the French windows of Snowdrop Cottage warming the room and me, I pick up another postcard and begin to read:

2nd January 1948

My Darling Frankie,

Oh, how I miss you.

I know I've written before and told you this, but particularly today I miss you all the more. You see I have to make decisions about my future education.

Mother and Father want me to go to Oxford University. (Apparently I'm clever enough, who knew?!) But I really want to go to an art school to study painting, which as you know, other than you is my one true love.

Oh Frankie, how I wish you were here to talk to.

Forever yours,

Lou x

I scribble a note in my book – *Oxford*.

Now we were pretty certain that Rose (or "Daisy-Rose" as Malachi was insisting we now call the camper van) had been owned by the mysterious Lou, I had decided to try to return the postcards to her, or if for some reason Lou wasn't around any more, to her family at least.

Malachi thought I was mad, and told me in no uncertain terms that I'd never be able to trace her, but I disagreed. There had to be something in the cards that would help me, and so far this morning I'd already found out that Lou was fairly local to St Felix – some of her early cards to Frankie were sent from places not that far from here. She'd bought the camper van she'd called Rose in 1964 with some money she'd made from painting. Now this last card told me she might have gone to Oxford University. I felt I was already starting to piece Lou's story together very nicely indeed, and I still had many more to read yet.

I didn't know what it was about the cards that made me so interested in them. Perhaps it was their age – some of them were over seventy years old. Or perhaps it was the exquisite notes of love that one person had sent to another. It was heart-breaking to think that someone so young was already experiencing the agonising pain of love and loss at such an early age, and not only that, that they had carried that pain for so long.

I read some more of the cards, trying desperately to read between the lines to find any clue that I can.

However, although I deduce Lou did eventually go to Oxford to study, other than that there doesn't seem to be anything else out of the ordinary. They all begin *My Darling Frankie* and end *Forever yours, Lou*, and nearly all of them mention at some stage how much Lou misses Frankie and how she wishes she could be with him, but what I do find as I organise them into chronological order is that there appears to be a huge gap. The cards start in the forties and continue with an average of three a year through to the sixties, and then there's a gap before they start up again in the late eighties and continue through until the end of the century.

Why did they stop for so long? I wonder, as I look at the pile of cards on the table next to me. It makes no sense for them to stop and then start again?

What happened to Lou for twenty years that meant she stopped wanting to write to Frankie?

I re-read the cards from the eighties onwards. Lou doesn't mention a husband or a family in any of them, so that was unlikely to have been what stopped her writing. She mainly talks about her career as a painter, and all the places she visits and people she meets. She doesn't mention any significant events that might have affected her life and either prevented her from writing to Frankie or made her not want to. It was very odd.

I get up and go downstairs to make a cup of tea. As I'm waiting for the kettle to boil, I'm still churning this mystery over in my head. Suddenly, it hits me. Without making my tea, I run back upstairs, grab my phone and dial.

'It's me,' I say breathlessly into the receiver.

'Hullo, me,' Malachi replies calmly at the other end. 'What's up?'

'There are more postcards,' I say, not wasting any time.

'More postcards? Where?'

'If they're not in Daisy-Rose, then they have to be somewhere else.'

'How do you know?'

I tell Malachi about the huge gap in the dates on the cards.

'It's possible, I guess.'

'It has to be – otherwise why would Lou stop writing?'

'There could be many reasons.'

'No, I've been through all of them. I'm certain there are more.'

'Look, do you want to come over and discuss it?' Malachi asks. He sounds very relaxed, and I'm sure I can hear the sea in the background and the cries of gulls. 'I'm not up to anything this evening, are you?'

'Er . . . no.'

'Great. Ralph and I are parked up on the cliff overlooking the bay. It's a gorgeous sunset this evening.'

'I know. I can see it from my window. What do you mean you're parked up? Are you in a car?'

'Noo, as if. We're in Pegasus.'

'What's Pegasus?'

'My van, of course!'

'Oh, *your* camper van. I forgot you had one too – sorry.'

'You'll find us easily enough. It's a green and cream bay.'

'Where you're parked is?'

'No, my van is green and cream – it has a bay window. Remember I told you about split screen and bay windows?'

'Oh yes, so you did.'

'So we'll be seeing you soon then?'

'Sure, okay, I'll walk up. It'll take me a few minutes, though, if you're where I think you are – it's a fair way from here.'

'No worries, we're not going anywhere. We'll see you in a bit.'

Assuming it will be cold up on the cliff, I pull on a sweater before locking up the house, then I make my way through the town and up along the cliff path until I see a green and cream camper van parked up. It's pulled off the road on to some rough grass, and as I get closer I see Malachi and Ralph sitting amiably next to each other on a rug to the side of it. They're facing the sea, and they both look so peaceful as they sit gazing out into the sunset that I almost don't want to go over and disturb them.

But my movement disturbs Ralph; he turns his head and barks at me. Malachi puts his hand on his back to quieten him, then he sees me coming across the grass towards them and waves.

'I almost didn't want to interrupt you,' I tell him, as I arrive next to them. I pat Ralph's head and he licks me. 'You both looked so calm there looking out over the ocean.'

'Nature at its finest,' Malachi says quietly, looking back towards the sunset. 'God is definitely showing off his skills tonight.'

'It's very pretty,' I agree. 'So how come you're parked up here?' I ask, looking at the van. 'Is it allowed?'

Malachi shrugs. 'Sort of. I can park here temporarily, but I can't park overnight.'

'Why would you want to park here overnight?'

Malachi turns to me, grinning. 'To camp, of course! If the sun is like this this evening, imagine what it will be like in the morning – glorious!'

'I guess.'

'Bob's yard doesn't quite have the same views, plus I've seen that vista a few too many mornings already.'

'You're sleeping in your van?' I ask in surprise. 'What – all the time while you're here?'

'Nope, not all the time while I'm here, all the time full stop.'

I look at him, puzzled. 'You live ... in *this*?' I turn to the camper van now. It's in a lot better state than Daisy-Rose. Malachi obviously dotes on it. Even though the sun is fading fast in the sky, I can see clearly how the paintwork and chrome have been polished to perfection.

'Yup, I most certainly do.'

'Why?'

Malachi laughs. 'Why not?'

'But where do you keep all your stuff?'

'In Pegasus.'

I look inside the van now. Like the outside it's pretty much spotless. There are dark green leather seats, which like Daisy-Rose's red ones match the exterior paintwork perfectly, a little kitchenette with a cooker, fridge and sink, and in the back I can see folded down and already made up with a fluffy duvet a large, comfy-looking bed.

'There's a Portaloo inside there too, in case you're wondering,' Malachi says, watching me. 'I don't like to get caught short.'

'I wasn't wondering actually. But where do you keep all your things – your bits and pieces?'

'Do you mean clothes?'

'Well, yes, and other things.'

'What other things do I need?'

'I don't know – toiletries, personal possessions, that kind of stuff.'

Malachi jumps up and climbs into the back of the van. He slides a cleverly hidden drawer out from under the bed area. It's filled with neatly folded jeans and T-shirts. Then he slides open a tiny cupboard built in to the pale wooden units, and in it I can see a few toiletries, books and cooking utensils.

'You want to see my underwear too?' he asks, reaching for another handle.

I hurriedly shake my head. 'But still, it's a very minimal way to live.'

'In comparison to . . . you, I suppose? I bet you brought more stuff to St Felix in one suitcase than I have in this van.'

'Not at all.' I choose not to tell him I'm expecting several internet deliveries from various clothes shops over the next few days to top up what I consider a meagre supply of outfits for my extended stay.

'I like it.' Malachi climbs down from the van again. 'It suits me, and my way of life. I like to keep things simple and Pegasus helps me to do that. Now, have you eaten yet? Ralph and I were going to barbecue some sausages tonight. You are most welcome to join us as long as you don't eat Ralph's share.'

'Oh, I don't know . . .'

'Come on, you haven't even talked to me about these post-cards yet?'

'Well, okay then. I guess a barbecue might be quite nice this evening.'

'Quite nice? Ralph, this lady has quite obviously never tasted our barbecued sausages. They're heaven sent – aren't they, boy?'

Ralph barks his agreement.

'Exactly! Now you sit down here.' Malachi pulls a folded-up camping chair from the back of the van and assembles it for me. 'And admire the wonder in front of you, and then when the sun goes down you can enjoy the wonder of Malachi's home cooking!'

Eleven

The smell coming from the disposable barbecue that Malachi has produced from the camper van is delicious. He also produces two bottles of beer from his mini-fridge, and while we wait for the sausages to cook we amiably drink our beer while watching the sun go down over St Felix Bay, me on the picnic chair, Malachi perched on the step of the camper van.

'You see,' Malachi whispers, 'isn't this glorious?'

'I never said it wasn't, did I?'

'You could do this all the time when Daisy-Rose is complete.'

'Perhaps.'

'Why not? What could be better than this – fresh air, fabulous views, great food and freedom?'

'I'll give you the fresh air and fabulous views, but I'll reserve my judgement on the food until it's cooked.' I smile. 'But I have to admit it does smell good.'

'You wouldn't like the freedom of travelling around in a van then?'

'Er . . . no.'

'But why – it's the best thing I ever did. I'm not tied down to any one place, and I can go where I like when I like.'

'It might suit you to live this bohemian life, but it's not for me.'

Malachi leans forward and turns a couple of the sausages over on the barbecue with a fork.

'Tell me something you'd miss?'

'A comfortable bed for one.'

Malachi grins. 'I'll have you know my bed is super comfy – you can try it if you like?'

'I'll take your word for it. Hot running water then?'

Malachi shrugs. 'Plenty of showers at campsites. There is actually a portable gadget that you can buy now that's supposed to give you a warm shower at the end of the day – it uses solar panels to heat the water.'

'No, not for me, thanks. I prefer my showers to be private affairs.'

'How very disappointing.' Malachi's eyes sparkle as he glances at me. 'I've always found the best showers to be shared ones . . . '

'And what about space?' I continue hurriedly, before my cheeks flush too red. 'You might be able to live like this, but I certainly wouldn't be able to.' The camper van was lovely like this on a pleasant summer's evening, all open and inviting, but what if it was raining and you were shut up inside with all the doors and windows closed? I shudder; being trapped in that tiny space didn't bear thinking about.

Malachi doesn't appear to notice my anxiety. Instead he gestures out in front of him at the horizon. 'You can't get more space than that – it's infinite.'

I look out at the view again. I couldn't argue with him.

'It suits a certain type of person,' I begrudgingly agree. 'But I'm not one of them.'

'By a certain type, you mean me, I suppose?' Malachi stands up and climbs into the van, returning with two plates, some cutlery and the bowl of salad he'd prepared earlier. 'Bread?' he asks.

'Yes, please.'

He leans back inside the door and lifts a bread-board with a knife and a crusty loaf balanced on it back outside on to the tiny table I'd assembled while Malachi was lighting the barbecue.

'Help yourself!' he announces, gesturing to the spread. 'Most of the sausages are done to perfection, even if I do say so myself.'

We gather our food and then sit back down again.

'What do you think?' Malachi asks after a few minutes.

'You were right, it tastes lovely, thank you.'

'Just *lovely* – not amazing, astounding or divine?'

'You can barbecue a sausage, I'll give you that.' I wink at him.

'Praise indeed!' Malachi breaks off a piece of sausage and gives it to Ralph, who gobbles it down gratefully and then immediately goes back into begging mode. 'So, you were telling me before about why this lifestyle suits me and not you.'

'Was I?'

'I think so. Tell me more.'

I think for a few moments. 'It's just you're that type, aren't you?'

'And what *type* is that?'

'You're quite chilled and relaxed. You don't need material possessions to make you happy, or career success. Having a lifestyle like this is what makes you happy.'

'You almost sound envious.'

'Perhaps I am, a little.'

'Why?'

'I don't know. I sometimes feel like I've never found my place in life.'

'Go on.'

'A comfortable place. I don't mean a physical place – like a town or a house or something – I mean a place in life that I feel content with, that I'm happy to be in. Does that sound weird?' I take a swig from my bottle of beer, feeling slightly embarrassed.

'Not at all. People pay a lot of money these days to *find themselves*. They're not really finding themselves, they're finding a version of themselves they feel happy to be for a while.'

I think about this.

'We all change through our lives, and what you're happy to be when you're twenty is unlikely to be what you're happy being when you're older.'

'That's very true.'

'I'm sure what you wanted when you were twenty is not what you want in life now, is it?'

'I'm not sure I've ever known what I really wanted.'

'Come on, everyone has some dreams or goals – there must be something either now or in the past you yearned for.'

Again, I take a moment to think. 'I always knew I wanted to work in design.'

'How?'

'I liked it at school.'

'Design or art?'

'Art, I guess.'

Malachi nods.

'When I was young my goals were all about getting qualifi-cations so I could go to art college – GCSEs first, then A-levels, then my degree.'

'Nothing else?'

I smile. 'Other than losing a couple of dress sizes, I wanted to see Wham! in concert!'

'Wham!?' Malachi looks puzzled. 'You're not that old, are you?'

'No, my friend and I were a bit different – we loved the eighties when everyone else was loving Windows computers and MSN chats.'

'Is this friend Daisy?' Malachi asks gently.

'It is. Was. Yes, Daisy.'

'What about after you'd qualified as a graphic designer and you'd started working – then what?'

'Career progression was my only goal. That and the weight thing – still!' I smile, but Malachi remains solemn.

'Only your career?' he asks. 'What about your personal life?'

I hesitate. There is something else, but I'm not sure I should tell Malachi.

'Is it to do with Daisy?' he asks perceptively.

I nod. I play for time by giving a grateful Ralph another piece of sausage. Malachi silently continues to eat his food while he waits for me to elaborate. 'You don't have to tell me if you don't want to,' he says eventually, when I don't speak. He puts his knife and fork down on his plate. 'We can just sit here silently eating sausages for the rest of the night. I realise they do require a certain reverence to enjoy them at their best.'

He stands up and removes the last of the sausages from the barbecue. He puts them on a clean plate and rests them inside the van out of Ralph's reach. 'They'll be even better when they're cold,' he says, lifting his beer and sitting down again.

I'm grateful to him for trying to put me at my ease. 'You see the thing is . . . ' I try, then I hesitate. 'You see it's like this . . . '

Malachi simply waits. 'Another beer?' he asks, as he finishes the last of his.

I nod hurriedly and do the same to mine, while Malachi gets up and reaches into the camper van fridge.

'I always wanted what she had,' I suddenly blurt out, as if Malachi's head buried in the little fridge made telling him easier.

Malachi calmly removes his head from the fridge and his body from the camper van. He takes the tops off both beers and passes me one.

'What did Daisy have?' he asks, sitting down on the step again.

'She had everything,' I say, as words escape from my mouth in a sea of liberation. 'From the minute I met her she had it all. She was pretty and funny, and she knew how to talk to people. She never had any problem getting boyfriends, and she was always invited to all the parties. She was even good at schoolwork – she did much better than I did in our exams.'

Malachi nods. 'Didn't you go to parties then, or have boyfriends?'

'Yes, but I only got invited because I was Daisy's friend.'

'And the boys?'

'I always got the ugly ones, after Daisy got first pick.'

Malachi looks at me with disapproval. 'If I'd said that about women I'm sure you'd have had something to say about it. Were the boys really that bad?'

'I guess not. It just felt like I always got second choice.'

'That's not always a bad thing. I remember in my courting days I was often considered the ugly one.'

I open my eyes wide. 'Hang on just one minute. Firstly, how could you ever be considered the ugly one? If you'd been my second choice I'd have been extremely happy.'

Even in the dim light, I'm sure I detect a warm flush on Malachi's cheeks.

'I'm very pleased to know so,' he says quietly.

'And secondly,' I hurriedly continue before it gets awkward. I'm already regretting my last words – it must be the beer. 'What do you mean in your *courting* days? Who calls it "courting" any more, and even if you do, why don't you do it any longer?'

Malachi stands up and stretches. 'I think Ralph might need a walk,' he says, looking at the dog currently fast asleep on the rug that he had been sitting on earlier.

'He's sound asleep! Stop trying to change the subject. You made me talk about stuff that makes me uncomfortable, now it's your turn.'

Malachi doesn't sit back down again; instead he leans up against the side of the van.

'Why do you think I travel around in this on my own?' he asks.

'I don't know. You said you liked it.'

'I do, most of the time, but it can be quite lonely sometimes. Sometimes I miss having a permanent place to call home.'

'Why don't you find one then?'

'Easier said than done now, I'm afraid.'

'Why?' I wonder if Malachi doesn't want to settle down, or if he can't afford to. I hope I haven't put my foot in it. I didn't want to upset him.

But Malachi simply looks up into the clear night sky. 'Do you ever wonder what's up there?' he asks.

'Planets?' I suggest, wondering if he was going off on one of his tangents again.

'That's what they'd have you believe.'

'Who?'

'Those that doubt.'

I'm not sure what to say. This was Malachi doing that thing he did so well – not making a lot of sense.

'Doubt in what?'

Malachi opens his mouth to answer, but suddenly the loudest clap of thunder I think I've ever heard crashes over our heads, and from nowhere large raindrops start pelting from the sky.

'How is that even possible?' I cry, as a wind suddenly whips up too, and we hurriedly gather all the things from outside the van and stash them inside. 'It was a clear sky only moments ago.'

But Malachi is strangely silent as we close the back of the van with Ralph inside and climb into the front seats.

'Anything is possible, Ana,' he says as he starts up the engine. 'Anything, if you know what I do. Now, I'd better drive you back to your cottage before we cause any further freak weather conditions that can't be explained.'

Twelve

Malachi drives me back to the cottage. We don't talk any more about the weather or indeed ourselves, instead we talk about his camper van and how the refurbishments he's done on it might compare to the ones on Daisy-Rose.

'We never talked about the postcards,' I say, as Malachi pulls up at the cottage. 'We got a little side-tracked talking about me!'

'You say that like it's a bad thing.' Malachi switches off the engine and turns to look at me. 'So what's the issue with the postcards?'

'I think there's a significant number missing. If I had those I'm sure I could find Lou and return them all to her. I've learned a lot about her already just by reading the first cards.'

'You're determined to do this, aren't you?'

I nod.

Malachi thinks for a moment. He stares out of the windscreen into the now darkened street.

'Deltiology,' he says, without explanation.

'What?'

'Deltiology – it's the name for the study and collection of postcards. It comes from the Greek word *deltios*, which means "writing tablet" or "letter".'

'Does it now. And just where are you going with this?'

'Postcards are the third most popular collection hobby after stamps and currency.'

'Are you simply trying to impress me with your knowledge?'

Malachi turns to look at me again. '*Hmm*, now who do you know that might have an insight into those worlds?'

I stare at him, puzzled.

'Someone who deals with collectors of antiques and other such things in his daily business?'

I'm still none the wiser, but Malachi just waits.

'*Oh!*' I exclaim as the penny finally drops. 'You mean Noah.'

'Took you a while – I really didn't want to go with the flood references again.'

'Do you think he might know something?'

'I think he might be able to put you in touch with someone who does – but it's a very long shot that you'll be able to actually trace those particular cards.'

'Malachi, I could hug you!'

'You're welcome to if you want?'

'Bit difficult in here, there's not a lot of room. But thank you.' I squeeze his hand instead. 'That's a really good suggestion.'

Malachi looks down at his hand where I've just touched it. 'No, Ana, thank you.'

'What for?'

Malachi shakes his head. 'No matter. Now be away with you, go get some sleep, and tomorrow you can go and find Noah, while I of course will be slaving over Miss Daisy-Rose for you.'

I smile at him and open the door of the van. Then I climb

out and slam it shut again, waving as he drives away down the street.

I shake my hand a little before I reach for my key. *What is that – pins and needles?* I wonder. My palm is tingling in a very odd way.

But by the time I've opened the door, gone inside and put the kettle on the tingling has gone, so for the time being I think no more about it.

The next morning, I set off early for Noah's shop.

It's another gorgeous day in St Felix and the sun warms my thoughts as well as my body as I walk along the narrow streets to Noah's Ark.

Contrary to what I'd thought when I left London, I was really beginning to enjoy my stay here. The people seemed lovely and the weather for the most part was glorious, and even when it wasn't, the rain and storms that would occasionally break up the fine weather were dramatic and enjoyable too, as long as you were inside in the warm and dry watching them through glass.

I'd phoned home a couple of times. Home being my neighbour, Helen, who I'd asked to keep an eye on my flat while I was away. Luckily Helen had a key and it wasn't a big ask – she only had to pick up any post and tend to the few plants that would need watering while I was away – but it was good to know someone was watching over my little place, and I'd promised her lots of clotted cream, scones and jam when I returned home.

I'd also texted my mum and told her where I was staying temporarily. I don't know why really. Mum lived in Cardiff with her new partner, so me being down here in Cornwall rather than London wasn't really going to make that much difference to our occasional phone calls and texts.

It had saddened me when I realised how few people would actually care that I'd be here in St Felix for a few weeks rather than in London. I was a freelance designer so I didn't have a boss to report to; all any client cared about was that my deadlines were met and that I produced quality work for them.

The only other person I'd texted had been Peter, Daisy's husband, to tell him that I'd found the camper van and that I'd be staying here temporarily until I could drive it home.

Pete had seemed pleased I was staying and had told me yet again how much Daisy had loved it down here.

The shop is open when I arrive. I push open the door and the little bell rattles instead of rings above my head again.

Jess immediately appears from the back. Even if the bell wasn't working properly, she seemed to know when anyone was entering the shop.

'Hi again,' she says, looking pleased to see me. 'I didn't expect to see you back so soon.'

'I was looking for Noah actually,' I say, as Jess's smile broadens even further. 'Is he in?'

'It's his late start today. We're rarely busy first thing, even on a Sunday, so we take it in turns to come in early. You can probably catch him at his cottage, though, if it's urgent?' Jess looks intrigued as she waits for my answer.

'Oh no, it's nothing urgent. I don't want to disturb him at home. It can wait.' I smile at her and turn as if to leave.

'A message then?' Jess pipes up behind me, so I turn back again. 'I could give him a message when he comes in?'

'No, really, it's fine, Jess, I'll pop back another day.'

Jess looks desperately at her watch. 'He usually walks Clarice about now,' she suggests hurriedly, 'you might find him on the cliff path above Porthhaven beach?'

I smile at her. 'All right, I'll bite. Which one is Porthhaven? I get confused – there are so many little beaches here.'

Jess grins, knowing she's reeled me back in. 'That's what comes of living on a peninsula. I was the same when I first moved here too – it's so confusing! Porthhaven is the one they let dogs on in the summer. All the others ban them – mean bastards, I say. Why shouldn't the doggies have their fun too? But it's the families, isn't it? They think we're not going to pick up the doggie doo-doos.'

I grin.

Jess shakes her head as though she's ashamed of herself. 'That's flippin' Noah's influence for you – doggie doo-doos! I'd just call it dog shit.'

'Well, I guess it's a little politer. Anyway, Clarice can't have much doggie doo-doo, can she – she's tiny.'

'You'd be surprised.' Jess rolls her eyes. 'When I signed up to work in an antiques shop I didn't sign up to being a dog walker too! But then I guess Noah didn't really sign up to taking on a small dog either when he agreed to take on the shop.'

'Oh?' Now I'm the one who's intrigued.

'Yeah,' Jess continues keenly. She seems to revel in discussing Noah with me. 'It was his aunt's shop before and Noah only took it on a few years ago, but with the shop came Clarice – it was part of the deal – so he's kind of stuck with her now. Not that I think he minds, though – he dotes on that thing when no one's looking. Real softie, he is, our Noah.'

I nod. 'So he changed the name then, when he took the shop on?'

'Oh no, the shop was called that before, his aunt Harriet doted on Noah too. Never had any kids of her own, so she spoilt her only nephew when she could. I think she thought if

102

she called the shop after him, Noah would feel obliged to keep visiting her when he grew into an adult and then one day take over the running of it, and she was right.'

'That makes a lot of sense. I didn't think a man would call a dog Clarice.'

I'm surprised actually just how much I have thought about Noah since I met him.

'Nah, it's after Clarice Cliff, ain't it – the famous ceramic designer?'

'Yes, I've heard of her.'

'Good. Not everyone has.'

'I studied art at college. Well, graphics, but we covered different designers in my foundation year.'

Jess nods her approval. 'So, are you going to go and find him? Noah, I mean. I'm sure he'd be pleased to see you.' She looks so eager that I hardly dare say no. 'If you're not going to go,' she adds, the disappointment clear in her voice, 'you can leave a message with me and I'll be sure to pass it on.'

'Okay,' I say, giving in. 'I'll head over to the beach and see if I can find him and Clarice.'

Jess claps her hands in glee. Subtlety was obviously not one of her strong points.

'If I don't find him, though, could you pass a message on?'

'Of course! Anything.'

'Just tell him I need his advice about something.'

'Ooh, really?' Jess rubs her hands together now.

'I'd love to tell you it's something exciting, Jess, but it really isn't.'

'Ana, anything that doesn't involve holiday-makers, fishing boats or tide times is exciting around here.'

I smile again. 'Let me find Noah first, and perhaps he'll tell you about it later, then you can judge for yourself whether it's exciting or not.'

Like Jess had said, St Felix sits on its own tiny peninsula that juts out into the Atlantic so it has several sandy beaches, the most northerly of which is favoured by surfers because of the huge waves that often crash dramatically on its shore. There is a tiny beach by the harbour, which can only be viewed at low tide, and another long stretch of sand popular with families runs below the coastal path I walked along a couple of days ago. But the beach I'm heading to now, Porthhaven, is as Jess had rightly pointed out the only one that dogs are allowed on in high season.

From my viewpoint high up above the beach I look down on to the sand.

There are a few dogs running around, chasing balls and splashing about in the waves, but I can't see Clarice amongst them, neither can I see Noah in amongst the small group of dog owners that are gathered down there having a chat.

I watch the dogs for a few moments, and I'm about to turn and head towards the street where Jess has kindly informed me Noah has a small cottage when I hear a friendly 'Hello' behind me.

I jump.

'Whoa, you don't want to be jumping like that all the way up here,' Noah says. 'It's a long way down.' He tugs on Clarice's lead to pull her away from what she's currently sniffing.

'You surprised me, that's all.'

'Sorry. You looked like you were enjoying watching the dogs having fun down there?'

'Yes, I was, but I was looking for you actually.'

Now it's Noah's turn to look surprised.

'Jess told me I might find you here,' I explain. 'I wondered if you might be able to help me.'

Clarice is obviously keen to get going again, and she pulls on her red lead.

'We can walk and talk if you like?' I suggest.

'We haven't got much more walking to do,' Noah says. 'She's already had a run around on the beach and whatever she thinks' – he looks purposely at Clarice – 'she only has little legs! What about if we walk up to that bench next to the coast-guard lookout and take a seat for a bit?'

'Sure, sounds good.'

After we've climbed even higher up the hill we seat ourselves on a small wooden bench that looks out over much of St Felix and the surrounding sea. While I tell Noah exactly what Malachi and I had discovered in the camper van, Clarice takes a nap on the grass in the warm sunshine.

'Very interesting,' Noah says, when I've finished. 'So how can *I* help?

'I hoped you might be able to help me trace the rest of the postcards. If I can find the missing cards, I'm sure I can trace Lou and return them all to her or even to her family if she's not around any more.'

'Yes, sadly there is that possibility,' Noah says, thinking. 'From what you say she must be what – seventy, eighty years old?'

'I think a little older according to some of the dates on the postcards and what she was doing at that time. Malachi thinks I'm mad trying to find her – he thinks we should just leave it alone – but there's so much love in those cards from Lou to Frankie and she wrote to him for so long, the postcards must be very special to her, like Frankie was.'

'Malachi – that's the guy you were with in the pub the other night?'

'Yes, that's right. He's the mechanic who's helping me to do up Daisy— I mean, Daisy-Rose. That's what we're calling the van now we've discovered Rose was her original name. Daisy was what I wanted to call her – it's a long story,' I add.

'I see,' Noah says thoughtfully. 'And this Malachi doesn't think you'll be able to find Lou?'

'He's doubtful. So, do you think you might be able to help me? I know it's a long shot, but I thought with you being in the trade and everything, you might have more of an idea of where I should start looking?'

Noah continues to gaze out into the distance. He appears to be thinking about something.

'I— I can't pay you or anything,' I continue, wondering if it might be better to let him think. 'I mean if I don't find Lou I guess you can have the postcards to sell. They might be worth something?'

Noah turns towards me. 'Don't be silly, I don't want to be paid, and anyway I doubt the postcards are worth all that much. Their sentimental value is high, but that's about it.'

'Oh . . . ' My head droops forward.

'You're just lucky I'm a bit of a romantic at heart,' Noah adds quickly, before it can droop any further.

'You will help then?' I ask keenly, looking at him again.

'Yes, I'll help you.'

I feel like clapping my hands in glee like Jess had. But I restrain myself and instead say, 'That's wonderful, Noah, thank you so much. So where do you think we should start looking first?'

Thirteen

We walk with a now refreshed Clarice back to Noah's shop.

'Jess told me you inherited Clarice and the shop from your aunt,' I tell him, as we stand back to allow a car to pass us on the narrow street.

'Yes, that's right. I didn't mind the shop part too much – I was at a stage in my life where I needed a bit of a new start, and an old antiques shop that already had my name seemed as good a place to begin again as anywhere.'

I wonder why he'd needed a fresh start, but I don't ask. It wasn't really my business, was it?

'But taking on this little madam,' he says, putting Clarice back down on the ground now the car has safely passed, 'well, that was a whole different ball game. I'd never had a dog before and when I'd imagined owning one, I'd always thought it would be a big dog. Clarice, you may be many things, but you're no Great Dane!'

Clarice turns her head and gives Noah an indifferent look.

'My friend had a big dog. He's lovely but he's a handful.'

'Oh yes, you said – a Burmese Mountain dog, wasn't it?'

'Good memory! Yes, it was, well, is – he's still about.'

'But sadly your friend isn't.'

'No.' I'd almost forgotten how much I'd told Noah about Daisy the first time I met him up on the cliff.

'Again, I'm sorry. I know how hard that can be.'

'Yes, it's still a little raw.'

That was an understatement.

'I bet it's a lot more than that,' Noah says perceptively. 'She was obviously a very good friend for you to travel all the way down here and then stay while you have an old camper van done up in her name.'

'How did you know all that? I didn't tell you.'

'You told me enough just now for me to put two and two together along with what you'd mentioned before.'

'You sound like Malachi.'

'The mechanic?'

'Yeah, he's like you – perceptive.'

'I'll have to meet this Malachi one day. I can't say I know of him?'

'I don't think he's been in St Felix that long. He's only here temporarily to look after the garage.'

We've reached the shop. Noah opens the door, and while the little bell rattles above he holds the door open for me to go through.

'Damn thing,' he says, looking up at the bell. 'I've tried fixing it, but to no avail. I'll have to get a new one sometime.'

There are few people browsing inside the shop and Jess is behind the counter.

'Ah, you found him then,' she says, looking pleased.

'She surely did.' Noah leads Clarice through the shop towards the back room. 'I'll just get Clarice settled and then we can talk some more, okay? She'll conk out once she's been fed and watered after her long walk this morning.'

'Sure, that's fine.'

'So . . . ' Jess asks, as soon as Noah has left the room. 'What's all this about then?'

I have to admire Jess's honesty. Most people would have been a little more discreet with their enquiries.

'I told you before,' I say, pretending to string her along a little, 'I need Noah's help.'

'Yes, but with what? Come on, I'm dying here. Nothing exciting ever happens in this shop. A pretty woman coming in here wanting help from Noah to me is akin to a particularly thrilling episode of my favourite soap – don't leave me with the *doof doof* moment, Ana!'

I grin at her *EastEnders* reference. 'I need to find some postcards, that's all.'

Jess's expectant expression drops a tad.

'Postcards,' she repeats. 'Is that it?'

'They're not just any postcards.' As quickly as I can I tell her all about Lou and Frankie.

'That's very cool,' she says, when I've finished. 'Nothing like that could ever happen now – everyone's texts and emails will end up being deleted in the future. There'll be no permanent record of people's love for each other, which is a real shame.'

I hadn't thought about it like that.

'All the more reason for us to try to reunite these cards with either their owner or their owner's family then.'

'Yeah . . . ' Jess is obviously considering something. 'There is one thing though.'

'What's that?'

'What if the owner didn't want her family to know about the

109

cards, and that's why she hid them? Maybe Lou was having some sort of clandestine affair with this Frankie and by returning the cards to her you'll blow up all sorts of trouble?'

'No,' I say confidently. 'It wasn't an affair, far from it. The cards I've read are full of unrequited love from one person to another. It's beautiful not sordid.'

'Ah, okay,' Jess says, seeming to accept this answer readily. 'Well, you've come to the right person. Noah loves a good puzzle – he'll enjoy trying to help you solve this one. I remember when—'

'Thank you, Jess,' Noah says, coming back into the shop. 'Don't you have customers to see to?'

'Yes, boss.' Jess salutes, then she rolls her eyes at me.

'Would you like to come through to the office?' Noah asks, beckoning me across the shop. 'It's just this way.'

Entering Noah's office at the rear of the shop feels like stepping back in time. It looks like one of those offices you might see in an old black and white film or a fifties drama on the television.

At one end of the cream-coloured room there is a solid dark-wood desk with a green banker's desk lamp standing on it. Matching wooden shelves neatly stacked with books and files in colour-coded rows run along one wall, and a few framed oil paintings and watercolours hang neatly in groups on the others.

'Take a seat,' Noah says, gesturing to a wing-back leather armchair. It has maroon buttons holding down the upholstery all along its back, and I wonder as I sit down on the warm leather how many other people have sat ensconced within its protective sides before me.

'Can I get you some tea or coffee?' Noah offers. 'I've just had one of those fancy machines installed.'

I'm surprised. 'Coffee would be great, thanks.'

'Cappuccino? Latte?'

'Cappuccino, please. One sugar.'

'Coming up. Our little kitchen is only next door, so I'll be right back.'

I watch him go through another door that adjoins the office, which he leaves slightly ajar, and I can just make out Clarice dozing happily in her basket on the floor against some pale-wood cupboards.

I hear the gurgling of a coffee machine doing its thing, and shortly Noah returns with two cups of frothy coffee.

'Thanks,' I say, as he passes me one. 'I have to say when you said you'd got a coffee machine I was quite surprised. Everything else in here is so old, and this' – I lift my mug – 'is so modern.'

'Not everything I do is anchored in the past, you know,' Noah says, surprising me again by looking a little hurt at my comment.

'Oh no, I didn't mean any offence,' I reply hurriedly. I didn't want to upset him, not now he'd said he would help me. Actually, no, it was more than that – Noah was a nice, kind man and I didn't want to offend him full stop. 'I meant it's a welcome change, and it makes lovely coffee.'

Noah looks at me suspiciously, and then he smiles. 'Good recovery.'

'Thanks.'

'It was probably me anyway – I'm a bit touchy when I think I'm being criticised. I know you weren't,' he says, holding up his hand to quieten me when I try to pipe up again. 'It's just . . . well . . . apparently I'm too sensitive.'

'Who told you that?'

'Jess, and a few other people.'

I think about this while I take another sip of my coffee. 'Do you want my opinion?' I ask a little shyly, putting my mug down on a coaster on the table next to me. After all, Noah and I had only met a few days ago.

Noah screws up his nose, and I notice under his glasses he has a few freckles scattered haphazardly across the bridge. 'Do I?'

'I don't think I've ever met a man that's too sensitive. Usually you can hit them with a brick and it will still bounce off them without making any sort of dent – metaphorically, of course.'

'Of course,' Noah says, grinning now. 'Well, thank you, I'll take that on board.'

'Good.'

We hold each other's gaze for a few seconds. Then Noah hurriedly blinks and pushes his glasses up his nose, even though they don't appear to have slipped at all.

'Right, about these postcards,' he says in a business-like voice now. 'I can make some calls for you. I know a few people in the trade. Even though I've had a fair few cards in the shop over the years, I'm no expert.'

'That would be great, thanks. Tell me honestly, Noah, do you think we have any chance of finding them?'

Noah sighs, 'I'd like to say yes – it's such a touching story that to give it a proper ending would be lovely. But in reality, I think you might be better using the cards you already have to try to trace Lou.'

I nod despondently.

'I'll do my very best none the less,' Noah says brightly. 'It's not often I have a damsel in distress asking for my help … especially one as pretty as you.'

Noah's cheeks flush so pink, they're almost the same colour as my chair, but instead of thinking it odd for a man to blush so profusely, I actually find it very endearing.

St John's Academy
Sixth Form Leavers' Ball, 2004

'Where's Dave?' Daisy shouts in my ear, trying to get her voice heard over the sound of the thumping music. The DJ is currently playing Britney Spears at full blast, and the dance floor is crammed with eighteen-year-old girls and boys in their prom dresses and tuxedos dancing the night away, seemingly without a care in the world.

Because of my 'little problem' we're standing on the sidelines as we so often did at these events.

'I don't know. I haven't seen him in a while.'

'I bet he's up to no good!' Daisy shouts again.

'Look, I know you've never liked him, but he's okay. Really, he is.'

Daisy looks at me and shakes her head.

'It's okay for you with your *oh, so perfect* A-star boyfriends. Those types of boys aren't interested in me, are they? Anyway' – I shake my head – 'I prefer them a bit rougher around the edges. They're more *interesting.*'

'Interesting – is that what you call it? I call it trouble.'

'Dave is not trouble, he's—' But I'm cut off mid-sentence by the music suddenly being turned off and the lights switched on. There are loud boos and jeers from the dancers, and Daisy and I blink under the bright fluorescent glare above us as we watch the head of the sixth form climb up behind the DJ's desk and take a mic from him. A uniformed police officer joins him.

'I'm sorry to put a stop to your enjoyable evening,' Mr Grayson says, looking quite pale, which I suspect is not due to the harsh lighting. 'But there's been a ... *situation* outside in the playground, and I've been asked by the police to put a stop to the music while everyone is questioned.'

'*Questioned*?' Daisy hisses in my ear. 'It must be bad if they want to question us.'

'This could take some time,' Mr Grayson says apologetically. 'So I ask that you are all patient and co-operative, and then the police can get their job done as quickly as possible.'

'What's happened, Mr Grayson?' someone shouts from the crowd. 'Has someone been murdered?'

There are *ooh*s and *aah*s from the floor, and much muttering and discussion suddenly breaks out.

Mr Grayson waves his hand to quieten everyone down. 'No, of course not. But there has been an issue.' He glances at the policeman standing to his left.

The officer nods his agreement.

'Well, it's more of an incident really – an incident involving drugs and a nasty fight ... ' Mr Grayson hesitates again. 'With a knife.'

More *ooh*s and *aah*s.

'Now before the police begin questioning you all, can anyone who knows David Skinner well come forward first, please, as they would like to talk to you immediately.'

I'm aware of several heads swivelling in my direction. Weakly, I turn to Daisy.

But instead of gloating, I feel Daisy gently take my hand, and with everyone staring at us she guides me safely through the crowd towards the police officer.

It was not to be my last experience of dating a 'bad boy'.

Fourteen

That afternoon I'm back at my cottage sitting in my favourite spot looking out through the French windows. The day has remained bright and sunny, and in amongst the cry of gulls and the sound of gentle waves rolling in across the bay, I can hear the sound of excited children playing on the sand with their families.

I'm reminded of a time when I'd taken a day trip to Brighton with Daisy and her family. I'd had a lovely time playing with the boys on the sand making sandcastles and paddling in the sea. We'd eaten fish and chips and then ice cream, and walked along the prom and the pier. I'd felt absolutely exhausted at the end of the day but extremely happy too.

It wasn't just Daisy I missed but her family as well. Peter had kindly said I could visit them any time I wanted to, and I had a couple of times – I'd taken the boys for days out to give Peter a little break – but I found it heart-breaking spending time with them, all too aware that Daisy wouldn't suddenly be popping by to join us or waiting with a cup of tea and a biscuit when I dropped them off at the end of the day, eagerly wanting to know everything we'd been up to.

I'd never been lucky enough to find anyone I wanted to spend the rest of my life with like Daisy had, let alone someone that I wanted to have a family with too. Recently I'd been starting to wonder if I ever would.

I shake my head. 'That's enough wallowing for today,' I tell myself. 'Time up.'

I allowed myself an indulgent trip down memory lane once every day, which usually resulted in a few tears, but I'd noticed since I'd been here in St Felix those trips were becoming shorter and, dare I even think it, marginally less painful each time.

I pick up the small pile of postcards I've chosen to re-read. They are all dated from the mid-sixties.

The first one has a picture on the front of Tower Bridge in London.

> 10th June 1963
>   My Darling Frankie,
>   You'll never guess, I've started a new
> hobby – painting!
>   I really enjoy it, it's so relaxing, and my teacher
> at the evening class I go to says I'm quite good. I
> knew I should have gone to art school all those years
> ago ... I'm joshing with you! I love my new job at
> the solicitors, and I wouldn't change it for the world.
> Except of course if you were close by ...
>   Forever yours,
>   Lou x

The next one is from November that same year. It's a postcard of St Michael's Mount at Marazion.

14th November 1963

My Darling Frankie,

Guess what, I sold a painting!

Our class had a small exhibition and a very nice lady said she would like to hang one of my paintings on the wall of her flat. I can hardly believe it!

Perhaps one day I'll be able to paint you? I know it would be the best painting I could ever do.

Forever yours,

Lou x

The card after that has a seasonal picture of a cheery Robin with a bright red breast.

23rd December 1963

My Darling Frankie,

I just wanted to wish you a very Happy Christmas.

I'll be spending mine this year back in Cornwall with Mother. It will be nice just the two of us, but I'm sure we will miss Father terribly.

I hope you have a lovely time with your family.

Forever yours,

Lou x

Then there's a slight gap because the next card is from August 1964. This time it's an arty-looking one of some strange sculptures with holes in the middle.

4th August 1964

My Darling Frankie,

I'm sorry I haven't written for so long; I've been

incredibly busy! You'll never guess ... I'm giving up
my job in the solicitor's office.

I'm going to give my painting a real go. I hope I
might be able to make a modest living from it. I'm
hardly a Hockney or a Warhol, but I'm told my paintings
are a little different and I've sold quite a few recently.

Exciting times. I wish you were here to share
them with me.

Forever yours,

Lou x

The last from this batch is a picture of a sunny day on
Newquay beach.

3rd September 1964

My Darling Frankie,

What do you know? I've bought myself a little
runaround from the proceeds of my painting! It's a
brand new Dormobile camper van, and I love her!
She's ruby red and cream and is by far the loveliest
thing I've ever owned.

I hope to travel the country finding inspiration for
my painting. (Don't worry I won't be turning into one
of those newfangled hippy types!)

I will of course write and let you know how
I get on.

Forever yours,

Lou x

So Lou probably first began painting in the sixties, and she
purchased Daisy-Rose in 1964 brand new. I'm quite impressed.

I'd never had a brand new car myself, always preferring to buy second-hand – new cars lost so much value the minute you drove them off the forecourt. I wonder if Lou was Daisy-Rose's only owner before my Daisy bought her last year? Then I remember one of the later postcards. I'd read through them all so fast yesterday that I hadn't really taken everything in properly.

I look back through the cards again, which I have tried to organise in small piles on the sitting-room coffee table. I was going to have to find a better way of cataloguing them; one strong gust of wind through the French windows and they'd be all over the place in seconds. In the later ones there is no mention of Lou selling Daisy-Rose. She talks about growing older and about not travelling so much any more, and there's a definite change in tone from her early cards, which are so vibrant and full of life. On one of the very last her writing is much shakier and harder to read:

12th April 1999

My Darling Frankie,

I went up to London today to see one of my paintings being hung in the National Gallery – only for a temporary exhibition, mind, but what an honour!

I couldn't take Rose, as I had to go by train, but to be honest it was quite a relief. I've been finding it harder and harder to manage her with my arthritic hands and I'm afraid the time is coming when I may have to let her go, and buy something a little easier to manage.

She's been such a part of my life for so long, I'll be dreadfully upset to give her up.

I just wish you could have shared some of our happy times with us.

 Forever yours,

 Lou x

I wonder what happened to Lou and Rose after that? I think, as I gaze at the picture on the card, which is of Nelson's Column in Trafalgar Square. *Did Lou sell Daisy-Rose then? Did she stop writing to Frankie?* I can hardly bear to think about the other reason she might have stopped writing. Lou would have been about seventy in that last card according to my calculations, maybe a bit younger. Surely she'd gone on to live many more years after that?

I sit and ponder what I know already, looking partly at my many notes and partly at the postcards covering the table, hoping they might be able to throw some new light.

I knew Lou had originally lived in St Felix when she was young. As I'd discovered with Malachi, the first postcard dates from 1945, and by what she wrote I'm guessing she must have been about fifteen years old. She did well at school and went on to Oxford University to study law – I know that because one of the postcards was from Oxford itself and told Frankie all about her first term there. She must have passed her exams if she went on to work in a solicitor's office at a later date, perhaps in London? A card had been written from there and had mentioned her job, but that could have been one of a few places she might have worked. There would have been time for her to have moved around before she gave it all up to paint in the mid-sixties; it isn't always clear whether the pictures on the front of the cards from that time have any relevance to what Lou is telling Frankie.

I think about what it must have felt like for a woman in the sixties to suddenly have the freedom to make her own decisions and not to have to rely on a man to support her. It was clear from the messages that Lou had never married or had children, but she seemed to have had quite an interesting and fulfilling life without them – even if she did pine for Frankie through most of it.

Lou never made mention of any relationships of the romantic kind, but then I guess she wouldn't; the postcards had been written to her one true love and even if she hadn't actually sent them to him, she was hardly going to tell him all about her love life, or lack of it, was she?

I sigh. Was this really all I had to go on? There was no way I would be able to trace a woman called Lou who lived in Cornwall when she was young, went to Oxford University in the late forties and might have worked in a solicitor's office in London in 1963 – it would be virtually impossible.

I think again, and the postcard with the holey statues catches my eye. Could the artistic part of Lou's life throw up something I hadn't thought of before?

I look at all the later cards I have once more. It seems that Lou had been quite the successful painter in the end. After her earlier excursions to other parts of the UK, and then her painting tours around the country with Rose, she seemed to have settled back in St Felix in the late eighties; partly, it seemed, to be near to her elderly mother, who when the cards start up again in 1987 appears to be in poor health, and partly because she seemed happy painting in and around her home town once more.

Wait a minute! I suddenly think. *Someone in St Felix must have lived here in the eighties and they would surely remember a woman called Lou who painted from a red camper van!*

Of course. I sigh. *Why didn't I think of this earlier?* I'd been so transfixed on tracing Lou's life, that I hadn't considered the answer could be right here on my doorstep.

I look at my watch – it was just past six o'clock.

I think a quick drink at The Merry Mermaid might be in order tonight, I tell myself. *And a little chat with my friend Rita.*

I head down to the Mermaid at 7 p.m. after I've showered and freshened up.

The bar is already busy when I arrive but I manage to squeeze on to a free bar stool and wait for Rita or Richie, who are both running around behind the bar tonight, to spot me waiting.

Rita catches my eye when she's pouring a pint of beer.

'Ana, love!' she calls, smiling at me. 'I'll be right with you. Just give me a moment – it's mad in here tonight!'

'No worries!' I call back. I'd rather wait until Rita has time for a quick chat anyway.

I look around the bar while I'm waiting. There is the usual mix of holiday-makers and locals. They're easy to tell apart as most of the holiday-makers look like they've had a bit too much sun today, and they're generally a little bit pink and tend to be in shorts and T-shirts, or flowery dresses and sandals. The locals are also in casual dress, but instead of a touch of sunburn, they all have that healthy relaxed glow and gentle tan that comes from spending a lot of time outdoors in clean air and plenty of sunshine.

I spot Ant and Dec from the bakery sitting at one of the window tables having a meal. Ant waves, and I shyly wave back, secretly pleased he's remembered me amongst his many customers.

'Now then, my love, what can I get for you tonight?' Rita

says from the other side of the bar. She looks very flushed and sounds slightly breathless.

'Can I have an orange juice with some fizzy water and ice, please?'

'You surely can, my love.' Rita scoops a shovel of ice into a glass, then she reaches down under the bar and retrieves a bottle of orange juice, which she deftly opens with the bottle opener attached to the bar. 'Would you like bottled water or soda?'

'Soda is fine, thanks.'

Rita moves a little way along the bar, lifts a nozzle attached to a pipe and squirts fizzy water into my glass.

'There you go, my lovely,' she says. 'That'll be two pounds eighty-five please.'

I thrust a five-pound note towards her.

Rita taps the till, then she produces my change.

'Can I have a word when you've got a minute, Rita?' I ask. 'I know you're really busy right now, but maybe later?'

'Of course, just give me a few minutes to clear this lot. One of our bar staff has called in sick tonight so we're rushed off our feet. What with the weather today, we've got the world, his wife and all his grandchildren in here tonight!'

As Rita moves along the bar to take the next person's order, I take a sip of my juice and look around the room hoping I might see someone I know, like Noah or Jess. Even Malachi would do, so long as I didn't have to sit here on my own.

Now that's not fair, I tell myself, turning back towards the bar when I don't see anyone. Malachi is a nice guy, a little bit eccentric perhaps, but his heart is in the right place.

'Busy in here tonight, isn't it?' a voice comments next to me, and I turn to see Ant from the bakery. He's wearing a bright green checked shirt with red trousers, and in his hand he holds two empty glasses. His gaze is locked hopefully in Rita's direction.

'Yes, it is,' I reply, relieved to have someone to chat to. 'Have you been busy in the bakery today?'

'Too right we have. Sometimes Dec and I manage a Sunday off, even in the summer months. But there was no chance of that today – manic all day. We had to call extra staff in to help out. That's why we're in here tonight. I said to Dec, "There is no way I'm cooking tonight, we're eating out!" So here we are! What have you been up to today – out enjoying the sunshine like everyone else?'

'Oh, this and that,' I tell him, not wanting to have to explain too much. 'I visited Noah's Ark – the antiques shop?'

Ant gives up trying to catch Rita's eye and turns fully towards me. 'Yes, I know it. Noah is a lovely guy. Quiet, mind. Well, quiet compared to me, I guess! But we see him about with his little dog and he always stops to chat.'

I nod. Everyone always seemed to have something good to say about Noah.

'Do you know Malachi?' I ask. 'He's doing up a vehicle for me at Bob's Bangers. That's why I'm staying here really, until the work is done.'

'No, I can't say I do. I didn't even know Bob had anyone working with him.'

'Malachi is looking after the place while Bob is away.'

'Ah, I see. Yes, Richie, I am waiting!' Ant calls sternly as Richie approaches. 'Only joking around.' He winks. 'You're a bit busy in here tonight, aren't you?'

Richie rolls his eyes. 'Tell me about it. But I can't complain. The till is constantly ringing and that's always good to hear!'

'Our usuals, please,' Ant says, passing him the glasses. 'Would you like something—?'

'—Ana. No, thank you. It's very kind of you, but I have this.' I lift my glass.

Ant looks around while he's waiting for Richie to bring his refills.

'On your own, are you, Ana?' he asks, his dark eyebrows rising in surprise.

'I only popped in to ask Rita something. I had no idea it would be so busy though. She's a bit tied up at the moment.'

'And could be for some time by the looks of it. Would you like to join us at our table until she's free?'

'Oh, I don't know – I don't want to impose.'

'Nonsense, darling, you won't be. We've eaten now, and to be honest when you work with someone *and* live with them, anyone new to talk to always goes down a treat. And we won't bite. As I'm sure you've gathered by now, we're very friendly, and very gay!'

I smile at him. 'Well, if you're sure, then I will, thanks.'

When Ant has his replenished drinks, I follow him across the pub. He introduces me to Dec and I take a seat with them, pleased not to be on my own any more.

'So what is it you're so desperate to ask Rita about?' Ant asks bluntly.

'Ant!' Dec admonishes. 'It might be private. He always dives straight in with his size twelves,' he says apologetically to me.

'I've never known you to complain about the size of my feet,' Ant responds quick as a flash to Dec, and then winks at me.

'Trust you to lower the tone,' Dec says, disappointedly shaking his head. 'I can't take him anywhere.'

I smile. These two were quite the double act in their own right, even without the names!

'I wanted to ask her if she knew anyone who lived here in the eighties. I'm looking for someone who I'm pretty sure lived in St Felix then, and I hoped they might remember them.'

'The eighties, *hmm*?' Dec says. 'Well, we certainly weren't here then, were we, Ant?'

'Nope. I was at primary school then in Portsmouth, and you were what – already out working?' Ant grins.

'If you were at primary school, I'd have been at secondary, that's all, and you know it!' Dec chides. 'I'm not *that* much older than him,' he says quietly to me. 'But Ant always has to make a thing about it. Now, the eighties – I don't know much about them other than it was a great decade for music.'

'It was, yes,' I agree.

'Although you don't look old enough to remember the eighties,' Dec says kindly. 'Does she, Ant?'

'You've had some great Botox if you do ...' Ant looks closely at me.

'No, I was born then, that's about all I remember. I just really like the music from that decade.'

'Good taste,' Dec says approvingly. 'Now,' he adds, 'who do we know that might have been here then? What about Lou?' he asks Ant.

'Lou?' My ears prick up. Surely she wasn't actually still here?

'Lou works at the post office. She's been here donkey's years, hasn't she, Ant?'

Ant nods.

'Did this Lou ever own a camper van, do you know – a red one?'

Dec shrugs. 'Not that I know of. Come to think of it, I don't even think she drives, does she, Ant?'

'No, I don't think so. She said something about it when she was in the shop once – about how she wishes she'd learned when she was younger.'

'Oh, that's not who I'm looking for then. You see the person I'm hunting for is called Lou too, so when you said her name I wondered for a moment if it might be her. But she definitely drove a red VW camper van.'

Dec looks at Ant with a puzzled expression.

'It's all a bit confusing, I know,' I say apologetically.

'Just a bit, sweetie,' Ant says. 'So why are you looking for this Lou?'

I tell Ant and Dec all about the camper van and then the postcards. In fact, I tell them everything I know so far, and just like Noah and Jess before them, they too are equally intrigued by Lou and Frankie's story.

'It's very romantic,' Ant says, when I've finished. 'But how odd she should write the cards and not send them. The pain of unrequited love ... ' He sighs wistfully.

'I think you're on the right path looking for someone here who was around at that time,' Dec says more practically. 'This place used to be inundated with artists in the past, but you'd think someone would remember her. I say definitely go and see *our* Lou. If anyone knows, she will.'

Fifteen

According to Ant and Dec this other Lou lives in Bluebell Cottage on Jacob Street.

First thing the next morning I head up there hoping to catch her in, but after I've knocked on her door a couple of times and rung the bell, there's still no answer, so I walk back down the hill towards the post office to see if she's there instead.

'Hi, is Lou at work today?' I ask a jolly-looking woman at the main shop counter. I hope Lou isn't working behind the glass of the post office counter, because there's already a long queue winding its way around the shop of people waiting to draw their pensions, post parcels and get official forms stamped. However, behind the glass I can only see a young man looking quite weary at the thought of this queue he has to work his way through over the next half an hour or so as he stamps yet another pension book.

'No, my dear, sorry. Lou's had to rush off up to the hospital. Her nephew's wife gave birth last night and they've all gone to the hospital to be with her.'

'Is that Poppy who owns the flower shop?' I ask, putting two and two together. 'Jake's wife?'

'Yes, it is. Know them, do you?'

'Sort of. I'm renting their cottage in Down-along.'

'Ah, yes, Rose's old cottage. That's what they've called the little girl – Daisy-Rose – after Poppy's grandmother and ...' She puzzles for a moment. 'Her great-great-grandmother, I think it was – the one who started the flower shop. Anyway it's a very pretty name.'

'Yes, it is,' I say, thinking first about my Daisy and then about the camper van. What were the chances – two Daisy-Roses in St Felix? There was definitely something special about those names and this town.

'Anyway the little baba is doing well, but Poppy's had a bit of a rough time of it, so I hear – Caesarean,' she whispers. 'So Lou's taken some time off to help out when she comes out of the hospital. It's Jake's busy time of the year at the nursery, and poor Amber will be run off her feet in that shop without Poppy – they'll need all the help they can get! Thank goodness they let the National Trust take over the running of Tregarlan last year.'

'Tregarlan – that's the old manor house up on the hill?'

'Yes, that's right. Poppy inherited it when old Stan died. Wonderful place, it is now. They've made a lovely job of doing it up.'

I nod, suddenly aware that there's a small queue beginning to form behind me.

'Ooh, listen to me gabble on!' the woman says. 'I could talk for Cornwall. You only came in to ask after Lou. Shall I tell her you called when I see her?'

'No, it's fine, really. I'll catch up with her when she's slightly less busy, but thank you,' I say, beginning to edge away. 'You've been very helpful.'

'Okay, my lovely!' she calls, turning to her next customer. 'Now, Sidney, what can I get you? Scratch cards, is it today, now you've got your pension?'

I leave the shop and walk down the street.

So that's that particular line of enquiry over. There was no way I was going to bother a stranger with my questions when she had all that to deal with. It wouldn't be fair, and anyway she might not even have known this other Lou, let alone know where she might be now. I'll have to think of something else.

I decide to take a walk up to see Malachi. I hadn't seen or heard from him since the night we sat out under the stars together, and I was keen to see if he'd had time to do anything to my Daisy-Rose over the weekend.

The garage is quiet as I make my way through the gates and around the back. Ralph barks as I enter the yard and wanders over to see me, but there's no sign of Malachi.

'Hello, boy,' I say, ruffling his head. 'Where's your master, eh? Is he here?'

'I am indeed!' Malachi calls, pushing himself out from underneath Daisy-Rose on a little wooden trolley. 'I was just doing some work on the engine.'

'How's it going?' I ask, walking over towards the camper van as Malachi rolls himself off the trolley and stands up. He grabs his customary rag and wipes his hands.

'Very well, actually. I've done some ringing around and I can definitely obtain all the parts we're going to need. Most of them are winging their way to me as we speak.'

'Great – any timescale yet?'

'All in good time is all I can promise right now, I'm afraid.'

I nod. 'Sure.'

'Are you still in a hurry to get away from St Felix? Aren't you enjoying your time here?'

'Yes I am, very much. A lot more than I thought I would.'

'Good, I'm glad to hear it. Tea?' Malachi offers. 'I'm just about to make one. No, wait!' he says, holding up his hand. 'You're a coffee person, aren't you? I can do either.'

'Yes, I am, but how did you know?'

Malachi taps the side of his forehead. 'Intuition,' he says, grinning. 'Coffee, milk and one sugar, right?'

'Yes, spot on.'

'Be right back.'

I sit down on a small pile of tyres while Malachi goes off to make us coffee, and I stare at Daisy-Rose.

Even though Malachi doesn't seem to have done all that much structural work on her yet, and she is still missing some major parts of her 'anatomy', Daisy-Rose does look a little happier as she stands calmly in the yard today waiting for the next part of her transformation.

'It must be because you've had a little clean, eh?' I ask her. 'Has that made you feel a bit better?' And then I feel my cheeks flush. Why was I talking to a motorised vehicle? I must have been spending too much time with Malachi!

But Lou had seemed totally besotted with this vehicle, and she'd talked about her in the postcards like she was an old friend. Daisy-Rose had accompanied Lou everywhere, in what I suppose must have been quite a solitary existence once she started to paint professionally. Lou certainly never spoke to Frankie about having any other friends; she talked about occasionally going to galleries and to exhibitions of her paintings, but I got the feeling she was a bit of a loner at heart, and other than her constant yearning for Frankie was actually quite happy that way. Perhaps Daisy-Rose was her only true friend?

'What ya thinking about?' Malachi asks, emerging from the garage with two mugs in his hands. 'I hope instant is all right. We don't have any fancy frothing machines here.'

I'm reminded of Noah with his coffee machine and I smile. 'Instant is just fine, thank you. I was just thinking about Daisy-Rose and Lou, and all the places they went together. It's like the van was Lou's best friend in all the years she had her.'

'Maybe she was. They say these camper vans all have their own personality, that's why people love them so much.' Malachi turns a bucket upside down and sits opposite me.

'Is Pegasus your best friend then?' I ask jokily.

'The van Pegasus?'

'Yes, of course the van! I didn't mean the flying white horse, did I?'

Malachi shrugs. 'You might have. No, Pegasus isn't my best friend. Ralph here is.' He pats his dog, who rolls over in the sun and looks at him enquiringly.

'Really?' I ask, surprised at this. 'I mean, you hear people say that their dog is their best friend, but do you really think that?'

'I do. Why is that so odd to hear? We've been everywhere together, haven't we, boy? We've been in all sorts of weird and wonderful situations, and we've always come out of it unscathed.'

'Unscathed is an odd choice of word. Makes me think you've been up to no good together!' I grin, but Malachi is thoughtful with his reply.

'Nope, quite the opposite, in fact,' he says, shaking his head. 'Always good. At least we try to make it that way.'

I'm about to ask him more when he says, 'Why do you find it so odd that I have a dog as my best friend and Lou had a camper van? Just because *your* best friend was a human – that's seen as normal, I suppose?'

'Well, yes.'

'And normal is always good?'

'Er . . . not always, but in this case at least I could talk to my best friend.'

'I can talk to Ralph.'

'He doesn't answer back though.'

Ralph barks. Malachi grins.

'In a way you can understand,' I insist.

'Says who?'

I shake my head. There was no point arguing with him about this. 'Okay, but don't even try to tell me that this van here talked back to Lou.'

'Why are you so obsessed with people talking back, answering your questions, boosting your self-confidence?'

'I am not.'

'Did Daisy boost your self-confidence? Was she always telling you that you looked nice, or you'd done well, or everything would be okay?'

I stare down into my coffee – he'd mentioned Daisy's name.

'No,' I say quietly.

'Really? Think about it.'

I should have told him it was none of his business. I'd only known Malachi a few days, and he was asking me questions that I wouldn't have answered for anyone, but there was something about him that I trusted: an openness, a sincerity. I couldn't put my finger on it, but I knew that however I answered he wouldn't judge me.

'Daisy looked after me,' I offer. 'I mean she looked *out* for me.'

135

'Sure it wasn't your first answer?'

'Maybe a little. But she was always the confident, successful one ... she always knew best about everything. I could only hope to be like her.'

Malachi sits quietly. He rhythmically strokes Ralph, running his long fingers over his short pale coat, and for the briefest of moments I wonder what it would feel like to feel those long fingers running over me.

I jolt myself sharply from that thought. 'Daisy was my best friend,' I say, standing up. I put my coffee cup on the ground. 'And I won't have anyone sullying my memories of her.'

I prepare myself to leave, and then realise I'm hesitating because I expect Malachi to do something to prevent me.

I look at him, but he still has the same serene, calm expression on his face as he gazes up at me.

'Aren't you even going to apologise?' I ask.

'Why would I do that? I haven't said anything wrong. You're the one who's about to storm off because you don't like your own reaction to my question, not because of anything I've said to offend you.'

I stare at him. Infuriatingly, he was right.

'How do you do that?' I sigh, sitting back down again on the tyres.

'Do what?'

'Twist things around. Have you been a psychiatrist or a therapist or something like that in a previous life? They do that sort of thing – analyse what you say and turn it to their advantage.'

Instead of giving me his usual quick flippant answer, Malachi considers this.

'A therapist ...' he says, like he's running through a list in his mind. 'Nope, I don't think so.'

He grins, and I shake my head.

'Talk about maddening!' I say, lifting my cup of coffee back up off the ground. I take a sip, and I'm pleased to find it's still warm enough to drink.

Malachi grins. 'You're not the first to say that.'

'I'm not surprised.'

'Any time you want to talk about Daisy, you just let me know,' Malachi says, with an unusually earnest expression on his face. 'We're always here to listen, aren't we, Ralph?'

Ralph looks up at him and yawns.

'I'll think about it,' I tell him, genuinely meaning it. 'Now, hadn't you better be getting back to work?'

Malachi shakes his head. 'Slave driver,' he says, climbing up from his bucket and stretching.

'Oh, I'm tough all right,' I say, finding my eyes drawn to Malachi's biceps. As always his overall sleeves are rolled up, and I can't help but watch how they tighten then relax while he stretches.

'But not as tough as you think,' Malachi says, and he holds his hand out to pull me up.

I take it, and as I do I feel it again, the same thing that I had on Saturday night when I got out of his van.

Something very odd but very pleasant surges right through me whenever I touch Malachi, and it's something I've never felt before.

Brighton University campus, 2006

'You're doing what?' I'd exclaimed, as Daisy had sat and calmly told me about her plans. 'You ... you can't just throw it all away.'

'I'm not throwing it all away, Ana, I'm following my heart.'

'But hearts can be wrong,' I'd said weakly. I knew I was fighting a losing battle. When Daisy made her mind up about something, that was it, and neither I nor anyone else could budge her.

'Not this time. I love Peter, and he loves me. We want to make a future together.'

'But what about your education, your career? We've both worked so hard to get here, Daisy.'

'I can still have a career if I go and live in Scotland with Peter. It's only until he finishes his architecture course, and then we'll probably move back down south again. Maybe I can pick up where I left off?'

But we both knew that was never going to happen.

Part of me was appalled that Daisy was giving up her place at university, but part of me was a tiny bit – no, make that a lot – jealous. She'd found love, real love, and a person she wanted to spend the rest of her life with. I was pleased for her, really I was, even though I knew that our friendship would never be the same again.

Daisy had found someone who was more important to her than me, and there was nothing I could do but get used to it.

Sixteen

I leave Malachi working on Daisy-Rose, and I make my way back down into the town, intending to go back to my cottage and do some work. I'm just heading down Harbour Street, dodging in between the holiday-makers dawdling along the cobbles, when my phone rings.

I feel my heart lift when I see Noah's name on the screen.

'Hi, Noah.'

'Hello! You knew it was me?' He sounds pleased.

'Yes, I added your name to my phone yesterday, remember?'

'Oh— oh right. Yes, of course.' He clears his throat. 'I have a little bit of news for you ... about the postcards?'

'Wow, already, you move fast!'

'Yes ... er ... it's not amazing news, but it's a start. I have a friend – well, more of a colleague really – who runs postcard fairs. There's a large one being held in Truro, and there will be a dealer there who specialises in Cornish postcards – it's a bit of a long shot, I know, but it's all I have right now I'm afraid.'

He sounds so apologetic that I feel quite sorry for him. It was obvious Noah desperately wanted to help.

'When is the fair?'

'Tomorrow and Wednesday.'

'Oh, I thought it would be over a weekend?'

'These sorts of fairs usually are, but this is very specialist – it's targeted at dealers rather than the general public – that's why I thought it might be worth a shot.'

'Great. How do we get there? I— I mean how do I get there?' I hurriedly correct myself.

'I could drive you if you like?' Noah suggests, trying to sound casual, and I can just imagine how uncomfortable this is making him. 'I know the way, and correct me if I'm wrong, but I don't think you have a vehicle here, do you, until your camper van is fixed?'

'No, I don't, you're right. If you're sure?'

'It would be my pleasure,' Noah says, sounding as though he's smiling at the other end of the phone. 'Shall I pick you up at your cottage at say nine a.m. so we can get a good start. It would be best to get there nice and early if we can.'

'Nine would be lovely. Thank you so much for this, Noah, I really appreciate it.'

'Like I said, it's *my* pleasure. See you tomorrow at nine then.'

I end my call to Noah and find he's not the only one smiling. I knew this was a really long shot, but it was the first one I'd had so far. I wasn't sure why reuniting these cards with their owner had become so important to me, but it had, and now I'm determined to give it the best go I can.

The promising start to the weather doesn't last long, and by lunch-time dark clouds have blotted the sun's best attempts to shine. As the rain begins to splatter against the French windows, I find myself quite happy to spend the rest of the day in the comfort and dry of the little cottage. I had plenty of work to be getting on with, and now I was going to be heading up to Truro tomorrow with Noah, the more I got done today the better.

Malachi phones me in the afternoon to ask me about paint for Daisy-Rose.

'I can't quite find the exact colour of red,' he complains. 'It's annoying because I want this refurb to be as close to the original as possible.'

Malachi and I had discussed what Daisy-Rose might look like when she was finished, and we'd both been in agreement that we wanted to restore her to her former glory. He had seemed relieved when I'd agreed to this, and when I'd asked him why, he said he thought I might want to paint her in all sorts of 'weird and wonderful colours and patterns' because of my design background. I just wanted Daisy-Rose to be returned to the sort of condition she was in when Lou had first owned her – it seemed like the right thing to do.

'Malachi, it's fine,' I reassure him now. 'Stop fretting. Are we talking darker, like a maroon, or brighter, like a pillar box red or even a scarlet?'

'Oh no, not that different,' Malachi insists. 'The shade I've found is very similar to the original Rose, only it's a metallic burgundy rather than the original matt.'

'Will anyone other than you actually notice?' I ask, not for the first time today smiling at the end of a phone. I was so pleased about Noah's lead on the postcards that this just seemed like such a minor problem.

'Probably not, no,' Malachi admits.

'Would I have noticed if you hadn't told me about it?'

'I highly doubt it,' Malachi replies dejectedly.

I felt bad as he was obviously trying very hard with this

restoration. The postcards had been taking up so much of my thoughts that I'd forgotten why I was actually here in St Felix in the first place. And Daisy-Rose *was* going to be mine when she was finished. Perhaps I should show a bit more interest?

'So you've got the red sorted. Now, what about the cream?' I ask, hoping to convey the level of interest that Malachi obviously wanted to hear from me.

Daisy-Rose had originally been split into two colours: a deep red that made up her bottom half, and a warm creamy colour covering her top. This was particularly attractive at the front, where the cream dived into the red in a beautiful curve, with the letters VW circled in silver across the middle of the two.

'The cream is not a problem,' Malachi replies, and I'm relieved to hear his voice returning to his usual upbeat tone. 'It's a pretty standard shade for refurbs on vehicles of that age.'

'Great ... well, I'm sure whatever red you choose will look wonderful on her. You're doing an amazing job, Malachi.'

There's a slight pause and the line goes silent.

'Are you still there?' I ask, wondering why he hasn't replied.

'Yeah, I'm still here. I was just thinking.'

'About?'

'Two things actually – the first is that you're calling Daisy-Rose *she* and *her* now.'

'Am I? I hadn't noticed.' That wasn't strictly true – I had noticed my feelings towards the camper van starting to change. Whereas to begin with all I saw was a battered, rusting old vehicle that was going to cost a lot of money to repair, now I was beginning to see the possible attraction of this vintage van when Malachi had completed his renovations.

'Yup! It's a huge step forward from when you were calling her *it*. She's obviously starting to work her magic on you ... '

'So, what's the second thing you were thinking about?' I ask hurriedly.

'You're sounding very chipper today – something must have happened. What is it?'

Malachi was always so perceptive.

'Nothing much,' I reply, trying to play it down. 'Noah thinks he might have a lead. We're going to a postcard fair tomorrow in Truro to see if we can find anything out.'

'Are you now? How very cosy . . . '

'Hardly. I'm sure a postcard fair in an old church hall will likely be quite cold and chilly actually.'

'Ho ho, very funny! I hope you have a wonderful time. Just you remember who suggested you ask Noah in the first place?'

'Yeah, yeah, what would I do without you, Malachi?'

Malachi goes strangely silent again.

'You don't need to worry about that for a while yet,' he eventually says in a quiet voice. 'Just appreciate me while you can.'

Seventeen

Noah pulls up outside Snowdrop Cottage at exactly 9 a.m. the next morning.

'Good morning,' he says, as I climb into his Land Rover next to him. 'How are you feeling today?'

'Hopeful,' I reply honestly, 'but realistic too. I don't know how much we'll be able to find out but I'm looking forward to trying.'

'Good,' Noah says, moving away very slowly along the narrow street. 'I actually meant how are *you*, but the rest was good to know also.'

I feel myself blushing. 'Sorry, I'm probably a little bit too excited about this.'

'Well, that's a first I must say. I don't think I've ever taken someone to any sort of fair, let alone a postcard one, who has felt like that.'

He takes his eyes from the windscreen for a moment and smiles at me.

'How's the shop?' I ask, as we pull out on to the main road that leads out of St Felix.

'Good, good. I've left it in the more than capable hands of Jess today. Don't tell her I said that.' He grins.

'She is a big help to you, isn't she?'

Noah nods. 'I couldn't believe it when she just rolled up on my doorstep one day asking for a job. I'd just lost my previous helper, and when I say lost, I mean she died – she didn't just leave.'

'Oh no, I'm sorry.'

'Don't be. Hetty was the biggest pain ever. She'd worked alongside my aunt for years, so I had no choice but to continue working with her when I took over. She came as part of the fixtures and fittings of the shop.'

'A bit like Clarice.'

'Clarice is an angel compared to her.' Noah shakes his head. 'Don't tell anyone I told you this, but I actually called her "Hetty Hitler" behind her back she was that bad.'

I stifle a giggle.

'Nothing I ever did was right,' Noah continues, 'or more like it wasn't as good as my aunt did it. She made my life a misery for the first few months I had the shop, then one day I couldn't take it any longer and I put my foot down.'

I couldn't imagine Noah putting his foot anywhere other than perhaps in his mouth. 'And what happened?'

'She didn't speak to me for a week. She still came into work, mind, just didn't speak. I think she thought I was going to give in, but I didn't. For once I held my ground with her, and then one afternoon she just caved in and suddenly offered me a cup of tea like nothing had ever happened. I accepted, and after that we got on. When I say got on, we co-existed together in the shop and I was allowed to do things my way a bit more without constant interference. Hetty would still *tut* and pull

146

disapproving faces a lot of the time, but at least she let me be the boss in my own shop.'

'And now you have Jess.'

'Yeah, like I said before she's a great help, although why she wants to work in an old antiques shop when she's just completed a history degree is beyond me, but she seems happy.'

'Maybe she wants to stay local for a while. Do her parents live around here?'

'No, I don't think so. I think she came here on holiday then just decided to stay. She's a bit of a free spirit is Jess. I'm sure she'll change her mind about working for me one day and just flit off somewhere else.'

'I'm sure she wouldn't just leave you in the lurch. She thinks too much of you to do that.'

Noah shrugs. 'Perhaps. But in my experience even the most reliable people eventually let you down.'

He doesn't expand on that statement so I don't pry. We've joined the A30 now, and Noah puts his foot down on the accelerator and moves through the gears as we quickly speed up.

'So, Ana, tell me about you?' Noah asks, seemingly happy to change the subject. 'What do you do?'

I tell Noah all about my job, and he seems very interested. He asks all the right questions, and nods and smiles in all the right places.

'And you're happy doing that?' he asks, as we overtake a horsebox.

'Yes, I think so, for now anyway. I trained long enough to do it, so I guess I'd better be.'

'That doesn't sound very positive.'

'It is, perhaps I didn't say it right. What I meant was, I am happy doing this for now, but I'm not sure I'll want to do it for ever. I think we need to move on in life, to evolve and grow, and often what you're happy doing now isn't what you'll be happy doing in a few years' time, is it?'

Something about what I've just said sounds familiar . . .

'Very true,' Noah agrees.

'I mean, what did you use to do, before you took over the shop – I bet it wasn't antiques, was it?' I ask, and then I suddenly remember. *It was Malachi! He said something similar to me about people changing outside his camper van the other night.*

'No, far from it,' Noah agrees, but he doesn't offer any further information on what he had been doing.

'But you're happier now than before?' I try, hoping this will prompt him into telling me more. Noah was being very guarded about this.

Noah considers my question. 'My life *is* very different from what it was before, and yes, I'm happy, but whether I'm happi*er* . . . ?'

I glance out of the window. This was getting more than a little awkward. Why didn't he just tell me what he used to do? What was the big secret?

'Let's talk about these postcards,' Noah says, steering the subject away from himself. 'If we *were* lucky enough to find them, what help do you think they'll be to your investigation?'

'It's hardly an investigation. I'd just like to return them to Lou if possible, and if that's not possible for whatever reason, to her family at least.'

Noah nods. 'Sentimental value?'

'Yes, but it's more than that . . . ' I hesitate.

'Go on.' Noah slows down as we approach a roundabout.

'I kind of want to know what happened.'

'To Lou?'

148

'To both of them. I thought to begin with I was just caught up in the romance of it all, and to a certain extent I guess I am, but there's also this big mystery that I want to solve. Why write postcards to someone for so long but never send them, and why hide them away in an old camper van and then leave them behind when you sell it? So much of this makes no sense, yet I really *want* it to make sense. Does that sound mad?'

Noah shakes his head. 'Nope, that sounds like perfect sense to me.'

'Really?'

'Yep, I hate puzzles that can't be solved – drives me insane.'

'Is that why you're helping me?'

'Partly.' Noah turns his gaze away from the road to me for a second, then just as quickly he returns it. 'And partly because I like you.'

I wasn't expecting that.

'What I mean by that,' Noah hurriedly says, 'is I like the fact you want to help someone and you're prepared to put yourself out to do it.'

'Thanks,' I reply sheepishly. 'That's nice of you to say.'

Noah doesn't look at me this time and simply nods his acknowledgement.

We chat amiably for the rest of the journey about more mundane subjects – like the weather, Noah's shop and St Felix. Then eventually Noah glances in his rear view mirror, indicates and turns the steering wheel of the car.

'We're here,' he announces, as we pass a red and white sign that says *Welcome to St Michael's Hall*. 'Let's hope St Michael is feeling kindly towards us today!'

The fair is much busier and much larger than I'd been

expecting. In the hall I manage to count at least seventy stalls and most are offering a mixture of picture postcards, but some seem to specialise. Some stall-holders only sell seaside post-cards or ones that are pre-nineteen thirties, or from the war, the fifties or sixties or of animals and birds. There is even a man only selling postcards of the West Country.

'The guy we want is at the back here,' Noah says, guiding me through the crowds until we reach a middle-aged couple sitting behind a large table filled with boxes and boxes of cards that are filed in categories such as South West Cornwall, North Cornwall, Penzance, Newquay and Land's End.

'Good morning,' Noah says, sounding much more assertive than I've ever heard him before. This was obviously his com-fort zone, in amongst dealers and buyers. 'Noah Lawson.' He holds out his hand to the man and then the woman. 'Good to meet you both. I believe we have a colleague in common – Geoffrey Harcourt?'

'Yes, I know Geoff,' the man says. 'Haven't seen him in a while, mind. How's the old devil doing?'

'Very well, apparently. I spoke to him only yesterday. He was telling me that you'd be exactly the person to speak to if I was trying to find a particular sort of postcard.'

The man's face reddens. 'I— I don't deal in them sort of cards any more,' he fervently insists, glancing hurriedly at the woman. 'Honestly, Mary, I don't. Cross me heart.' He makes a cross on his cardigan with his finger, then he looks back up at Noah again. 'If it's that type of thing you're looking for, then you'd be best seeing Kevin on stall forty-five. I believe he has a lot of *that* sort of thing hidden under his table.'

I try not to grin as Noah hastily shakes his head. 'No, you misunderstand. I— well, we' – he gestures to me –'are looking for a set of postcards probably written fairly locally between the mid-sixties and the late eighties.'

'Twenty years!' The man's bushy eyebrows rise. 'That could be a lot of cards.'

'Yes, it's likely it is,' I join in now. 'They were sent, well, not sent ... They were all written by one person always to the same recipient, but what makes them unusual is they were never posted.'

While the man pulls a perplexed face, Mary, who I assume must be his wife or partner, speaks for the first time, 'That sounds interesting, love. What do you mean exactly by they were written but never posted?'

I'd been pretty sure I'd be asked this today so I've prepared a condensed version of the story so far. After I've told them everything I know as swiftly as I can, I produce one of the cards as a sample.

Mary takes it carefully from me, pops on the glasses that are hanging around her neck, and reads:

30th May 1953

My Darling Frankie,

Today is my half-day, so I decided to take a bus to Mevagissey. It's a very pretty little harbour town, and there are fishing boats bobbing about merrily on the water just like on the front of this card!

I sat in the sunshine and watched people getting ready for the Queen's coronation. The bunting they were hanging looked so gay as the red, white and blue fluttered happily in the sea breeze.

I'll be watching the coronation with Mother and

Father at our neighbours' house. They have bought a
television set especially for the occasion – very grand!
It makes me wonder who you will be watching with?
Oh, how I wish this special day was something we
could share. In fact, I wish we could share every day,
and that would make them all extra special.

Forever yours,

Lou x

'Aw, that's lovely. Look, Colin.' She passes the card to Colin
who retrieves his own glasses from his cardigan pocket and he
now reads the card.

'Very nice,' he says, passing it back to me.

'*Very nice*!' Mary explodes with indignation. 'That right
there, Colin, *that* is romance. A word you quite clearly wouldn't
understand if it was tattooed backwards across your forehead
so you read it in the mirror every morning!'

I can't help but laugh.

'These men, love,' Mary says sadly, shaking her head at me,
'they don't understand what we want, do they? A petrol station
bunch of chrysanthemums on our birthday just ain't gonna cut
it. I bet this one doesn't buy you flowers from no petrol station,
does he? He looks better brought up than that.'

'He doesn't buy me flowers at all,' I hurriedly insist, even
though I'm enjoying Mary's rant. She opens her mouth again,
but I just manage to finish speaking before she pounces on
Noah. 'We're not together, you see. Noah is just helping me
out with my search for the cards.'

Mary tips her head to one side. 'Aw, really? Shame, that –
you'd make a lovely couple, wouldn't they, Colin?'

Colin is having a sip of his tea and he jumps as Mary's elbow jabs into his ribs, just managing to prevent his drink from spilling over the side of the polystyrene cup.

'Er ... yes, I suppose so.'

I glance at Noah – his usually pale cheeks look as warm as mine feel.

'So, you've obviously not come across anything like these cards then?' Noah says, clearly deciding the best course of action is to continue as if nothing has happened.

Colin shakes his head.

'If I give you my business card, would you give me a call if you do, please?' Noah makes it sounds like an order rather than a request. He pulls a card from the pocket of his jacket and hands it to Colin.

'Wait a minute,' Mary says, thinking. 'We can't help you, but what about Alistair? He's always on the lookout for cards with interesting messages on them. Some people collect cards because of what they've got written on the back as opposed to the collectors who choose them based on the pictures on the front.'

'Who is Alistair?' Noah says, looking around. 'Is he here?'

'I haven't seen him. It's possible he couldn't get anyone to look after his shop today. He has a small shop up in Newquay – Beachcomber Antiques – it might be worth you trying there.'

'Thank you.' I smile at Mary, and as I do something catches my eye. It's a postcard of Brighton. I pick it up and look at it while Noah gets further instructions from Colin on how we might find Beachcomber Antiques. It's a view I remember well from my university days, of Brighton pier. I turn over the card and find it's dated *4th July 1986*.

Having a lovely time, it says in faded blue biro. *Saw a Duran Duran tribute act last night. Not as good as the real thing, but better than the comedian we saw the night before – he was blue! Missing you, wish you were here. Jenny xx*

'How much?' I ask Mary.

'Take it,' she says kindly. 'We only get pence for the more modern cards.'

'The eighties are modern, are they?'

'In the world of postcards, they are. The most sought after are from the late eighteen hundreds through to the end of the Second World War.'

'Really, as far back as that?'

Mary nods. 'The early cards were used back then like we use text messages now, as a way of quick communication. There were often several postal deliveries a day in this country at that time, so people could send a card in the morning letting someone know what time to meet them later in the day. Or what time they would be arriving on a train or a bus.'

'Gosh, I hadn't thought about them like that. I just think about postcards as something people send when they're on holiday, and even that's fading out now, I guess.'

Mary nods sadly. 'Yes, in the future there'll be no record of wonderful romantic messages like your Lou was sending to her Frankie. Everything digital that's not deemed important will simply be deleted. How our descendants will ever know anything personal about us, I don't know.'

'You're the second person to say that to me,' I say, thinking of Jess. 'Perhaps someone needs to start a campaign to bring back the traditional ways of communicating.'

'It's been tried, my love. No one is interested apart from a few die-hard purists. Such a shame, but that's the way of the world these days.'

'Yes, isn't it. Well, thank you for this. I have a bit of a thing

154

for the eighties, and I went to uni in Brighton, so this card fits both bills!'

'You're very welcome. I do hope you manage to find this Lou. Wouldn't it be wonderful to reunite her with her cards after all this time? I wonder what she's doing now.'

I'd been wondering that a lot too.

'Thanks for your help,' Noah says, shaking both their hands again. 'Most appreciated.'

'Good luck!' Mary calls as a parting gesture. 'Let me know how you get on.'

'I'll send you a postcard if we're successful!' I call back, as Noah guides me away through the hall.

'They were very nice,' I say, as we step outside again into the fresh air. The hall had been quite stuffy, filled with so many people and old paper.

'Nice, but sadly not all that helpful.'

'Why not? They've given us another lead?'

Noah smiles.

'What?'

He shakes his head. 'Nothing. Yes, this Alistair might be helpful, who knows.'

'Should we go now?' I ask. 'That's if you have time, of course. How far is it to Newquay from here?'

'About half an hour. I have time if you do?'

'I have lots of time,' I say, thinking about Malachi and Daisy-Rose. 'In fact, I have all the time in the world right now.'

Eighteen

I wait for Noah in the Land Rover while he quickly calls Jess to check that she's getting on okay.

'Everything all right?' I ask, as he returns to the car.

'She seems to have everything under control.'

It's my turn now for a knowing smile.

'What?' Noah asks, starting the engine.

'I was smiling because you know you needn't worry about Jess, and yet you still do. Why don't you trust her?'

'I do trust her.' Noah reverses out of our parking space and we drive to the gate.

'You don't behave like you do.'

Noah, waiting for a break in the traffic so he can pull out safely, simply shrugs. 'I'm just looking out for my business, that's all, and I haven't known Jess all that long. Like I said, she just sort of turned up on my doorstep one day asking for a job.'

'Sure ...' I say, looking out of the passenger window. 'I guess that would be it.'

'What's that supposed to mean?'

I turn back. 'It's just you're very secretive about your

156

life – protective even. I doubt you trust anyone really, let alone Jess.'

'Just because I don't share every part of my life with everyone I meet' – Noah pauses to accelerate quickly out into the traffic – 'it doesn't mean I'm secretive or untrusting of people.'

'I just get that vibe from you, that's all.'

'Let me guess,' Noah says, glancing at me quickly. 'You're one of these people who share every part of their life on social media. I bet you have Instagram and Facebook and Twitter, and you're on them all the time.'

'That is where you're very wrong. Yes, I have all of those apps on my phone but I very rarely use any of them.'

'Really?' I detect a hint of approval in Noah's voice.

'Really. I mean they're good for keeping up with friends and family, or finding out news and stuff, but that's it. I just find it all so . . . ' I search for the right word, 'fake.'

Noah nods approvingly. 'Me too. Jess is insisting we need a Facebook page for the shop but we have a small website already, so I can't see why I need that too.'

'I suppose that's the way a lot of business is done these days, and Jess is young so she knows no other way.'

'You're hardly old yourself,' Noah says. We've pulled up at a set of traffic lights, so he's able to look at me this time for more than a couple of seconds.

'I'm thirty-two.'

'Like I said, hardly old.'

'How old are you then?' I'd guessed in my head he'd be in his late thirties, but it was difficult to tell – he dressed older and often had the manner of a more mature person.

'I'm thirty-six, no sorry, make that thirty-seven. My birthday was last week.'

'Cancer,' I say knowingly.

'What?'

'Your star sign – it's Cancer. My friend was into all that kind of stuff. I couldn't help but absorb some of it.'

'Yes, I am. I have no idea what that means, though?'

'You're emotional, sensitive and private, you can be difficult to get to know, but once you do get close to someone, you're very loyal to those you hold dear.'

Noah doesn't comment. 'What are you then?' he asks instead.

'Capricorn – we're practical and goal driven, and usually successful, often later in life.'

'Only that?'

'A Capricorn can often be seen as cold and unfeeling, which is usually not the case at all – they've just chosen not to show their feelings to you.'

Noah smiles. 'Do you believe any of that?'

I shrug. 'Some perhaps. Daisy was quite resolute about it all, as she was about most things.'

'You obviously miss her a lot.'

I just nod.

'Do you think this is one of the reasons you've set your heart on finding Lou – to take your mind off your loss?'

I stare hard at him. 'No.'

'I didn't mean any offence by that. I just meant sometimes, when we're grieving heavily, to have something else to focus your mind on can help ease the pain a little.'

'Perhaps it is diverting my thoughts a tad,' I admit, 'but that doesn't mean I've forgotten her. Far from it.'

'I never said you had.'

There's silence between us for a moment.

'I'm sorry,' I apologise, 'if I snapped at you. It's just since I've been in St Felix I've found myself thinking less and less about Daisy every day, and that makes me sad.'

'That's not necessarily a bad thing, though,' Noah suggests gently. 'It's part of the grieving process, and it means you're starting to heal.'

'You sound like you know what I'm going through?'

'Are you hungry?' Noah asks, deftly changing the subject. 'We just passed a sign for a service station up ahead – we could get some coffee and maybe a sandwich?'

'Sure.' Noah quite obviously doesn't want to talk about his past with me, and who was I to push him about it if he wanted to keep that chapter of his life private.

At the service station we manage to get cups of hot Costa coffee from a machine and some reasonable-looking sandwiches, then we return to the car to eat and drink.

'Sorry it's not more glamorous,' Noah says, taking a sip from his cappuccino. 'I guess we could have stopped for something when we got to Newquay.'

'It's fine, I'm quite hungry. Plus this way we can people watch, which I love.'

'What's so interesting about watching people coming out of a service station?'

'Are you kidding? You can tell a lot about someone by what they've bought – take that woman over there, for instance. She's carrying a salad and a diet drink, so she's obviously watching her weight.'

'Or she just wants to be healthy?'

'Perhaps, whereas this guy has a large bag of sweets.' I squint a little. 'And a can of Coke.'

'What are you deducing from that, Sherlock?' Noah asks,

looking amused. 'That he doesn't care about himself because he eats sugar?'

'Yep.'

'Or . . . ' Noah says, looking hard at the man. 'He's buying it for his child as a treat on a long car journey?'

Our eyes follow the man across the car park, and Noah is proved right as he opens up the back door of his car and hands the sweets and Coke to a young boy.

'Impressive,' I say approvingly. 'He still shouldn't be giving the kid all that sugar, though, so technically I was right about him not caring.'

'Is that a Capricorn trait too?' Noah asks, his eyes twinkling behind his glasses. 'Having to be right all the time?'

I grin. 'Perhaps.'

'Right, enough character assassination for now. We'd better get going. Are you ready?'

'Yup.' I take his sandwich packet and throw it into a nearby dustbin with my own rubbish, then I climb back into the car. 'Let's go.'

Beachcomber Antiques is located just outside the town of Newquay. It looks more like a converted barn than a shop, and has its own little car park, so Noah pulls up on the sandy-coloured gravel and we climb out.

'Phew, it is open,' I say, trying to sound positive as I see a sign hanging outside the entrance. 'So that's a start.' I'd tried phoning the shop on the way here but no one had answered, and I'd wondered if we were going to arrive and find it closed.

As we walk towards the barn, our feet crunching on the gravel, we find the shop is not only open but quite busy too.

'After you,' Noah says, holding out his hand.

160

'Thanks,' I say, going through the door. 'Gosh!' I look around me in wonder as I enter the shop. 'This place is amazing.'

Inside the barn we find a cornucopia of what I'd politely call junk, but what I'm sure Noah will think are interesting and fascinating artefacts. They're hung from the roof, stacked up on tables, displayed on the walls and sometimes protected in glass-fronted cupboards. Each way we turn there is something new to see.

'Impressive,' is all Noah says as he looks around him.

'Thank you,' a voice, appearing to belong to a large stuffed black bear standing on its hind legs, politely says.

I glance at Noah, but he's smiling at the elderly man who appears now from behind the bear.

'Is this your shop?' Noah asks.

'It is indeed, young man.'

'You must be Alistair then?' I ask eagerly.

'Again, guilty as charged. What can I do for you both?'

'We're looking for some postcards,' I begin. 'A particular set of postcards ... '

I tell Alistair the same condensed version of the story I'd told Mary and Colin.

'I see,' is all he says when I've finished.

'And Mary thought you might have seen something like them,' I add. 'She said you specialised in interesting messages on cards.'

'I do indeed. *Hmm* ... now, let me think,' he says, rubbing at his white beard. 'There *was* a set of cards a while back. Interesting lot – the seller said he found them stuffed inside an old tyre he bought for his VW camper van.'

'That could be them!' I say excitedly. 'Do you still have them?'

Alistair shakes his head. 'Sadly, no.'

I sigh with disappointment.

'When did you sell them?' Noah asks steadily.

Alistair pulls a face. 'A few weeks ago, I reckon. I remember because the guy bought quite a lot of stuff from me. He was one of these interior designer chappies. You know – they buy old reclaimed stuff when they're doing up people's houses for them. It makes their clients seem interesting because they've got a lot of old stuff, even if they really aren't.'

'What did he want some old postcards for then?'

Alistair shrugs. 'He said something about a screen – he got that from me too. He was going to paste the cards on there, I think. He was interested in the messages, though, not the picture side of them. He bought a lot of my cards, not just the ones you're looking for.'

'Découpage,' I say, with a tinge of disappointment. 'I bet he was going to cover the screen with the cards then varnish over them. Damn.'

'Do you have any records of this sale?' Noah asks, not sounding in the least bit disillusioned by this news.

'As a matter of fact, I do.'

'So you'd have a name then?'

'I can do better than that, my friend. He had everything delivered, so I should hopefully have an address too.'

I can't help but smile as we follow Alistair back over to his shop counter, where he proceeds, in between customers, to look through his records on a very old computer that matches the rest of the shop perfectly. It seemed luck might be on our side once more.

'What do you think to the shop?' I ask Noah, as we stand back to let Alistair serve another customer. 'It's a lot like yours, isn't it, only yours is much tidier.'

'This place is way cooler than my shop,' Noah says. He picks up a wooden elephant from the table next to us and turns it over to look underneath. 'It's a real treasure trove of goodies. Alistair has a wonderful eye for what's going to sell. Madam,' he says suddenly, stepping forward. 'I wonder if I might interject for a moment?'

I watch as Noah expertly proceeds to sell the woman the wooden elephant to go with the several carved pieces she already has on the counter. Then he steps back to let Alistair complete the sale.

'That was very smooth,' I whisper. 'Quite the charmer, aren't you, when you want to be?'

'Selling antiques is about the only time my talk is smooth,' he says, rolling his eyes. 'The rest of the time I'm usually putting my foot in it and saying the wrong thing to people.'

I shake my head. 'Well, I think you've been quite wonderful today. I've been very impressed.'

'Thanks,' Noah says, blushing a little. 'I'm not completely useless then.'

I'm about to tell him in no uncertain terms that he's very far from that when Alistair suddenly jumps up in front of his computer screen. 'Got it!' he says joyfully. 'Thirty-first of May – a job lot of two hundred and twenty postcards was bought by . . . oh, wait.' He grimaces slightly. 'I'm not supposed to tell you, am I – client confidentiality and all that.'

'Ah, no, indeed,' Noah says calmly. 'Perhaps you'd be good enough to try phoning your client, though, and ask him if he'd mind if we spoke to him about the cards?'

Alistair nods. 'Of course.' He picks up the receiver of his landline telephone and dials, then turns secretively away from us as though that will make the call more private.

'Let's go over here while he phones,' Noah says. 'We don't want to get him into trouble after he's been so helpful.'

We wander over to the other side of the shop while Alistair makes his call.

'*Great news!*' we hear him holler a few moments later. 'I couldn't speak to my client, but I spoke to his partner instead and he'd be more than happy to help you.'

'That's wonderful,' I say, as we hurry back over.

'Let me just write down his details,' Alistair says, grabbing a pencil and some paper. 'We delivered all the items to a Mr Oliver Jackson at this address in Penzance.'

I grin excitedly at Noah, but he just looks calm and composed as always.

'Here you go,' Alistair says, handing me the piece of paper. 'I can't guarantee the cards haven't been covered in glue and slapped on a nineteen thirties modesty screen. But for your sake, I hope not.'

'Thank you so much for your help, Alistair,' I say, glancing at the paper. 'You've been very kind.'

'Nonsense, I should be thanking you for adding to that sale from earlier. If you ever want a job,' he says to Noah, 'give me a call.'

'I will,' Noah says. 'And thanks again.'

'Why didn't you tell him you had your own shop?' I ask, as we leave the barn and head to the car.

'Didn't seem necessary,' Noah says, unlocking the doors. 'We got what we wanted, didn't we? Never show all your cards, Ana. Always keep something in reserve. Ana?' he enquires, when I don't respond. 'What's wrong?'

I've opened the door of the car but I'm still standing outside staring at the piece of paper.

'What's up? Didn't he write it down correctly?'

'Yes, it's all here all right.' I climb into the vehicle.

'Where does it say we have to go to then?'

'Oliver Jackson,' I read. 'Jackson's Interiors, 88 Thatcher Street, Penzance.'

Nineteen

After I've got over the shock of the eighties-sounding address, Noah calls the phone number that Alistair has added to the paper to see if we can go over and visit today. But now there's no reply, so he leaves a message asking if Oliver or his partner can call us back.

'Shall we head back?' Noah asks. 'There's not much more we can do until we hear from him.'

'Yeah, that sounds like a good idea. Let's go home.'

Noah pulls away from the Beachcomber Antiques car park and we begin our drive back to St Felix, which Noah says should take just under an hour if the traffic is good.

'Interesting that you chose to use that word before,' Noah says, when we've been travelling a few minutes.

'What word?'

'Home. When I suggested we head back you said, "Let's go home."'

'So?'

'Well St Felix isn't your home is it? It's only temporary.'

'Maybe I meant let's go back to my temporary home then? Why does it matter?'

166

'It doesn't. I just thought it was interesting you should call it that. You must feel quite comfortable there already.'

I think about my little cottage and how I was looking forward to getting back to it, putting the kettle on, making a hot drink and seeing what the weather was currently doing to my view through the French windows.

'I do actually. It's such a pretty cottage I'm staying in, I really like it.'

'What about the rest of St Felix?'

'It's a nice ... no, make that a *lovely* Cornish seaside town. Probably one of the best I've visited. I like the people and the scenery, especially the beaches. I can imagine when all the visitors have left it will be even better.' I wink at him, but he's concentrating on the road. 'Why are you asking me all this?'

'No reason, I just wondered what you thought to it, that's all. After coming from London, it must seem like such a change.'

'It's very different from London. I don't think you can really compare them, can you? You've obviously been to London?'

'Oh yes,' Noah says knowingly. 'I've been.'

'And what did you think?'

'Loud, noisy, dirty – everything St Felix isn't.'

'You hated it then?'

'I didn't say that. There's a buzz to London that you only get in a big city. New York is very similar. However much I love the calm and tranquillity of St Felix, when the tourists have diminished slightly' – he winks at me now – 'it doesn't have that same unique energy you get from city living.'

'You lived there?' I ask, surprised to learn this.

'For a while.'

'What did you do there?'

'This and that.'

'*This and that*! What were you – a Cockney wide boy wheeling and dealing?'

Noah laughs. 'No, far from it. I was in the Met.'

For a second I think he means an art gallery, but then I remember the Met is in New York. 'You were in the police!' I ask, a little too incredulously.

'Is that so hard to believe?'

'Yes— I mean, no. I . . . ' I'm not sure what to say. Noah was tall, yes, and I could just about imagine him in a police uniform pounding the beat. He had a long purposeful stride when you were walking next to him, but his general demeanour was not that of an officer of the law. He was too shy, too nervous, too . . . Then I remember the way he'd dealt with people today: his cool, calm presence and his authoritarian manner. 'Sorry, I just didn't expect you to say you were a police officer. Gosh, did you go straight from that to running an antiques shop? I bet that was some leap.'

Noah doesn't say anything. He pretends to concentrate on the traffic, suddenly feeling the need to check all his mirrors.

'This traffic is looking quite heavy up ahead. I think I'll turn off up here and take a little detour. We don't want to get caught in the evening rush.'

I look at my watch – it said ten to four. Not much chance of an evening rush quite yet, but I just nod and sit quietly in the passenger seat. Noah quite obviously didn't want to talk any further about his past. In fact, I got the feeling he'd said more than he wanted to already.

'Thanks for driving me today, you've been a great help,' I tell him, when we eventually arrive back in St Felix. The rest of our journey had been quiet with occasional bouts of polite conversation about things we passed on the road.

'I'm a good chauffeur,' Noah says, turning off the engine. He turns to me and smiles.

'You've been so much more than that and you know it. You discovered all the right people to see, and you knew all the right questions to ask them. I couldn't have done it without you.'

'Even if we are returning home with no postcards.'

'But we have another lead.' I cringe inside – I hadn't meant to bring up the police again, but I front it out. 'We just have to hope that this Oliver hasn't done anything yet with the cards, then he might let us buy them off him.'

'It's possible, I suppose.'

'Have a little faith, Noah. This *will* work out. I know it will.'

'You're a very positive sort of person, aren't you?'

'Am I? I don't think of myself like that at all.'

'I think you are. It's quite endearing that you have so much faith that things will come good in the end.'

'Why shouldn't they? We're doing a good thing, aren't we, attempting to reunite these cards with their owner?'

'I guess so, but life doesn't always treat the good all that well.'

'No, you're right there.' I think about Daisy for a moment, then I wonder what he'd meant by that statement. Was he talking about himself? 'Maybe this time it will. You'll let me know if Oliver calls?'

'Of course, the minute he does.'

I reach for the handle on the car door to get out. Then I change my mind and turn back towards Noah. Before I have time to change my mind, I put my hand over his and lean in to kiss him gently on the cheek. 'Thank you for today,' I say, squeezing his hand. His face is part shock, part pleasure as I open the car door. 'See you soon, I hope?' I add, before stepping down on to the cobbles.

169

Noah, still looking a little dazed, nods silently as I reach for my keys. I turn away to let myself into my house, and hear the car being put into gear and then slowly pulling away.

As I step inside the cottage I can't help but look down at my hand. Touching Noah had felt very different from when I'd touched Malachi the other day.

But why?

Twenty

The next day I make the now familiar walk up the hill to see Malachi.

I hadn't heard anything further from Noah about Oliver and the postcards, except a short text late last night from him to tell me Oliver hadn't got back to him and if he didn't by lunchtime today he would phone him again.

It was good of Noah to go to so much trouble for me when he didn't have to, but now I understand why he seemed to be enjoying our task so much. His previous life as a police officer in the Met must have been a lot more exciting than his current life here in St Felix; perhaps he was relishing the thrill of the chase once more, even if it was only the pursuit of a few vintage postcards. I'd really enjoyed spending time with him yesterday, and I'd been allowed the chance to see another side to him that his guise as mild-mannered antiques shop owner had prevented me from seeing before. However, I couldn't help wondering what might have changed not only his personality but his career path too.

A car horn hoots behind me, making me jump, and before I

have time to turn around a green and cream camper van pulls up alongside the pavement.

'On your way up to see me, are you?' Malachi calls through the open window.

'As a matter of fact, yes, I am.'

'Want a lift?'

'Sure.'

I climb into the van next to Ralph, who sits in between Malachi and me on the long leather seat. He gives my arm a friendly lick as I squeeze in next to him.

'Beautiful day,' Malachi says, as he indicates and pulls back out into the road.

'Isn't it just. I've been quite lucky with the weather since I got here – there's been sun every day.'

'So what are you on your way to see me about?' Malachi asks. It's nice to see him out of his overalls again. Today he's wearing pale blue jeans, ripped at the knee, heavy Timberland-style boots and a black T-shirt with an obscure heavy metal band's logo on the front. 'Or are you just checking up on me?'

'No, not checking up. I just wanted to see you again—'

'Stop right there!' Malachi interrupts, grinning. 'That's enough for me.'

'—*to see you again*,' I repeat, 'to find out how Daisy-Rose is coming along.'

'Ahh, you know how to shatter a man's dreams.' Malachi turns the wide cream steering wheel and we pull up in front of Bob's Bangers. 'Can you get the gate for me? I had to lock up before I went out to get parts for *your van*!'

'Sure.' I grin back. 'Where's the key?'

'In the pocket of my jeans.' Malachi winks.

I hold out the palm of my hand.

'You can't blame a man for trying!' Malachi retrieves the key from his pocket, passes it to me and I go to open the gate for him.

As I follow the van around to the back of the shed, I notice that there's an empty spot where one of the vintage show cars is missing.

'You sold one then,' I say to Malachi, after he's parked Pegasus and wandered back over to me with Ralph. 'One of the cars out front.'

'Yes, does that surprise you?'

'Nope, you've certainly got the gift of the gab.'

'I wish I'd sold a few more. I'm sure Bob will be disappointed that all I've managed to do while he's been away is sell one vehicle and do up another.'

'Do you know when he's coming back then?' Malachi was talking like Bob was due back any day, and I desperately hoped that didn't mean he'd be leaving soon. I'd got used to Malachi and his ways, and I was enjoying spending time with him while he renovated Daisy-Rose.

'Nope, he rang the other day to find out how things were going. Said he might be gone some time yet and could I keep covering, which of course I told him I could, just in case you were worried ...'

'No,' I reply innocently. 'Why would I be worried?'

'Ah, you'd miss me if I wasn't here, wouldn't you?' Malachi nudges me playfully with his elbow. 'Go on, say it! You know you would.'

I turn away from him and pretend to inspect Daisy-Rose. Today she not only looks brighter and a little shinier than I'm used to seeing her, but I notice Malachi has substituted her missing door with a replacement that's currently pale blue.

'She's looking a lot cleaner now, isn't she?' I say positively. 'And she's almost got all her parts.'

'She's a fair bit more than *cleaner*!' Malachi insists. 'You're only looking at her exterior. She's virtually had a whole new engine and I've ripped out all her old insides, not just the seats like before. Currently I'm in the process of acquiring new cupboards and kitchen equipment for her interior which, by the way, reminds me – you still haven't told me about the sleeping arrangements yet.'

'Sorry?' I ask, turning to face him again.

'Do you prefer to be on top or down below?' His dark eyebrows move up and down suggestively.

'I'm assuming,' I reply straight-faced, ignoring his innuendo, 'that you're talking about a bed for Daisy-Rose?'

'Yeah . . . although if you want to share with me *those* sorts of preferences too, I wouldn't be averse to listening.'

I sigh heavily and turn away from him again, but secretly I quite enjoy his flirting. It's a long time since anyone has flirted with me, even if it is just a bit of fun.

I inspect the inside of Daisy-Rose now. Malachi is right – she has had all her old shabby interior removed and I'm quite shocked to see her so empty.

'She's stripped bare,' I say almost to myself.

'You what?' Malachi pipes up behind me. 'Did I hear the words *stripped bare*?'

'Daisy-Rose is!' My face flushes so I keep it turned from Malachi. 'So what would you suggest in the bed department?' I ask. 'For the van!' I insist, without even waiting for his answer.

'*Daw*, party pooper! It's quite simple really – you have three choices. A rock and roll bed, like we discussed before – by day it's your back seat, then at night it folds out to become your bed.'

'Like a bed settee?'

'Yep, exactly that.' Malachi jumps up past me into the back of the van. 'You have two sizes of that – full or three quarter.' He demonstrates this by holding his arms across the inside of the van. 'It really depends on how many people you want in the bed at once ...'

'*Malachi.*'

'All right!' He rolls his eyes. 'Your other options are a bed up in the roof when we put in the pop-up. Kids are often better in those. Or, of course, no bed at all, only seats. But in my experience a seat is never as *comfortable* as a nice bouncy bed ...'

He grins, and I shake my head.

'It really depends, Ana,' he says, sounding serious now as he jumps back down from the van, 'on what you're going to do with her once I've finished the renovations. We've talked about the basics but not what we're actually aiming for.'

'I'm still not really sure. Perhaps you'd better do it in a traditional fashion with one of those rock and roll beds, then if I end up selling her at least it will be saleable.'

Malachi is strangely silent. He casually leans his back up against Daisy-Rose, his arms folded and his legs crossed.

'I'm guessing by your silence you don't approve?'

'No, not at all. I think a traditional approach is always best with these types of conversions, unless you have in mind exactly what you want to do – like turn your van into a coffee outlet or a sandwich shop.'

'I'm sensing a "but"?'

'Your senses serve you well, boss. Didn't you tell me that your friend Daisy wanted you to do something with this van, something that will make you and others happy?'

I nod. 'I knew you were going to bring that up.'

175

'Even more impressive, telepathic skills too!'

'But what am I supposed to do with it?' I say, ignoring Malachi as usual and standing back to look at Daisy-Rose. 'I'm sure she's going to look fabulous when you're finished, Malachi, of that I have no doubt, but driving around in her for more than a few days certainly isn't going to make me or anyone else happy. I'm not cut out for this kind of living.'

'Says you.'

'Are you saying I don't know myself?'

'Nope, not at all. What I'm saying is, how do you know until you try?' Malachi pushes himself away from the van in one easy movement. 'Right, I think it's time for coffee. Want one?'

I look at my watch. 'Sure, why not, coffee would be great, thanks.'

Malachi smiles. 'I don't want to hold you up if you need to be somewhere.'

'No, it's not that. It's— Look, why don't you make the coffee. In fact, why don't I make the coffee while you unload your parts from Pegasus, and then we can talk?'

'Sounds good to me, boss! Milk, three sugars please. Heaped ones too.'

I make us two cups of coffee in the little office, which looks very much like I imagine most mechanics' offices to look – a little bit grubby and a lot messy. There's a grey metal filing cabinet on one wall and a cheap desk on the other covered in papers. It looks like someone's left the office in a bit of a hurry there's so much clutter everywhere, and I hope it's not Malachi that's been making the mess in Bob's absence. There's a calendar on the wall above the tea- and coffee-making equipment, and I'm pleased to see it doesn't have a half-naked woman on it but rather a bright red car. According to the calendar it's a 1984 Audi Quattro.

'And there you are again,' I say, acknowledging the eighties iconic car. 'How come all these eighties things keep popping up all the time? It's very strange.'

While I wait for the kettle to boil I can't help but compare this office with Noah's immaculate offering, which I'd sat in only a few days earlier. The two couldn't be more different, but then neither could the two men with whom I was spending much of my time here in St Felix.

'I've been very lucky to find both of you,' I say to the empty office.

The kettle boils and I pour water on to the instant coffee I've added to the mugs, then I grimace as I measure three large spoons of sugar into Malachi's mug. *How does he stay so slim if he has such a sweet tooth as this*, I wonder.

I couldn't help but notice this morning Malachi's rather toned muscly body as I'd sat next to him in his van. His T-shirt was even tighter today, and its sleeves that little bit shorter, so not only was I treated to another glimpse of his fine biceps but also to the beginning of a black ink tattoo on the upper part of his arm. It looked very much like the base of an intricate Celtic cross, but I decide I'd need to see the rest of it first before I could verify that.

I wonder as I walk back across the yard carrying two mugs of coffee if he has any more tattoos scattered about his body – it might be quite nice to find out one day . . .

'Was it warm in the office?' Malachi asks, taking his mug from me. 'You look a little flushed.'

'No, not really,' I say quickly, hiding my embarrassment. What was I thinking? Malachi's flirting was starting to rub off on me. 'I must have stood too close to the boiling kettle, that's all.'

'Ah,' Malachi says, seeming to accept this ridiculous excuse for my pink cheeks. 'So now, tell me why you're so concerned about time today?'

Malachi, Ralph and I sit amiably in the morning sun together while I tell Malachi all about what happened yesterday with Noah and the postcard fair.

'Sounds promising, doesn't it?' I ask, at the end of my tale.

Malachi shrugs. 'Let's just hope this Oliver hasn't plastered them all over his screen yet.'

'Well, yes, I think we're all hoping that.' I was surprised Malachi didn't seem as excited about our discovery as I was.

'Sounds like you and this Noah had a good time yesterday.' Malachi looks down into his mug and swirls the remains of his coffee around.

'Yes, Noah is a nice man. He's been very helpful.'

'*Nice* ... that's a very interesting word. It can have so many meanings.'

'What do you mean?'

'Well, is Noah nice in that he's pleasing, agreeable, amiably pleasant and kind? Or is he nice because you can't find a more exciting adjective to describe him?'

'The first, obviously.'

'Really? Because in my experience using the word *nice* is a very dull way to describe someone. Perhaps he is quite dull, though?'

'Noah is far from dull actually. He may seem quiet and calm on the outside, but on the inside I think he's quite a deep and complex man.'

'Oh, really?'

Malachi sounds surprised by my statement, but he's much less surprised than I am to hear myself saying it. 'Yes, really.'

'Sounds like you got to know him *very* well on your day out together.'

'We talked about things, yes, if that's what you mean? We were in the car for quite some time travelling. Like I said, he's a nice, kind man.'

Malachi smiles knowingly.

'What now?'

'Nothing, just thinking.'

'About?'

'About Daisy-Rose,' Malachi says, jumping up. 'And how much work I have to do on her before she's ready for you to drive away. Assuming, that is, you're still wanting to drive away as soon as possible?' He looks at me with a questioning expression.

'Why wouldn't I?'

Malachi shrugs. 'I don't know – you tell me?'

'I have no clue what you're talking about, but then I often have no idea about what's going on in your head, Malachi.'

'That's probably for the best! Now, if there's nothing else? I'd best be getting on. Time is money as everyone here is so keen on saying.' He jumps up, picks up a screwdriver and heads towards Daisy-Rose's door. Ralph lifts his head from where he's been dozing in the sun in case anything interesting like a walk is about to take place, then when he realises it's not, he immediately drops it down again and goes back to sleep.

I stand up and collect Malachi's coffee mug with the intention of taking it back to the office with my own, when something occurs to me and I hesitate.

'Something up?' Malachi asks, turning around just as he's about to climb into Daisy-Rose.

How did he know I'd hesitated? He'd had his back to me just now.

'No, it's nothing – it can wait.'

'Sure?'

I nod. 'Yeah, everything is just fine. I'll wash these mugs for you, then I'll leave you be.'

'Okie dokie!' Malachi calls cheerfully. 'You know where I am if you want to talk about anything, though.'

It's only as I walk back towards the office that I realise what a strange contradiction this is. Not Malachi's words – his offer had been genuine, of that I had no doubt. What's strange when I think about it now is how reassuring the thought of unburdening myself to Malachi is. While in reality the prospect should feel odd, given that I hardly know him, it actually feels very comforting indeed to know he is there.

Twenty-One

'Do you want the good news or the bad news first?' Noah says, when I answer my ringing phone later that day. I'm just settling down to do some work in my favourite spot beside the French windows. I would have liked to be sitting outside in the sunshine that's currently pouring down on to the balcony but my laptop just won't play ball. As hard as I try I can never see the screen properly when I'm outside in the sun.

'Er . . . good?' I suggest, hoping this is the right way around.

'Right, Oliver phoned me back and he did have the postcards like Alistair said. And the way he's described them, it sounds like they're definitely our cards.'

'Yes! Go on. Wait, is the bad news he used them for découpage on his screen?'

'Nope, that's not the bad news – that news is he's since got rid of them.'

'*Noo!* Where?'

'To an auction house in Penzance. He gave them the cards to sell with a job lot of other stuff.'

'But . . . please tell me there's a *but*?'

'*But* the second bit of good news is the auction is this Saturday. So we can still bid on them!'

'*Yay!*' I fist-pump the air. 'This is wonderful. We shouldn't have any problem buying a few old postcards, should we?'

'I doubt it, unless the cards are in a lot with something that's very desirable. Oliver said it was just a load of old bits and pieces that he hadn't used in past jobs.'

'Great. Are you free to come to an auction this Saturday, though? Won't it be one of your busiest days?'

'Don't worry, I'll sort it. I haven't come this far to bail on you now.'

'Thank you, Noah.'

'It's my pleasure, Ana.'

It seems like for ever until Saturday comes.

I pass the time by working feverishly to get my latest project done before its deadline, popping up to see how Malachi is doing with Daisy-Rose, and generally enjoying the delights of seaside living – including morning and evening walks along the cliffs breathing in the sea air.

On one of those walks I bump into a tired and pale-looking Jake. He's pushing a small blue pram as far as he can before the path becomes inaccessible to wheels, and walking next to him is a dog that looks like it might be some sort of basset-hound cross.

'Hello!' I wave cheerfully as they approach.

'Hey, how's it going?' he whispers, nodding at the pram.

'Whoops, sorry,' I apologise, whispering now too. I bend down and stroke the dog.

'It's fine. I'm just being extra careful, that's all. This one's a terror for not sleeping. We find taking her out for long walks in the sea air the best way to get her to nod off and stay like that for a while! And Bill doesn't mind, do you, boy?'

The dog looks up at Jake and pants his agreement. I stand up again and take a peek over the side of the pram. 'She looks like butter wouldn't melt,' I say, seeing a fast asleep rosy-cheeked baby wrapped up in a pale yellow blanket.

'Tell me about it. Poppy is exhausted, though – she's barely getting any sleep at night. I try my best but I don't quite have the right equipment for feeding Daisy-Rose, if you know what I mean.'

'Has she tried expressing?' I ask. 'My friend had a baby that wouldn't sleep too. She was like a walking zombie for months.'

That had been Daisy's first son, Jacob. I'd tried to help her as best I could at the time, but I'd felt utterly useless.

'Yeah, but madam here won't take milk from a bottle! I never had this with my other two – they were angels compared to this – but maybe I've forgotten. Time does funny things to the mind. I have two older children,' he explains, 'from my first marriage. All grown up now, thank god. I don't think I could have handled this and two young children!'

'It is tough,' I say, still thinking about Daisy.

'Thank goodness we have Lou around – my aunt. She's been a godsend to us both helping out. Anyway, enough of my woes. How's your stay? Is the cottage behaving itself?'

'The cottage is fab, thanks. Yes, everything is going very well. I'm really enjoying being here in St Felix.'

'St Felix *is* gorgeous. I sometimes think I don't appreciate the town anywhere near enough. But that happens, doesn't it, when you live somewhere, whereas you as a visitor see all its glory.'

'I do indeed,' I agree, looking at the view.

There's a shuffling sound from inside the pram and Jake's

face turns even paler. 'Got to go!' he hisses. 'I can't have her waking yet. I need to let Poppy get some sleep!'

'Go! Go!' I say, laughing.

'See you around!' he whispers, and I watch him head back down the hill with Bill, furiously rocking the pram as he goes.

As I walk back down the same way at a more relaxed pace, my mind turns again to Daisy and her children.

Queen Charlotte's Maternity Hospital, March 2011

'He's beautiful,' I say to Daisy, as I stand by her bed in the maternity unit.

'Would you like to hold him?' Daisy asks. She looks weary, and there are dark blue-grey smudges under her eyes.

'Sure.' I hold out my arms, and Daisy places a heavy bundle in them.

'He hardly stopped crying last night. The nurse had to come and take him off me for a bit so I could get some rest.'

'He looks like a little angel right now.' I stare at the baby in my arms, and for the first time ever when faced with a newborn baby I feel a swell of love.

'*Looks* being the appropriate word! I'm kidding – I'm sure we'll get along just fine when we get home, won't we, Jacob?'

'Ooh, is that what you're calling him? Good name – solid.'

'It's after Peter's grandfather but I quite like it too.'

'Hello, little Jacob,' I say softly, as the baby in my arms opens his eyes. He squints up at me and wiggles his tiny fingers. 'I'm going to be your Aunt Ana.'

'You're going to be more than that, I hope,' Daisy says, looking up at me. 'You're going to be his godmother too.'

So just when I was afraid we were going to grow even further apart now Daisy was married and had a child, instead I was pulled in even closer. And when Daisy had a second son two years later, I was asked to be godmother to little Harry too.

Even though Daisy was no longer with us, I would for ever be a part of her family, and for that I was truly grateful.

Twenty-Two

'Ready?' Noah asks on Saturday as we set off for the auction.

'Yep. You?'

Noah nods. 'Sure am!'

He sounds quite excited and I'm pleased. I loved Noah's enthusiasm for this project. It made a change from Malachi's unusually reserved comments about it all, but I couldn't complain; his enthusiasm went into Daisy-Rose and for that I was very thankful.

'Have you been to an auction before?' Noah asks.

I look over at him in the driver's seat. Today he's wearing dark navy chinos, smart shoes and a white shirt with a tiny blue check running through it. It could only be described as smart casual, but it was very Noah.

'Nope, never. I'm assuming you have, though.'

'Yes, many times, it's good fun. So what's your budget for the cards?'

'Er . . .' I hadn't really thought about it. I just desperately wanted to come away with the missing postcards. 'I'm not sure really?'

'We'll need to agree a limit before our lot comes up, otherwise it's quite easy to get carried away once you begin bidding.'

'I just really want those cards, and I don't mind if we have to pay over the odds to get them.'

Noah glances at me.

'It won't come to that, though, will it?' I ask anxiously. 'I mean who else is going to want some old postcards?'

'You'd be surprised. The thing is we don't know what else Oliver put in the auction with them. From what he said I don't think it will be anything particularly sought after, just a few bits and pieces that he had cluttering up his office.'

'Good.'

'But auctions can be funny things,' Noah continues. 'The lots you think will sell for a good profit quite often don't, and then things you have little hope for can go for a lot more than they're worth if there are two or more people after them.'

'Well, I'm prepared to bid higher than anyone else,' I say with confidence. 'We *must* get those cards, Noah. I'm absolutely certain they will fill in the missing gaps about Lou and Frankie. In fact, I know they will.'

We arrive in Penzance at the auction house, and pull up in the only free space available in the large car park.

'Busy, isn't it?' I say, as we lock up the Land Rover and make our way towards the entrance.

'I thought it would be. This is one of Cornwall's biggest auction houses. I've bought and sold things here before and they usually get a good turnout.'

That thought doesn't fill me with joy. The more people that were here, the more likely someone else would want to bid on my cards.

I smile to myself as we queue up at the reception desk to

register. I was calling them 'my cards' now. I'd taken this project very much to heart, and I was determined to return these unique and special things to their rightful home.

'Hello, Noah,' the lady behind the desk says in a broad Cornish accent. 'We haven't seen you in a while, my love.'

'Hello, Moira,' Noah says, looking pleased she'd remember him. 'No, it's been some time since I was last here.'

'After something special, are you?'

Noah shrugs. 'We'll see how it goes.'

Moira taps the side of her nose and winks. 'You do that, my love.' She checks Noah's name off against a long list on her computer, then she scribbles a number on a card and passes it to him. 'Here you go, my lovely, best of luck. But maybe you won't be needing it – I see you've brought your own Lady Luck with you today.' She smiles with curiosity at me.

'Ana is just one of my customers,' Noah insists, his neck reddening above his collar. 'She's looking for a few bits and pieces today too.'

'Hi,' I say, feeling a little awkward. I didn't mind Noah referring to me as a customer, but I would have preferred it if he'd called me his friend instead.

'Well, good luck to you as well, my dear. I hope you find something here you like today.'

Noah hurriedly pulls me away from the counter before I have a chance to reply to Moira.

'Why did you do that?' I ask, pulling my arm away from his hand.

'Sorry, I didn't want to seem rude, but it's not a good idea to show too much enthusiasm for anything while you're in here – if someone overhears you it might affect the bidding and I thought you might mention the cards.'

189

'I might be a novice at this but I'm not that silly,' I insist, even though he was right – I *was* about to tell Moira exactly what my interest was in today.

'Sorry, my mistake.'

'You don't need to keep apologising. It's fine, honestly. Should we take a look around and find *our lot*?' I whisper the last part.

Noah nods.

We walk slowly around the various tables in the centre of the room, rifling through cardboard boxes filled with anything from vintage records and old books to china and costume jewellery. Each one is labelled with a small white sticker dictating its lot number.

'Let's try the rest of the room,' Noah says, when we don't find Oliver's lot on the tables. 'I wish Oliver had known what his number was going to be, then this would have been a lot easier.'

'Nice pun,' I say, tearing my eyes away from an old box of records.

'What?'

'A *lot* easier – I assumed you meant to say that.'

'Oh ... no, not really,' Noah says, sounding distracted. 'But I get it now, very good.'

We continue now around the edges of the room, where most of the furniture in today's auction is located. We walk past cabinets, mirrors, chairs and even wardrobes, all with the same little white stickers on, but we don't see any postcards. Just when I'm starting to wonder if the cards are actually here, we stumble upon an old wooden trunk tucked away in a corner. The lid of the trunk is open and as we both peer inside, we see a Tiffany-style lamp with a brightly coloured glass shade, a few small metal sculptures of people and some pieces of flowery china. Noah moves a few of the things aside so we can see what else is in there, and we find a bundle of garish-looking fabrics, an old battered teddy bear and a large ornate box covered in découpage that might once have been used for jewellery. 'Bingo!' Noah whispers, lifting the box from the trunk. 'This must be it.' He glances quickly at me before opening the lid.

'The cards!' I cry joyfully, as we both look inside and see several large piles of postcards bound together with brown string. Then I quickly lower my tone. 'Is it them?' I ask hurriedly. 'Can we get them out to check?'

Noah lifts one of the bundles of cards from the box and turns them over so we can see the writing. 'It's them,' is all he says, before putting the cards swiftly back in the box and closing the lid. He tucks the box back at the bottom of the trunk, then he hesitates. 'Oh ... ' he says, lifting up the teddy bear now.

'What? What's wrong.'

'Nothing is wrong,' he says quickly, inspecting the ear of the bear, then giving it a quick squeeze before putting it back in the trunk and attempting to cover it with some of the fabrics. 'Just as long as there aren't any teddy bear experts bidding today. Come on,' he says, beckoning me away this time instead of dragging me. 'We need to move away from here. We don't want to draw any extra attention to this lot.'

'What's up?' I ask, as we take one of the seats in front of the auctioneer's block.

'I'm no expert but I'd say that bear might be an early Steiff.'

'What's that?'

'It's *the* most sought-after type of bear for collectors. Steiff is a German manufacturer and they still make toys today, but their early bears sell for *a lot* of money.'

My heart sinks. 'But what makes you think it's a Steiff?'

'To be honest, it's just a hunch. It's the shape of him, his eyes, the colour of his fur, the fact when I squeezed him he made a crunchy sound like he was filled with excelsior – it's a type of wood wool stuffing rather than a softer kapok. He doesn't have a button in his ear – the classic Steiff logo – but there's a tiny hole where one might have been.'

'Do you think anyone else will have noticed him?'

'Possibly. Bears always sell well at auction, but if that's a Steiff, or someone suspects it might be, we could well have quite the battle on our hands when it comes to Lot 105.'

Twenty-Three

The room eventually fills with people – so many, in fact, that not everyone gets a seat and there are a large number standing around the edge of the room as the bidding begins.

This crowded scenario should have made me nervous, but as I wait with anticipation for our lot to come up, I find I'm feeling more excited than anxious at being in this confined environment.

I watch carefully as the auctioneer whizzes through each item, taking his time if it's a popular one or moving on quickly if it's not. I'm surprised to see that not every lot sells, and I secretly pray that ours might be one of those unpopular ones, so we can buy my cards quickly and easily.

Much faster than I'd expected we reach Lot 100. Not long to go now. It's the box of records I'd been nosing around earlier. I sit up a little in my seat.

'Lot 100,' the auctioneer says from his elevated position, 'is a box of vinyl records mainly dating from the mid-nineteen eighties. I'd like to open the bidding at thirty pounds.'

There's silence in the room.

'No, twenty pounds then? Ten pounds?' he asks hopefully.

I put my hand in the air.

'Ah, a lady with good taste, I see,' he says, pointing to me. 'You can't be old enough to remember the eighties, though, can you, miss?'

There are a few titters from the other bidders, and I smile.

'Do I hear fifteen pounds then?' he asks, looking around the room. 'Fifteen pounds? Thank you, sir.'

I turn back to see who else is bidding, but there are too many people in the room to see.

'Do I hear twenty pounds?'

I thrust my hand in the air again, and the auctioneer nods at me. 'Thank you, miss.'

'Twenty-five pounds, sir?' he says, looking out into the room at my rival. 'No, it's with the lady at twenty pounds then ... going ... gone!' He bangs his wooden gavel down hard. 'Number, please?'

Noah looking a little bewildered holds up his card.

'Very appropriate,' the auctioneer says. 'Number one hundred and eighty.'

'Is that our number?' I ask, looking in astonishment at Noah as the next lot begins immediately.

He shows me the card.

'Wow ... ' I say under my breath.

'Something wrong?'

'No, on the contrary, everything is just right.'

I watch the next two lots unfold and then Lot 103 begins.

'The next lot is a box of Volkswagen sundries including an original steering wheel, rear view mirror, hub caps and tyre cover. I'd like to start the bidding at one hundred pounds.'

I thrust my hand in the air.

'Steady,' Noah whispers. 'You still have the important one to come yet.'

'Malachi can use these,' I say, my hand going in the air again as I'm immediately outbid. 'I saw them earlier – they look in great condition.'

'Are you sure they're for the camper van *you* have, though?' Noah asks. 'I thought you said you had one from the sixties? These parts are for a 1976 model.'

I stare at him.

'Miss?' the auctioneer asks. 'Do I have a hundred and sixty pounds?'

I shake my head. 'Thank you,' I whisper to Noah, 'I was getting a bit carried away.'

'I told you it was easily done. Let's just concentrate on Lot 105.'

I nod and sit back in my seat. That was close – I'd nearly used up the postcard budget on something I wouldn't have been able to use. I'd have looked a right idiot presenting that lot to Malachi and then finding out it was for a bay window camper van and not a split screen.

Ooh, I'd remembered the difference.

'Lot 105,' the auctioneer announces, and I jump in my seat, 'is this handsome oak trunk.' He gestures to where his assistant is displaying it. 'It has some very nice detailing on the metal-work, as you can see, and it's filled with various objets d'art including some hand-dyed silk fabrics, a Tiffany-style lamp and a pretty rose-patterned tea service.'

Yes! He hadn't mentioned the postcards or the bear!

'I'd like to start the bidding at fifty pounds.'

Noah grabs my hand, and for a moment I think it's a romantic gesture of support, but then I realise it's to stop me bidding too early.

'No? Shall we try thirty pounds then?' the auctioneer says, looking around the room. 'Thank you, madam. Now, do I see thirty-five pounds?'

Noah allows the bidding to get to sixty pounds before he releases my hand. 'Go for it,' he whispers. 'But don't get carried away.'

'Sixty-five pounds – my eighties friend is back in the game, thank you, miss,' the auctioneer says, acknowledging my new bid.

The bidding very quickly escalates to a hundred pounds and then one hundred and fifty.

'I think someone suspects the same as me about the bear,' Noah says, looking around. 'This could get expensive, Ana.'

'I don't care. The cards are coming home with me.' I wave my hand in the air again to raise the bid to one hundred and seventy. It's just me and one other bidder now.

Please stop before two hundred pounds, I think, raising my eyes to the ceiling. At this rate I'd have no budget left for the van, and I didn't want to be the one to tell Malachi he would have to compromise on his renovations.

'It's with the lady at one hundred and ninety pounds,' the auctioneer says. 'Two hundred pounds?' he asks again. The other bidder shakes their head. 'No?' The auctioneer looks around the room. 'Anyone else?'

I grab Noah's bidding number and hold it to my chest. *Please . . .*

'It's in the room at one hundred and ninety pounds then. Going once, going twice. Sold to my eighties friend!' He bangs his gavel hard on the desk.

'*Yes!*' I shout, punching the air.

Everyone laughs.

'Sorry,' I apologise, holding up our number.

'One hundred and eighty. Yes, I remember,' the auctioneer says, grinning at me.

'We did it!' I whisper excitedly to Noah.

'Correction – *you* did it,' he says, smiling at me. 'Well done.'

With the auction still going on, we leave the room and make our way to the reception desk again to pay for the two lots we've won.

'Well done, lovey,' Moira says, as I count my cash on to the desk. 'You've got a nice pair of lots there. Just between the two of us, I thought that bear might be a Steiff.' She looks at Noah. He silently nods his agreement.

'That's great, but I didn't buy it for that – I bought it for the cards in the jewellery box,' I say happily.

Moira looks puzzled. 'You spent one hundred and ninety pounds, actually over two hundred pounds with our fees, on some postcards – they must have been special. Were they sent from Queen Victoria to Prince Albert?'

'Not quite. It's more that they have a sentimental value, so they're very special to me.'

And hopefully to Lou and Frankie, I think, as we drive home with the trunk and the box of records in the back of Noah's car, and a very happy me in the front, a pile of postcards on one knee and an old teddy bear on the other.

Twenty-Four

I spend the next couple of days poring over the new batch of postcards I now have in my possession. As I'd hoped, they cover the missing twenty years of Lou's life and are fascinating to read.

It seems that after she bought Daisy-Rose her life changed completely. She very quickly went from being a new artist who sold the occasional painting to a prolific painter, who not only made a living from her works of art but was much sought-after too.

She appeared to have toured the country with Daisy-Rose acting as a sort of muse-cum-companion to her. The more Lou travelled with her camper van, the more successful she became.

This card of the Yorkshire moors from 1971 perfectly sums up what Daisy-Rose meant to Lou:

> My Darling Frankie,
>   I'm here in God's own county! Yes, that's right —
> Yorkshire. And I can confirm that if it does indeed
> belong to God, then he chose very well!

Rose and I are here touring areas I've never visited before, and more importantly never painted. The scenery is breath-taking, and I've been very inspired. We've camped in some very remote areas, and have spent several days without seeing a soul, but as long as I have my Rose for company, I never feel truly alone.

Forever yours,

Lou x

They seem to have toured all over the place during the seventies, with Lou stopping to paint when she felt inspired to do so, and when the eighties arrived it seems Lou and Rose's travels took them even further afield with new countries added to their ever growing list of travels.

This postcard to Frankie from 1985 with a photo of the Eiffel Tower on the front is one of my favourites from this bunch:

My Darling Frankie,

I'm sending you this card from Paris! Can you believe it? Rose and I have made it across the Channel! I was honoured to be asked to come over here to teach a class of French art students – they were very eager and talented, and I'm not sure what help I was to them, but they seemed very grateful to have me there.

Now Rose and I are touring France together and having a wonderful time. We're a bit early for the Beaujolais Nouveau race but I'm enjoying the odd glass of wine while I'm here – it would be rude not to.

*I still wish you were here with us – even after all
these years.*

Forever yours,

Lou x

The postcards are very entertaining, but more importantly they help me piece more of Lou's life together. Now I have a fairly complete picture of a young girl who followed her parents' wishes, went to a traditional university and came away with a very good qualification in law, but after doing what was expected of her she eventually followed her heart and pursued what became a very successful, and by the sounds of it lucrative, career as an artist, where she was able to not only paint for a living but also travel the world while doing so.

However, what the postcards still don't bring me any closer to discovering is how I'm going to find Lou so I can return the cards to her.

I sigh as I sit back in the armchair and let the sun that's pouring through the French windows warm my face. It was a welcome change from the cool, wet weather that had blown in across the sea this morning. As so often happened here, what took place in the sky in the morning was no indicator as to what might take place later in the day.

There must *be something in the cards that might be a clue*, I think, as I stare into space. *But what?*

I'm jolted from my thoughts by someone knocking at the front door. I go downstairs to see who it is and I'm pleased to find Noah standing self-consciously on my doorstep.

'Hello,' I say, 'this is a surprise.'

'Yes, it is. I mean, hi there.' He hurriedly holds up a carrier bag. 'I have these, you see – I mean I have fish – mackerel to be precise. A grateful customer brought them in to us after we helped him with his mother's house clearance last week. I mean it was the house clearance that was last week, not when the fish were caught. They're very fresh. Caught this morning.'

'Yes, I gathered that.' I smile.

'Sorry ... only Jess doesn't like mackerel apparently. First I've heard of it, though.' Noah shakes his head as though that was one of the things Jess should have put on her CV before coming to work in the shop. 'I wondered if you might be able to use them?'

'Don't you like them either then?' I ask.

'Oh yes, I love mackerel, but there are too many here for one person and I wondered if you might like them? They're very tasty barbecued.'

'That's very kind of you. I love fish, but sadly I don't have a barbecue.'

Noah holds up his other hand. 'It's only disposable,' he says innocently, waving another bag at me, 'but it would do the trick ... I could light it for you if you want?'

'And stay to cook and eat the fish, I hope?'

Noah's face reddens.

'Sure.' I grin. 'Why not – come on in. Can we barbecue on the balcony though? I don't have a garden here.'

'If the wind is in the right direction, we can,' Noah says, looking pleased. He follows me inside. 'I've come prepared. I brought firelighters and matches in case you didn't have any.'

'Matches, I can do. Firelighters, I doubt it. You took a bit of a chance, didn't you?' I say, taking the fish from him and placing it on the kitchen draining board. 'What if I didn't eat mackerel, like Jess?'

'This was all Jess's idea actually. I was unsure to be honest – it seemed a bit forward just turning up on your doorstep, but she was very keen on the idea.'

That made more sense. I was finding it hard to believe Noah had decided to do all this himself. It was so bold, and not like Noah at all.

'Well, it was a very good one. When do you want to eat – now or later?'

'The barbecue will take a little while to heat up, so shall I make a start now? I'll need to clean the mackerel first, but at least they won't need de-boning.'

I'm amused that Noah, as a man, assumes he'll be the one barbecuing, but I don't disagree. 'I wonder if the bakery will have any bread left now?' I look at my watch. 'It's a bit late but they might have something. Some fresh bread and salad would be perfect with mackerel.'

'Sounds great to me. Do you want to pop down and see while I get this set up upstairs?'

'Sure. I'll just grab my purse first.'

I leave Noah cleaning the fish in the kitchen while I sprint upstairs to fetch my bag. I can't help popping into the bathroom to check what I look like while I'm up there. I hadn't been expecting any visitors – Noah was lucky I was still wearing jeans and hadn't slipped into my comfy PJ bottoms as I often did when I was alone.

I run a brush through my hair, stroke some mascara over my eyelashes, then add a dash of gloss to my lips for good measure. I'm not really sure why I felt it necessary, but I didn't want Noah to think I didn't care about myself. Then without thinking about it any more I grab my bag and head back downstairs to the kitchen.

'How's it going?' I ask.

'Good, good. I'm nearly done here. I'll go upstairs in a minute and get the barbecue going if that's okay with you?'

'Sure, I won't be long. I'll go to the bakery and if they don't have any bread I'll try the supermarket.'

'Great, see you in a bit.'

I leave Noah at the cottage and head towards the bakery, surprised at how much I'm looking forward to this impromptu barbecue with him. I hadn't really had any particular plans for this evening and the thought of hanging out together was a very pleasant one indeed. As I hurry along Harbour Street I'm relieved to see the bakery *is* still open, even though their pavement sign has already been taken in.

'Hello!' I call, popping my head around the door of the empty shop. 'Anyone home?'

Ant appears from the back. 'Well, good evening, young lady, you're a bit late today, aren't you? We're just about to shut up for the night.'

'Yeah, sorry. I just wondered if you had any bread left? It's a bit of an emergency.'

Noah barbecuing mackerel could hardly be classed as an emergency, but in the bread sense it was.

Ant doesn't seem fazed though. 'Any type in particular?'

'Something to go with barbecued mackerel if you have it?'

'Nice. Hold on just a minute, I'll see what we have.'

Ant disappears out back again, and returns a few seconds later with a wholegrain bloomer and a crusty French stick. 'Any good?' he asks, waving them at me like flags.

'Perfect, thank you. How much?'

'On the house, lovely. They'll only go to waste otherwise. We haven't got all that much left today – a couple of loaves for us to take home, that's all. We don't often have a surplus, but if we do we take it to the old folks' home up the road.'

'That's good of you.'

'You have to do your bit, don't you. So, what's the occasion?' Ant asks, wrapping my loaves in white paper. 'Solo barbecue, is it?' He asks this question innocently but glances up at me with mischief in his eyes.

'No, I have a guest . . .' I reply, with just enough mystery to pique his interest.

'Let me guess, would that be our local antiques dealer by any chance?'

'It would! How did you know?'

'Ah, news – well, gossip – doesn't take long to travel here in St Felix. I hear you went to an auction together the other day too?' He raises his dark eyebrows suggestively.

'Yes, but that was to do with my missing postcards,' I protest.

'And did you find them?'

'We did actually.'

'Wonderful, and did you speak to our Lou?'

I shake my head. 'No, I didn't want to disturb her. I know she's really busy helping Poppy and Jake right now.'

'She is that. Bonny baby, though – have you seen her?'

'I have, out with Jake. Very pretty.'

'Jake, or the baby?' Ant winks. 'Talking of local hunks . . . back to this blossoming romance of yours . . .'

'No such thing!' I grin. 'Now, you're sure I don't owe you anything for the bread?'

'Nope. You can just owe me the first dibs on any gossip, okay? I want to be the first to know when you two go official, so I can spread the news accordingly.'

I shake my head. 'You'll be waiting a long time then! Thanks

204

for this' – I tap one of the loaves of bread – 'very generous of you.'

'Any time!' Ant calls, as I leave the shop. 'Enjoy your evening!'

I head back the way I came but not before I've detoured via the supermarket. I grab some salad bits – coleslaw, tomatoes – and, at the last minute, a bottle of Pinot Grigio that's on offer by the till. Then I walk back through the town to Snowdrop Cottage.

'I'm back!' I call, as I stash my salad in the fridge and wine in the freezer so it chills super-fast, and then leave the bread on the kitchen table. But there's no reply, so I climb the stairs and wander over to the now closed French windows, where I find a very chilled Noah sitting out on the balcony next to a smoking barbecue placed safely on two upturned terracotta flowerpots.

He waves, so I pull open one of the glass doors.

'Sorry, I had to close them up,' he says. 'I didn't want any smoke to blow back inside your house. Luckily for us, though, the wind is blowing in just the right direction to take the majority of it away from us. How was your shopping trip?'

'Good. I got everything we should need.'

'Great. I'm just about to put the mackerel on so everything is looking rosy.' He smiles.

'I've only just put the wine in the freezer, but it should chill quite quickly in there. I'll prepare the salad while you get the fish going and we'll meet back here for wine in a few minutes, shall we?'

By the time I head back upstairs to the balcony carrying two glasses and a bottle of wine in an ice bucket that I found at the back of one of the kitchen cupboards, the barbecue is well under way.

'It smells amazing,' I say, putting the ice bucket and glasses down on the small wrought-iron table. I sit down on the second of a pair of matching chairs at the opposite end of the small balcony to where Noah is cooking.

'Don't they?' Noah agrees. 'Nothing beats fresh mackerel cooked out in the open like this. Especially when you're sharing it with good company too.'

'And good wine,' I say, feeling the need to deflect his compliment. 'Well, I can't guarantee it's good, but at least it's chilled. Would you like some?'

'Please.'

I half fill the large glasses with wine.

'This is a very well-equipped property,' Noah says, holding his glass up to the light to examine the contents. 'Decent size wine glasses *and* an ice bucket – what more could you want?' He swirls the wine around in the base of the glass before tasting it. 'Very nice.'

Shirking all the wine formalities, I take a sizeable gulp from my glass.

'Yeah, not bad for a supermarket.'

'I see you've put your new housemate in pride of place,' Noah says, looking in through the French windows. 'He looks right at home on the sofa there.'

'Yes,' I agree, looking at the old bear we'd brought back from the auction. 'He's quite cute, isn't he?'

'Does he have a name yet?'

'No, I just call him "Bear". I'm thinking he'll be a nice mascot in the camper van when it's finished, though.'

Noah nods.

'Although, if you think he might be valuable I'd be happy to give him to you. As a little thank you for all you've done.'

'No, don't be silly. He's yours now – you won him fair and square.'

'If you're sure?'

'Absolutely. So how is the camper van coming along?'

'She's coming along really well ... I think so anyway. And Malachi seems pleased with the progress he's making.'

'I haven't come across this Malachi yet. Does he ever leave that garage?'

'Yes, he actually lives in his own camper van, called Pegasus of all things!' I find myself smiling as I think about Malachi. 'You might have seen that around – it's green and cream, and he also has a golden Labrador called Ralph. I'm surprised you haven't bumped into him walking Ralph when you've been out with Clarice. I'm guessing there aren't that many places to walk dogs around here.'

Noah shakes his head. 'Nope, doesn't ring any bells. What does he look like? I couldn't really see him properly when we were in the pub the other night.'

'He's tall, about your height, I guess. He has dark curly hair and green eyes, but not your usual pale green – his are a really bright green. Erm ... he's pale skinned, but he has little freckles. He dresses very casually – jeans mostly, quite often ripped, and he wears T-shirts with motifs on the front like rock bands and stuff. He's quite muscly too,' I say, happy to think about Malachi's arms once more. 'Not muscly like a body builder, just very fit, you know?'

There's silence.

I pull myself from my very pleasant reverie to find Noah tending to the fish on the barbecue. 'Oh, and he's Irish,' I finish. 'But he's from the north, not the south, I think ... Either that or somewhere close to the border – his accent is neither one nor the other.'

Noah glances up at me from his position bent over the barbecue. 'Sounds like you've got to know this Malachi very well indeed if you can give that detailed a description of him. In my experience most people are usually much vaguer when it comes to describing someone they hardly know.' Noah re-folds the tin foil around the mackerel once more. 'Almost ready,' he announces, giving me the briefest of glances. He sits back up on his chair and reaches for his wine again, then he takes a long slow sip.

'Do you mean in your experience of taking witness statements?' I offer, wondering if something is wrong. He's gone very quiet all of a sudden.

'Yes, exactly that.'

I look over the balcony at the view. The sun isn't quite ready to set, yet it's still managing to impart a warm golden glow to not only the sky but the sand and sea down below us as we sit in silence on the balcony.

Has reminding Noah of his time in the police force offended him in some way?

'You don't like talking about your time in the police, do you?' I ask bluntly. There was no point tiptoeing around it – Noah was making it very clear.

'Not really, no.'

'Okay then, I won't ask any more about it.' I stand up. Even though we were outside, you could cut the atmosphere with a knife. 'I'll go and fetch the rest of the food from downstairs if you think the fish might be ready soon.'

'Can I help?' Noah asks, obviously sensing the tension in my voice. He stands up as I pull open the door, looking concerned.

'No,' I reply curtly. 'I'll be just fine, thank you.'

Well, that was awkward, I think, as I load a tray up in the kitchen with everything we might need. It wasn't like I was trying to be nosy asking about the police, just making conversation. I'd given a detailed description of Malachi because he was so easy to describe and he was such a character, plus it was easy to describe someone you liked and found attractive . . .

I clap my hand over my mouth.

I don't know if I'm more shocked at the realisation that I do indeed find Malachi *very* attractive, or that I think I might know why Noah had gone all cool with me upstairs.

It wasn't reminding him of the police force that Noah had found annoying, his annoyance had come from the fact I was attracted to Malachi.

Could it be that Noah was jealous?

Twenty-Five

I climb back up the stairs with the tray piled high with plates, cutlery, a breadboard and the rest of the food, wondering if I'm imagining things.

Noah wouldn't really be jealous of Malachi, would he? Surely not. No, I must have been right in the first place, it must be the police thing. And anyway, he had nothing to be jealous of – Malachi and I were just friends.

As I reach the French windows, Noah jumps up from his chair to open the door for me, then he insists on taking the tray and putting it on the table next to the ice bucket.

'I re-filled your wine while you were downstairs,' he explains eagerly. 'I hope that's all right?'

'Yes, thank you.'

'And the mackerel is finally done!' He smiles at me and I smile back, glad everything seems back to normal between us again.

'Great. Let's eat then.'

Yes, I'd definitely got the wrong end of the stick downstairs.

Noah seemed a lot happier now. Maybe I'd just read his mood wrongly? After all, I didn't really know him all that well.

We chat while we eat, but only about neutral things like the weather and Noah's customers that day, and as quickly as the mackerel disappears so does the wine.

Noah pours our last two glasses and puts the empty bottle back in the ice bucket.

'You were right about that mackerel,' I tell him, as I take my glass and lean back in my seat, with the comfortable drowsiness that often follows a good meal and plenty of alcohol just starting to overcome me. 'It was delicious. Thank you for cooking it.'

'My pleasure ...' Noah begins, then he grimaces. 'Ana, at the risk of ruining things again, I have to say it – I'm *so* sorry if I put a damper on things earlier. It's been such a lovely evening and I do apologise if I spoilt things before.'

'Don't be silly, Noah, it's fine,' I reply, shrugging it off. 'I totally understand there are things that you'd rather keep private.'

'Thank you. I don't like to talk about my time in the police, you're right. I find it very difficult, very difficult indeed.'

I knew I'd got it wrong. *Jealous! As if, Ana!* I berate myself. *You're not in some rom-com movie here. This is real life.*

Noah looks hesitant, but continues when I don't immediately say anything. 'You see, it's like that was another me. That me feels like a different person from the one I am now, and I don't recognise him any more. Does that sound weird?'

'No, not at all,' I assure him. Now I know exactly where he's coming from, I feel myself physically relax. 'I feel a bit like that about Daisy. We were together for so long as a pair that now she's not here any more, I feel that I'm not really me without her.'

Noah nods, but sensing there might be more, waits for me to continue.

'Even after she met her husband we'd still go out with each other all the time,' I tell him, 'and we'd talk on the phone nearly every day. Now there's just this huge void in my life and I don't know how to replace it, or even if I want to. Something has been taken from my life I'll never ever get back, and I don't know how to continue living my life without Daisy in it.'

I gasp for air like I've just emerged from under water. Where had that all come from? I've never told anyone before that's how I felt about Daisy. Until I'd heard the words coming from my mouth to Noah, I wasn't even sure *I* knew that's how I felt. Now here I was sitting with not exactly a stranger, but with someone I didn't know all that well, and I was telling him exactly how I was feeling, and how I'd felt every day since Daisy died.

Noah nods empathetically. 'I completely understand. Truly I do. When something is a part of your life for so long, a very important part of your life, to even try to imagine a life without that thing or that person in it seems impossible. Believe me, I've been there.'

'So how did you get through it? I assume you have – you're talking about it as though it's in your past?'

'It is ... mostly. How did I get over it?' Noah smiles ruefully. 'I came here to St Felix and I started a new life running an antiques shop. *This* is my life now. The old one sometimes feels like it never happened at all, but I know it did. However much I try to block it out of here' – he taps his forehead – 'I still feel it in here.' He puts his hand on his chest.

I desperately want to ask him what it was he was trying to block out. It was clear from what he was saying that Noah didn't leave the police on good terms, and that whatever happened to him changed him considerably. Sensibly, this time I keep my questions to myself.

'People have told me that St Felix is a good place for fresh starts,' I tell him, 'and it obviously worked well for you.'

'Yes, I suppose it did. Maybe it will help you too?'

'But I'm only here for a while, then I'll be moving on. My stay is temporary. I can't see St Felix healing all my wounds in a few weeks.'

Noah's optimistic expression fades. 'Perhaps a few weeks is all it will take for you?' He takes a slow sip from his glass and glances out at the ever reddening sky.

'Perhaps. I doubt it, though. I've a feeling it's going to take more than a quick holiday in Cornwall to heal all my wounds.'

'Do you feel like you've been brought here for a reason?' Noah asks suddenly, turning back to face me.

'How do you mean?'

'Well, it always seemed odd to me that I left the force having absolutely no idea what I was going to do next, or where I should go to do it. I was in a bad place, Ana, really I was. I was totally lost.'

Again, he doesn't enlighten me as to why.

'And then my aunt,' he continues, 'who had had perfect health all her life, suddenly with no warning dies peacefully in her sleep and leaves the shop to me in her will. I'm not sure what would have happened to me if that hadn't occurred. At first, I wasn't keen on leaving London and coming here, as you can imagine. The last thing I wanted to do was leave everything I knew and start again in a remote Cornish seaside town where I'd holidayed as a child, but now I know it's what saved me.'

I listen silently to Noah.

'It might sound a little crazy, but sometimes it feels like this was all orchestrated to happen like this.'

'How do you mean?'

'I often wonder whether I had to leave the police so I could go on to do something better with my life that wouldn't have happened if I'd stayed with them. I'm still to find out what that is, but if it's just so I can run a little antiques shop that brings a few people pleasure, then I guess I'll have to accept that.'

'Doesn't the shop bring *you* pleasure then?'

'Yes, but I always have this nagging feeling there's more to it. I'm just being silly probably.'

'You could be right, I suppose. Daisy had a great belief in destiny and things happening for a reason. She used to say we all had paths that we had to follow – we could step off the path occasionally but eventually we'd be guided back on to it.'

'That's a nice way of thinking about it. Do you believe that?'

'I'm not sure what I believe any more. Losing Daisy has shaken any little belief I might once have had. I've never been very spiritual. Daisy was always the one for that kind of thing.'

'I'm not usually into that sort of stuff either. I just have this nagging thought that keeps occurring. Weird, really.'

'Not necessarily. But to answer your earlier question, I don't think I've been brought here for any other reason than to collect Daisy-Rose and drive her home, sad as that may be.' I think about this for a moment. 'You aren't suggesting that Daisy had to die to help *me* in some way, are you?' I ask, suddenly appalled. 'Because if you are—'

'No, no, not at all,' Noah insists. 'I would never be so insensitive. What I'm trying, obviously very badly, to say is that perhaps something good can come from her death. Perhaps

214

you've come to St Felix not simply to collect an old camper van but to do something else as well?'

'Like?'

'Take those old postcards, for instance,' Noah says, gesturing to the sitting room. 'If you manage to trace Lou and return the cards to her, won't that be a good thing to come out of this? You wouldn't even be here if it hadn't been for Daisy, would you, so you never would have found them in the camper van.'

Technically, it was Malachi that found them, but I decide not to point this out.

'*If* I ever manage to trace Lou, then yes it would be a good thing.' I sigh. 'But it's a very big "if" right now. I've read through all the new cards several times and I haven't got any more clues from them at all. It's so frustrating.'

'I hope you don't mind but I had a quick look through them while you were out.'

'Nothing much in them that's going to help us, is there?'

'*Hmm*, that's not strictly true . . .'

'Why, what did you find?' I sit forward excitedly.

'Let me fetch the cards,' Noah says, getting up. 'I notice you file them all in date order – very efficient. I like that.'

Noah goes through the French window and then returns shortly afterwards with several postcards in his hand.

'Look at this one first,' he says, handing me a card. 'It's from Brighton and it's dated June 1987.'

My Darling Frankie,
    You'll never guess what? I found a photo of you in
a local newspaper today!
    Some of my paintings are being shown in an

215

exhibition here in Brighton, and the paper was
simply lying around in the foyer of my hotel. I
couldn't believe it when I flicked through and saw a
photo of you.

I recognised you straight away. Even though
you'd aged a little (like we all have!) I still knew
it was you immediately. Your lovely eyes are still
the same as I remember them, and you're just as
handsome too.

It made my day – no, my whole year.

Forever yours,

Lou x

'Now here's a follow-up card written only days afterwards,'
Noah says, handing me that one now. 'This one has St Felix
on the front.'

My Darling Frankie,

I was so excited to see you again – if only in a
photo – that I've decided to paint you!

It will be one of my first portraits as I've always
stuck to landscapes before as that's what people seem
to like. But I know I can do this particular subject
justice, as it's always been one of my favourites!

I'll let you know how I get on.

Forever yours,

Lou x

'Now the third card,' Noah says, handing it to me. 'St Felix
again, but it's dated a few months later.'

My Darling Frankie,

I finished it! And I'm so proud; I really think I've done justice to you. I think I've worked harder on this than any other painting I've ever done, but I enjoyed it so much more too.

I'd like to hang this on the wall of my studio here in St Felix, but I think people would ask who the handsome man was! So I'll hide it away somewhere where only I can see it.

I'm so pleased I picked up that newspaper. In the early days Mother kept me informed of your news and what you were up to, but just lately I've been wondering what and how you're doing again, and now I know.

Congratulations to you. I hope your family are proud.

Forever yours,

Lou x

I look up at Noah. 'I read these before, but I'm not sure why you're so excited. All we know is that Frankie was in a local paper and that Lou was proud of what he'd done. But he could have done anything. So how does that help us?'

A knowing smile crosses Noah's lips. 'Local newspapers keep records, and if their digital records don't extend that far, old copies are often backed up on microfiche.'

I look blankly at him.

'Come on, Ana, keep up!'

'We're not all ex-cops,' I say, raising an eyebrow. 'Just tell me.'

'If we can find out which newspaper this was, and I doubt

there were that many local to Brighton back then, we can see if we can view some of their past copies. If we can, all we have to do is look at the ones from June 1987 and hopefully this Frankie will be named in one of the photos . . . If we can trace who Frankie is—'

'We might be able to trace Lou too!' I squeal excitedly. 'You're amazing, Noah!' I jump up and hug him, then without thinking I kiss him on the cheek. 'Thank you.'

Noah blinks calmly behind his glasses, but his cheeks tell a different tale. They're now very pink indeed.

'It's my pleasure,' he says, in an equally calm voice. 'We can do this, Ana. If we stick together, we can do this. I know it.'

Twenty-Six

'Guess what's happened?' I say breathlessly to Malachi, when I visit him the next day at the garage.

'You've fallen madly in love with me and your heart at just the mere sight of me has started beating wildly out of control?' He slides himself out from underneath Daisy-Rose, the usual mischievous grin on his face.

'Ha ha. Actually, I walked up here quite quickly so that's why I'm breathing a little heavily.'

'Shame. So, what's all the excitement?' Malachi pulls himself up, then cleans his hands on a rag from his pocket. 'Wait, should we get coffee first?'

Malachi makes the coffee this time, then while we perch on our usual bucket and tyres I tell him all about what has happened with Noah, leaving out anything I didn't think was relevant, like Noah's jealousy and the kiss . . .

'So you two had a barbecue together . . . very nice. Is that what you always do on a first date?'

'What do you mean?' I ask, thrown by his question. I'd been expecting him to ask me more about Frankie and the newspapers.

'Have you forgotten already? I'm hurt,' Malachi says dramatically, tossing his head to the side.

I stare blankly at him.

'Our moonlit barbecue,' Malachi reminds me, 'where I think you said my sausages were the best you'd ever tasted.'

'I don't think I said that exactly, did I?'

'Close enough. So you barbecued with Noah too . . . I should be hurt, but fish?' He pulls a face. 'I suppose you had a loaf of bread with your fishes? That's so Matthew 14:13-21, not Noah at all.'

'Ha ha, very funny,' I say drily.

'So Noah thinks he can find this Frankie from the newspaper, does he?'

'If we can find the newspaper that Lou saw him in. It's a bit of a long shot but we don't have anything else.'

'Worth a try, I guess.'

'I think so. Noah is ringing around today to see if we can view the records of local papers at that time.'

'What would you do without him, eh?'

'He's been very helpful with the postcards, that's for sure. Just like you've been with Daisy-Rose,' I add hurriedly, in case there's a repeat of last night's jealousy but the other way around. However, I was sure Malachi's flirting was just high spirits on his part; he was probably the same with all women . . . not that I'd ever seen him with any.

'She's certainly coming on,' Malachi says, looking at the van. 'As you saw last time you were here, she has all her doors now and a new front light, and just this morning I've given her a brand new windscreen. I've patched up all the rust now, so I'll be ready to start spray-painting her very soon.'

Daisy-Rose currently looks like a patchwork quilt of many

shades: there's her original red, the pale blue door, many patches of pink where Malachi has touched up her rust spots, and one small square of new metallic dark red paint on her side.

'I've tested the new colour,' Malachi says, pointing to the new patch, 'and I think it's going to look pretty amazing on her.'

'I agree. She's going to look wonderful, of that I have no doubt. You seem to be making so much progress – every time I come here she looks different. I have to give it to you, Malachi, you certainly work fast.'

'I have had a bit of help,' Malachi admits. 'A couple of lads from the town come in and help me some evenings.'

'Do they? I didn't know that.'

'Yeah, I wouldn't be making this much progress without them. I'm not a magician, you know?'

'There was me thinking you were working miracles all on your own, when all the time you had help.' I laugh, but Malachi sighs.

'Chance would be a fine thing,' he mutters. 'Miracles aren't allowed yet.'

'What do you mean?'

'Nothing,' he says hurriedly. 'Forget I said anything. Being so quiet here at the garage has helped too.'

'I wonder why that is. The rest of the town seems so busy.'

Malachi shrugs. 'Me being so quiet means your van gets completed quicker and you get to leave here all the faster. So it's all good.'

Was that such a good thing now? I was beginning to wonder . . .

'Everything happens for a reason,' I say, without thinking. 'Oh, someone else was saying something similar to me only yesterday.'

'Someone being . . . Noah?'

221

'Possibly.'

'And what made him come out with that little bumper sticker gem?'

'Don't mock him.'

'I'm not ... but it is a favourite slogan that people hook into to make bad things happening to them seem good.'

'I quite like it actually.'

'Oh, do you?'

'Yes.'

'Give me an instance then.'

'Of?'

'Of everything happening for a reason.'

'Well, I can't right now ... I'd have to think about it.'

'You see?'

'I see nothing, only a lack of memory, that's all. Hang on a minute ...' I think hard again, determined to prove him wrong. 'There was a time when Daisy and I were at university.' I glance at Malachi.

'Go on,' he encourages.

'Well, Daisy decided she was giving it all up to follow her boyfriend, Peter, up to Scotland.'

'And?'

'And I thought at the time she was making a terrible mistake giving everything up like that for a man, but it turned out really well for her. She was happy, they got married and they had two gorgeous boys together.'

'And?' Malachi asks. 'There has to be more to that story if you want me to accept it as proof that everything happens for a reason.'

I shrug.

'Okay ... how did you feel when Daisy left?'

'Awful.'

'Did you hate her for leaving you?'

'A bit,' I admit. 'But everything turned out all right in the end.'

'For her or for you?'

I think about this. 'For both of us, I guess.'

'Why? I know why for Daisy, you just told me that. But why for you in particular?'

'It made me more determined to do well at uni, I suppose.'

'You suppose, or it actually did?'

'I asked you once before if you'd ever been a shrink in a past life,' I joke. 'And you said no, but you sure sound like one sometimes!'

Malachi seems to consider this. 'Look, I'm just trying to help. If you don't want my help ...' A look of rejection settles on his face.

'You can stop the play-acting!' I think again about Brighton. 'Okay, yes, it definitely made me more determined and more independent too. I'd always relied a lot on Daisy before – she was the driving force in our relationship. When she left I had to grow up, stand on my own two feet a bit more. It changed me.'

'For the good?'

'Yeah, I'd say so.'

Malachi holds out his hands in a 'there you go' gesture. 'You see, something good came of something you perceived to be bad at the time. It often does. It just takes people a while to see it sometimes.'

'So you agree with Noah then?' I ask, equally triumphant. 'Everything happens for a reason?'

'Never said I didn't agree with him, did I?'

'Yes, you did, you said he was spouting bumper sticker nonsense.'

'I was just testing you, that's all. I just wanted you to justify what he said and you did.'

I shake my head. 'You can be so infuriating sometimes!'

'But loveable too?' Malachi pouts.

'Occasionally . . . ' I say begrudgingly. 'I should have known you'd be into that sort of stuff anyway.'

'What sort of stuff?'

'You know – alternative healing, spiritual stuff.'

'And why would you think that?' Malachi asks, his eyebrows rising.

'Things you say.'

'Like?'

'Right, stop asking me for proof all the time. I'm not a prosecuting attorney.'

Malachi grins. 'Sorry. Yeah, I am quite open to all that sort of thing as it goes.'

'Good.' I look down into my almost empty coffee cup.

'What's up, Ana? There's obviously something bothering you. Let me guess, it's something you can't explain, right?'

I nod. I had to talk to someone about it and Malachi was the only person I could think of who might understand.

'*Is* it something spiritual?'

'No,' I snap. 'Why would you say that?'

'What you were saying before, that's all. No need to bite my head off.'

'Sorry. Like I said, Daisy was into all that kind of thing. It was one of the few things we disagreed on.'

'I see. So is that what's bothering you – something to do with Daisy?'

I glance up at Malachi, still wondering if I should share this with him. He does seem genuinely interested and eager to help.

'It's going to sound silly if I tell you.'

'Why don't you try, and I'll decide that.'

'Okay ...' I take a deep breath. 'So since I've been here in St Felix there have been ... well, how can I put it ... there have been these signs.'

'What sort of signs?'

I should feel awkward telling him this, but strangely I don't – it actually feels like the most natural thing in the world now I was finally doing it.

'Did I ever tell you how Daisy and I met?'

'I think so, over a love of eighties music – yes?'

I nod. 'Well, since I've been here I keep seeing all these eighties references. First it was the *I heart the eighties* sticker in the window of Daisy-Rose – don't get rid of that by the way, will you?'

'I wasn't intending to.'

'Then when Noah and I were searching for the postcards, I was given a postcard from Brighton dated July 1986. Daisy and I went to university in Brighton.'

Malachi nods. 'Go on.'

'Oliver Jackson, the guy that put the postcards in the auction, his address was 88 Thatcher Street.'

'Nice one.'

'And when Noah and I went to bid on the postcards our bidding number was one hundred and eighty, and I bought a box of eighties records there too. That one's a bit vague, I know, but the others ...'

'No such thing as coincidence, Ana, if that's what you're about to say.'

'Do you really think so?'

'What's more important is what you think. Actually no, what's important is what you feel.'

'How do you mean?'

'Try not to let your rational mind do the thinking on this one. Try to remember how you felt when you saw those eighties references.'

'All right ... er ... I was happy, I guess.'

'Because?'

'Because they reminded me of Daisy.'

'That can only be a good thing – am I correct? So does it matter if they actually *meant* anything?'

'I didn't say I thought they did, did I?' I snap. 'I was asking for your opinion.'

Malachi grins. 'No, that's true, you didn't, but is it possible they could?'

'How do you mean?' I'm curious to find out Malachi's view, even though I really don't want to believe anything weird is going on.

'Did those "signs", shall we call them, come at a time you needed some reassurance?'

I think about this. 'Yes, possibly.'

'There you go then.'

'There I go what?'

Malachi sighs. 'Look, Ana, I don't know what it is you want me to tell you, but if you don't want to believe, then nothing I'm going to tell you is going to make you change your mind.'

'So you *do* think something odd is happening?'

Malachi stands up. 'Come back and see me when you've opened your mind to the possibilities.'

'What's that supposed to mean?'

'That's my phone ringing,' Malachi says suddenly.

I'm about to say I can't hear anything when I hear the sound of a phone ringing in the office.

'Catch you soon, Ana,' he says, taking my mug from me, and before I have time to reply he strides quickly away in the direction of the office with Ralph trotting loyally at his heels.

Twenty-Seven

'Fancy a trip to Brighton?' Noah asks me later that same day.

I'd just been coming out of the bakery after collecting my lunch when my phone had rung.

'Why Brighton? Oh, have you found something?'

'Yes, it seems there were two local papers in Brighton in 1987 – *The Gazette* and *The Post*. *The Gazette* is still running and says it has a complete back catalogue of its copies on microfiche. It's just in the process of transferring them to computer files apparently. *The Post* no longer exists but was bought by the same company that owns *The Gazette*. A lot of their old copies are on a newspaper archive website, but I've checked that already and I can't find copies from the dates that we want. So the only way we're going to be able to one hundred per cent check is to visit the head office and go through their records.'

'And they're all right with us doing this?'

Noah hesitates at the other end of the line. 'I may have had to call in a couple of favours ... but I think it should be fine.'

'Favours from whom?'

'That doesn't matter. All you need to know is we'll be able to see the newspapers from June 1987, and then we should hopefully be able to find out who this mysterious Frankie is at long last.'

After much discussion over the next twenty-four hours, much of which is me telling Noah he can't possibly drive us all the way to Brighton, and Noah ignoring me completely by discussing which route we should take, we eventually agree to drive up one day and back the next. I'd suggested the train, but that seemed to involve an even longer and more tortuous journey than I'd taken to get down to St Felix in the first place, so by road it had to be.

'Are you sure?' I'd asked Noah, for probably the tenth time since he'd suggested it, the night before we were due to set off. 'You really don't have to go to all this trouble for me. I'm sure there are better things you could be doing.'

'Ana, what you fail to understand,' Noah had said, 'is that this is by far the most interesting thing I've had to do since I came here to Cornwall. It's testing my grey matter.' He taps his head. 'And for that I should be grateful to you, not the other way around.'

So on Friday morning at the crack of dawn we set off on a journey that Noah's satnav suggests should take us just over five hours to complete.

'Music?' Noah asks, as we begin to travel along the A30.

'Sure,' I agree, trying not to yawn. It was 5 a.m., a time I rarely saw unless I was going through one of my bursts of insomnia.

Noah fiddles with his car radio, and Pirate FM the local Cornish radio station comes on. 'And now on Pirate FM, for all you early risers, we're going back to the eighties. Here's Wham! to wake you up!'

I can't help grinning as the voice of George Michael fills Noah's Land Rover. It was happening again. Was this a sign to let me know I was on the right track with this jaunt along the south coast?

'What are you smiling about?' Noah asks. 'I didn't think anyone had much to smile about at this time of the morning?'

'The eighties,' I say, gesturing to the radio. 'My favourite era.'

'Oh yes, of course – well, enjoy.'

Something else that Noah and I had disagreed on before we left was driving – namely, who was going to do it. I had suggested we take turns as it would be a long journey, but Noah had insisted that he drive, saying his insurance didn't cover guest drivers. I could have argued that my insurance would cover me to drive his car, but there seemed little point. Once Noah made his mind up about something, I was learning it was very difficult to change it, but I quite liked that about him. The more time I spent with him, the less I was seeing the meek, mild-mannered antiques shop owner that I'd first met and the more he was allowing a poised confident personality to show – perhaps that was his old self. And not for the first time I wonder again what had happened to change him.

'Ana,' I hear myself being called softly from close by. 'Ana, time to wake up.'

I open my eyes and see Noah watching me.

'Wha— Oh no, did I fall asleep?'

'You did, round about Bodmin.'

'And where are we now?'

'Just past the junction for Lyme Regis.'

'Oh, I'm so sorry.'

'It's fine. I've been happy listening to the radio – although we left Pirate FM a while back. I'm now on Radio 2.'

I take my eyes from Noah and look through the car window; we appear to have stopped at a service station.

'Sorry it's not more glamorous again. I only seem to take you to service stations, but it was the only place I could find along here.'

'This is fine. Is it still breakfast time?' I ask, looking at my watch and seeing it says a quarter to eight.

'It is. Hungry?'

'Sure am.'

We manage to buy two overpriced coffees and a couple of muffins from a coffee shop with a queue that snakes around the room and out of the door.

'Again, sorry it's not more glamorous,' Noah repeats.

'One – stop apologising,' I say, as I sip on my coffee and immediately feel the warmth of freshly brewed caffeine seeping through my veins, shaking me into a more alert state. 'Two – you might not have noticed, but I don't really do glamorous.' I gesture to my jeans and trainers. 'Comfort is much more my bag. And three – these blueberry muffins happen to be one of my personal favourites, so I'm quite happy with this meagre yet very tasty breakfast.'

Noah smiles. 'Good, I'm pleased to hear it.'

We set off again from the service station with Noah promising that we are already halfway into our journey, and me promising to stay awake this time.

'You're very cute when you snore, though,' Noah says, grinning.

'I was snoring earlier?'

'It was more like a gentle purr really. Quite sweet actually.'

I roll my eyes. 'I can't believe I was snoring! In case the walls

231

are quite thin at our hotel, I'll ask for our rooms to be well away from each other so I don't disturb you.'

Noah takes his eyes from the road and glances at me to see if I'm joking. Relieved to see I am, he turns back.

'At least you found somewhere at such short notice.'

'Yeah, it's just budget but it should be fine.'

'I could have driven there and back in one day, you know?'

'Don't be daft! It's bad enough you driving all this way for me without killing yourself, or me for that matter. We'll go to the offices, hopefully find what we're looking for, then we can relax for the evening before driving home tomorrow.'

'I'm looking forward to it,' Noah says cheerfully. 'I don't get away from St Felix enough these days.'

I did get away, but secretly I was looking forward to it too. Partly because I was going back to a place I had many happy memories of, and partly because I was going there with Noah.

We arrive in Brighton just before lunch, and we park the car in a multi-storey car park that had been recommended by the hotel.

'Lunch?' Noah suggests. 'It seems ages since breakfast.'

'Definitely.'

We find a nice-looking pub, and order some drinks and a couple of baguettes with a portion of chips each.

'The newspaper offices aren't too far from here,' Noah says, looking out of the window. 'We should be able to walk there easily enough.'

'Yes, I know.'

'I forgot you knew the place well. When were you here?'

'2004 to 2007.'

'Has it changed much since your uni days?'

'From what I've seen so far, not that much actually.'

'Did you enjoy your time here?'

'Yeah, it was mostly good.'

'Mostly?'

'Same as all things, isn't it? Some good things, some bad. Most of my memories of uni are good, some not so.'

'Are you going to elaborate?'

'Rather not.'

'Sure, I understand. Some things are best kept in the past.'

I'd only been thinking of when Daisy had left Brighton to go up north, which at the time had been pretty traumatic for me, but I had a feeling my bad memories were nowhere near as stressful or traumatic as Noah's.

After lunch we head off to the newspaper offices, which are in a big building a short distance from Brighton's sea-front.

'Here goes,' Noah says, as we enter through a revolving glass door. 'Keep everything crossed.'

We walk through a large foyer with modern, leather-look sofas arranged behind Perspex coffee tables that have newspapers and magazines arranged neatly on them.

'Good afternoon,' a young immaculately dressed male receptionist says brightly, as we approach his desk. 'How can I help?'

'We're here to see Josh Walker,' Noah replies confidently.

'One moment.' He taps a button on his desk and fiddles with his headset. 'Who may I say is here?'

'Noah Bailey, and Ana— Oh, I'm so sorry, I don't know your surname?' Noah looks mortified.

'It's Bennett, and don't worry about it – why would you?'

Noah turns back to the receptionist. 'Noah Bailey and Ana Bennett. Josh is expecting us.'

The receptionist nods and listens intently to his headset. 'I do apologise – no one on Josh's extension seems to be picking up. I'll try the next desk.'

I glance at Noah. Surely we hadn't travelled all this way and his contact wasn't here?

'Oh hi, Juliet,' the receptionist says eventually. 'I'm trying to locate Josh. He has two visitors waiting for him in reception.' He listens, presumably to Juliet. 'Oh right, yes ... uh-huh ... sure ... Yep, I'll tell them.' He removes the headset. 'It seems Josh has had to step out, but Juliet has agreed in his absence to help you with your enquiries today. I do hope that's all right?'

Noah looks a little annoyed.

'If you'd like to take the lift up to the second floor, Juliet will be there to meet you,' he continues. 'If I can just give you these to wear first.' He hands us two lanyards with *Visitor* written across them. 'If you could wear these at all times while in the building, we'd be most grateful.'

'Thank you,' I say, taking the lanyards. 'Come on, Noah.'

Noah reluctantly leaves the reception desk.

'I'd specifically arranged to speak with Josh,' he mutters, as we wait for the lift. 'I'm not happy.'

'Perhaps this Juliet will be able to help us even more?' I say, as the lift arrives and we step inside. 'Remember everything happens for a reason. You said so yourself.'

Noah grimaces at my reminder.

We arrive on the second floor and the lift doors open.

'Hi, you must be Ana and Noah,' a youngish woman in casual yet fashionable attire says as we step out. 'I'm Juliet.' She holds out her hand for us to shake. 'Sorry Josh couldn't be here, but he's told me all about the editions you're wanting to look through. Hopefully we should be able to help.'

Juliet guides us to a small room lined with shelves covered in black files. There are several machines that look a bit like big old computer monitors on one side of the room with some of the box files already placed next to them.

'These should be all the microfiches you will need to see to cover the newspapers you've requested. Do you know how to work the reader?'

To my surprise Noah nods. 'Yeah, I've used them before.'

'Good.' Juliet hesitates. 'Is there something in particular you're looking for in the editions you requested?'

'Yes,' I begin, 'a per—' but Noah interrupts me.

'We're not exactly sure, Juliet. Do you mind if we just take a look?'

'Not at all,' Juliet says. 'Josh said that's what you wanted to do. It just seemed such a precise request, so I assumed there must be something equally specific you were looking for?'

'We'll let you know how we get on,' I say politely, while Noah is already loading a small thin piece of film into the viewer.

'Sure. Let me know if you need any help.' Juliet gives one last inquisitive look in Noah's direction before leaving us alone in the room.

'That was very rude,' I say, pulling up a chair and sitting down next to Noah. 'She was only trying to help.'

'I didn't mean it to be, but she's a journalist, isn't she?'

'So?'

'In my experience, any sniff of a juicy story and they'll be all over us in an instant asking questions and poking their noses in.'

'But we don't have a juicy story.'

Noah turns his head from the screen to me. 'Lou and Frankie's story could turn into a very interesting one, if we ever find either of them. You may think it's just a few old postcards you've found, but I can almost promise you it will very likely be so much more than that, and if it is, the papers will want a part of it, of that you can be sure.'

'How do you know?'

'Call it gut instinct. Now we need to get reading before our friend Juliet comes sniffing back.'

Twenty-Eight

It only takes us about fifteen minutes to feed through all the microfiches that contain newspapers from June 1987.

'Are you sure that's everything?' I ask Noah as we come to the final page. 'We've been through them all and there are no Frankies or a Francis mentioned anywhere.'

'Yeah, it would appear so ... Damn, what was Lou talking about when she mentioned a local paper?' He gets up and paces a bit around the tiny room.

'Have we missed one, do you think? These newspapers came out on Wednesdays and Thursdays, so shall I check those days in June 1987 and double-check we've seen a newspaper corresponding with all the relevant dates?'

'Worth a try,' Noah says, still pacing.

I quickly use my phone to Google a calendar for 1987, then I cross reference the Wednesdays and Thursdays with the newspapers we've seen.

'Yep, we've seen all the editions that would have come out then,' I tell Noah sadly. 'This can't be right. In June 1987 Lou said she'd seen Frankie in a local Brighton newspaper – it said so on the postcard.'

'*Hmm* ... I'm missing something, I know I am,' Noah says, his forehead wrinkling. He lifts his glasses and rubs the bridge of his nose. Then he stares at the box files. 'Wait a minute ...' he says, dropping his glasses back down so he can see properly. 'Lou said she'd read the paper in June. What if it wasn't a current copy – what if it was an old edition someone had left lying around?'

I digest this while Noah traces his hand along the shelf and then pulls out another file.

'You mean she might have read a copy from May 1987?'

'Or even earlier, I guess,' Noah says, lifting some more microfiche film from the file and placing it under the reader. 'Let's hope not for our sake, eh?'

We have to run a few papers under the microfiche reader before we find it.

'There!' I say, pointing at the screen magnifying the page in front of us. 'Can you make that picture any bigger?'

Noah pushes a couple of buttons, and the black and white image becomes larger but also grainier.

It's a photo of four men wearing running gear. They have their arms around each other and look like they've just finished a race.

The headline over the photo says *LOCAL MEN FINISH LONDON MARATHON IN AN ELECTRIFYING TIME*. Then the copy underneath reads: *Four Brighton men, who all work together at local firm Johnson's Electronics, successfully completed the London Marathon last Sunday. The colleagues, who train together regularly at Brighton Bombers running club, ran the entire 26.2 miles together, crossing the line in just under four hours. This is the tenth Marathon that the men have completed and they have so far raised nearly £10,000 for Cancer Research UK between them.*

There are no names listed, but what I'd so nearly missed in the tiny photo was that just above their running numbers on the front of their white vests the men all have their names emblazoned in large letters. There's a Joe, a Harry, a Duncan, and a Frankie.

'This must be him!' I say, looking even harder at the photo. 'But why doesn't it say his full name? They always put people's names and usually their ages too in newspapers.'

'Are you sure that's him?' Noah asks, leaning towards the screen to peer hard at the photo with me. 'How can you be sure?'

'I can't . . . but I think it is. Call it gut instinct,' I say, smiling. I turn my head and find my face centimetres from Noah's.

Realising our closeness, he too turns, and for a moment neither of us speaks.

'We should print this out,' he says quietly, not moving.

'We really should.'

'So, how are you getting on?' Juliet asks cheerfully, as she comes bowling through the door.

I jump up as Noah hits the print button.

'Fine!' I say in a shrill voice, blocking Noah behind me, who I can hear hurriedly tidying up the files and snapping them shut.

'Find what you were looking for?' Juliet asks, desperately trying to see behind me without appearing too obvious about it.

'Yes, thank you, we did. It's very kind of you to help us like this.'

'I don't believe we had much choice,' Juliet says, her face still smiling brightly but her voice hardening. 'Josh said someone from the local police station rang up and demanded you be given free rein over the files for an hour.'

I glance back at Noah, who I'm pleased to see has finished his rather hasty tidy.

'And very helpful it's been too,' Noah says, gathering the copy of our page from the printer. 'I hope we've not been too much trouble, Juliet?'

Juliet doesn't say anything. She looks curiously at the page in Noah's hand.

'Well, thanks again,' I add, reaching out my hand. Juliet shakes it dubiously. 'It's all been most informative.'

'Yes,' Noah repeats, doing the same. 'Very useful indeed.'

We leave the newspaper offices like two naughty school-children, virtually throwing our lanyards at the receptionist in our haste to escape. Then we walk as quickly as we can down the street together, not stopping to speak until we're a safe distance away.

'Why do I feel like we did something in there we weren't supposed to?' I ask, as we turn a corner and Brighton sea-front comes into view at the bottom of the street. 'We only looked at a file that wasn't offered to us. We hardly committed a crime.'

'I know. I think it was Juliet – she was acting very oddly for someone who was just there to show us a few files, even for a journalist!'

'Do you think so too? I thought it was just me!'

'Nope, your instinct serves you well. We'll make a copper of you yet!' Noah's face, so full of life and excitement one moment, falls in an instant. 'Sorry, I got a bit carried away there. Forgot where I was.'

'That's okay. Is that similar to the rush you used to get when you were in the police?'

'A bit, yeah, but being a real police officer isn't like being one on TV, you know – all guns and car chases. There's a lot

240

of thinking and paperwork that goes into solving crimes before you get any sort of rush.'

'I can imagine.' Noah had said 'solving crimes'. I wonder if he was a detective in the Met? 'Well, whatever we just experienced, what happens next? I definitely think that the photo could be of Lou's Frankie. That runner seems the right sort of age – he looks in his mid-fifties, doesn't he?'

Noah pulls the photocopied page from his pocket. 'Yes, I'd say so,' he says, looking at it.

'That matches with the timescales Lou talks about in the postcards. So if that is our Frankie in the picture, how are we going to trace him? We don't have his full name.'

'Ah, we might not have his name . . . ' Noah says, as we arrive at the bottom of the road and a strong gust of wind hits us now we're directly on the sea-front, forcing him to turn away from it to protect the paper. 'But what we do have' – he folds the paper and slips it safely in his trouser pocket – 'is the name of a running club, and possibly more importantly, the name of a business, both of which Frankie was involved with in 1987. It's a long shot, but I've solved crimes in the past on even longer ones.'

I smile up at him. 'Do you *really* think we can find him?'

Noah nods. 'Absolutely, and I won't be able to rest until we do.'

In celebration of our successes this morning we decide to buy ice creams, and while we enjoy the soft sweet Mr Whippy cones we sit on a bench on Brighton's famous promenade watching the world pass by. Well, I do. Noah is concentrating hard on his phone screen right now, while his ice cream remains untouched in his other hand.

'Your ice cream will melt,' I tell him, as I watch the white whip on top of his cone gradually softening.

'*Hmm?* Oh yeah. Do you want it?' he asks, as if it's just a bother to him being there in his hand. 'I haven't touched it.'

'I know you haven't, that's why it's melting. Just as well it's not very sunny at the moment or it would be in a pool around your feet by now.' I smile at my joke, but Noah still looks at his phone, attempting to scroll down the page with one hand.

'Look, give it here and I'll hold it for you,' I tell him, taking the cone from his hand. 'What are you so engrossed in on there?'

'I'm trying to find out if that electronics business still exists. I think it does, but under a new name.'

'Frankie's business?'

'Of course, Frankie's business! Sorry,' Noah apologises. 'I didn't mean to snap – I'm just determined to trace him, that's all.'

I'm beginning to see just what Noah would have been like when he was in the police force – he was very focused on the job in hand. Perhaps he'd become too obsessed with a case and something had gone wrong?

'That's okay. I'm just happy someone is helping me do this – I'd have been useless at it on my own.'

'Do you think so? I reckon you'd have been great. You're very switched on.'

'Am I?'

'Yeah, I think so. Okay, let me test you – what do you think our next move should be?'

'Eating this ice cream?' I pass Noah's cone back to him.

'And after that?' he asks, before expertly removing all signs of melted ice cream with his tongue in one long satisfying lick.

'Er . . . ' I say, losing my train of thought slightly as I watch him do this. *Damn, what did Noah just ask me? Oh yes, our next move.* 'I think we should find the running club first,' I say confidently, hoping to hide my hesitation. Noah's treatment of the ice cream cone had thrown me right off course.

'Why?'

'Well, in that photo the runners all seemed very close. In my experience people bond much more over a shared interest or pursuit than they do at work.'

'Nice thinking.'

'Thanks. So is the running club still going?'

'It is. I've already checked and I have a contact for it.'

'Great. So what about this business – have you tried Companies House?'

'Just on it when you passed me back my ice cream. You see – you do know what to do.'

'But it's more fun doing it with you,' I say, without thinking.

Damn. Had the ice cream numbed my brain? Why did I say that aloud?

Noah's cheeks pink slightly. 'Thanks,' he says, sounding genuinely touched. 'I'm having fun doing this with you too.'

In a repeat of our 'moment' in front of the microfiche, we hold each other's gaze for a touch longer than is necessary.

And in another repetition, yet again an intruder breaks this moment.

'Flood!' a voice says behind me, and I look back to see a youngish fair-haired man in jeans and a T-shirt with his arms folded staring at us. 'Sorry, it's Inspector Flood now, isn't it?' he grins. 'Or was. Well, Inspector, I never expected to find you on Brighton sea-front littering. Do I have to pull you in for questioning?'

Twenty-Nine

Noah and I both stare in shock from the man to the floor, and we see a blob of white ice cream that had once belonged to Noah's cone melting slowly on the tarmac by his feet.

Noah grins first at the ice cream and then up at the man. Leaping up from the bench, he holds out his hand.

'Jonesy, man, good to see you.'

The handshake rapidly turns into a manly hug.

'Foxy said you were coming down,' the man says, grinning at Noah. 'I thought you might have popped in to see us?'

'Flying visit.'

Jonesy looks down at me still sitting on the bench.

'Sorry. This is Ana Bennett, a friend of mine,' Noah says, introducing me. 'Ana, this is Adam Jones. We worked together when I was in the force. I was stationed here in Brighton, before I went to London.'

'He says worked together,' Adam says, with raised eyebrows. 'But technically he was my superior officer when I was just a lowly detective constable.'

'Hello,' I say, standing up. 'Nice to meet you.'

We shake hands. 'Likewise,' Adam says. He looks between us. 'So what are you doing here – day out?'

'Something like that,' Noah says.

'You can't be here on official business. Foxy said they'd pensioned you off from the Met after . . . well, you know.'

'Yes,' Noah says hurriedly, 'a while back. I live in Cornwall now.'

'Cornwall – well, that's a change from the smoke. What do you do down there?'

'I run an antiques shop,' Noah says, with a hint of embarrassment.

'Antiques . . . ' Adam looks surprised. 'Well, I guess that's a nice slow pace of life?'

'Yes, better for the old ticker than running around with you lot.'

'Talking of running around, I'm afraid I've got to go,' Adam says, looking at his watch. 'I'm on duty.' He grimaces. 'Are you two around tonight? It would be great to catch up, Flood, if you're free for a drink?'

'Er . . . ' Noah hesitates.

'Yes, I'm sure we could manage that,' I answer for him. 'We don't have any plans tonight, do we?'

Noah shrugs.

'Where's good around here these days?' I ask Adam. 'I was at university here but that was a good few years ago now.'

'Surely not *that* long ago?' Adam says, winking at me. 'Far too young. How about we go to the old haunt, Flood? Remember?'

'Yeah, I remember.'

''Bout eight?'

Noah nods.

'Great, looking forward to it. See you guys later.'

I sit down again while Noah watches Adam walk away for a few moments before sitting down next to me.

'Bit of a blast from the past?' I ask, when he doesn't immediately say anything. 'It can really throw you when you see someone you haven't seen for a long time.'

'Yeah, Jonesy, Foxy and I were quite close when we worked here together. I was their sergeant when they were both constables.'

'But you became an inspector when you went to London?' I ask. This was the most Noah had ever told me about his past.

'Detective inspector. Jonesy and Foxy were promoted to detective sergeants not long after I left. Probably did them good me not being around.'

'Or you gave them a good training?'

'Perhaps.'

'Was it Foxy who you had to pull in a favour from before we came here?' I ask.

'Yes. But I told him not to mention it to anyone else. Trust Foxy to tell Jonesy – they were always a bit too close.'

Noah is lost again in his own memories.

I feel some spots of rain begin to hit my arm, and I look up to see the pale seal-grey clouds from before have darkened making the sky above us look heavy and bruised.

'I think we'd better go and find our hotel,' I say to Noah, before I stand up. 'Otherwise we're going to get soaked.'

Noah doesn't budge; he still stares at nothing in particular in front of him.

'*Oi, Flood!*' I cry, making him jump. 'Time to move.' I point up at the sky.

'Sorry, miles away.' Noah stands up. Then he grins when

he realises what I've called him. 'Yep, that was my nickname. Original, eh?'

'I've heard better.'

'Did you say something about heading to the hotel?'

'I certainly did. Let's go, and you can tell me more about your time here in Brighton on the way and whether there's another reason apart from the obvious one why they call you Flood ...'

We grab our overnight bags from the car and walk to the hotel.

'Hi,' I say to a glum-looking receptionist. 'We have a couple of rooms booked? In the name of Bennett.'

'One moment, please.' The receptionist looks at her computer screen. 'Yes, I have you down here but only for the one room?' She stares at me reprovingly as though I've made a mistake.

'No, I definitely booked two rooms. I rang yesterday when there was nothing available on your website, and you said you could just squeeze me in as you'd had a cancellation.'

'That wasn't me, I wasn't in yesterday. You probably spoke to Helen or Joanne.' The receptionist checks her screen again. 'Sorry, it's just the one room that's been allocated in your name.'

'Well, do you have another room available?'

'No, sorry, we're fully booked tonight.' She looks from Noah to me. 'Your room can be made up as a twin if that helps?'

I glance at Noah. He shrugs.

'This really isn't acceptable,' I tell her. 'We're not a couple. We're ... colleagues.'

'That's as maybe,' the receptionist says stoically, 'but I still don't have more than one room available.'

'Look, I don't mind sharing, Ana, if you don't?' Noah says

helpfully. 'It's only for one night, but I completely understand if you don't want to. I leave the decision entirely up to you.'

'We can throw in a complimentary breakfast if that helps?' the receptionist offers, staring at her screen again. 'I see here you haven't booked any. Our way of apologising for the mix-up.'

I want to suggest a greasy fry-up really wasn't going to make up for the lack of a room, but instead I sigh heavily. 'Okay, sure. I guess we haven't got much choice. A lot of the other hotels around here were fully booked too.'

'It's a busy weekend here in Brighton,' the receptionist says, sliding a couple of forms for me to sign across the top of the desk. 'There are several events on including a vintage car rally and a fun run.' She rolls her eyes. 'You'd think they'd learn to keep them apart by now?' She retrieves the signed forms and hands me two key cards. 'It's room number eighty-four on the third floor. There are stairs just through there and a lift. On behalf of the hotel I can only apologise for the mix-up, and I hope you enjoy your short stay with us. If there's anything else I can help you with, just let me know. Oh, and I'll send someone up to make up your extra bed.'

'Thanks,' I say begrudgingly, as Noah picks up our bags and we make our way to the lift.

'Are you sure you're all right with this?' Noah asks, as we wait for the lift to arrive. 'We could just drive home if you'd prefer?'

'Are you kidding? Not when there's a chance of us finding out more about Frankie tomorrow. Also, we've got your buddy to meet up with tonight. That will be nice.'

'Yes, I suppose,' Noah says, sounding less than enthusiastic. 'Well, if you're sure.'

'I don't mind unless' – I turn and wink at him – 'you're the one who actually snores! Then you and I will be falling out very quickly, Inspector Flood.'

But as I climb into the lift beside Noah, I can't help but glance again at the cardboard sleeve our key cards are wrapped in.

We were in room 84 – that had to be a good sign, didn't it?

Thirty

After we've unpacked the few things we've brought with us, we decide to head out in search of food before we meet Adam later.

'So,' I ask, while we're waiting for our pizzas to arrive in a little Italian restaurant not far from our hotel. 'What do you suggest next in our search for Frankie?'

'Well I haven't had too much luck finding this business,' Noah says, fiddling impatiently with his empty glass. 'It seems it ceased trading a few years after that photo was taken, seemingly in shady circumstances too.'

'How do you mean?'

'Officially the company just went into liquidation, but unofficially it looks like some dodgy dealings from the owner might have caused the firm's collapse.'

'So it's unlikely we'll be able to trace *any* of the staff then, let alone a man who worked for them in 1987.'

'Probably not. But I think the running club is our best bet anyway. Luckily for us it's still going. I'll ask Adam tonight if he knows anything about it. If not, we have the contact number listed on their website – we can call that and see if they have any member lists dating back to the eighties.'

'Good plan.'

'I try.' Noah winks.

'I know I've said this before, but thanks for helping me with all this, Noah. I really would be lost without you.'

Noah just smiles. 'Again, it really is my pleasure. I just hope we find something and this isn't simply a wild goose chase.'

'Even if it is, I'm having a really good time chasing this particular goose.'

'Me too, Ana. Me too.'

After supper, Adam is already waiting for us when we arrive at The Angel's Feather pub, and he has a friend with him.

'Foxy!' Noah says, hugging a smaller man with red hair who looks a similar age to Adam. 'Great to see you, man!'

'Hope you don't mind me tagging along?' Foxy says, grinning. 'Had to see you, Flood, when Jonesy said he was meeting up with you tonight.'

'What are you having?' Noah asks, looking elated to see his old buddies again. 'First round's on me.'

Adam and Simon (as I quickly find out Foxy's real name is) are a lot of fun. There's much teasing, mainly of Noah, and many trips down memory lane, all of which result in long, often hilarious, stories about their time in the force together.

But I don't feel left out, far from it. The boys are keen to involve me in their exploits, partly I suspect because they have someone in their midst who hasn't heard all their tales before, and partly so they can embarrass Noah as much as possible.

Three rounds later (I'm not allowed to buy a round, however much I insist) it's Noah's turn to go to the bar again.

The boys are all drinking pints of beer, and I'm now on

orange juice after three very full glasses of white wine, which I'm already regretting.

'So how did you two get on with your trip to the newspaper?' Simon asks, while Noah is at the bar and Adam has gone to the gents. 'Flood wouldn't say what it was you were looking for, only that he needed a favour.'

'Thanks again for getting us in there. It was very helpful actually.' I pull out the photocopied sheet from my bag that Noah has given me to look after. 'It's a long story but we're looking for this man.' I point to the person I desperately hope is our Frankie.

Simon peers at the photo. 'I'd like to tell you I know him, but he's not familiar. That's probably a good thing in my case, eh?'

'Definitely.'

'I know the running club, though. My wife runs with them – well, I say run, it's more of a jog, but it seems to keep her fit. I sometimes think she only goes for the social life.' He lifts an imaginary glass. 'They seem to end up in the pub after every training session. She and a load of mates are doing the fun run through the city tomorrow.'

'Yeah, I heard about that. Will there be many people from the club there?'

'A fair few, I expect. My wife and her mates are all running for Cancer Research.'

'Good for them.' I look at the photo again. 'Like these guys.'

'Yeah, over twenty years later and still no cure.' Simon shakes his head. 'Bloody awful disease.'

'Isn't it.'

'What are you two looking so down about?' Adam asks, arriving back at our table.

'Ah, nothing,' Simon says. 'I was just telling Ana here about the fun run tomorrow.'

'Pain in the arse for our uniforms with all the road closures et cetera but it raises a lot of cash for the charities, so we can't complain too much.'

'Why don't you and Flood come down,' Simon asks. 'I'll be cheering Lucy on from the sidelines, but I might be able to ask a few of her running buddies if they knew your guy back in the day.'

'That would be wonderful, thank you.'

'Any friend of Flood's is a friend of ours. You are just friends . . . ?' Simon asks, raising his eyebrows suggestively. Adam grins.

'*Yes*, we're just friends.'

'Shame, 'bout time Flood got himself a nice girl again. And you, Ana, are by far the nicest girl I've seen him with in a very long time, if not ever.'

'Why are you making Ana blush?' Noah says, swaying a little as he brings a tray of drinks over to the table.

'Because we're saying nice things about her, of course!' Adam says, grinning at him. 'And wanting to know why she's hanging about with a reprobate like you?'

After a few more rounds of drinks and much more banter between the boys, eventually we stagger out of the pub on to the pavement outside.

'Where are you two staying tonight?' Simon asks, taking a few gulps of fresh air into his lungs.

'A hotel just off the sea-front,' I tell him. I'm by far the most sober person of the four of us, but even I feel quite giddy as the cool salty air slaps our faces and tries to knock some sense into us.

'You could have stayed with Lucy and me if you'd said you were here overnight,' Simon says, slapping his own face to try to knock some sense into himself.

'Maybe they wanted a bit of privacy,' Adam says, nudging him. 'Nice little hotel – adjoining rooms and so on.'

'Actually we're in the same room,' Noah says, his brain obviously not running through with his lips first what he should and shouldn't say. 'Twin!' He waggles his index finger at them, and they giggle and jeer.

'They only had one room,' I try to say above all the whistling and catcalling. 'They were fully booked.'

But it falls on deaf ears, and as we walk back to our hotel with the boys accompanying us as apparently it's on their way home, there's much mention of dark horses and all-nighters.

'Seriously, though,' Adam says, when we reach the hotel, and while Simon and Noah are hugging each other goodbye but actually looking more like they're trying to hold each other up. 'You're a good girl, Ana, and Flood is a good boy . . . I mean *man*! He deserves someone like you after what he went through.'

'What did he go through?' I ask, hoping Adam will spill the beans.

Adam pats me on the shoulder. 'A good woman, that's what every man needs . . . eh, Foxy?'

'What?' Simon says, swaying back over to us with his arm around Noah's shoulders.

'We need a good woman!'

'You speak for yourself – I'm happily married. Well, most of the time.' He winks at me. 'Talking of which I'd better get back to her. We'll see you tomorrow then?' he asks, while Adam says his goodbyes to Noah now.

I nod. 'Yep.'

'There's some shindig after at one of Lucy's running mates' – you can come to that too. I could do with someone to talk to who doesn't go on about blisters and runner's nipple all the time.'

I grin. 'We'll see.'

We wave to Adam and Simon, who wander off along the road happily together, each one holding the other up. Then we head inside the hotel and up to our room.

Suddenly, I was more than a little apprehensive about sharing a room with Noah. I knew what he was like sober, and more to the point I trusted him, but what I didn't have any experience of was a more than a little drunk Noah.

In the last couple of weeks I'd seen Noah change from a quiet, unassuming person to a self-assured businessman at ease in his world of antiques, and then tonight I'd watched him morph again into a lively and boisterous ex-copper, happy and supremely confident amongst his old buddies. I liked a little bit of all those Noahs, but what I didn't know was, which was the real him?

I don't have to worry too much.

After we get upstairs to our hotel room, no sooner are we through the door than Noah immediately flops on his bed. Well, I say 'bed'; it's a bed settee that's been made up in our absence by one of the housekeeping staff. Noah is so tall that his feet hang over the edge of it.

'Are you all right?' I ask, removing my jacket and hanging it over a chair.

'*Mmmhmm,*' Noah mumbles, his eyes shut. 'I'll just lie here for a bit . . . Top night, though.'

'Yes, it was. Right . . . Well, I'll just be in the bathroom then.' I grab my pyjamas and my toiletry bag, and scuttle into the bathroom to get ready for bed. When I come out Noah hasn't moved but there's an odd purring noise coming from his bed.

I go over to him and gently remove his shoes. Then I try to cover him up with the duvet but find it's trapped underneath him, so I fetch a spare blanket from the cupboard and place that over him instead.

I hesitate over Noah's glasses – probably best if I remove those too as I very much doubt he sleeps in them. Very gently I pull them off, then fold them and put them on the nightstand next to him in case he should need them in the night. Then before I go to my own, very comfortable-looking king-size bed, I take one last look at him.

Noah looks quite different without his glasses. He was handsome with them, but without I can see all his features in more detail and he's actually quite striking. His cheekbones alone would put many a male model to shame, but it wasn't that: there was something familiar about his face, comforting even. Looking at him I feel something unusual stir inside me, and I realise it's not some strange feeling I've never felt before, some random butterflies being unleashed in my tummy at the sight of a handsome man. No, this feeling is one I haven't felt in a very long time.

Looking at Noah makes me feel happy. Very happy indeed.

Thirty-One

The next morning after we've had our complimentary breakfast, we walk down to the sea-front to find Simon and watch the fun run.

Noah has been quiet all morning. He'd apologised for immediately falling asleep last night soon after we both woke up. He'd also thanked me for removing his glasses and shoes and covering him up, saying it really wasn't necessary but he was glad I had.

'How are you feeling now?' I ask him as we walk. 'You didn't eat much breakfast.'

'Delicate.'

'Ah, the sea air will soon help with that!'

Noah grimaces.

My phone beeps in my bag. I pull it out and see Malachi's name on the screen. 'It's from Malachi,' I explain for Noah's benefit.

Hey, how's it going in sunny Brighton?
    I hope you and Noah are behaving yourselves ;)

Just thought I'd send you this photo of Daisy-Rose. She had her first coat of paint last night. Doesn't she look fine?

Hope you've found out lots of info on our Lou.

Ralph is missing you, and I guess I am too a little bit.

M x

In the photo, Daisy-Rose looks almost unrecognisable from how I remember her. Her patchwork effect has disappeared, and she almost looks like a different vehicle with a new coat of paint. I fire off a quick reply:

Photo: Amazing, thanks.

Info: Coming slowly.

I think for a moment.

Behaviour: Impeccable.

A x

As quick as a flash a reply comes whizzing back.

Re. Behaviour: Just as well you took Noah with you and not me then, eh?! ;)

'Everything okay?' Noah asks casually, as we turn a corner and find ourselves slap bang in the middle of everyone preparing for the race. There are people everywhere with runners and spectators mingling together, and there's a huge banner over the top of road that runs next to the promenade saying *START* on one side and *FINISH* on the other

'Er ... he was just sending me a photo of Daisy-Rose.' I

enlarge the photo so the text disappears from the screen and show him. 'She had her first coat of paint yesterday.'

A couple of runners jog slowly past us warming up.

'Very nice,' Noah says, looking briefly at the photo. 'Did he say anything else?'

'Yes, he was just asking how we were getting on ... with our search,' I add quickly.

'Ah.'

'If only that camper van could talk,' I say, staring at the photo again. 'I'm sure she'd be able to tell us exactly who Lou was and where we might find her, then we wouldn't have to be here worrying about finding Frankie. Malachi can do many things for Daisy-Rose, but he can't give her a voice.'

'No, indeed,' Noah says, looking around him. 'So now we *are* here, we'll just have to carry on with Plan B.'

I glance at Noah. He sounded a bit like he had the night of the barbecue – sort of cool and detached. *Was* it Malachi that was bothering him? Just as well he hadn't seen what he'd written in the text then!

'How's it hanging, folks?' Two arms wrap themselves either side of us and Simon's head appears through the gap. 'Ooh, nice camper van,' he says, looking at the phone in my hand. 'Is it yours?'

'Yes, it is. A friend is doing it up for me. He's just sent an update.'

'I bet that's taking a while. A mate started something similar a couple of years ago and he's still doing it.'

'I bet he's not working on it full time, though. Malachi is. Well, in between jobs at his garage, but he's very quiet at the moment so he's getting on with it superfast.'

'How long has he been repairing it?'

259

'A couple of weeks. This is what it looked like before.' I show Simon a photo Malachi sent me just before he started working on Daisy-Rose.

'And he's done all this in two weeks? What is he, some sort of superhero?'

'He's a hard worker.'

'He'd have to be working twenty-four hours a day to get that done in a fortnight.'

I look at the photo again. I guess Malachi had done quite a lot in the short time I'd been in St Felix – I hadn't really thought about it properly.

'He has a bit of help, though.'

'Ah, you didn't say he had a team working with him. Well, that's different. But still, they're doing brilliantly.'

I decide not to tell him Malachi's team consisted of two local boys who popped in occasionally after school.

'So, enough about Malachi, the *magical* mechanic,' Noah says, quite obviously changing the subject.

Simon raises his eyebrows.

'Let's talk about what we're really here for today – this race, and more importantly, to talk to members of the running club.'

We hang around the race start with Simon introducing us to a few members of the Brighton Bombers running club, but no one we speak to has any recollection of a Frankie. In fact, most of the runners we speak to weren't even involved in the club in the eighties.

'Here's your coffee,' Noah says, handing me a paper cup after he's gone to fetch hot drinks for all of us. 'How's it going?'

The weather, although apparently perfect for running, is chilly for spectators and I'm glad of the warmth as I take a sip of my frothy cappuccino.

'Not great. Most of the runners haven't finished yet. Simon keeps pulling over anyone he knows when they cross the finishing line, but no one seems old enough to remember our Frankie. He's gone to cheer on Lucy now. He reckons she'll be finished soon.'

We watch the runners pour over the line, scanning them for a Brighton Bombers running vest, but trying to talk to anyone when they've just run ten kilometres is difficult as all they want to do is grab their medal and a drink of water, and find their loved ones.

Simon appears through the crowd after a bit with his arm around an attractive woman who I assume must be Lucy. She's wearing a finisher's medal over her pink and navy running vest. She looks hot, but not too dishevelled like many of the runners we've seen finishing.

'This is Lucy, my wife,' he says proudly. 'Lucy, meet Ana and Flo— I mean, Noah.'

'Hi, good to meet you,' Lucy says brightly, shaking our hands. 'So you're the infamous "Flood" that Simon is always talking about?'

'Hush, woman,' Simon says. 'Don't make his head any bigger than it is already.'

Noah grins. 'How was your race?'

'Good, thanks, new PB. It wasn't really about time today, though – we were raising money for our charity.' She holds out her shirt, and I swallow hard when I realise what it says: *Breast Cancer Research*.

'Great cause,' Noah says. 'Does your running club often raise money for that charity?'

'Not always. We like to vary it, but my running mate today was keen to do it for them this time because her grandmother

261

died of the disease. Where is she?' Lucy looks around. 'She was with us just now, Simon.'

Simon shrugs. 'I asked Lucy this morning about the club members' records for you, and she doesn't seem to think they'll still have them dating back as far as you want to go.'

'Yeah, sorry,' Lucy says, turning back to us. 'We went all digital a few years ago – I'm not sure what happened to the old records. Maureen might know, I suppose?'

'Maureen?' Noah asks.

'Yeah, she's my mate's mum. I think she was involved in the club in the eighties. You should ask her. We're all going back to my mate's house for a post-run get-together – it's like a tradition. I'm sure you'd be most welcome. It's a sort of open house thing.'

'Lovely!' Noah says, while I'm still thinking. 'If you don't mind us tagging along.'

'Not at all. There will be loads of people from the club there. I'd be very surprised if you can't find what you're looking for at that gathering.'

Lucy's friend lives in a large detached house on the outskirts of Brighton so we grab a lift from Simon and Lucy.

'You're very quiet,' Noah says to me in a low voice, as we sit together on the back seat. 'Everything all right?'

'Yes . . . ' I whisper back. 'It was just Lucy's charity. It threw me a bit.'

'Because it's the same kind of charity that Frankie was supporting? Yeah, I noticed that too – what are the chances?'

I shake my head. 'No, I was a bit thrown because breast cancer was what my friend Daisy died of.'

Noah's face pales. 'Oh god, I'm so sorry, I didn't realise.'

'Why would you? Coincidental on both counts, that's all.'

262

'Perhaps. In my experience coincidence is rare though.'

'How do you mean?'

'I don't know exactly yet. Time will tell.'

'What are you two muttering about in the back there?' Simon asks. 'Whispering sweet nothings in each other's ears, no doubt!'

'Si, stop it,' Lucy says. She turns back towards us. 'Sorry about my husband – it's a laugh a minute living with him, as you can imagine.' She rolls her eyes, and we smile politely.

I'd thought Noah and I might feel awkward crashing someone else's party – after all, we didn't know the hostess, only one of the guests – but the do extends right through the large house into the extensive and beautifully manicured gardens at the back, and there are so many people milling around with drinks and plates of food in their hands that no one notices a couple of interlopers.

'I'll go and look for Maureen,' Lucy says shortly after we arrive. 'See if she can shed any light for you. Help yourself to food and drink, won't you?'

Noah and Simon dive right into the buffet – Noah's delicate constitution from earlier obviously a distant memory – while I help myself to a glass of orange juice. Feeling self-conscious in the room full of strangers, I turn around and look at the walls of the kitchen we're currently standing in while I sip on my juice.

That's interesting, I think, staring at a cluster of prints hanging on one of the walls. *Why does that seem familiar?*

My attention has been caught by a picture of some mountains, probably in Scotland by the look of them. They're behind a lake – no, make that a loch – and in front of the loch is a fisherman. Next to the fisherman is a huge pile of fish that he's already caught.

Nothing unusual in that – hundreds of pictures of Scottish mountains and lochs must have been painted over the years, but this one is different. The colours of the mountains are not the traditional ones but much bolder, brighter shades, and the same is true of the lake, which instead of being a more realistic pale blue-grey is a vibrant shade of azure blue more suited to a Mediterranean landscape than a Scottish one.

I move closer to the picture, and realise that it's not actually a print as I'd first thought but an original oil painting. I'm just trying to make out the signature when someone taps me on the shoulder.

'Ana, I can't find Maureen, but this is her daughter, my friend—'

'Juliet!' I exclaim, as I turn around and recognise the young woman from the newspaper offices yesterday. 'Gosh, what a coincidence!'

Juliet looks as shocked to see me as I am to see her standing right in front of me holding a tray full of sausage rolls.

The tray tips, and Lucy, more on the ball than either Juliet or me, swiftly catches it and straightens it up again. 'How do you two know each other?' Lucy asks in amazement.

'We don't really,' I reply, the first to recover. 'We met yesterday at *The Gazette* offices.'

'Yes, that's right,' Juliet says now, her voice returning. 'What a small world.'

Like yesterday, Juliet is smiling, but her smile doesn't extend to her eyes.

'I'm sorry if we're intruding on your party,' I apologise, wondering if this is what's upsetting her. 'Lucy said you wouldn't mind.'

'Noah is an old friend of Simon's,' Lucy explains. 'He's only here for a couple of days so I said they could come along. That is okay, isn't it, Ju?'

Juliet nods. 'Of course,' she says in an overly bright voice. 'The more the merrier.'

'Great spread.' I hear Noah's voice behind me. 'I should thank the hostess – Juliet!' he exclaims, seeing her. 'What are you— Oh, wait . . . ' he says, catching on much more quickly than me. 'You *are* the hostess, right? You're Lucy's mate.'

'I am indeed. Good to see you again, Noah.'

It feels to me like Juliet's pretence is put on mainly for Lucy's benefit and not ours.

'Noah and Ana are looking for someone they think was a member of the running club in the eighties,' Lucy explains, oblivious to everything else that's going on. 'I was going to ask your mum about it but I can't find her.'

'Migraine,' Juliet almost snaps. 'Gone home.'

'Oh, that's a shame,' Lucy continues. 'I thought she might be able to help. Sorry' – she shrugs at us – 'I tried.'

'You're looking for one of the guys in the newspaper photo, right?' Juliet says, looking accusingly at us. 'You left it in the microfiche reader,' she explains, when we don't answer. 'You didn't quite tidy everything away.' She glances meaningfully at Noah.

'Yes, that's right,' Noah says, fronting it out. 'Do you know any of them?'

'I should do – one of them is my grandfather.'

Thirty-Two

'*Your* grandfather?' I ask, completely aghast. 'But ... how? Why—'

'What my somewhat bemused friend is trying to ask,' Noah says, stepping in, 'is firstly, which *one* of the men is your grandfather?'

'The one with *Frankie* written across his chest.'

I look at Noah, hardly able to contain my excitement, but he remains cool and calm.

'The Frankie in the photo is your grandfather?' Noah confirms.

Juliet nods. 'Frankie wasn't his real name, though – his real name was John, and Francis was his middle name. John Francis Kennedy.'

'JFK,' Noah says, again working this out faster than I can. 'Nice.'

'That's why he was nicknamed "Frankie". He was always called John until the sixties, and then he decided it best to lose the initials.'

'I didn't know that?' Lucy says, looking in astonishment from Juliet to us and then back again.

'It's true,' Juliet insists. 'So why are you looking for him?'

'It doesn't matter,' I hear Noah saying, as I'm about to tell her the whole story. 'The Frankie we're looking for was called that as far back as 1945, wasn't he, Ana?'

I nod.

'So I very much doubt it's the same person.'

'Good. I mean, that's a shame.' Juliet smiles a much warmer smile now. 'Anyway, if it had been him you were looking for, you'd have been out of luck, I'm afraid. My grandfather died almost thirty years ago, not long after I was born.'

'Oh, I'm sorry,' I hear myself saying.

'That's okay,' Juliet says matter-of-factly. 'Shame you had a wasted trip. I guess I could have told you that yesterday if you'd said what you were looking for in the newspapers.'

'Yes, I suppose you could.'

'But you're more than welcome to stay and enjoy the food,' Juliet says, looking at Noah's plate piled high with food. 'There's plenty to go around. Now I must get these sausage rolls on to the table. Nice to see you again.'

'Just one more thing, Juliet?' I ask, before she leaves.

'Yes?'

'I was just admiring your pictures on the wall behind us. You've got quite an assortment of styles hanging up there. This painting here,' I say, pointing to the painting of the loch, 'where did you get it?'

Juliet's face stiffens again. 'I can't say I remember. Why?'

'No reason. I just quite like it, that's all.'

'Didn't your grandfather give you that?' Lucy says, looking at the painting too. 'I'm sure you told me he did.'

'Oh, *that* painting. I thought you meant the one next to it. Yes, he did. Just before he died.'

We all stare at the painting now.

267

'It's good, I like it. Also, that's unusual too,' I say, pointing up a little higher on the wall. 'Is that artwork from the band Dire Straits you've got framed up there?'

'Yes,' Juliet says, obviously relieved to move attention away from the Scottish painting. 'It's a cover from one of their singles. Most people think I was named after Shakespeare's Juliet, but the truth is my parents were huge Dire Straits fans in the eighties and their song "Romeo And Juliet" came out the year I was born, 1981, so they called me after that. It's a bit of a family joke.'

'Ah, I see. That's very cool. Well, I think we'd probably better get going,' I say to Noah. 'Everyone has been most helpful, but we don't want to outstay our welcome and we've got quite a long journey back to Cornwall.'

Noah looks sadly down at his plate of untouched food. 'You're probably right,' he says. 'I'll just go and say goodbye to Foxy, I mean, Simon.'

Juliet can hardly hide her delight that we're leaving. She virtually escorts us out of the front door.

'Sorry I couldn't be of more help in your search,' she says, at least attempting to look sorrowful. 'I do hope you find who you're looking for eventually.'

'Oh, we will,' I assure her. 'Of that I have no doubt.'

'I'm sorry this trip turned out to be a waste of time,' Noah says, as we walk away from the house in the direction of the hotel so we can collect our bags. 'I had such high hopes for it too. I was sure that Juliet was hiding something. Maybe my instincts aren't quite as sharp as they used to be.'

'No, I think they're spot on actually,' I reply, walking calmly alongside him.

'How do you mean?' Noah stares in surprise at me. 'What do you know, Ana?'

'I know that Juliet wasn't telling us the truth for one thing.'

'How? Much of what she said actually matched up with what I already knew. The owner of the electronics firm *was* called Kennedy – I found that out on the internet – so the Frankie in the newspaper photo not only worked for Johnson's Electronics but he owned the company too.'

'Yes, that part is likely true, but one minute she's telling us her grandfather died just after she was born, and the next, he gave her that painting.'

'So?'

'Well, for one, who gives artwork to a newborn baby? And two, even if they did, I happen to know that that picture is from the late eighties or possibly even early nineties, and Juliet, as she just told us, was born in 1981.'

'How do you know that? Did it say on it when it was painted? Did the artist date it?'

I shake my head. 'Nope, not that I saw. But I know that artist went to Scotland around the end of the eighties, and so the painting must have been done around then.'

Noah just stares at me. Then I see it click in his eyes as it registers in his brain. 'It isn't, is it?'

I nod. 'I'm pretty sure it is. I think that painting was done by our Lou, and the reason I know that is because she wrote to Frankie all about her trip to the Scottish highlands and that very fisherman in one of her postcards.'

Thirty-Three

The next day I wake up back in my bed in Snowdrop Cottage.

Our journey home had been a long one after an accident caused long tailbacks on the A30, but we didn't mind too much as it gave us plenty of time to discuss our next move.

Noah said he was going to run some checks with his ex-colleagues to check that this John Francis Kennedy *was* actually dead, and that it wasn't another thing Juliet was lying to us about.

But why would she? I'd argued. What possible reason would Juliet have for lying to us about that, or anything else to do with Frankie for that matter?

I turn this thought over in my head as I stare at the ceiling. My job today was going to be to try to trace Lou through her paintings. We knew now that her name was Lou Adams, because I'd seen the signature *L. Adams* in the corner of the painting. I was sure this had to be one of Lou's paintings from when she took a trip to Scotland, because the style – the bold colours and large brush-strokes – were just as she'd described to Frankie many times on the postcards as the way in which she painted.

I lean over and pick up a postcard from the table next to the bed.

Even though it had been late when we'd finally got in last night, I'd searched through the postcards until I found the couple I was looking for. The first had been sent in October 1989 and, along with the second one, told me everything I needed to know:

My Darling Frankie,

I'm up here in Bonny Scotland. In the Highlands to be precise, and I can confirm it is very Bonny indeed!

Rose and I took quite some time to get here. Rose (a bit like me!) is getting on a bit now, and likes to take her time to get anywhere!

But I'm so glad we came, the scenery is to die for – a painter's paradise.

Today I stopped and sketched a fisherman I found on the shores of Loch Lomond. He'd had quite the day and had already caught a huge pile of trout, but he was kind enough to give me one, which I barbecued that night. It was delicious and so fresh! I think you would have loved it.

Forever yours,

Lou x

Then there was the follow-up postcard dated February 1990 some four months later:

My Darling Frankie,

Remember the fisherman in Scotland?

When I got home I painted him and the loch, and

the beautiful mountains that surrounded him. I used
some garish colours that I absolutely love when the mood
takes me – not to everyone's taste, but this style is very
popular if you market it in the right places. I think
I'm going to keep this one, though, as I do with all my
paintings that remind me of particularly happy times.

 Forever yours,
 Lou x

The painting hanging in Juliet's kitchen was definitely the same one as Lou was describing in the cards, I was sure of it, but how had it really come into her possession? The story about her grandfather John Francis Kennedy just didn't add up – if he *had* given it to her, why try to hide it from us? He wasn't our Frankie so there was no need.

I sigh. 'Oh Lou,' I say to the empty bedroom, 'please stop hiding and show yourself to us soon.'

While I'm waiting to hear back from Noah, I get ready to take my usual walk up the hill to see Malachi, but just as I'm about to head out of the door someone knocks on it.

'I was just about to walk up to see you,' I say, as I open the door to a grinning Malachi.

'I know, I mean I guessed you would as soon as you got back, but I was in the town and I thought I'd drop in on you for a change.'

He holds up two coffee cups with lids.

'I didn't know what sort of coffee-making facilities you'd have here,' he says, peering into the kitchen, 'so I came prepared.'

'I am equipped with the basics – like a kettle! But thanks,' I say, standing back to let him in. 'That's kind of you.'

'All right to bring Ralph in?' Malachi asks.

'Sure, he's house-trained, unlike you!'

I find a bowl and fill it with water for Ralph, then I lead them both up the stairs and into the sitting room.

'I'll open up the doors again now I'm not going out,' I tell him, unlocking the French windows. 'It's a gorgeous day.'

'Isn't it?' Malachi says, following me while Ralph has a sniff around the lounge. 'Shall we drink our coffee out here? Whoa, what a view!' he exclaims, going immediately to the edge of the balcony. He gazes out over the beach and onwards into the sea – calm today with just the lightest of breezes to stir its waves into tiny peaks as they wash gently across the pale sand.

'It is pretty special, isn't it?' I say, sitting down on one of the chairs. I tilt my face up and let the sun warm my cheeks.

Malachi passes me a coffee. 'Skinny vanilla cappuccino – just as madam likes.'

'Thanks.' I take a sip. 'Wait, how did you know? We've only had instant coffee at your workshop before.'

'I guessed,' Malachi says, sitting now too. 'Bit of a hobby of mine. I usually get it right.'

'Guessing people's coffee preferences?'

'That and other things.'

'Like?'

'All sorts – favourite drinks, sandwiches, positions . . . ' He winks at me. 'The list goes on.'

'I bet it does. What's my favourite *sandwich* then?'

Malachi looks at me with his head tipped to one side. 'Tuna and coleslaw,' he says after a few seconds.

'How'd you know that?' I ask, astonished.

'Told you – it's a hobby.'

'My favourite drink then? I'll make it easier – my favourite *soft* drink?'

'Diet Pepsi.'

'Very clever. I'm impressed. I feel I'm missing a trick somewhere, though.'

'Aren't you going to let me guess the last one?'

'*Hmm?*' I have to think about this for a moment. 'No!' I say when I remember. 'Definitely not.'

'Aw, please . . .'

'Guess my favourite takeaway instead,' I suggest.

'Easy – pizza, with tuna again and olives.'

I shake my head. 'You're a wizard . . . or a magician!' I smile. 'That's funny. Noah called you something similar yesterday.'

'Oh, did he?'

'Yeah, he called you "Magic Malachi", or was it a "magical mechanic"? I can't remember now.'

'So how did the two of you get on?' Malachi asks, without further comment on this nickname.

'Great, actually . . .'

I tell Malachi everything that happened in Brighton while we sip on our coffee, and Ralph finds a cool spot in the sitting room to snooze in.

'That's excellent, Ana,' he says, when I've finished. 'But I actually meant how did the two of you get on – like get on *together*?'

'Fine, why wouldn't we?'

'There was no slipping in and out of each other's . . . rooms then?' Malachi raises his eyebrows suggestively.

'No. Anyway, we shared a room. But before you start, it was only because there was a mix-up with the booking and they didn't have any other spare rooms to offer us.'

'She got that right at least,' Malachi murmurs into his coffee cup before taking a sip.

'What did you say then? Who got what right?'

'I *said* you could have at least got that right. How hard is it to book a room?'

'I did book two rooms – I know I did. Perhaps it was a glitch in the computer system?'

'Maybe. So you shared a room – and . . . ?'

'And nothing. Noah had quite a lot to drink with his police mates. He just crashed out on the bed when we got back to the room last night. *His* bed,' I maintain, before Malachi starts. 'Not mine.'

Malachi shakes his head. 'What a waste,' he says, looking up at the sky.

'Excuse me?'

'I mean, you're a beautiful woman, Ana. What a waste as a man sharing a room with you and passing out due to alcohol. That wouldn't have happened if I'd been there.'

'Oh, and what would have happened then? You're very sure of yourself.' I grin, assuming this is going to be one of Malachi's usual wind-ups.

Malachi, who like me has been sitting with his face turned to the sun up until now, suddenly turns and gazes directly into my eyes so intensely that it makes me wish that I'd set the chairs a little further apart on the balcony. 'Ana, I'm going to ask you something now and I'd like an honest answer, please.'

'Okay . . . '

'Do you find me attractive?'

'What kind of question is that?'

'A pretty straightforward one, I'd have thought.'

I sit back a little so I can look properly at Malachi. This

morning he's wearing his customary jeans – black today with just the one small rip at the knee. He's teamed them with a black sleeveless T-shirt; this one has some sort of white feather design on it. His muscly arms reveal more of his tattoos than I've seen previously, and as I look up into his face I'm mesmerised by his large green eyes that gaze intently back at me under a halo of his shiny, yet always scruffy curly black hair.

'You'd have been just my type a few years ago,' I tell him honestly.

'Oh yeah, what type is that?'

'A bad boy.'

Malachi's eyes open wide with mock outrage. 'How *very* dare you?' He grins now. 'There's not a bad bone in me.'

'No, I don't mean you *are* bad, I mean the way you look is. It's not clean cut, is it? It's ... rough, rugged even. It's like you're more Johnny Depp than Tom Cruise.'

Malachi doesn't look too impressed.

'More James Dean than Clark Kent then?' I improvise, trawling my mind for appropriate comparisons.

Malachi nods his approval. 'I'll take that as a compliment. James Dean is the ultimate iconic rebel. So you like a bad boy then?' he asks, his eyes twinkling.

'I did. Nearly all my past boyfriends have been a bit ... ' I don't want to offend him by choosing the wrong word. 'Let's say they were outsiders, quite often on the wrong side of the law.'

'I can't imagine you with someone like that.'

'Because I appear so strait-laced now? Yeah, I've dated a few naughty boys. Daisy hated it – she always warned me I was going to get hurt and she was usually right.'

'Why do it then if you knew it was going to end badly?'

'I wanted to rebel, I suppose.'

'Against?'

I think about this. 'Do you know, I've never thought about it before?'

'Think about it now then.'

I shrug.

'Were you rebelling against Daisy by any chance?' he asks quietly, obviously anticipating my response.

'Why would I do that?' I snap. 'She was my best friend. Why would I rebel against her?'

'Whoa, steady! Calm down, it was just a suggestion. What *were* you rebelling against then?'

I think again, his suggestion nagging at me. 'I guess Daisy *was* always Miss Perfect,' I admit. 'We used to laugh about how she was always right. She always knew the right things to say, she always did the right thing too. She even married a Mr Right. You couldn't find a better man than Peter. I certainly couldn't anyway, so I guess that's why I went for the boys and then the men that I knew would let me down eventually.'

I glance at Malachi. He just nods and waits for me to continue.

'I was never going to match up to her, was I, however hard I tried? Daisy was perfection in my eyes; with her *perfect* hair, her *perfect* skin, her *perfect* family and her *perfect* life!' I slap my hand over my mouth. Where had all that come from? I sounded so bitter.

'It's okay to think these things, you know?' Malachi says gently. 'You've not said anything bad about her. Just how great she was. It can be hard to know someone you consider to be a flawless human being. It can make anything you do seem very inadequate. But there's rarely a flawless human being, Ana. Everyone has their faults.'

'But she was my friend, and she's not here now. I don't want to think badly of her – I want to remember her as she was.'

'And you will do, with much love and affection. But now you've got to stop living your life in her shadow. Her life has ended and yours goes on. But how you choose to live it is up to you. This is the Ana show now – you're a solo artist, not part of a double act any longer.'

I stare at Malachi. 'Who made you so wise?' I ask, suddenly realising he's actually talking a lot of sense.

Malachi shrugs. 'It's a gift.'

I smile. 'And so cocky too?'

'Years of experience.'

I shake my head and sit back in my chair. The sun is currently fighting with a bank of fluffy white clouds that have floated across the sky while we've been talking, so I'm able to look directly up into the sky without blinding myself.

'So, back to my earlier question,' Malachi asks. 'Do you find me attractive or not?'

I have to admire his persistence, and his sheer audacity.

'Yes, and no,' I tell him seriously, removing the grin from my face.

'*Hmm* . . . I'm not sure I like the sound of that. Explain.'

'So I told you before you would have been just my type in the past and that I've dated many a boy like you.'

'Yes, but I'm hardly a boy.'

'Okay, a man then, but now I think I want something different. My life has been so unstable since Daisy died, I think my priorities have changed and I need some stability in my life again. Daisy used to provide that stability, but now . . .'

'You need to stand on your own two feet?'

'Yes, I think so.'

'No need for a man then?'

'Well, I wouldn't say that. Maybe a different sort of man, that's all – one that can provide me with some stability. Before I'd have been happy to whizz around on the back of a Harley-Davidson, but now I need someone with something a bit more substantial.'

'Like a camper van?' Malachi suggests, his eyes twinkling.

'Ha, maybe? I was thinking of something a little more reliable.'

'Shame.' Malachi shrugs. 'Ah, well, you win some, you lose some. I don't mind being your James Dean, but the question is, who will be your Clark Kent, or even your Superman?'

Thirty-Four

While Ralph snoozes peacefully in the sitting room, Malachi and I spend another relaxed hour or so on the balcony together, talking about St Felix, Daisy-Rose and just life in general.

Malachi, I've come to realise, for all his chat and swagger, is actually very insightful when it comes to discussing things of a philosophical nature, which surprises me. I attempt to discover where he formed his interesting beliefs and opinions. Did he go to university? Had he been on a debate team at school? Had he had a spiritual experience as a child that had led to his views?

However, Malachi is vague when I ask him about his childhood and growing up, much like Noah when I'd asked him about his time in the police force, so eventually I find it best to leave it be when no answers are immediately forthcoming.

I'm about to suggest some lunch might be an idea sometime soon when I hear a knock on the door downstairs.

'I'll just see who that is,' I tell Malachi.

'Sure,' Malachi says, stretching out in the sun, which is now shining fully down on the balcony. 'I'll have to get back to the garage soon, though. Daisy-Rose won't spray-paint herself. Last coat today!'

'It's Sunday!' I call as I head down the stairs. 'The day of rest.'

'No rest for the wicked!' I hear Malachi call back. 'And according to you I'm a very bad boy indeed!'

I'm still smiling as I reach the door and pull it open.

'Noah, hi,' I say on seeing him. 'How are you on this lovely day? Isn't it gorgeous out there?'

'Bit hot for me actually,' Noah says, stepping inside the door. 'I burn far too easily in this weather.'

I think of Malachi stretched out in the sun upstairs. How opposite could two men get?

'You seem very chipper anyway,' Noah says. 'I thought you might be a bit down after our trip.'

'Nope. I'm just as positive we're going to find Lou as I was before. If not more so now we have her name. Anything on that yet, or on the mysterious JFK?'

'No, sorry – Sunday, isn't it? Most of my guys will be off today. We only work Sundays if we have to.'

I notice Noah is talking about the force in the present tense now since Brighton, and not in the past. I find myself wondering if this is a good thing?

'I should be able to find something out either tomorrow or Tuesday at the latest though. So what have you been up to this morning? Did you find the relevant postcards?'

'I did, yes, and Juliet's painting *is* the one Lou talks about in the cards. I'm certain of it now.'

'Very strange,' Noah says, shaking his head. 'Very strange indeed.'

'So how come you're here? I thought you'd be run off your feet in the shop today?'

281

'I had some errands to run in the town so I took an early lunch. We're not actually that busy. All everyone wants to do today is laze on the beach in the sun, not wander around a dusty old antiques shop.'

Noah's shop is far from dusty but I don't mention this. I've suddenly remembered that Malachi is upstairs, and even though I wasn't a hundred per cent sure whether Noah *was* actually jealous of Malachi, I knew him finding out he was upstairs wouldn't be a good thing.

'So, anyway,' Noah says, when I don't speak. 'I was wondering if you'd like to join me for a barbecue again later? The good weather is supposed to last well into the evening. The sunsets over Porthhaven beach can be pretty amazing in this weather.'

Was I hearing this correctly? Was Noah suggesting a romantic evening watching the sun go down together, just the two of us?

'Jess suggested Porthhaven so we can bring Clarice,' he continues. 'She's bringing the salad, I'm doing the fish and we wondered if you'd like to come – and if you do, if you'd bring some wine or a dessert perhaps?'

Ah, not quite so romantic after all.

'Sure, that sounds great. I'll bring both.' I'm keen for Noah to leave as soon as possible. Knowing Malachi, he'll come bounding down the stairs at any minute spouting all sorts of innuendo – harmless to me, but perhaps not quite so harmless to Noah.

'Ana, I just had a great idea!' I hear from upstairs, almost before I've had a chance to finish my thought. 'In this wild-child life you once led, did you ever go skinny-dipping?'

I stare with horror at Noah. He looks equally as dismayed to hear the voice as I am.

'There's a really quiet little cove I know.' Malachi's voice sounds even closer, and I can hear him leaping down the stairs two at a time. 'How about it some … Oh, hello stranger, you must be Noah.'

Malachi comes bouncing into the kitchen with just as much energy as he'd descended the stairs. He holds out his hand, and Noah shakes it reluctantly.

'This is Malachi, Noah,' I say, introducing him as the two men shake hands.

'I guessed as much,' Noah says, wriggling his fingers a little after they part company from Malachi's.

That's odd? Did he feel the same thing I did when I touched Malachi's hand?

'Noah just popped round for coffee. He's been updating me on the camper van's progress,' I add hurriedly, looking at Noah. 'And Malachi has just invited me to a barbecue,' I tell Malachi. 'Oh, I mean the other way around obviously!' I feel my cheeks redden.

'Great night for a barbie,' Malachi says approvingly. 'Good call that.'

'Would you like to come?' Noah asks politely, but I detect reluctance in his offer.

'I'm grand,' Malachi says 'Three's a crowd and all that!'

'I'm sure we could stretch to four.'

'Four? Who's the fourth?' Malachi asks. 'I assumed this was to be a romantic evening for two, watching the sunset together.'

He heard?

Noah suddenly looks very uncomfortable, as though he should have thought of this idea too.

'Jess, who works alongside Noah at his antiques shop, is coming too,' I say quickly to try to cover his embarrassment. 'So really, you'd be most welcome, Malachi.'

'Well, that's a date then!' Malachi says, grinning. 'What shall I bring – meat? Ana knows all about my prize-winning sausage, don't you, Ana? Said it's the best she's ever had ...'

I shake my head reprovingly at Malachi, and then I turn back to Noah. He eyes Malachi with indifference.

Ah, what a fun evening this was going to be. At this rate I'd spend my whole night trying to stop Malachi from winding Noah up, and attempting to stop Noah from injuring Malachi ...

Thirty-Five

That evening we're all set up on the beach: four adults, two dogs, two barbecues – one for fish and one for meat – three cool boxes, two chairs and a scattering of picnic rugs.

Malachi is tending to his sausages in a relaxed fashion, turning them occasionally with some silver tongs in between swigs from his bottle of beer. Noah is slightly more attentive to his fish, never stepping more than a few feet from his barbecue for even a minute. Jess is sitting cross-legged looking out at the sea with a bottle of beer in one hand and a dog ball in the other, and I'm sitting on one of the chairs trying to relax while the two dogs chase each other around my legs.

Clarice and Ralph have taken to each other immediately. I had wondered when it was being discussed about bringing them whether they would get on. They were very different dogs – Clarice was tiny, yappy and seemingly quite uptight, and Ralph was big, bouncy and as relaxed as they come – but they'd hit it off straight away when Clarice had picked up Ralph's ball and run off with it, and the latter, after looking in

285

horror at Malachi for a moment, had given chase. They were still playing together almost an hour later.

'Another beer, Jess?' Malachi calls, as he opens up the cool box.

Jess looks at her bottle. 'Yeah, why not?' she says, smiling at Malachi.

Malachi prises the lid off a bottle of beer with the bottle opener from the cottage that I'd had the foresight to pack, and passes her the beer.

'Cheers, Mal,' she says informally.

'Malachi, thanks,' Malachi says, raising his eyebrows at her. 'Beer, Ana?'

'Sorry, I keep forgetting,' Jess says, her cheeks reddening.

I lift my bottle and shake my head at Malachi. 'No thanks, still have plenty here. So ...?' I ask, looking between Malachi and Jess. 'Have you two met before – you seem like you might have?'

'No, don't think so,' Jess says almost too quickly. 'I'd remember if we had, I'm sure.'

'Nope,' Malachi says, tending to his barbecue. 'Definitely not.'

I look across at Noah, who's also watching this exchange with interest. He shrugs.

'You'll be able to do this all the time when Daisy-Rose is up and running, Ana,' Malachi says, changing the subject. 'Quick drive out to the sea, barbecue on the beach, then camping under the stars.'

'Sounds idyllic but there aren't too many beaches in London.'

Malachi and Jess exchange anxious glances. *What is it with those two?*

'So what *are* you going to do with the van when it's finished, Ana?' Jess asks. 'Have you decided yet?'

'No, I still don't know. When I first came here to St Felix, deciding what I was going to do with Daisy-Rose seemed an age away. But Malachi has made so much progress so quickly, I guess that day is looming closer all the time.'

'You don't need to sound so serious about it,' Noah says, letting his fish be for a moment. He picks up his beer and sits down in the empty chair. 'You're making it sound like the day of reckoning.'

'I hardly think it's anything like that,' Jess says sternly. 'I mean . . .' She stares with wild eyes at Malachi.

'I think what Jess might be trying to say' – Malachi casts a reproving look at Jess – 'is that deciding what to do with something as fun and exciting as a camper van shouldn't really be looked upon as a chore.'

'*Yes*, that's exactly what I meant.' Jess nods enthusiastically. 'You should look upon it as a new start to your life, Ana.'

'How is owning Daisy-Rose going to be a new start? Lovely though I'm sure she's going to be when she's finished, where on earth am I going to park her when I get back to London? I have enough trouble parking my bike on the rare occasion I ride it.'

'You could leave her here if you want to?' Noah suggests casually. 'I have quite a bit of space in the yard at the back of the shop where I park my Land Rover.'

I think about this. It would certainly solve one of my problems.

'You wouldn't mind?'

'Of course not. On one condition though.'

'What's that?'

'You occasionally come to visit her, and the rest of us in St Felix.'

'Of course.' I feel my heart swell at the thought of having a reason to return to this quaint little Cornish town, and to Noah. And not for the first time, we hold each other's gaze for a tad longer than is necessary.

'That's grand that you have somewhere to park her,' Malachi says, interrupting our moment, 'but you can't just leave her sitting in a yard all day.'

'She's not a dog, Malachi!' I grin. 'I'm not asking you to leave Ralph locked up in Noah's back yard all day.' I look for Ralph and see he's currently chasing Clarice around a large rock for a piece of driftwood that they've claimed as their new toy.

'I know, but I just hoped you'd have better plans for her, that's all.' He wanders over to tend to his sausages, a sulky look on his face.

'I would do if I could think of any, but what you have to remember, Malachi, is I'm a graphic designer who lives in a small flat in North London. What use do I have for a camper van in my life?'

'I've worked my socks off doing her up for you,' Malachi mumbles, poking at his sausages. 'And now she's just going to sit rusting away in the back yard of an antiques shop.'

I hold my hands up to the others in a 'what should I do?' gesture.

'Are you *absolutely* sure you can't think of anything you'd like to do with Daisy-Rose when she's finished?' Jess asks, glancing at Malachi. 'I mean you've changed such a lot already since you arrived here in St Felix, maybe by the time you leave you'll have changed your mind about this too?'

How would Jess know I'd changed? I had, yes, I couldn't deny it. St Felix had helped me clear my head, that was for sure, and I did feel better for coming here, but how would Jess know that? What had Noah been telling her?

'It's good you think that, Jess,' I say, glancing at Noah. He looks as puzzled by her statement as I am. 'But I don't think I've changed so much that I'm going to give up my job and live out some sort of hippy-style fantasy travelling around the country in Daisy-Rose.' I smile at my joke, but Malachi just makes a huffing noise and Jess looks sadly down into her beer bottle.

'All right!' I concede, standing up and going over to Malachi. 'How many more days do you think you'll need before Daisy-Rose is finished?'

Malachi looks up hopefully from his sausages and considers this. 'Four, maybe five.'

'That's perfect. I have Snowdrop Cottage until next Saturday. How about I promise to think really really hard about what I can do with Daisy-Rose in the remaining days I have left here? How does that sound?'

I hear Jess clap her hands together in delight, but Malachi still seems gloomy. 'Good, I guess,' he admits. 'But it will be a shame to see you go whether you go with or without Daisy-Rose. We'll miss you, won't we, Noah?' he prompts, glaring at him.

'Er ... yes. Yes, of course we will.' Noah, startled, looks up from his beer bottle. 'The place won't be the same without you.'

'I'm sure Noah will be glad to see the back of me. I've had him careering around the country for two weeks on something akin to a wild postcard chase. He'll be glad of the peace.'

Noah doesn't reply.

'How's that going?' Jess asks keenly. 'Noah told me what happened in Brighton. Have you found anything more yet?'

'I haven't had much time today, but I did take a little look on the internet before I came out and there are quite a few paintings listed on eBay by an L. Adams. They're all in that same bright bold style too. I'm positive this L. Adams is our Lou.'

'Is there anything else on there about her? Jess asks. 'Like a Wikipedia page?'

'Not that I can find.'

'Social media?' she suggests. 'Does she have a Twitter or Facebook account? Maybe she puts her paintings on Instagram?'

I smile. 'If our Lou is still alive, and I pray she is after all this, she's likely around eighty-eight years old. I very much doubt she tweets!'

Everyone laughs, including Jess.

'Worth a shot,' she says, shrugging.

'Jess, anything is worth a shot right now,' Noah says, getting up to check his fish again. 'We're so short on leads that I might have to borrow Clarice's if we don't find any soon.'

The food is eaten much faster than it takes to prepare it. I'm careful to eat equal amounts of sausages and fish, so I don't show any favouritism. More beer is downed and we're now all sitting wrapped up in jumpers and blankets as the evening begins to chill – Noah and I still on the picnic chairs, and Malachi and Jess down on the rugs as we witness the dramatic sight of a beautiful blood red sun slowly sinking down beneath the sea.

'Isn't nature wonderful,' I sigh, breaking the silence that's engulfed our little camp for the last few minutes.

'When you witness sunsets like this, it makes you wonder just how many other people must have sat watching the same thing before us over the years,' Noah says, glancing across at me. 'Things change and times move on, but nature remains the one constant.'

I look down at Malachi and Jess, and smile as I see them

290

curled up next to each other on the rugs apparently asleep. Malachi is lying on his back with his hands behind his head, and Jess is using Malachi's legs as a pillow while she snuggles under one of the picnic blankets to keep her warm.

'Look at the kids,' I whisper jokingly to Noah. 'They're all worn out.'

Noah smiles. 'I think it more likely all the beer they both consumed rather than acute tiredness that's put them to sleep.'

'They were behaving oddly earlier, weren't they?'

'When?'

'When I asked whether they'd met before – they went all cagey.'

'Maybe they have, and they don't want us to know about it.'

'Why, though?'

Noah smiles. 'Ana, not everyone wants their secrets known to all and sundry. The trend these days is to share everything – it's supposed to be healthy – but sometimes things are best kept hidden.'

I assume he's thinking of his time in the Met again.

'You've known Jess a lot longer than me,' I say, pretending I don't know what he's referring to. 'What's she like?'

'How do you mean?'

'Does she talk about a lot of deep stuff to you?'

'Not that I'm aware of. How do you mean, "deep"?'

'Like philosophical stuff – the meaning of life, that kind of thing.'

Noah thinks about this. 'I suppose she does some-times. Why?'

'It's just Malachi does the same. I know you're not keen on him, but he's a really good listener and he has some really good advice about . . . well, life.'

I can feel Noah bristle across the rugs.

'You don't need to worry you know?' I tell him. 'We're just friends. We were actually having this conversation earlier before you arrived at the cottage. How he'd have been just my type a few years ago.'

'Oh, yes . . . ' Noah shuffles uncomfortably in his seat.

'But how he's very definitely not now,' I emphasise.

Noah looks across at me. 'I see . . . May I ask what *is* your type now?'

I look at him, my brain willing my mouth to say the word *You*.

'I'm not sure I have one,' I hear myself saying instead.

Malachi sighs heavily on the rug below us, but he doesn't appear to wake up.

'That's probably a good thing. Leaves your options open.'

'Yeah.'

We look at the sky again. The deep magnificent reds are fading now into paler oranges and yellows.

'It was good of you to offer to let me keep Daisy-Rose in your yard,' I tell him after a bit.

'It's not a problem at all – I have plenty of space. I was actually considering renting that space out to one of the holiday cottages for parking as we're so tight for that in St Felix.'

'Well, it was once an old fishing town – I doubt they had much need for car parks.'

'No, indeed.'

Jess sighs this time. She moves her head a little on Malachi's legs, then is still and silent again.

'I'll miss this place when I go,' I say, still staring at the sun, which is barely visible now over the sea. 'I've had fun here.'

'I've had fun you being here too,' Noah says, gazing out over the ocean as well. 'It won't be the same when you go.'

We both look across at each other, then immediately turn back again.

I shiver. Now the sun has gone completely, there is no warmth on the beach at all. The only heat is the little bit still coming from the now empty barbecues.

'Are you cold?' Noah asks. 'Have my jacket. I don't need it. I have a sweatshirt on underneath.'

Before I have time to say no, he's unzipped his big North Face jacket and brought it over to me. He kneels down and wraps it gently around my shoulders.

'Thank you,' I say, looking at him.

Noah's hands haven't left my shoulders, and his face is still level with mine; we can do nothing but stare into each other's eyes.

Without thinking any further about it, I take my chance and reach my face forward until my lips touch Noah's. In what feels like for ever but is likely only a few seconds I feel him give a tiny jolt, but then he immediately relaxes and presses his lips firmly on to mine. He lets go of the jacket, and as I turn further in towards him it falls on to the sand but neither of us cares. Noah's hands are now cupping my face, and our kiss becomes less experimental and more wanting as we explore each other's lips and then mouths.

We break momentarily to catch our breath.

'Noah,' I gasp, 'I ... I didn't expect you to kiss like that. You're quite the dark horse.'

'Clark Kent ...' I'm sure I hear whispered behind me. I turn around, but Malachi and Jess are still sound asleep on the rugs. Perhaps it was just the sea breeze catching on the rocks or whipping along the sand, but I was sure I had heard those words.

'Did you hear that?' I ask Noah.

But Noah is only interested in returning his lips to mine.

'Wait just one moment,' I ask him.

'What's wrong?' Noah asks anxiously.

'Nothing, I just want to do this.' I gently lift his glasses from his face and put them carefully in the pocket of his hoody.

'Now then, Superman,' I tell him, running my fingers seductively down his cheek, 'show me what you've got.'

Thirty-Six

I awake the next morning and stare up at the ceiling of my bedroom in Snowdrop Cottage. Nothing odd there – it's what I usually did when the morning light began to stream through the thin curtains to wake me.

But today something doesn't feel right. I'm used to being awoken by the noise of a seagull tapping around on the roof or an early morning delivery van passing down the narrow street on its way to the harbour, but today I realise I've been woken by the sound of gentle snoring.

And then I remember . . .

I close my eyes and quickly run over the events of last night after I'd kissed Noah on the beach.

While Jess and Malachi had continued to doze on the rugs, I'd gathered our things and Noah had tethered the also sleeping dogs with their leads.

'Will they be okay?' I'd asked worriedly.

'Jess and Malachi? They'll be fine.'

'No, I meant the dogs. Should we take them with us? Clarice, at least.'

Noah had grinned. 'Not if you want any peace. Clarice will scratch at the bedroom door all night unless you let her in, and I'm sure we really don't want a small dog watching us when we get back to your cottage!'

'No, you might be right there.'

'Jess will take Clarice back to her house, no problem, and Ralph will stay with Malachi. The tide is as far in as it will come so nothing will happen to them, I promise. Unless you'd rather wake them?'

I'd shaken my head. Where I was going with Noah and what I was planning to do with him was not something I wanted to share with Malachi or anyone else.

'Not changing your mind, are you? Would you rather stay here?' Noah couldn't hide the tinge of disappointment in his voice.

'No, of course not. I still want to go – but I think we should leave a note.'

Noah had waited patiently as I scribbled a quick note and tucked it under Pegasus's windscreen wipers. Then without looking back, we'd run hand in hand across the sand towards the steps that led back up to the town, quickly slipped on our shoes and continued to run back to Snowdrop Cottage, stopping occasionally to steal another breathless kiss from each other when we could bear the wait no longer.

When we'd finally got back to the cottage, I'd struggled to get the key into the door because Noah had his arms wrapped around my waist while his lips caressed the back of my neck, making it extremely difficult to concentrate on something usually so simple.

Finally I'd got the door open and we'd fallen inside with our lips locked together. I'd closed the door to the outside world with my foot and then, without speaking, we'd quickly made our way up the stairs to the bedroom where we'd remained for several eventful hours before falling asleep in the early hours of the morning.

I feel my closed eyes screw tightly together, partly from embarrassment and partly from pleasure as I remember what those few hours had consisted of.

Noah might appear quiet, calm and perhaps a little bit dull, but that was quite the opposite of the man I found myself with in Snowdrop Cottage last night. In the same way as antiques shop Noah had proved himself a different person to Detective Flood, the man I'd spent last night with seemed like another version of him altogether. Once Noah's glasses were removed, he was passionate, loving and extremely sexy, and I found myself having to remember on more than one occasion just who I was with once the bedroom door had closed.

You really are Clark Kent, I think, smiling to myself.

I realise the snoring has stopped, and I open one eye.

'You *are* awake?' I hear Noah say, and he sits up in the bed next to me as I open the other eye. 'I wasn't sure. You were pulling a very odd face – part happy, part pained.'

'Facial exercises,' I improvise. 'I do them every morning before I get up.'

'I don't know why?' Noah says, leaning over the top of me. 'I think you look beautiful.' He leans down a little further and kisses me. I find myself immediately responding, and then I hesitate.

'Something wrong?' Noah asks, sensing my reluctance.

'No, no, not at all – bathroom!' I roll out of bed, suddenly aware I'm naked, but I front it out, literally, and make my way to the bathroom.

'Oh lord,' I whisper, as I sit on the toilet. 'What have I done?'

Then I wail again as I wash my hands and see myself in the mirror for the first time this morning.

It's a good job Noah hadn't replaced his glasses before he kissed me just now, or beautiful would have been the last adjective he'd have been using to describe me. Hideous, gruesome or even scary might have been a better way to describe how I looked this morning.

I had smudged mascara under my eyes, making me look like Noah had punched me rather than seduced me last night, and my hair – well, it was quite clear that it hadn't been brushed after we'd arrived back from the beach yesterday, and after a night of bedroom gymnastics now looked gale-force wind-swept. The overall effect looked like I was auditioning for a part as one of Macbeth's witches rather than the romantic lead in a new rom-com.

I tidy myself up, wrap a bath towel around me and head back to the bedroom, but Noah has gone. Not without making the bed, I note – this was more like the Noah I knew. He must have replaced his glasses!

I hear him climbing back up the stairs and he appears at the bedroom door. 'Breakfast?' he asks cheerily, pushing his glasses up his nose.

'I'm not sure what I have in . . .'

'Not a lot, I just looked. I'll pop down the road and get us something. Back in a bit.'

'Sure,' I agree, grinning manically, but Noah kisses me anyway before bounding back down the stairs two at a time.

You have a lot of energy, I'll give you that, I think, and I grin.

By the time Noah returns, I've got myself dressed into some blue jeans, a striped red and white T-shirt and my flip-flops.

I've opened the balcony doors to let some fresh air in, and I've attempted to organise some breakfast things for whatever Noah was going to bring back from his excursion.

'I just popped to the bakery,' he says, laying some paper bags on the table. 'I got some Danish pastries and two coffees – cappuccino, isn't it?'

I nod. 'This is very kind of you.'

'Nonsense, least I could do after, well ... you know?'

I nod and busy myself with transferring the breakfast on to a tray.

'It's funny,' Noah says, thinking, 'Ant was very insistent that I buy a Belgian bun as well as the Danish pastries. Why would he say that, do you think?'

I smile. Word sure spread fast in St Felix ...

'No idea. Shall we eat on the balcony?' I ask brightly. 'It's a lovely sunny morning again.'

'Sounds perfect.'

We eat our pastries and drink our coffees in the morning sun. We don't talk about last night as such, only discussing Jess and Malachi and the barbecue. There may not be an elephant in the room while we sit out here in the fresh sea air, but it feels like there's a huge something on the balcony with us that neither of us dare mention.

'Thanks again for offering to keep Daisy-Rose in your back yard,' I say, finishing off the last of my coffee. 'That was good of you.'

'Maybe I won't have to offer my services any more,' Noah says, smiling knowingly.

'How do you mean?'

'Well, I thought you might consider staying a while longer in St Felix now ...'

'Why would you think that?' I ask foolishly.

Noah's expectant expression diminishes slightly. 'I don't know ... perhaps because of what happened last night? I don't know about you, but that meant something to me. It's not something I have a habit of doing, I can assure you.'

Oh lord ...

'I thought we were getting on well, Ana. I really like you.'

'And I like you too, Noah, but—'

'—but not enough to want to stick around – I get it. Sorry, silly mistake to make.' Noah looks down at the half-eaten pastry in his hand. He lays it down carefully on his plate, still looking at it.

'No, it's not silly,' I protest. 'You just took me unawares, that's all. I wasn't expecting you to say that.'

Noah glances up at me now. 'What *were* you expecting me to say then? Thanks for last night, I've got what I wanted, now I'm out of here?'

That *was* more like what I was used to.

'No, of course not. But ... my stay in St Felix ... it was never going to be permanent, was it?'

'Apparently not.' Noah stands up. 'Perhaps I'd better leave. I've made enough of a fool of myself already. If I stay and keep talking I might end up looking like a complete idiot!' He makes his way towards the open French windows.

'No, please don't go,' I say, grabbing his arm. 'Like I said, you took me by surprise.'

'I knew I shouldn't have listened to Jess,' Noah mumbles, pulling his arm away as he stomps inside.

'What do you mean "listened to Jess"?' I call, following him. 'What's she been saying?' I chase after Noah as he heads for the stairs.

300

'It *really* doesn't matter now,' Noah calls, as he disappears down the staircase. 'You've made your feelings very clear. I should be grateful to you – at least you haven't strung me along.'

'Noah, stop it, *please*! It does matter.' I thunder down the stairs after him, but my foot lands awkwardly in my flip-flop and I stumble down the last couple of steps, landing in a heap on the hard kitchen floor.

'Ouch!' I cry, just as Noah reaches for the front door handle. He turns to see me rubbing my foot.

'Are you okay?' he asks, rushing back. 'Have you hurt yourself?'

'Nothing broken,' I say, attempting to stand up.

Noah silently takes hold of me and helps me up.

'I'm fine, really,' I tell him. 'I thought I might have hurt my ankle but it seems fine now I've put weight on it. It's just my pride that's a bit bruised, and probably my bum.'

'I think that might be my problem too,' Noah says, moving away from me now I'm upright again.

'Your bum or your pride?' I ask, smiling a little.

To my enormous relief, I see a half smile twitch at Noah's lips too. 'The latter.'

'I'm sorry I didn't say the right thing upstairs,' I tell him. 'You took me by surprise.'

'I know – you keep saying that. Look, don't be sorry. Your answer was honest, and I always appreciate honesty. Even if I don't always like what I hear. I read the situation incorrectly, that's all. As often happens to me in matters of the heart, I got it wrong. I should be the one apologising.'

'Don't start that again! I thought I'd cured you of saying sorry.'

Noah gazes thoughtfully at me. 'Ana, you've cured me of

301

much more than that. If you only knew how much you've actually done for me.'

Then he turns and quietly lets himself out of the door, while I can only stand and watch him go.

Thirty-Seven

'Hey, Malachi,' I say sadly, as I open the cottage door later that morning. I'd rushed downstairs hoping it would be Noah returning, and I feel guilty that I'm disappointed it's only Malachi and Ralph.

'Not interrupting anything, am I?' Malachi says, peering behind me.

'No, why would you be?'

'I just wondered if yer man Noah was still here. I got your note,' he says, pulling a piece of paper from his pocket. '*Very* nice!'

'No, he's not,' I reply gloomily. 'Do you want to come in?'

'What's wrong with you?' Malachi says, beckoning Ralph inside and closing the door behind them. 'I thought you'd be all rainbows and unicorns this morning. *Oh* . . . was his unicorn a little disappointing last night?'

'Malachi! Is that all you think about?'

'Well—' Malachi begins, but I cut him off.

'Forget it, I don't want to know, and for your information, Noah was amazing last night.'

'*Amazing* … High praise indeed. So where is he now – resting?'

'I don't know, probably at his shop.'

Malachi scans my face. 'Uh-oh, that doesn't sound like the happy afterglow of someone who's had an *amazing* night. What happened?'

'Come upstairs,' I say, beckoning him towards the sitting room, 'and I'll tell you.'

'Ah,' is all Malachi says, when I've finished telling him a very condensed version of the events of last night, and a very detailed one of what had happened this morning.

The French windows are still open, but we've retreated indoors because grey clouds are beginning to multiply and join together in the skies now the tide has changed direction.

'*Ah* – is that all you've got to say?' I ask incredulously. 'Usually I can't stop you talking and giving me your opinion.'

'A man's pride can be easily dented,' Malachi replies, scrunching up his face, 'and it sounds like you've knocked a great big wedge in Noah's.'

'Why? I didn't say he'd done anything wrong. In fact, quite the opposite …'

'All right, enough details! No, you didn't say that, but you did turn him down.'

'No, I didn't … I just panicked a bit when he seemed to assume I'd be staying here in St Felix. Like us spending the night together automatically meant we were a couple.'

'Did he actually say he wanted to be a couple?'

'No, but he asked if I might consider staying on longer.'

Malachi looks thoughtful for a moment.

'Why don't you?' he suddenly asks.

'Why don't I what?'

'Stay on a bit longer here when Daisy-Rose is finished. What's the rush to get back to London? You told me yourself your job is very freelance, and you can work from wherever you need to as long as the work gets done. Why not work from here?'

'I— I don't know. I do have to go back to London some-times, though, to oversee projects occasionally.'

'We're not exactly in outer space here, are we? There are trains, roads, even flights if you needed to be somewhere superfast.'

'But I'd have nowhere to live,' I say, desperately trying to think of reasons why this idea isn't practical. 'I can only keep the cottage until the end of the week, then some other holiday-makers will be moving in.'

As I hear myself say this, I immediately feel very sad at the thought of leaving this little house with its quirky living arrangements and beautiful view through the very windows we're sitting next to.

'There are other cottages, Ana, and you know it. Yes, a lot of the property here is let to holiday-makers, but your rent must be extortionate in London, so even if you do have to pay a little over the odds, compared to renting there it's got to be an improvement. Unless you don't *want* to stay ...'

I think quickly what it would be like to live here, and it doesn't take a lot of thought to realise that I've felt happier in the couple of weeks I've spent in St Felix than in the whole two years I've been renting my flat in North London.

'Yes, but still,' I add, avoiding his question. 'I can't just up sticks and move, can I?'

'Why?' Malachi demands. 'Tell me one thing that's stopping you? You have very few people you can call friends where you are now. What little family you have lives mostly in the south of the country, so it won't be a lot harder to see them when you need or want to, will it?'

How did he know that, I wonder? I'm sure I haven't talked to him about my family.

'And think of Daisy's boys. How much would they love coming to stay with Aunty Ana by the seaside? You could give them some magnificent holidays here.'

Now that thought does cheer me. Jacob and Harry would love it here; we could have some wonderful times if they came to stay, and I could give Peter a break occasionally too.

'But if I did come to live here that doesn't mean Noah and I necessarily have to be in a relationship.'

'No one said it did. You obviously aren't that keen on him.'

'I never said that. I do quite like him ... Actually, no, I like him a lot.'

'And so, what's holding you back?'

I hesitate – it sounded silly, even in my head.

'He's too nice.'

'How can someone be *too* nice?'

'I'm just not used to it, that's all, and it's not just Noah, everyone here in St Felix has been lovely to me – you, Ant and Dec, Jake, Jess, even Rita from the pub. Everyone is too kind.' I feel myself welling up a little, and I turn away from him to compose myself.

'You can't have too much kindness in your life, Ana,' Malachi says softly. 'If only there were more places like St Felix in the world, it would make my job so much easier.'

'What do you mean *your* job?'

'Spreading sunshine into people's lives, of course,' he says quickly, then he winks. 'A bit of Malachi charm works wonders – that and my infamous coffee-making.'

I have to smile. 'Yeah, yeah. Although I must say you've been my saviour since I've been here, Malachi. I'm not just talking about Daisy-Rose – you've sat and you've listened to me, given me advice – actual good advice, not just some text book nonsense, and most importantly, you've been my friend.'

Malachi looks quite touched.

'I've never had a male friend before, not a platonic one anyway. You're like having a gay best friend. Except you're not.'

'No, I'm not, not this time anyway.' He pauses to think, as if he's considering saying something. I'm about to ask him what he means by *this time* when he speaks again. 'I've really enjoyed spending time with you too, Ana,' he says, looking earnestly at me. 'It doesn't always work out that way, but this time you've been a delightful charge.'

'Why do you keep saying *this time*? What's going on?'

'How are those signs coming on?' Malachi asks, standing up and going outside to the balcony.

'I haven't seen any lately. The last one was at Juliet's house when she said she'd been named after a Dire Straits song from the eighties. But don't change the subject, what do you mean by *this time*?'

'So you'll definitely think about it then?' he asks, leaning on the balcony railings and looking up. 'Staying in St Felix? I really think you should.'

I get up now and join him outside.

'I'll think about it, okay?' I reply. 'But I have to do something else first.'

'What's that?'

'Make peace with Noah. Apparently I've dented his pride . . . ' I look wryly across at Malachi.

'Just my opinion,' Malachi says, holding up his hands. 'But I

307

think if you can make peace with Noah, everything will work out just fine for both of you.'

'How can even *you* possibly know that?'

Malachi looks up into the sky again, and I follow his gaze.

'Whoa – how is that possible?' I say, staring up at the sky.

'Anything is possible if you believe, Ana.'

Malachi and I stand side by side on the balcony, gazing up in wonderment at the clouds, which have managed to form a perfect 8 and a perfect 0 above us.

Thirty-Eight

I walk towards Noah's Ark later that day still thinking about the clouds.

I'd never seen anything like it – it had been truly amazing. A complete coincidence, of course, I'm trying to tell myself as I walk. Clouds made funny shapes all the time, and it just so happened that these clouds had formed something I was searching for at the very moment I was looking at them.

Some people would call that a sign …

No, I shake my head. It wasn't possible. But what about all the other times that eighties things had popped up when I'd been wondering if I was on the right track? Was that just coincidence too?

Ah, where are you when I need your spiritual input, Daisy? I think, glancing up at the sky again. *You'd have definitely had your own take on this. One I would have likely pooh-poohed though. I never took much notice when you tried to tell me about these things – I sort of wish I had now.*

Even when Daisy had been very ill in bed one day and had tried to talk to me about an afterlife, I'd tried to change the subject …

'Thanks for taking the boys out today, Ana – both Peter and I really appreciate it.'

'You know I enjoy it just as much as they do, if not more!' I smile at my friend propped up on several white pillows in her bed. It was only a double, but Daisy's frail tiny frame made it look super king-size she took up so little space in it. 'How are you feeling today?'

'Not good,' Daisy admits, which I'm surprised to hear her say. She always tried to put a positive spin on things however bad they were, especially her illness. 'I don't think I've got much longer, Ana.'

'No, don't you be saying that,' I tell her, getting up and pretending to arrange the flowers the boys had chosen for her this afternoon: pink roses and tiny white alstroemeria. A bit traditional for me, but they had liked them and thought their mother would too. 'You'll live for ever.'

'Sit down, Ana, please,' she says, and I notice how much of an effort it is for her to tap the bedclothes.

I do as she asks.

'Now, I know we've discussed what I want to happen when I've gone regarding the boys and my funeral.'

I look away. I hated talking about this.

'Ana, please listen.'

I reluctantly turn back.

'But I want to tell you something else. I know you don't believe in any of my "nonsense" as you like to call it, but I do. When we die, Ana, it's not the end, I'm convinced of it. Our spirits go on to do even greater work than they've done here on earth, helping those that need a little push in the right direction and guiding those in need back on to the right path.'

This was making me feel decidedly edgy, but I continue to listen to my friend. Who was I to deny her this when she was going through so much?

'I know you don't believe, Ana, and that's fine, really it is – we can't all be the same and the world would be much poorer for it if we were, but I'm going to make you a promise, my friend. When I die— No, let me continue,' she says, when I try to interrupt. 'When I die, I'll be looking down on you and Peter and the boys. I'll watch out for you and I'll help you if you need me. I don't know how I'll do this, Ana, but I just know I will. I'll send you a sign to let you know I'm there. I've tried to talk to you about signs before, haven't I?'

I nod.

'A lot of people only see white feathers as being a sign that an angel or a spirit, or whatever you want to call them, is present, but there are so many ways of being sent reassurance that you're doing the right thing or are on the right path – you just have to look for them.'

'Can you make sure your signs are fifty pound notes?' I ask, smiling at her. 'It would be really handy to find a few of those lying around every now and then.'

Daisy smiles now too. 'I'll do my best,' she says. 'But I will send you a sign that I'm still with you, I promise. Don't forget to look for them, will you?'

'I won't,' I agree, mostly to appease her.

'Promise me, Ana?'

'I promise.'

*

I stop for a moment on Harbour Street and stare up at the sky.

'Is it you?' I whisper, as holiday-makers surround me and

people have to sidestep to pass me by. 'Are you sending me the eighties signs to let me know I'm on the right track?'

'Are you okay?' someone asks, and I'm forced to come back to earth again.

'Oh, hello,' I say to Amber from the florist. 'Sorry, I'm causing an obstruction.'

'It's fine,' she says calmly. 'Sometimes you have to stop and think when you need to.'

'What's that?' I ask, noticing a floral arrangement in her hand.

'This? It's a delivery. It's for a customer's eightieth birthday. They're holidaying in Seagull Cottage up the road, so it's easier for me to walk it to them than get the van out.'

'It's pretty,' I say, looking at the flowers in the arrangement.

'Yes. It's a bit too traditional for me – roses and alstroemeria – but it's what they wanted. The two together mean love and friendship. It's what we specialise in at The Daisy Chain – flowers with special meanings.'

'I think their meaning is spot on,' I agree, still staring at the flowers. 'Spot on for me anyway.'

Amber doesn't seem to think there's anything odd in my statement, and she simply smiles. 'That's good to know, Ana. I'm so pleased I could help.' Then she continues on her way along the street, and I, with a big smile on my face, continue in the direction of Noah's Ark.

'Hi, Jess,' I call, as I open the door of the antiques shop, and as usual the bell rattles above me. I walk over to the counter where she's cleaning a silver tea service. 'Is Noah about?'

'Ana, it's you,' Jess says, looking a little flustered. 'Er, no, Noah's gone down to Marazion – some house clearance thingy.'

'Oh.' With my newly found buoyant mood I'd been all

312

geared up to apologise to Noah and hopefully carry on where we left off, if he still wanted to.

'He should be back soon, though?' Jess adds hopefully. 'Do you want to wait?'

'Erm ... ' I look around. I wanted to see Noah, but I didn't really want to spend the sunny afternoon in an antiques shop. 'I might pop back later.'

Jess looks downcast. 'It might be just as well,' she shrugs. 'He wasn't in a very good mood before he left.'

'That might have been my fault, I'm afraid.'

'Ah ... I did wonder, but I didn't like to ask. Noah was in no mood for chit-chat earlier.'

'No, I'm sure he wasn't. I think I offended him this morning.'

'Oh, really?' Jess's ears prick up. 'So he did stay over at yours after the barbecue then? We ... I mean *I* thought as much.'

'It's fine, Jess. I'm sure you and Malachi discussed where we'd gone when you awoke on the beach and found we weren't there.'

'*Yes*, that would be it ... on the beach.' Jess grins at me, her eyes wide.

But my eyes narrow. 'What is it with you two?' I ask. '*Had* you met Malachi before last night?'

Jess's eyes widen even further and she looks up at the ceiling.

'Er ... Yeah, sort of.'

'When?'

'Er ... in the pub. The pub ... yes, that's it. I didn't remember him to begin with, though – I think I'd had a bit too much that night.' She rolls her eyes dramatically and lifts an imaginary glass.

'But he remembered you?'

'I think so. Maybe you'd best ask him?'

313

'I will.'

'So . . . Noah stayed at yours last night, eh?' Jess says, leading the conversation back to Noah. She winks at me. 'I'm glad. It's about time he got some action.'

'*Jess!*'

'It's true. I've never even seen Noah *look* at a woman in all the time I've been here. Not in the way he looks at you anyway. The man is besotted with you.'

I feel my cheeks redden. 'That's a bit strong, isn't it?'

'Nope. He was smitten the moment he bumped into you eating your fish and chips, I reckon. All he needed was a little push in the right direction. Actually make that a great big shove!' She smiles knowingly and folds her arms.

'Noah said you were always keen for us to spend time together. Why is that?'

'I just want to see him happy, and I reckon you, Ana, could be just the person to make that happen. The guy needs a break after what happened to him.'

'What did happen to him?' I ask. 'Noah won't discuss it. He just closes up when I try to talk to him about it.'

Jess hesitates, obviously debating whether she should let me know or not. She looks around the shop. It's not particularly busy, and as far as I can see there are only a lady and a small child looking at some china figurines in the far corner.

'I'm not sure whether I should be the one to tell you,' she whispers anxiously. 'It might not be right. They might not like it.'

'Who might not?'

Jess wrings her hands together and hops uneasily from one foot to the other.

'Please, Jess. I might be able to help. You obviously know something?'

But my plea is broken by the sound of the shop bell making a noise; this time it has a half rattle, half ring to it, as though it's recovering its voice after a bout of laryngitis. Jess stares with alarm at the bell, and we watch the elderly lady and the child leaving through the door.

I look twice at the lady – isn't that the same woman who woke me on my journey to St Felix? It sure looks a lot like her. I'm about to say something when the little girl speaks.

'Every time you hear a bell ring an angel gets their wings,' the little girl sings, looking at the bell above her head, and I forget about the woman for a moment and smile. The line was from one of Daisy's favourite movies – she always made us watch *It's a Wonderful Life* every Christmas. I stare silently at the woman and the child as they leave the shop, but before the door has time to close Noah appears in the entrance. He looks surprised and then annoyed to see me, and I'm shocked at how much his annoyance hurts.

'Noah!' I say, wanting to rush over and hug him. 'You're back. Jess said you were in Marazion.'

'I was,' Noah says, calmly closing the shop door. 'The house clearance turned out to be a bit of a dud. Is Jess helping you this afternoon?'

I nod vaguely.

'That's good,' he says, and before I have time to say anything, he walks straight past me across the shop towards his office. 'I'll be in here doing the accounts if anyone should want me, Jess,' he calls from the door. 'Don't disturb me unless it's important please.' And he closes the door firmly behind him.

I look helplessly at Jess, but she doesn't seem as thrown by Noah's behaviour as I am.

'I'd say you were pretty important.' She grins, nodding in the direction of the office. 'Wouldn't you?'

I take a deep breath and march across the shop towards the office, then I pause just a moment before knocking forcefully on the door.

'Yes?' Noah's tired voice asks from inside. 'What is it, Jess?'

'It's not Jess,' I say, opening the door. 'It's me.' I step inside the room before he has a chance to turn me away, then I close the door behind me.

Noah is sitting behind his desk, and I notice he has yet to start work on any accounts. 'What do you want, Ana? I think we said everything earlier, didn't we?'

I shake my head. 'I didn't tell you how sorry I am for . . .' I hesitate; how to say this? '. . . letting you down.'

Noah looks back at me, his expression not giving anything away. 'You didn't let me down. I just got the wrong end of the stick, that's all. It's fine, it happens.'

'No, it's not fine.' I go over to his desk and sit down in the chair opposite. 'I was a bit shocked, that's all, and so I wasn't honest with you about my true feelings.'

'Which are?'

'Which are . . . that I'm truly flattered that someone should want me to stay somewhere to be with them. It's never happened before. Usually it's completely the opposite.'

Noah's stark expression lifts slightly, and I see the compassion and kindness I was used to seeing in his eyes begin to flood back into them.

'You surprise me,' he says, not moving in his seat.

'It's true. And for someone to ask me to stay with them in a place I actually like is a double bonus. And I do like it here in

316

St Felix. It's so beautiful and joyful, and being here makes *you* feel beautiful and joyful too.'

'So you do actually *want* to stay then?' Noah asks, as if he needs to confirm everything so he doesn't get it wrong again.

'I think so – if I can make it work I do. If I can find a place to stay and I can continue to freelance from here then, yes, I think I'd very much like living here.'

Noah nods. 'I'm glad you changed your mind. If that's all?'

His tone surprises me. *What have I said now?*

'What is it? I've just said I'd like to stay here, haven't I?'

Noah stands up and goes over to the door.

'Yes, you've told me you'd like to stay if you can find somewhere to live and make your job work, and how beautiful it will be living here, and those reasons are all admirable and I'm pleased for you, really I am.'

'But . . . ?' I just don't get why he's being all weird.

'But it's quite clear I don't feature in any of those reasons. So, although I'm delighted for you that you'll be staying on in St Felix, forgive me if I don't get out a bottle of champagne to celebrate.'

He opens the door.

I glare at him for a moment, and then I stand up and march across the office. Noah obviously thinks I'm going to head straight out of the door because he opens it a little wider for my exit. But instead I grab the door and slam it shut.

'Now you listen here!' I tell him, seizing him by the shoulders and slamming him up against the wall.

I'm not sure who is more surprised by this action, Noah or I. Noah isn't exactly small, and pushing his tall, muscular body up against the wall has taken more strength than even I knew

I had. I continue to summon this strength as I speak to Noah.

'It's taken a lot of guts to come here and tell you all this,' I say, removing my hands slowly from his shoulders. 'Admitting I was wrong and opening my heart up to you. So the least you can do is show me some respect by actually understanding what I'm trying to tell you.'

'Which is . . . ?' Noah asks, straightening his glasses where they've been knocked a little to the side with the force of my shove.

'That I care about you,' I say, my voice calming, as my heart quickens. 'That I like spending time with you, and I'd like to spend more time getting to know the real Noah, the one you keep hidden from everyone.'

I blink as I look up at Noah. That speech was as much of a shock to me as the physical force that had spilled from me moments ago.

'The real Noah? I don't know who you've been spending time with but there's only one of me.' Noah smiles, obviously trying to lighten the tension between us.

'No, there isn't only one of you. There's antiques shop Noah, and then there's bedroom Noah, and then the one I know the least about, policeman Noah.'

'You make me sound like a children's book character.' Noah smiles again, but instead of smiling back I find myself enraged again.

'Stop it,' I tell him. 'Stop trying to hide from me. You can't expect me to open up to you and then you just pull away again.'

I stare up at him, suddenly realising that what Noah says next is going to be crucial to what happens between us. He seems to realise the same.

'Policeman Noah is the someone I used to be,' he says quietly.

I stand back from him slightly to give him space. 'You saw a little of him in Brighton, but I stopped being him years ago.'

'Why, though? You seemed so happy when you were back with Simon and Adam.'

Noah pulls himself away from the wall and proceeds to prowl around the room.

'If I tell you, I'll tell you quickly . . . but there's to be no pity.' He looks at me, waiting for my agreement.

I nod.

'Take a seat then,' Noah says, gesturing to the red leather armchair I'd sat in the first time I was here in this office.

I do as he asks.

'As you know,' Noah says, suddenly becoming very formal as he paces around his office, 'I used to be in the police force in Brighton.'

I nod again.

'Then I was offered promotion to the Met in London. With hindsight, I probably should have never left Brighton – I was happy there,' he adds, almost wistfully. Then he shakes his head, forcing himself back into his formal mode again. 'But promotion is promotion and so I moved to London.'

'Sure,' I say, waiting for him to continue. It was odd sitting here in the leather chair with Noah pacing around me. He was being so proper and official I almost felt like I was being questioned for my story in a police interview room.

'So, to cut a long story short,' Noah continues, not making eye contact with me, 'I was undercover on quite a big job. Drugs,' he says firmly, as though that explained everything. 'But then things went a bit off course.'

'Go on.'

'My partner, who was also undercover with me . . . they . . .

319

Well, they . . . ' Noah stops pacing and swallows hard. 'They double-crossed me,' he says rapidly, as though getting it out in the open quickly will make it easier to hear.

'And?' I ask gently, acutely aware this was something very painful Noah was dragging up just to please me.

'Let's just say the gang I was undercover with didn't take too kindly to the news I was actually a police officer and not one of them.'

'What did they do?' I ask quietly, knowing whatever it was it wasn't going to be good.

'They roughed me up a bit.'

'A bit?'

'Okay, a lot. They beat me so badly they left me for dead, and abandoned my body in a back alley behind some bins.'

My heart twists inside me as my hand covers my mouth. 'Oh god, no.'

Noah nods, looking at me now.

'But you survived. How?'

'I don't know really, it's all a bit hazy. I must have fallen in and out of consciousness for a while, but then I think someone found me and called the emergency services. The next thing I knew I was in hospital – intensive care, a drip, the whole caboodle,' Noah explains matter-of-factly, but I'm still horrified.

'What do you mean you *think* someone found you? Didn't they wait with you? Tell their story to the police?'

'No, no one could ever trace them. But I knew someone was there, Ana, because they spoke to me for ages, kept telling me it was going to be all right and to hang on in there. They saved my life, but I was never able to thank them. It was like they just disappeared, right before the paramedics turned up. They said I was on my own when they got there.'

320

This was so awful. I couldn't bear the thought of Noah lying abandoned in an alley all alone, afraid and in pain. I wonder who the person might have been who'd kept him going, and why they'd left without anyone seeing them.

Noah is still looking uncomfortable. He swallows again, and I sense there is more to come.

'What is it, what haven't you told me?'

'You should probably know,' he says calmly in a low voice, 'that the partner who double-crossed me wasn't just my partner at work, she was my partner at home too.'

My eyes open wide. I can barely believe any of this, let alone this latest bit of information. 'You were double-crossed by your *girlfriend*? No way!'

Noah nods silently.

I take a moment to digest this. Noah's girlfriend had been the one to blow his cover? That had to be *the* worst form of betrayal. She must have known what would happen to him. What sort of scum would do that to any human being, let alone Noah? He was so kind and lovely.

'I should add,' Noah says, actually looking ashamed, 'we shouldn't have even been working on a case together. It's not only frowned upon in the force, it's actually forbidden. I should have trusted my instincts.'

'No!' I cry. 'You mustn't blame yourself. It wasn't your fault. You trusted someone and they let you down. It was her, not you.'

This whole story had explained so much to me about Noah, why he was anxious and edgy in one situation, and then so confident and happy in another. The self-assured, easy-going Noah was the real him, the mouse-like nervous Noah was a persona that had been forced upon him by someone else's selfish and ultimately vicious act. No wonder he was slow to trust, and so hurt when his trust had been thrown back in his face.

By me.

I feel my hands ball into tight fists at my side.

Noah sees me. 'There's no point in you getting angry about it,' he says, smiling kindly at me. 'It was a long time ago now. My life has moved on to better places, and' – he pauses and comes over to me, kneeling down by my chair – 'better people.'

'I'm not only cross because of what happened to you,' I tell him, my eyes full of tears. 'I'm angry with myself for letting you down again.'

'What do you mean? You haven't let me down.'

'I did after we spent the night together. You put your trust in me, and I didn't tell you what I really felt. I was too scared to.'

'Ana,' he says, cupping my face in one of his hands. 'That doesn't matter now. You've been honest with me, and I've tried to be honest with you about everything. Now you know why I am the way I am, do you still want to be with me?'

I shake my head. 'You silly thing, of course I do! What do I need to do to show you . . . This?' I say, leaning forward and kissing him very firmly and extremely passionately on the lips. 'Well?' I ask, eventually pulling back from our kiss to look at him. 'How about that?'

Noah grins. 'Let's just try that again,' he says, pulling me to him this time. 'I need a tiny bit more reassurance.'

While Noah and I kiss again, I'm aware of a tiny bell ringing somewhere, but so caught up am I in our passionate embrace, I can't tell if it's in Noah's office or the shop.

The ringing stops, and then there's a different sort of ringing, but this time it's definitely the shop's telephone that's making the noise, because the tone is more muffled than before.

'*Noah!*' someone cries, banging frantically on the other side of the door. 'Noah, get out here quick. Juliet is on the phone, and she says she needs to talk to you about Frankie and Lou.'

Thirty-Nine

I'm silent as I stare at the sight in front of me. It's so beautiful and so perfect I'm almost lost for words.

'Something wrong?' Malachi asks, watching me. 'You're very quiet.'

'No, nothing is wrong, quite the opposite, in fact. Everything is very, very right.'

We're standing in the backyard of Bob's Bangers looking at Daisy-Rose, but it's not the Daisy-Rose that I'd gazed upon when I first arrived in St Felix and stood with Malachi on this very spot – this vehicle is a very different one indeed.

Instead of the rusty, ramshackle, worn-out old VW camper van which I'd wondered about saving at all, I'm looking at a flawless, shiny, sparkling reincarnation.

'Malachi,' I say, running my hand over Daisy-Rose's metallic burgundy paint that's sparkling under the bright midday sun. 'How have you done this?'

'A lot of sweat, a few tears and a smidgeon of Malachi magic,' he says, grinning. 'You like it then?'

'Oh my goodness, it's amazing. The transformation is

incredible. Look at this chrome,' I say, hardly daring to touch it in case I leave fingerprints. 'It's so shiny, and her new number plate – I adore that – where did you find it?'

Malachi taps the side of his nose as we gaze upon the number plate at the front of the vehicle: ANA 80.

'It's perfect,' I say, grinning at it. 'And those tiny daisies you've painted on her too. They're so pretty. I love them.'

'I thought you might,' Malachi says, looking pleased. 'Now do you want to see inside?' he asks, sliding open the side door. 'It's pretty neat, even if I say so myself.'

We climb in together after Malachi has opened up the matching striped pop-up top in the middle of Daisy-Rose's cream-coloured roof, so we can stand up easily inside without hitting our heads on the ceiling. He then proceeds to demonstrate tiny hidden cupboards, a compact little fridge and a spotless hob.

'And the bed,' he says, pulling at a small leather handle attached to one of the back seats, 'is right here.'

Before my eyes a huge, very comfortable-looking mattress appears made up of the back and base of the red leather seat. It fills the width of the van, and Malachi informs me it's the full-size rock 'n' roll bed we talked about. 'You'll need to get your own bedding,' he adds, almost apologetically. 'I didn't quite have time for that. Come on,' he says, jumping up on to the mattress. 'Try it out.'

For once I don't hesitate. I understand how Malachi works now, and I'm more than happy to be his friend. I feel comfortable in his presence, and more importantly I trust him. Eagerly I climb on to the mattress next to him.

'This is great,' I say, bouncing up and down a little. 'I bet this will be super-comfortable to sleep on.' I look around at the interior of the van again. It's absolutely spotless. 'Malachi, I still don't understand how you've managed to do all this in such a short space of time, but I'm so pleased you have. She looks amazing, she really does. Not only have you done me proud, but you've done Daisy-Rose and Lou proud too.'

Malachi looks touched by my words.

'You should have a drive in her later, before you take her on her big trip tomorrow,' he suggests. 'She won't need too much getting used to, but she will feel quite different to begin with if you're used to things like power steering.'

'Yes, I'll definitely do that. Will you come with me?'

'On your test drive, yes. But not to see Frankie – I think it should be you and Noah who do that, don't you?'

It seemed like forever since Juliet had rung the antiques shop a few days ago to speak to Noah, but the moment was still etched in my mind as clearly as if it had happened only minutes ago.

Noah and I had stared at each other for a few seconds before he had dashed out of the door and across the office with me close behind.

Then for an infuriating few minutes where I could only hear one side of the conversation, Noah had spoken to Juliet, nodding and smiling at various intervals, leading me to pray that we had at last found someone that might lead us to Lou.

'Well?' I ask, when he finally puts the phone down. 'What did she say?'

'Frankie is alive and well, and living in ... you'll never guess?' Noah teases.

'Where?' I demanded, jumping from one foot to another in anticipation.

'Newlyn.'

'Newlyn! But that's like what, half an hour from here?'

Noah nods.

'So were we right about Juliet? She was lying when she told us our Frankie wasn't her grandfather?'

'Yep, we were spot on, but she had good reason to lie. She thought the reason we were trying to find her grandfather, who apparently has been "on the run for years" as she put it, was to catch up with him for something he did in 1990.'

'What?' I ask, astonished to hear this. The story was getting stranger by the minute.

'Remember I said that Johnson's Electronics had closed down in shady circumstances?'

'Yes.'

'Well, apparently that was Frankie – he'd been misappropriating the company's funds to such a degree that he thought a prison sentence was on the cards, so he went AWOL.'

'How?'

'He simply disappeared, took on a new identity, came to live in Cornwall and he's been here ever since. Only his family know his true whereabouts.'

'So all this time we've been looking for a criminal?' I ask, trying and failing to hide the disappointment in my voice.

'*Well.*' Noah screws up his nose. 'Yes and no. The reason Frankie was taking money from his business was to fund some specialist treatment for his wife abroad. Remember Lucy told us Juliet's grandmother died of breast cancer? Apparently the treatment she was getting here just wasn't making any difference. So in desperation he took money from his business, money he really wasn't entitled to, but sadly he got caught and the rest of the firm's directors decided to press charges.'

'Really? Bastards!' I exclaim. 'How mean of them, they

could have shown him a little compassion.' I think of the photo of Frankie finishing the London Marathon with his arms around the rest of his team. How I hoped they weren't the same men who turned on him in his hour of need. 'Poor Frankie.'

'Yeah, you never know who you can trust,' Noah says, and I realise that the story has struck a chord with him too.

'So that's why Juliet became all agitated when we starting digging around,' I say, thinking how us suddenly turning up must have seemed to Frankie's granddaughter. 'She thought we were still chasing after her grandfather for a crime he committed nearly thirty years ago.'

'Yep, and when it was someone from the local police who asked her colleague to let me look at the old newspapers, that only made her suspicions worse.'

'Oh!' I say suddenly, realising something else. 'Is that why the women were running for Breast Cancer Research? In memory of Frankie's wife, Juliet's grandmother?'

Noah nods. 'Wait, how do you know it's in memory of? I didn't tell you she didn't survive.'

'Lucy said at the race they were running in memory of Juliet's grandmother. Plus,' I continue, as something else pops into my mind. 'There was a postcard. I didn't really think anything of it at the time, but Lou wrote to Frankie sympathising with him on the death of his wife – how she knew, I don't know, but she seemed to keep up with everything that was going on with him over the years. So why did Juliet suddenly decide to tell us about Frankie? Is that what his name is now?'

Noah nods. 'Yes, apparently he's always been nicknamed that. The JFK thing about the president was just a ruse on Juliet's part. Apparently she decided to tell Frankie all about us and the postcards – he'd been away for a few days and that's why it took her so long to get back to us. He was interested immediately and wants to meet us ... well, you in particular. He'd like us to bring the postcards and the camper van, if it's finished.'

'The camper van as well as the postcards – that's odd, isn't it? So he must remember Lou then?'

'According to Juliet, yes, he does, very fondly.'

I go to the door of the antiques shop and take a deep breath of fresh sea air. At last I was going to be able to take the cards back to the person who they had been meant for in the first place.

'Are you all right?' Noah asks, coming over to stand by me in the doorway.

'They're going home, Noah,' I say, tears forming in my eyes. I turn to him. 'Finally Lou's postcards are going home.'

And as we stand hugging in the doorway of Noah's Ark antiques, as clear as anything the shop bell rings above our heads.

We both look up.

'How is that working again after all this time?' Noah asks in amazement. 'I never fixed it?'

'Miracles happen, Noah,' I say, smiling at the bell. 'They really do.'

Forty

'That's it. Perfect,' Malachi says, as I attempt to steer Daisy-Rose around the local streets. 'I told you you'd pick it up eventually.'

Driving Daisy-Rose felt like I was driving a big old bus. Her cream steering wheel was wide and stiff to turn, and her gearbox – although perfectly restored by Malachi – needed quite some effort to move through the gears. Her engine was noisier than I was used to and her suspension made for a bumpy ride, but even with all her imperfections I felt a huge sense of enjoyment and pleasure while driving her.

Fellow drivers flash their lights and toot their horns in greeting, and pedestrians wave to us from the pavement, their happy faces lighting up our journey with smiles.

'That's it,' Malachi says, as I ease my way back into the yard. 'Easy does it.'

I pull up in the back yard of Bob's Bangers and pull on the handbrake, then I turn the key in the ignition so Daisy-Rose's gentle purring is quietened for the time being.

'What did you think?' Malachi asks from his spot next to me on the long leather seat.

'It's pretty special driving her, that's for sure. I don't mean the actual drive itself – I mean people's reaction to her. It's so friendly.'

'Yes, there's definitely something about a camper van that makes people smile. They're a very happy vehicle, so people enjoy seeing them as much as their owners enjoy driving them.'

'Thank you again, Malachi, for doing all this for me. I know I was paying you, and it's your job and everything, but I feel that you've put a lot of you into this transformation and that makes it extra special. Especially to me.'

Malachi looks visibly moved at my words. 'When you say transformation, you're not only talking about Daisy-Rose, are you?' he asks quietly.

'How do you mean?'

'I'm talking about you, Ana. You've been transformed since you came here to St Felix, haven't you?'

'I— I don't know. I guess maybe a little . . .'

'I think you definitely have. It's not only Daisy-Rose who's been restored to her former glory, you have too. You've healed since you've been here, Ana, and I've enjoyed being a part of your recovery.'

His words ring a bell. Hadn't Amber from the flower shop also told me that St Felix was a very healing place to spend time in?

'I suppose I am happier than when I first came here,' I say, thinking about this for the first time. 'I'm much more relaxed about life, that's for sure. I had a few issues before. I didn't like it if I couldn't control things and I worried about wasting time. I had a fear of crowds and enclosed spaces too, and that's definitely improved.'

Malachi nods in agreement. 'That's partly because you've accepted what you can't control, Ana. You accepted your feelings towards your friend Daisy, and you've moved on from being angry at her for dying, and as you see it, leaving you again.'

I try to interrupt, but he continues.

'You've also found someone else to fill her place – someone you can care for, and who will care for you too. Note I said "*fill* her place", not "*take* her place". No one will ever take Daisy's place, Ana, but Noah will do his very best to help you live the rest of your life the way it's supposed to be lived, with joy and laughter and love, and you will do the same for him.'

I gaze at Malachi, entranced by his moving and inspiring speech. 'I've asked you this before, Malachi, but who made you so clever? That's a very wise head you have on your fairly young shoulders.'

How old *was* Malachi? I'd always assumed he was in his late twenties, possibly early thirties, but his words and, in fact, his whole manner today had been mature beyond his years.

'Years of practice,' Malachi says earnestly. 'I'm truly glad I've been able to be with you on this journey, Ana, and that I've been able to help.'

'You have helped me so much,' I tell him. 'At first I thought you were a bit of a pain in the arse.' Malachi grins. 'But you've proved yourself to be an amazing friend.' I take hold of his hand, and again the strangest feeling overcomes me. I can only describe it as an encompassing and overwhelming sense of love.

'Who are you, Malachi?' I ask, looking down at his hand. 'I feel like I know you so well and yet . . .'

'You'll know soon enough,' Malachi replies, looking

unblinkingly into my eyes. 'Now, Ana, it's time to spread even more happiness to some other people's lives.'

He looks out of the windscreen and I see Noah coming towards us. He's carrying the box that I know holds all the postcards.

'Time to go,' Malachi says, opening the passenger door and climbing out of Daisy-Rose. He turns back and looks at me. 'This isn't the end, I promise. I'll be in touch again.'

What an odd thing to say, I think, watching him walk away from Daisy-Rose towards Noah. He pauses to shake Noah's hand, then he strides casually towards the office with Ralph at his side.

Noah climbs into the seat Malachi has just vacated and pulls the door closed.

'Ready to go?' he asks, and I notice he's wiggling the fingers of the hand that's just touched Malachi's.

I nod as I start the engine again.

'What did Malachi just say to you?' I ask, before putting Daisy-Rose into first gear.

'Nothing, he just shook my hand and walked away.' Noah looks down at his hand again. 'That guy has one powerful handshake. I can still feel it now.'

'Yeah,' I say, putting Daisy-Rose into gear and moving slowly away. 'He's something very special is Malachi.'

The short drive down the south coast towards Newlyn takes a little longer in Daisy-Rose than it might usually, but I soon get the hang of driving a camper van, and Noah doesn't look quite as scared as he had done when we'd first left St Felix.

'Take a right here,' Noah instructs, as we drive into the small harbour town. 'Yep, now left, then left again. It should be just along here somewhere.'

333

I slow down as we drive past a row of neat bungalows with pretty front gardens before Noah instructs. '*Stop!* It's this one.'

Luckily for me there's a fairly big space on the road in front of the bungalow, so I don't have to try anything too complicated when parking Daisy-Rose.

'We're finally here,' I say, looking at a large whitewashed bungalow with pink roses in full bloom climbing up its front wall.

'We are. You ready for this?'

'As I'll ever be. Let's go.'

Carrying the box of postcards, we walk up the gravel drive to the front door. Noah presses the doorbell and we wait.

After a few moments the door opens and an elderly man stands in front of us. A few decades may have passed since the newspaper photo was taken, but I can still recognise a handsome, if slightly older Frankie. He's tall, with blue eyes that still shine brightly amongst the many laughter lines that cover his face, but his white hair, that once would have been the thick dark mane I remember from the photo, is now thinning and heavily receding.

'You must be Ana and Noah,' he says, smiling. 'Juliet said you'd be calling this afternoon. I'm Frankie, come in.'

We're invited into a small but neat hallway, and then we follow Frankie through into an even tidier sitting room.

'Take a seat,' he says, gesturing to a comfy-looking sofa with brightly coloured cushions scattered across it. 'Would you like a cup of tea, or perhaps coffee?'

'Whatever is easiest,' I say politely.

'I'll put the kettle on for some tea then. One moment, I'll be back presently.'

Frankie shuffles slowly out of the room and heads presumably for the kitchen.

'See that picture over there,' I whisper, pointing to a framed painting on the wall. 'I bet that's one of Lou's. It's the same style as the one at Juliet's and the same as the ones I've seen on eBay.'

'Frankie was obviously fond of Lou as well if he hangs her paintings up on his wall.'

'Yes, it's good to see, isn't it?' I'd wondered a few times if I was doing the right thing in bringing the postcards for Frankie to see. After all, Lou had never sent them so maybe she didn't want him to ever read them, but seeing the painting only reinforced that we were doing the right thing. 'What's that smell?' I ask Noah, as a distinct whiff of something catches at my nostrils. 'It seems familiar.'

'I don't know,' Noah says, sniffing. 'It smells a bit like . . . '

'Paint!' we both say at the same time.

'It's oil paint and turps,' I say excitedly. 'You don't think that Lou might actually be here, do you?'

'Now *that* would be an amazing coincidence!'

'Malachi says there's no such thing,' I begin, but someone else comes through the sitting room door now. They're wearing a painting smock and wiping their hands with a cloth.

My heart, which had felt so euphoric just moments ago with expectation and hope, immediately sinks. The person looking eagerly at us may well be wearing painting clothes splashed with blobs and streaks of colourful paint, but this person can't be Lou, because standing in front of us is another elderly man, shorter and a little tubbier than Frankie, and this time with a full head of white curly hair. A pair of gold-rimmed spectacles balances precariously amongst his curls.

335

'Hello,' he says, smiling warmly at us like Frankie had done. 'You must be Ana and Noah.' He comes over and holds out his cleaner hand for us to shake. 'Thank you so much for coming to see us today. I should introduce myself. I'm Louis. But my friends call me Lou.'

Forty-One

A stunned silence fills the small sitting room.

'You . . . ' I stutter. '*You* are Lou? Postcard Lou?'

'Yes, Postcard Lou.' Lou grins. 'Not what you were expecting, eh?'

Frankie arrives back in the room. 'Kettle's on,' he announces. 'Ah, I see you've met my Lou.'

They gaze at each other with such a look of tenderness that I let out a small gasp. 'Sorry,' I apologise, my face flushing. 'I just hadn't ever thought you might be a man. I'd just assumed . . . ' My voice trails off.

'. . . I was a woman?' Lou smiles. 'I thought you might. That's why we told Juliet not to tell you I would be here.'

I just stare at the two of them. I can't help myself – I just hadn't seen this coming at all.

'Perhaps we should have,' Lou says, regarding me with concern. 'Are you all right, dear?'

'Yes . . . yes, I'm fine,' I say, my heart beginning to beat again. This was even more amazing than it had been previously. Not only had Lou loved Frankie unwaveringly for fifty years, but *she* had been a *he*. And now it appeared they were finally together after all that time. This story just got better and better.

'I'll get that tea,' Frankie says, heading back out into the hall. 'And we'd better make it good and sweet, I think, don't you?'

We sit down in Lou and Frankie's sitting room armed with tea and biscuits, and they begin to tell us their amazing story.

'It all started when we were at school, didn't it, Frankie?' Lou says, glancing at him with that same adoring look. 'We were friends to begin with, really good friends, and we did absolutely everything together, but it wasn't until we went on a school trip and shared a room that we started to realise it might be something more.'

Frankie nods. 'In those days being gay was completely frowned upon for anyone, let alone for two teenage schoolboys. If we'd tried to talk to anyone about it, they'd have told us to stop being silly, that we couldn't possibly know anything at that age, so we kept quiet and pretended everything was normal.'

'Until Frankie's father caught us one day hidden down by the harbour in St Felix,' Lou says. 'We weren't even doing anything particularly bad, only holding hands. He saw red and forbade Frankie not only from being friends with me but also from ever speaking to me again.'

'We, of course, ignored him.' Frankie's bright blue eyes twinkle with mischief as he remembers. 'But sadly he found out yet again when someone told on us. We never found out who, did we, Lou?'

Lou shakes his head. 'Can't trust anyone, can you?'

'No,' Noah agrees. 'You can't.'

I glance at him, while Frankie continues, 'It was after that second time that my family suddenly decided to leave St Felix for pastures new. More my father's doing, I think, than my mother's, but she had to go along with what he wanted. It was 1945, and she didn't have a lot of options back then. Even though she never said as much, she probably knew what I was like. They say mothers always know.'

'We missed each other terribly,' Lou says, picking up the story. 'I just couldn't imagine my life without Frankie in it. I was fifteen and it felt like the end of the world when he left. We were, of course, banned from contacting each other, and any letter I attempted to get to Frankie was simply returned unopened. Luckily, my mother, who I'm sure guessed what had happened, kept me updated with any gossip or news she heard about Frankie and his family. That's why I was able to follow what he was doing for so long. Our mothers kept in touch for years.'

'I had no idea,' Frankie explains to us. 'My mother kept the fact she was writing to Lou's mother very quiet. My father would have hit the roof if he'd found out. He had a filthy temper on him, which my poor mother fell foul of many a time.'

Frankie looks sad as he remembers.

Lou takes his hand. 'So I decided I would write to Frankie anyway by postcard. I think originally my idea was I might send them to him at some point in the future, but as time went by it became obvious that wasn't going to happen. I'm not sure why I kept writing them over the years ... possibly a part of me used them a bit like therapy – a way of getting my thoughts down on paper. And another part simply enjoyed feeling like I was still speaking to Frankie even though he was so far away from me.'

They look at each other again, gazing into each other's eyes in a way I was more used to seeing young couples do, but I guess Frankie and Lou were living their honeymoon years out now they were finally together again.

'You married, didn't you, Frankie?' I ask, eager for them to continue with their tale.

'I did,' he answers, turning back to me. 'In 1955. It was just expected of you in those days to get married and have children, so I did as society expected and toed the line. I did love my wife, though,' he insists, looking at a sideboard behind them with a large collection of photos displayed on it. 'She was a wonderful woman, but I always knew I was gay, and I think, god rest her soul, a part of her knew too. Nevertheless, we were happy in our own way and it tore me apart when she got ill.'

Frankie heaves himself up off the sofa and goes over to the sideboard; he lifts one of the framed photos and brings it over to show us.

'This is Lillian,' he says, glancing at the photo before handing it over to me. 'A better woman, mother and grandmother you will never meet.'

I look at the photo and see an attractive middle-aged woman. It has been taken on a beach, and the woman is laughing because her sun hat is blowing off in the breeze.

'Juliet said you know what happened to my business.'

'It's fine,' Noah insists. 'You don't have to tell us about that.'

'No, I want you to know everything. I know how much trouble you must have gone to searching for us to return the postcards. It's only right you should know the whole story.' Frankie sits back down on the sofa again, and I stand the photo frame on the table next to my armchair. 'Lillian had breast cancer – a real nasty strain of it that wasn't responding to any of the treatments the NHS could offer. We were desperate to do something, the whole family was, and no one could bear

340

to watch her going through the torture she was enduring day in, day out. Have either of you known someone with cancer?'

'I have,' I say quietly. 'My best friend.'

'Then you'll know you'd do anything to try to ease their suffering.'

I nod.

'It was my daughter who found a clinic in America that offered an alternative treatment, but the cost was astronomical, more money then I earned in a year. We talked about fundraising, but it was going to take for ever to raise that sort of money, so I told everyone I'd get it and that was when I took the money from the business. Not the whole lot at once – I'm not that stupid – but I had to get it quickly and I was careless about where I took it from, so as you both know I got found out.'

Frankie looks so ashamed of himself that I want to go over and comfort him, take his hand and tell him it's all right, but luckily Lou is there to do it for me.

'You did it for a good cause,' Lou says, patting his hand.

'The courts weren't going to see it that way, though, that was the problem. According to my lawyer it was looking very bad for me. So I did the only thing I could, I disappeared. It broke my heart leaving Lillian, but I couldn't risk going to prison and never seeing her again. I thought, stupidly perhaps, that if I disappeared for a while things might blow over, and one day I might be able to return to Brighton and my home. But sadly that never happened. Lillian's health deteriorated rapidly after I left. I don't think she knew I was gone she was so desperately ill. My children looked after her and kept me updated on her progress, but she never recovered. I couldn't even attend her funeral when it came just a few months later. I could only visit her grave afterwards to tell her how sorry I was.' Frankie actually begins to cry now. I grab a box of tissues next to me and take them over to the sofa.

'Thank you,' he sobs, pulling a tissue from the box. 'I'm so sorry to break down on you like this. The last thing you've come here for is to see an old man cry.'

'Nonsense,' I tell him, kneeling down next to him. 'Your story is inspirational. The only ones who should be ashamed about any part of this are the people who gave you up to the authorities. They should have understood and stood by you, not dropped you in it. People can be so cruel.' I glance back at Noah, wondering if he realises I'm referring to his past as well as Frankie's, but his face only shows concern for Frankie.

'You're a good girl,' Frankie says, patting me on the shoulder. 'I hope your friend's story had a happier ending?'

I shake my head. 'Sadly, no. But I'm coming to terms with it a little better now. St Felix is an amazing place – it has really helped me heal since I've been there.'

'St Felix *is* very special,' Lou says wistfully. 'I loved living there. I travelled all over the world with my paintings, but I never found anywhere that was as special as that little town.'

'I know. Your postcards documented so well how your career progressed over the years. It was amazing to read about.'

Lou looks towards the unopened box. 'No,' he says, like a dieter resisting the temptation of a cream cake, 'I must be good until we've told you the rest of our story.'

I get up and go back to my chair.

'So, after Frankie disappeared, he moved around a lot, didn't you?' Lou adds, prompting Frankie to continue.

Frankie nods. 'Yes, I couldn't really settle anywhere for very long, but I always felt a tremendous pull for Cornwall, the place of my birth. I didn't dare return to St Felix – too many

342

memories and too much chance of someone recognising me. Even though I'd left as a boy, there were still people alive that might know me, so I settled here in Newlyn. Big enough so I could blend in without anyone taking too much notice of me, but small enough so I could enjoy living here. What attracted me the most was the big artistic community that exists here. Unlike Lou, I'd never been much of a painter, but I liked looking at other people's work and it was that interest that helped reunite me with my first love once more.'

This was the part I was looking forward to. I sit forward a little in my chair.

'Did you see one of Lou's paintings in a gallery?' I ask eagerly. 'Is that how the two of you met again?'

'You'd think, wouldn't you?' Frankie says, smiling again. 'But no, it wasn't that. Do you want to tell them, Lou?'

'It was Rose,' Lou says, 'my old camper van. I was here painting one day – nothing odd in that as I'd often come down to Newlyn over the years to sketch and paint – but on this particular day I was just packing up after Rose and I had been parked on the harbour all day when she suddenly started behaving oddly.'

'How does a camper van behave oddly?' Noah asks, smiling.

'I still don't really understand to this day, perhaps she short-circuited or something, but suddenly her lights started flashing, and her horn – which was a manual one – began beeping. Then she began to move.'

'On her own?' I ask in astonishment.

'Her engine wasn't running, but she began to roll forward. I swear I didn't leave her handbrake off as I was always so careful about that, but roll forward she did. I just panicked. I was hardly a sprightly young thing – this was in 2001 so I was already seventy-one – but luckily I had my guardian angel on my side that day.'

'You did?' This story gets more amazing by the moment.

'Well, my guardian angel in the form of Frankie anyway.'

'I was just taking my daily stroll along the harbour,' Frankie joins in. 'I'd noticed a man painting earlier and had every intention of stopping to look at his work on my way back, but when I heard a horn beeping and saw the lights flashing on his camper van, I knew something must be wrong. But it was when the van started to move slowly forward on its own that I realised I had to do something, so I moved as quickly as I could along the harbour, which wasn't very fast even in those days, I can assure you. Oddly, that day I seemed to be able to sprint, so I caught up with the van, pulled open the door and jumped inside, and then I pulled on the handbrake just before the van reached the harbour.'

'Rose's front tyres stopped about this far from the edge,' Lou says, holding his hands a tiny way apart. 'It's a miracle Rose didn't end up in the water that day. I went to thank the kind gentleman who had saved us, and you can imagine what a shock I got when Frankie climbed out of the van.'

'I still can't believe you recognised me,' Frankie says, looking lovingly at Lou.

'I'd have recognised you anywhere,' Lou replies. 'But remember I'd seen that photo of you in the paper. The question is, how on earth did you recognise me?'

'You hadn't changed one bit,' Frankie says.

'Charmer.'

'And you've been together ever since?' I ask. 'And it's all thanks to Daisy-Rose.'

'Daisy-Rose?' Lou asks. 'Is that what you call her now?'

'Yes, I'd started calling her Daisy after my friend before we discovered the name Rose painted on her. So we decided on Daisy-Rose.'

'I like it,' Lou says, nodding, 'it suits her.'

'Would you like to come outside and see her, Lou?' I ask.

'Oh, lovey, I would, very much so.'

We all head outside, and as we walk down the front path together I hear Lou gasp.

'Are you all right?' I ask.

'Yes, yes, I'm fine, dear. I just can't believe how good she looks. Almost like the day I bought her.'

We walk out of the gate and stand on the pavement in front of Daisy-Rose.

Lou walks forward a little and places his hand gently on the side of the vehicle. 'How have you been, girl?' he asks. 'You're looking well.'

It's such a simple, yet heartfelt gesture, I feel tears spring into my eyes.

'Malachi, the mechanic who restored her for me, has done an amazing job.'

'He has indeed. Wait, what did you say his name was?'

'Malachi.'

'What a coincidence. The young lad I sold Rose to was called that.'

'Are you sure? What did he look like?'

'Oh, it was quite some time ago, wasn't it, Frankie? I never really wanted to sell Rose, but my eyesight isn't what it used to be and driving was becoming difficult. Luckily, I'm short-sighted so I can still paint.'

'It was in 2010, just after you turned eighty,' Frankie says, steering the conversation back on course. 'She was the star of the show at your eightieth birthday, remember?'

'Oh yes, that's right. Your great-grandchildren loved playing in her.'

'Do you remember what this Malachi looked like?' I ask again. It can't be the same one, surely?

'He was tall,' Frankie says, trying to recall the details. 'He had dark curly hair and he was Irish too. Yes, I remember, he was a bit of a charmer.'

This was a pretty accurate description of Malachi, but maybe it was just a coincidence.

No such thing as coincidence, Ana, Malachi's voice echoes in my head.

'It was all a bit strange,' Lou continues. 'This young fella just bowled up on our doorstep one day and asked if we'd be interested in selling Rose. I immediately declined saying she wasn't for sale, but he was persistent, wasn't he, Frankie?'

Frankie nods.

'Like Frankie said, this Malachi was a bit of a charmer. He'd certainly kissed the Blarney stone several times, I'd say, and by the time he'd finished I knew he'd be the ideal person to take on Rose. I couldn't drive her any more and I didn't want her to rust away outside the house – that would have been just too sad to watch – so we decided to let someone else have the joy of owning her.'

'He certainly seemed to know his stuff, that's for sure,' Frankie adds. 'I don't think I've ever heard anyone wax so lyrical on the delights of owning a VW camper van.'

'How old would you say this guy was?' I ask. After all, this had taken place eight years ago. If it *was* Malachi, he'd have had to have been pretty young at the time.

'I'm not sure – early, mid-twenties perhaps?' Frankie says. 'It's so difficult to tell these days with young people. I guess he might have been thirty at a push. He had a lovely dog with him, though. Oh, what did he call it?'

'Ralph,' Lou answers. I remember because he said he'd named it after Raphael. Another great painter, that's why I remember.'

Malachi had Ralph eight years ago? He must have been a puppy in that case then.

'Was the dog a puppy? I ask, hoping they say 'yes' so I can make some sense of this.

'Oh no – a fully grown golden Labrador. Lovely fella he was too, very gentle nature.'

I look at Noah. He looks as dumbfounded as I feel.

'Anyway,' Lou says, not noticing our bewilderment. 'We sold Rose, I mean Daisy-Rose, to Malachi and never saw her again. I'm surprised you bought her in such a bad state, though – he promised to look after her. If it is the same guy, maybe he felt guilty and wanted to help you restore her to her former glory. But this' – Lou runs his hand over Daisy-Rose's paintwork again – 'this is much better than her former glory. This is a whole new level of heavenly glory.'

Putting my many questions about Malachi aside, I show Lou around the rest of Daisy-Rose, including her spotless interior.

'Magnificent,' Lou declares. 'Truly magnificent.'

'We found the first batch of the postcards stuffed inside one of the seats, then some others hidden around the rest of her,' I tell him, as we make our way back inside the bungalow. 'The rest I managed to buy at auction to make the full set.'

'Amazing,' Lou says, shaking his head. 'I can't believe you found them all. Obviously I hid them because I didn't want anyone to read them. What I was writing was private, and even several decades later I was still worried someone would

347

see them and realise who they were written too – old habits die hard, I suppose.'

'But didn't you think to retrieve them before you sold Daisy-Rose?' I ask.

'After Frankie and I met up again, it was nine years before I sold the van. In that time I hadn't needed to write any more cards, plus, amazing as it might seem, I was a little shy of showing them to Frankie, so I kept them secret. So when the van went my old brain had forgotten that they were even in there.'

'Would you like to see them again now?' I ask, going over to the box on the table.

Lou and Frankie sit down next to each other, and I place the box between them on the sofa, then they lift the lid off it together and begin to read the first few cards.

Noah and I watch them, enjoying being part of such a special moment in their lives. I feel Noah's hand reach across the chairs to take hold of mine and he squeezes my hand. As I glance across at him I notice he has tears in his eyes.

I look at Frankie and Lou and realise they also are finding it difficult to hold back their emotions, so I give in and join them.

I let the tears flow down my cheeks for what we'd been able to achieve by returning the cards to this delightful couple, for Frankie and Lou and their remarkable love story, and for the very dear friend I'd lost but who had made it possible for me to be here, experiencing this incredible moment with all the wonderful people in this room.

Forty-Two

Noah and I stay with Lou and Frankie for another hour.

After the first few postcards, Lou and Frankie realise this was going to be a long and emotional journey they were undertaking in reading these declarations of love together, so they put the box down and agree to read the rest of the cards later when their guests have left.

'We should be going anyway,' Noah says, echoing what I've been thinking. It felt like we'd done what we came here to do, and now it was time for us to leave this couple to discover nearly half a century of love together, privately and in their own time.

'Oh, do you have to?' Lou pleads, heaving himself up off the sofa. 'It's been so lovely meeting you both. I really can't thank you enough for taking the time to return these cards to me, and for bringing Rose – I mean *Daisy*-Rose – to see me again.'

'Would you like you keep her?' I suddenly hear myself saying. 'It was my friend, the one I mentioned earlier, who told me I had to come down to St Felix to collect her and restore her to her former glory. It was her final wish. But she also said I had to do something with Daisy-Rose that would make myself and others happy. I'm sure you'd love having her back in your life again, wouldn't you, Lou? And I know it would make me extremely happy to give her to you.'

'Oh, my dear,' Lou says, coming over and hugging me. 'That's such a lovely generous thought, but I'm too old to be looking after a camper van now, even one as smart and sassy – looking as Daisy-Rose. No, you must keep her to enjoy, my darling Ana. She's yours now. Go out and enjoy her, she's a wonderful companion. Although,' he says, winking at Noah, 'I see you've already found one of those.'

'I have,' I say, reaching for Noah's hand this time. 'You're sure you won't change your mind?'

'Absolutely not.'

They walk us outside to where Daisy-Rose is waiting to take us home again.

Noah goes over to shake Frankie's hand, and Lou hugs me again.

'I honestly can't thank you enough,' he says, standing back to look at me. 'This has made my life complete now, having the cards to show my Frankie and seeing this old gal again.'

He puts his hand on Daisy-Rose one last time. 'What's that?' he asks, tilting his head to the side to listen. 'Oh, you think so, do you?'

He turns back to face me.

'Bit of a strange one this,' he says, 'but Daisy-Rose thinks you should paint.'

'What?' I ask, not sure if I'm more surprised by his suggestion or by the fact he appears to think a camper van is talking to him.

'She thinks you should paint. Are you artistic in any way?'

350

'Sort of. I'm a graphic designer.'

'Then expand, darling!' Lou says dramatically. 'Throw off your shackles and let your artistic side explode on to the canvas. Daisy-Rose will help you. She'll take you to all the best places for you to paint if you let her.'

'Okay . . .' I reply hesitantly. 'If you think so?'

'I know so, darling.'

I hug Lou again, then Frankie, and then Noah and I climb back into Daisy-Rose promising to come back and visit very soon.

Then we drive away, taking Daisy-Rose with us but leaving the postcards where they very much belong.

'What a day,' I say to Noah, as we drive back up towards St Felix. After my efforts earlier, I'd offered Noah the chance to drive Daisy-Rose home, which he'd gratefully accepted. We'd found a radio station playing an hour of eighties music on the little radio that Malachi had fitted into the dashboard, and I felt happy and relaxed as we journeyed to St Felix, our job done.

'It's been a pretty special one, hasn't it?' Noah says, glancing across at me. 'I'm glad I could share all that with you today, Ana.'

'And me you.' I think for a few moments while I listen to The Police singing on the radio. 'So many things were such a surprise today, like Lou being a man. How had we never thought of that before?'

'We just assumed, I guess. Their story was pretty amazing, though, don't you think?'

'It was. Imagine loving someone for all those years and not knowing if they would ever be yours again? Even though their love wasn't exactly unrequited, that sort of love when it's one-sided is such a hard thing to bear.'

351

'Yes, it is,' Noah says quietly, looking ahead.

'It was incredible what they were saying about Malachi, though, wasn't it? What are the odds of it being anyone other than our Malachi back in St Felix?'

'It would be an awful coincidence if it wasn't. I mean what would be the chances of someone else of the right age and the right description being called Malachi, equipped with an Irish accent *and* owning a dog called Ralph shortened from Raphael?'

'I know. Malachi always says there's no such thing as coincidences.'

'That's funny, Jess said something similar to me the other day too.'

'Did she? I always thought it was strange about those two. They clearly seemed to know each other at the barbecue, but wouldn't admit that they did.'

'Yeah, also Jess was acting really oddly before we left this morning. Kept telling me how glad she was that we were together at last, and how it meant so much to her. She kept looking at the shop bell every time it rang too. In fact, she was positively jumping any time someone came into the shop.'

'Malachi was saying some strange things too. I mean his behaviour is often quite unconventional, but this morning, it sounds weird to say it, it felt like he'd grown up, like he'd shed his Jack the Lad attitude and become an older and wiser person.'

Noah laughs. 'What a couple of oddballs we've got ourselves involved with.'

'But they mean well, and they were both always very keen for us to be together. When I first knew Malachi I thought he was flirting with me, but then I realised it was just his way. Whatever you may think of him, he really likes you, Noah.'

'I don't have a problem with Malachi. I did when I thought he might be after you.' He glances across at me. 'But now I'm fine with him. He seems like a good guy.'

'He is. He certainly worked his magic on this little lady that's for sure.' I tap the dashboard in front of me.

'He must have worked night and day.'

'Yes, I must pay him properly when we get back. I'll nip up to the garage first thing tomorrow. It'll be too late by the time we get back tonight. Is it okay if we park Daisy-Rose behind the shop now? There's no reason for her to be at the garage any more.'

'Sure, start as we mean to go on,' Noah says, reaching across and squeezing my hand briefly before returning his to the steering wheel in the correct ten to two position.

I smile at his correctness. I'd thought Noah very uptight when I'd first met him, but now I knew why, I completely understood, and even better, all his little idiosyncrasies made me like him even more.

'Ooh, I like this one,' I say, still smiling, as I hear Annie Lennox singing about angels on the radio.

I sing along, and to my surprise Noah joins in.

'What?' he asks, grinning at me. 'You're not the only one who has the monopoly on eighties music, you know?'

And we continue to sing happily along together until we reach home.

Forty-Three

The next morning I head up the hill towards the garage still singing.

Last night I'd spent the evening with Noah, and even though his house was just as smart and tidy as he was, I was glad to find that he yet again left that attitude at the bedroom door.

Without thinking, I head immediately around to the back of the garage.

'Can I help you?' I hear someone call from the office. Then I see a large round man walking across the yard towards me. He's wearing the same navy overalls that Malachi usually wore only in a slightly bigger size.

'Oh, hi, is Malachi around?' I ask, wondering who this is.

'Who?' The guy looks me doubtfully up and down.

'Malachi, the chap who's been looking after the garage in the last few weeks while Bob is away.'

'I'm Bob,' the man says, looking even more suspicious of me. 'And no one has been here since I've been away. I left on too short notice to get anyone to cover, so I don't know who you're talking about. There's no one called Malachi here, I can assure you of that.'

'B— but ...' What was happening here? Where was Malachi? 'If no one has been here,' I say, suddenly remembering, 'who sold the MG that you had parked out the front before you left?'

'How did you know about that?' Bobs asks, half in amazement, half in disbelief. 'I thought it had been stolen when I came back and it wasn't there, but when I went to the office to call the police I found the money in the safe with the buyer's details and a copy of the paperwork.'

'That was Malachi,' I say almost proudly. 'You should be grateful to him. He's kept this place ticking over while you've been gone.'

'Has he now?' Bob says, staring at me suspiciously again. 'Be sure to thank him from me then, *when* you see him,' he adds sarcastically.

'I will,' I say, marching away out of the garage and back on to the street. But I pause as I step on to the pavement.

What is going on?

I try ringing Malachi's mobile but an automated voice tells me his number is no longer in service. *Damn!* I rush back down the hill towards the cottage, for some reason wondering if he might be there, but as I hurry along Harbour Street my phone rings.

'Ana,' Noah says, sounding quite odd. 'Have you seen Malachi this morning by any chance?'

'No, I was just thinking of calling you. I went to the garage and Bob was back. He said he knew nothing about Malachi looking after the place while he was away.'

'Right ...' Noah says in the same dazed voice.

'What's wrong, Noah? You're starting to worry me.'

'You didn't notice a note or anything in your cottage this morning, did you?'

'No, I showered and everything at yours, didn't I, so I only nipped in there briefly to pick up the cash to pay Malachi. What sort of a note?' I ask uneasily. I didn't like the tone of Noah's voice.

'It's just I got into work this morning and found an envelope addressed to me stuck to the till. It was from Jess. She's gone.'

'What do you mean "gone"? She's left her job, or left St Felix?'

'Both. But there's a bit more to it than that. If Malachi is missing too, I think you might have a note somewhere as well. Are you far from your cottage?'

'No, I'm almost back there now.'

'Okay, I'll come over.'

'But what about the shop?'

'The shop can wait. This is more important. *Much* more important.'

I get back to the cottage and pull open the door, then I rush about the house looking for a note. I'm about to give up when I notice the French windows. Someone had used one of my lipsticks to draw an *8* on one glass door, and a *0* on the other. Without stopping to wonder who, I quickly unlock the doors and fling them open. It's then that I see it – a white envelope stuck with tape to the black wrought-iron balcony.

It has *Ana* written on the front in an ornate black font. I stand for a moment staring at the envelope. What was it going to say inside? Noah had sounded almost spooked when I'd spoken to him on the phone just now.

Unable to bear the suspense any longer, I tear the envelope away from the balcony and rip it open.

356

Inside the envelope is a postcard. It has a picture of a red camper van on the front.

I turn it over. The message is written in a tiny florid black handwriting, but it's not too small that I can't appreciate every word:

My dearest Ana,

By now you'll know that I've gone.

I was only ever going to be in your life temporarily, to help you and guide you back on to the right path.

Whenever someone is in trouble we are sent in to help, and boy, were you in trouble! You could never ask us for help – you were too proud to ever do that, but with the help of your friend Daisy I was able to come to you and assist you in your time of need. You made my mission so much easier to complete by eventually (you put up a good fight to begin with!) allowing me to help and advise you.

Noah is a good man, and as you now know he too has had his troubles in the past, but he, like you, was too proud to ask for help. So this was a double mission for my junior Jess and me. Jess is over the moon (literally, now she has her wings) that we were able to succeed, and I too am delighted that you and Noah will make each other happy for decades to come.

But much more than that, I want to tell you what a joy it was to be with you as you repaired yourself. As Daisy-Rose was brought back to life in front of me, so were you, Ana, and that is all the reward I could ever ask for – to see someone happy and filled with love again.

Take care of yourself, Noah and, of course,

Daisy-Rose. Lou was right – she will guide you in all your future endeavours now I am not there to look after you. But be assured, Ralph and I will always be here if you need us.

You only have to ask.

But for now, I must say farewell.

Always know, Anastasia, I will be

Forever yours,

Malachi x

As I stand on the balcony holding the letter I hear Noah let himself in downstairs, and then he comes bursting up the stairs grasping his own letter tightly in his hand.

'Did you get one?' he asks breathlessly, as he joins me out on the balcony.

'Yes, but mine was a postcard,' I say, holding it up for him to see. 'Quite appropriate, really.'

'What does it all mean?' Noah asks. I notice he looks very pale, even though I'm sure he likely ran all the way here.

I don't answer him. I look down at the card in my hand again.

'You're very calm, Ana,' Noah says. 'If your postcard says anything like what my letter does, then I'd expect you to be jumping around like me.'

'I think it probably does.' I pass Noah the card, and he passes me his letter from Jess.

Jess has been a little less eloquent than Malachi, but the essence of her letter is very similar to my card.

'Do you believe it?' Noah asks, passing me my card back. 'What they are suggesting? I mean it's all a bit strange, isn't it?'

'Does it actually matter?' I ask, turning Noah towards me so we look into each other's eyes.

'How do you mean?'

'I mean both Malachi and Jess helped the two of us when we needed it. In their different ways they were there for us, and they not only helped us with practical things like running your shop and restoring Daisy-Rose, they helped us to heal and make our peace with the past, and most importantly of all they helped us to find each other. So what does it matter who or what they are? We have them to thank for so much.'

Noah nods in agreement, then without speaking he pulls me to him and we wrap our arms around each other tightly in the silent knowledge that our friends and loved ones may be gone, but we will always have each other.

As I rest my head on Noah's shoulder, suddenly I see it.

'Look,' I say, pulling away from him a little. He follows my gaze.

We both stare up into the sky, where we see slowly forming in the clouds above us, a perfectly shaped heart, and in the heart are the numbers 8 and 0.

Then as quickly as it appears, it disappears, as the rest of the swirling clouds swallow it up again. But I know as I look up at the sky that the friends I've known and lost will always be there, watching me and loving me from afar.

Acknowledgements

What a joy it's been to be given the chance to return to the magical town of St Felix once more. I loved revisiting some old friends, meeting some new ones, and catching up on what's been going on with the town and its residents since *The Little Flower Shop by the Sea*. Fictional St Felix, as some of you may know, is inspired by the beautiful town of St Ives down on the far west tip of Cornwall. It's one of my favourite places to visit in the world, and many of the locations in St Felix are based on places you can see there. There is something very special about St Ives, and I hope in St Felix I've captured a little of its unique appeal.

Writing can be a very solitary experience, which much of the time I enjoy, but there are many who help and support us writers along the way, so I'd like to take a moment to thank just a few of them. Much love and thanks as always are sent to my amazing agent, Hannah Ferguson. Hannah and I have been together since the beginning, and I could wish for no better person to work alongside me, providing me with all the necessary encouragement and support in good times and bad.

Also, I am grateful to the whole team at my publishers Sphere and Little, Brown, without whom my books simply wouldn't appear on your bookshelves and digital devices! Thanks are sent to Maddie West, Tamsyn Berryman and EVERYONE who works with me on my books.

And lastly, the biggest thanks of all goes to my wonderful family – the ones who really matter. Huge hugs and much love to Jim, Rosie, Tom and our dogs Oscar and Sherlock. I simply couldn't do it without you. xx

Author's Note

What's in a name?

Anastasia – Resurrection
Noah – Rest and comfort
Malachi – God's messenger